Putney Ferret

Putney Ferret

How selfish can you be?

Freddie Hodgson

authorHOUSE®

AuthorHouse™
1663 Liberty Drive
Bloomington, IN 47403
www.authorhouse.com
Phone: 1-800-839-8640

All characters in this book are fictitious. Any resemblance to a real person, living or dead, is coincidental.

Published by AuthorHouse 10/31/2012

ISBN: 978-1-4670-0714-6 (sc)
ISBN: 978-1-4670-0716-0 (hc)
ISBN: 978-1-4670-0715-3 (e)

August 3rd, 2002

Hampshire, England

The party was in full swing when the old man said, 'Paul, we shouldn't be making a bloody monkey of him.' His brusque Teesside accent underscored his point. 'He's supposed to be celebrating his twenty-first birthday, not performing some kid's circus act.'

'Dad, you're talking rot,' Paul replied, his received pronunciation concealing northern England roots. 'And look, you've got soup running down your dress shirt. Your grandson is big enough to stand up there and perform a quick rendition on the fiddle. Just like he used to. Many here tonight can remember him doing it in his shorts.' There were titters around the table as Paul ensured close friends and extended family were in on the joke. The grandson finished the short violin solo, bowed, and Paul his father signalled to the hired-in Master of Ceremonies to commence the speeches. Three waitresses from a local catering company sped round the marquee, half-filling rented Champagne flutes with chilled Prosecco. Paul waited for the applause to die down before thanking friends and family for such a wonderful evening. He added a few special mentions, his own managing director for one, before reminding guests of the evening's purpose.

'Ladies and Gentlemen, Ladies and Gentlemen, as you tuck into some carefully selected local cheeses, I'd like to toast the man of the evening. On behalf of my wife Rosalind and I, I give you our one and only beloved son!'

The birthday boy stood up beside his own parents and grandfather, and stared across smiling faces, parents' family friends, his friends from university, one or two from school—they'd all raised their glasses to him. Several unrecognisable faces, presumably his father's colleagues.

'This evening,' Paul announced, 'we are reminded of the proud heritage of this family and its traditions.' The birthday boy smirked uncomfortably as his father presented him with a small box. The birthday boy peered in, and took out the gold signet ring.

'Try that on for size,' whispered Paul.

The son did as he was instructed then turned to the microphone. 'I feel like I'm getting married to my dad,' he declared. Laughter. His father leant across him and said into the mike, 'in a way he rather is!' More laughter.

The birthday boy gave his speech. Not the one he'd hope to give, but one that his father had insisted he help pen. The birthday boy had also hoped to read a brief poem he'd composed for the occasion, but his father had told him 'neither the time nor place, old chap.'

Everyone toasted his name, before sampling the artisan cheeses, alongside servings of port for those needing it. The dance floor began filling up, with all ages bopping away to a local cover band, chosen by Paul and his wife.

East Midlands, England

'Given it's your third and final warning, I regret to inform you that with immediate effect your contract with this club is terminated . . .'

The young man said nothing. Not even a last minute appeal from his growing fan base would save him from the sentence passed down by a man he'd idolised, seconded by the hastily arranged panel, on this balmy Saturday evening in August. 'I wish I could have given you one more chance, but I can't. Regretfully . . .' his rugby coach paused to gather himself, 'I consider this matter closed. Best of luck, but I do ask that you leave now. Goodbye.' The young man's legs began to shake. 'Goodbye,' the coach repeated calmly.

The young man picked up his holdall and slung it over his back, ruffling up his suit jacket across the shoulder, and turned for the door. Before leaving the committee room, he briefly glanced up at the gold lettered plaque that bore the name of every President of this famous Rugby Football Club since 1880, its founding year. He could still reel them off in sequence, something he'd done since a boy of 11. By then he'd already been a regular at the ground, stood alongside his father and uncle across countless cold Saturday afternoons, watching his warring heroes battle against the other elite clubs of English Rugby Union. They were now English and European Champions. His own talent had been spotted early and in his early teens he was playing County level. Physical and mental development came to him at a young age; he made the 'B' team at sixteen, the third youngest player in the club's post-war history to do so. He earned three caps for England

Under-17's. There was serious talk of him making the full England side. Offers from Wasps, Saracens and Quins quickly followed. All were turned down. Then, at nineteen came the offer he'd been waiting for. To play full-time, after finishing his university studies.

Tonight, barely a year since signing, he was banished from the only top flight rugby team he'd ever wanted to play for.

Pattaya, Thailand

He left the Yabba-Dabba-Doo! bar with his arms draped around two young women. It was way past three in the morning and the drunken threesome wove slowly through swaying revellers. Most of the tourists had long since gone, done with browsing for CDs, suitcases or sunglasses among the late-night market stalls. Moving away from the busy market area, the night air quietened, save the occasional tinny drone from a two-stroke moped as it zipped past, or a lonely cricket sawing in the grass strips lying alongside low, ramshackle fences. Strings of bead lights and neon signs hung haphazardly amongst lower branches of trees, tired and grimy like the folk lolloping home beneath.

They turned off into a narrow residential street and stopped outside a low-rise apartment building. The American girl appeared limp and tired.

'Time for my bed,' she yawned. 'Help me upstairs, honey. Gotta sleep.'

'Sorry love,' the young man replied. 'Got to take this 'un home.' He motioned to the equally weary Dutch girl beneath his right arm then gave the American a knowing wink.

'Okay, well see you two love birds around.' The American girl turned and slowly made her way up some wooden steps that led to her apartment.

The Dutch girl curled round to face him. 'I knew you'd pick me over her,' she slurred. 'Well let me tell you, Mr. Handsome Man, I picked you, remember that.'

'Will do. Now, what d'ya fancy doing?'

'Guess,' she replied then kissed him clumsily on the chin.

Her new, handsome friend looked at his watch. He'd need to make this a quickie if he stood a chance with the American before she dozed off. Eloise—was that her name?

'The beach!' the Dutch girl exclaimed, rummaging for a pack of cigarettes.

'Great. And we've got all the time we need,' he replied slowly.

Pristina, Kosovo

Sat at her desk in the European Assistance and Reconstruction (EAR) offices, the European Union advisor considered herself a bit of a cop-out. Tomorrow she'd be back home in England, leaving behind this new yet still broken country and its battered people. True, she'd return next June, but to what? Sure the development funds were seeing some good. But the tension here was notable and the peace brittle . . . she shuddered at the mere thought. It was 1900 hours, a full day's work despite it being the weekend. She placed the laptop in her briefcase then packed up the family photos she always took away with her. She stood and took one last look at the room that had been hers since June, before making for the exit and the awaiting transportation still laid on by NATO's KFOR forces. Her young driver, a Lance Corporal called Richards, drove her along the short, familiar route through the empty Pristina streets. Thousands had poured back there since the fighting between the Serbs and ethnic-Albanians had largely ended, and tonight the city sat quietly, still taking stock.

As former Leverhulme Professor of Geopolitics at Bristol University, she had spent twenty-five years specialising in the Balkans. Then in '98, as tension increased in Kosovo between Serbs and Albanians, the European Commission sought her out for policy advice. When fighting broke out a year later, her initial brief was to observe first hand the humanitarian situation, at great personal risk to herself, and report back to policy makers safely ensconced in Brussels. From June '99, when the whole country was placed under international control through the UN, she'd split her time between her home life in South West England and Pristina, advising those tasked with overseeing the EU's reconstruction and economic development effort on the ground. She wished her driver well, stepped out of the car and straight into the hotel bar. Beer in hand, she relaxed into her own thoughts. It was times like these when she was alone she often thought of what had truly drawn her towards Kosovo. And tonight it was a stranger's voice that would reawaken her.

'Miss Riley?' came a voice from behind her. She ignored it. Must be referring to someone else. 'Diana Riley?' the voice repeated. Diana froze. No one had called her by her maiden name in twenty years. She turned. At first she didn't recognise the man stood in front of her. He was tall and slim, his face weathered, but very handsome. She began focussing on the stranger's eyes. Kind eyes . . . and a memory began to surface. His olive-toned skin and strong jaw, they were still the same. The grey hair was different to how she'd once remembered it—rich and black, and through which she'd once idly pushed her fingers as they read together. But those kind, kind eyes, they would never grow old. And in that very moment, a dormant longing to meet him again one day, a hope carefully buried away for so long, abruptly re-awakened. Suddenly her heart was as it was on that night back in November 1981—light, jubilant, and skipping. That forbidden night they spent together, before he had to leave her, forever.

She smiled. And in that same moment, he smiled too.

ONE

Geoff Fox studied the café opposite and pondered. *How come so many of Putney Ferret's café-going residents sport signet rings? And how come they all seem to congregate in the same places, striking a somewhat similar pose?* Stood at his lounge bay window, Geoff trained his binoculars on one particular individual, presently sat at the table nearest the café door. He was someone who Geoff new too well, someone whose tireless commitment to convey a particular public image was matched only by his deep and proven aversion to public humiliation. Which was unfortunate because publicly humiliating his housemate was Geoff's third favourite pastime.

The instant Geoff had heard his housemate leave for his usual Sunday morning coffee opposite, he leapt from his bed, head still sore from last night, and set about his task: convince every living being located within a radius of fifty metres that the inhabitants of his home, No. 47 Ferret Rise, Putney Ferret, South West London, were actively engaged in very live, highly amplified, and wholly inconsiderate sex acts, and in so doing ruin his housemate's morning.

Phase One: the right dialogue. Finding the most authentic porn soundtrack possible would be easy, and Geoff immediately plumped for a box set with the rather ambiguous title '*A Mouthful of Europe—Culinary Skills for Amateurs*'. Certainly the movies featured several amateurs, but what they were up to didn't involve much cooking. Geoff quickly ruled out '*Nordick Horn of Plenty*'. It lacked any crisp dialogue, relying heavily on visuals. 'No good for today's purposes' he muttered, nonetheless making a note to return to it at the next quiet opportunity. Next up was '*Sweet and Sour Krauts*'. Another disappointment—its clavichord-heavy incidental music would betray its studio recording origins. No, for this morning's prank to succeed Geoff needed a movie with no music. Just simple dialogue between consenting adults, alongside

1

the kind of crass grunts and groans best saved for moments of private intimacy. Which is why Geoff finally opted for a DVD called '*Cremed Swedes*'.

Phase One completed, Geoff turned his attention to Phase Two: prepare the electricals. The ensuing cacophony had to prove nigh impossible to turn off, and getting this right took much concentration. In fact Geoff became so engrossed in the careful sabotage of relevant plugs, fuseboxes and other key constituents that he completely forgot the second reason for coming downstairs. Nor did he register several phone calls, or the return of his other housemate, Chris Reece, known to his friends as Kish, fresh and ruddy-faced from his regular ten-mile run around Richmond Park, and who was presently slumped on the sofa with his orange juice, watching on with interest.

Geoff slotted the DVD into the machine, then began encasing the entire DVD player with gaffer tape, until the disc door, the volume knob, and the off/on switch were entirely bound up. Assuming the remote would soon be impossible to locate (part of Geoff's plan), anyone trying to override a very loud DVD player would face considerable obstacles.

'Almost there,' Geoff puffed, resting his considerable weight on his right knee. A tiny piece of floating cartilage jerked across his patella. 'Oh y'bastard!' he shrieked, followed by a controlled ale-fed belch.

Quite the ambassador for the beer industry, thought Kish. Geoff then placed the DVD case back into the box when he noticed a folded letter inside it. It turned out to be a note from his proud, if phenomenally naive mother. He looked at the date at the top of the letter. 'Ten years ago. Still at Uni.'

Dear Geoff,

How are you darling? Enclosed is the cookery DVD box set you asked me to order on your behalf. I haven't opened it. For some odd reason, I had to prove I was over 18 years old—I can't think why. Contains some recipes involving hard liquor, or the use of sharp knives, maybe?

Anyway, I am sure you will get immense enjoyment from it. I also thought you could do with a new large non-stick saucepan, to replace the one you broke. Can't think how.

See you next week. Looking forward to seeing you in action. We are so proud of you! Love you,

Mum (and Dad) Xx

Geoff chuckled at the saucepan remark, and recalled a particular cricket match held in his University Hall of Residence corridor where his old pan was used as an improvised cricket bat. As he recalled, play was suspended when he accidentally buried it into a recently painted plaster wall whilst attempting an explosive clout to the imaginary boundary. This resulted in him having a pan with no handle and being banned from all Hall of Residence social events for a term. Geoff placed the note back in the box, then popped the window latch and slid the large sash window up enough to wedge two compact Bose speakers beneath it, both facing outward.

Kish booted up his laptop and went straight to Twitter and clicked on someone he followed called 'FerayNotFerret'. Written by an anonymous local, its almost surreal classist commentary was fast becoming something of a household favourite on Sunday mornings. Almost immediately Kish began to chortle.

'Jesus Christ, it's even worse than yesterday's toss,' he blurted, briefly glancing over to Geoff who was currently staring out of the lounge window. Powerfully built, his legs astride, Geoff looked quite imposing albeit in a hugging t-shirt and tight underpants.

'Are those my cacks?' Kish enquired.

'Ran out of my own, 'fraid to say,' Geoff replied casually, his back to Kish still. 'So I had to wear these until I've done the laundry.' Geoff motioned blindly over his shoulder toward the kitchen, then delved down to give his groin a thorough scratching (his trademark twitch as he preferred to call it) in full view of anyone unfortunate to be walking past No. 47 that very moment.

'You keep them,' said Kish, clocking the enormous black bin-liner slumped beside the washing machine. Geoff's monthly laundry. As his own clothing supply diminished, Geoff increasingly scavenged through his housemates' draws and wardrobes for something to wear. This morning, Kish could reasonably assume several of his own garments would be found in the bin liner, ruptured, irrevocably stained, or both.

'Good Morning,' Kish said suddenly. *Odd comment,* thought Geoff, his back still facing the room.

'Morning,' came a woman's voice.

Instantly, Geoff span around, and saw the attractive and slightly bedraggled female stood under the archway that led into the hall. Both she and Kish looked back at Geoff, who was still giving his trademark twitch a damn good seeing to. Casually he pulled his hand out and tucked it behind his back.

The young woman smiled at Geoff and walked into the room. 'Morning you,' she started. 'I thought I'd come see how that coffee you promised was coming along? The one you offered to make half an hour ago?'

Geoff smiled back, but said nothing. At least now he knew the other thing he'd come downstairs for. Trying to forget where her hands might have been in recent hours, Kish jumped to his feet and nervously extended his.

'Hi. I'm Kish.'

The woman politely shook his hand and then looked straight at Geoff. As she waited silently for a response, her smile gradually narrowed into something more edgy. Suddenly Geoff felt distinctly uncomfortable, and instinctively went to give his scrotum another nervous scratch, stopping himself at the last moment. He knew exactly what she was getting at. *Post-coital introductions.* Remembering girls' names after doing the dirty had never been a strong point for Geoff Fox. Especially when confronted on the matter by someone he'd met just hours before. He stood upright, and pushed his fingers through his thick, unkempt hair.

'Kish,' Geoff began confidently, 'may I introduce the lovely Elaine.'

'It's Lisa actually,' the woman interjected swiftly, and said 'well, you really meant it when you said last night would be your most memorable.' She chuckled nervously.

'Howsabout I get some coffee going?' said Kish and without waiting for a response, escaped through the archway into the kitchen, once again mystified how such a fat fart like Geoff managed to charm them. *Lucky sod.*

'You know, on second thoughts maybe I'll skip coffee,' Lisa replied, an Australian intonation looping upward, then eyeing Geoff said, 'Don't worry stud, I'll be gone in a jiffy.'

'Don't be silly. Stick around?' Geoff replied with as sincere a tone as he could muster. 'You know, chit-chat a little?'

'Well . . .'

'Excellent. Just give me a few minutes here with this thing?' Geoff pointed at the DVD.

'Oh, you mean the thing you forgot to tell me about when you jumped out of bed so energetically? You're clearly busy and I don't want to get in your way.'

'At least feel free to have a shower,' Geoff suggested. 'There's a towel, I think, in my bottom draw.'

'Thanks, I will. Mind if I wear this polo shirt back home? I can get it back to you, just I need to get back to my flat, and well my brother will be there and I want to look . . .'

'Certainly,' Geoff interrupted. He knew all too well what the morning walk-of-shame felt like, and Lisa's backless top with the deep plunge front would scream 'dirty stop-out' all the way back to her flat in . . . well he was buggered if he could remember such details. 'It actually belongs to our other housemate,' he continued. 'I'm sure he won't miss it.'

'Well I'll see you get it back.' And Lisa made for the stairs.

Geoff didn't reply. Getting it back might mean seeing her again, not something he'd given much consideration to. Upstairs, Lisa sighed. This morning, this guy seemed vague and distant, at odds with the amiable, disarming, if attached bloke who only last night had made her laugh out loud and feel terrific about herself for the first time in months. It was not as if she wanted anything different than he did. She'd have just preferred to leave his company with some mutual respect.

Hearing the bathroom door thud shut, Geoff exhaled loudly. 'Bloody Hell! She put me on the sodding spot there. No mercy shown! Lisa did she say she was? I could have sworn last night between shunts it was Elaine.'

'Evidently,' replied Kish, returning to the lounge. 'Fox, you really are a dirty hound, aren't you?'

Geoff smiled. 'Rather tidy wasn't she? I told her I was attached, and hey presto, she was all over me. I'm buggered if I can remember much at all about last night, mind.'

'Well I could fill you in on some choice moments. Can't imagine how Humphrey could've slept through it.'

'No, I mean I can't remember how she ended up back here. I'll have to retrace my steps. You saw me come in, right?'

Kish shrugged. 'I had an early night. Just remembered some repetitive banging.'

'That's unfair. Could have been Humphrey.'

'There are two things wrong with that comment. First off, the bangs accompanied, well . . .'

'Well what?'

'A yapping sound, like those made by a baby seal. Or a lap dog maybe. Whatever, it definitely sounded like some kinky role-play. And when I hear kinky stuff like that, I know it's down to you. And second, when was the last time Humph got any?'

Geoff stared at the lone individual sat drinking coffee across the road. 'Must be nearly a year. Poor sod. Meantime, me offering her Humph's polo shirt was a nice touch, don't you think? Sort of concluded our time together on a pleasant note.'

Kish always knew when Geoff sought affirmation. He also knew that Geoff was a bit of a player. But he'd never call him up on it. What with his own track record, he was hardly one to talk.

Geoff clapped his hands. 'Back to more pressing matters. How loud can we get this thing to play?'

'I'm sure it's ample for what you need,' said Kish.

Geoff studied his housemate sat outside the café opposite. 'Well Humphrey my friend, this morning, your tidy world of brown oxford brogues, moleskin trousers, and over-priced snowboarding jackets is about to get a thorough shafting.'

Having summarised his plan to Kish, Geoff got ready to press Play.

An introduction to the neighbourhood of Putney Ferret

Putney Ferret (pronounced 'fer'ay') is a small, affluent residential area located to the southeast of <u>Putney</u> in South West London. Designated a "Conservation Area", it comprises a main street, Ferret Rise, with several fashionable streets running off it, predominantly much sought-after Victorian terraced cottages and semi-detached homes, as well as more substantial Edwardian residences. At the last census, Putney Ferret was estimated as having 1050 residents, with 87% of property owner-occupied. The average salary per household is £196,000, comprising 1.7 wage earners. The average home value is £632,000 (March 2011). Average rent: £2310 pcm. Average number of children per household is 1.5; cars: 1.8 per household.

In 2011 Putney Ferret was awarded 'best for aspirant lifestyle' category by the magazine <u>Gentrifik</u>, and is a much sought-after haven for young social climbers and wealthy professionals.

History: Putney Ferret's name goes back to AD 1072 when . . .

TWO

Opposite No. 47 stood the 'Latte Pharté' café, the caffeinated jewel of Putney Ferret. It had a vivid blue and cherry frontage, housed in a well-appointed late-Victorian terrace. Mounted on its wall was a small, polished brass plaque that read '2009 Café with Best Ambience Award'. It was bestowed by The Putney Ferret Café-Society Association, a local club founded a couple of years ago and which enthusiastically plaqued several local cafés for a variety of merits, including *'Most Comfortable Sofa'*, *'Best café for tweeting'* and *'Best Cappuccino Foam Swirl'*.

The Latte Pharté sported several shiny aluminium bistro tables and patio gas burners along its frontage, made all the more pretty by terracotta window boxes, packed full of crocuses. In just a few months time, hanging baskets filled with trailing lobelias and fuchsias would also line the frontage, drooping verdant foliage into cafégoers' overpriced pastries. Inside, soft leather sofas surrounded an inviting fireplace, and the café's deep blue walls were lined with various watercolours painted by local artists, all bearing a sizeable price tag.

The early March sun had got several residents sitting outside the café, including one Humphrey C. Massey. He'd been on display there since around nine that morning, buried in his Mac laptop, making full use of the café's free Wi-Fi. Twitter was his home page, and he too was busy reviewing the tweets Kish had been cursing just moments before. Unlike Kish, Humphrey concluded this morning's diatribe was the mysterious FerayNotFerret's best yet. Pure genius in fact.

@FerayNotFerret:
Public, frankly aghast. Place littered with 'someones' using their Mac or Sunday Times for effect

@FerayNotFerret:
Surely anyone wanting to actually work would shy from sitting in most prominent and busy area of café?

@FerayNotFerret:
Too many people with macs sat as prominently-visible as possible #pretentious

Having sipped on a rapidly chilling latte, Humphrey C. Massey looked about him and tutted. Place was brimming with laptop-tapping pretenders. No doubt one or two were filling Facebook with all the usual drivel. Highly likely one or two were aspiring authors, fiddling on a plot that could only ever be self-published, if at all. Others no doubt were checking through their work email, relying on the weekend to maintain the illusion of competency during the week. He might be on a laptop himself, but unlike them, he knew he was real. After all, Humphrey *was* FerayNotFerret.

The Latte Pharté had long been Humphrey's hide from which he cast a critical eye on the scrambling frauds happily ambling around Putney Ferret, dreaming of owning a place there. When Twitter took off and the café's WiFi went free two years ago, Humphrey began writing as FerayNotFerret, offering up thoughts and observations to anyone who cared. As his tweets on 'Ferretisms' had became pricklier, so his readership grew, largely through one follower tipping off a friend to do likewise. By no means were all of his eight hundred and seventy three followers from the neighbourhood. One of them even claimed to live in Venezuela. Of course, Humphrey's craft now required he maintained total anonymity, at odds with a natural disposition to be noticed. He never published his location other than stating something nebulous like "*sat on Ferret Rise,*" or "*the café is brimming today*", and besides, even if his geographical location was known, hidden among so many Mac users and laptoppers, the true identity of FerayNotFerret was frankly anyone's guess.

Humphrey trained that same critical eye on a rather striking fellow who'd just sat at a table toward the end of the row. *Chancer. Game on.* Taking care not to appear concerned what others were up to (Humphrey often reminded his readers that this watching others only signalled one's own social inferiority), Humphrey studied the guy's demeanour: effortlessly relaxed in a blue moleskin sports jacket, wearing dark tan Oxford's paired with red trousers. Frankly the clothes said it all. Why, thought Humphrey, despite every attempt since university, could he still not quite pull that 'signature Ferret' look off, the same way that this—this Mr. Moleskin could? Humphrey stared uncontrollably as Mr. Moleskin read his battered Penguin Classic. Humphrey noted his well-nourished hair, stress-free complexion, and strong jaw. Mr. Moleskin never once looked up, but simply sat there with that utter, uncompromising self-confidence that comes with being at home in ones' own moleskin, oblivious to Humphrey's silent prostration toward him. *Look back at me*, Humphrey seethed silently. *Am I not at least worth consideration? Am I not real Ferret too?*

That precise moment, Humphrey saw the very thing that confirmed both his frustrations and Mr. Moleskin's provenance. Sat on his left little finger was pure Ferret itself: a gold signet ring. Humphrey nervously twisted his own signet ring. Any onlooker might not see any difference between the two men. But Humphrey knew better. He realised now where he stood in this two-person pecking order. Before him sat The Genuine Article, not even bothering to notice Humphrey, whose own provenance was betrayed simply by concerning himself with someone else's social standing. Humphrey counted to ten to calm himself. Clearly he should seek out an easier quarry this morning. Which is what he finally opted for, all the while chastising those oiks around him doing precisely the same.

Geoff teased out the gusset of his borrowed underpants from between his clenched buttocks and smiled at his housemate opposite. 'Bless his little cashmere socks,' he mumbled. Geoff had not missed anything from his vantage point, including a young couple with sunglasses on arrive at the table next to his housemate. Geoff observed the man of the duo opt for the outward facing seat then adjust his position so he was more side-on to his partner sat opposite, her back to the pavement. *Tut, tut. In seating protocol, surely it was still the female's prerogative to be sat facing outward?* Geoff raised his binos for closer inspection. The young man dumped at least a kilo's worth of crisp Sunday newspaper on the table, causing it to wobble. He then wedged some paper underneath one of the legs. Appearing satisfied, the young man sat back. Geoff studied his face, and for a second thought the man had something familiar about him.

'Can we get this over and done with?' asked Kish from the sofa. 'I'd quite like to pop over there myself. Elise and I had another bust up last night and quite frankly I'd like to get out the house to relax.'

Kish and Elise arguing? Nothing unusual with that, thought Geoff, his eyes now back on Humphrey.

The early spring air was cool and crisp, and Humphrey had come well wrapped. This morning he was decked out in a particularly expensive black and grey Salomon boarding jacket purchased only the day before at Putney Ski, the local winter sports outfitter of choice for discerning Ferret residents. Purchased courtesy of his ever-giving credit card, it was an expensive upgrade on his previous jacket, made unwearable following last weekend's unfortunate rooftop incident, courtesy of Geoff. Complimenting the jacket was his slate-grey Kangol beanie hat, a veteran of at least four snowboarding trips to Les Trois Vallées, or 'Mt Ferret' as the area had been coined more recently. And finally his favourite pair of red trousers. After the disappointing self-calibration against Mr. Moleskin earlier, Humphrey aka FerayNotFerret felt much better starting on the couple sat just one table along:

@FerayNotFerret:
Public! Faux Ferret Alert!

@FerayNotFerret:
Taken immediate, certain umbrage to this recently arrived duo and their outward deliberation

@FerayNotFerret:
Not-so-chirpy chap is her fiancé, judging by large vulgar engagement ring

@FerayNotFerret:
2 carats is my conservative guess: must be briolite or bought cheap from CongoBloodGems or such

@FerayNotFerret:
Just flicked a succession of brief glances to gauge her 'look n' feel'

@FerayNotFerret:
Certainly equestrian, less Windsor Park Polo, more Donkey sanctuary.

@FerayNotFerret:
I'd put a day's pay on her name not being Olivia, or a Carissa, more a Jackie or Charlene

When Humphrey eventually gleaned the lady's name, it was only fair he update his readership:

@FerayNotFerret:
Turns out our faux Ferret is called Shelley. A Shelley in Ferret of all places!

@FerayNotFerret:
Frankly if she were my fiancée, I'd have her adopt an alternative name

@FerayNotFerret:
Does Shel come with a matching surname? A 'Clodhopper' perhaps, or 'Buggins'

@FerayNotFerret:
Whatever, name surely appointed to an ancestor who worked in medieval pigcraft

@FerayNotFerret:
Or abandoned as a bastard upon frosted steps of some Victorian workhouse near Stepney.

@FerayNotFerret:
The fact she is wearing a Barbour quilt jacket, leads me to one conclusion

@FerayNotFerret:
She is desperately clambering up the very pole we true Ferrets are perched atop #greasypole

@FerayNotFerret:
Top marks for re-invention Shelzz, but alas you don't fool me
More spirited now, Humphrey turned his attention to describing Shelley's fiancé, who he'd just established was called Rob.

@FerayNotFerret:
Guessing likely profession of 'Rob' aka guy-next-to-me

@FerayNotFerret:
Based on dead cert financial indicators of footwear, collar position, Sunday paper, and hairstyle

@FerayNotFerret:
I conclude he is a colossal 'Trier', a sad parvenu, clearly not the real deal

@FerayNotFerret:
My guess is 27, and still works in a job requiring the wearing of a headset

@FerayNotFerret:
Mon-Fri 8.30-5pm, recites call-scripts down the phone flogging market research or add-on insurance 'products'

Yet with no hair wax, a thinker's look about him, and that beaten-up cardigan, he didn't appear like someone who'd sit comfortably in a call centre. Somewhat bothered, Humphrey went through other possible careers for this Rob chap. Approximately nine guesses later and Humphrey sat back, satisfied.

@FerayNotFerret:
A local journalist, readers. Unconfirmed but that's my guess. #ponceyjourno

@FerayNotFerret:
And by the looks of him, he's come to terms with imminent lay-off from his traditional newspaper

@FerayNotFerret:
Thx to the new dawn of online, astute commentators like me, and discerning readers such as you

@FerayNotFerret:
Which means he is probably on £30k? Assume therefore he's not residing in this postcode

Any sense of restoring equilibrium to his universe proved short-lived. Being sat on an endothermic aluminium seat for an hour had by now severely agitated Humphrey's old haemorrhoid friend, plus his bladder was rapidly filling up. But Humphrey had no intention of moving just yet. Humphrey then remembered his hot water bottle, tucked under his jacket—he'd use it as a nice, warming cushion. He looked about him. Unfortunately the place was bustling with the sort of people who'd question the provenance of someone producing something so domestic as a water bottle in Ferret, in broad daylight. For now he'd just have to remain stoic, and endure the irritated vein-end. Humphrey began searching for details on journalist salaries when a waitress came over to take Shelley and Rob's order.

'Hi there!' exclaimed Shelley, who then stood up and kissed the waitress on both cheeks. Known as Lucia by the few who chose to care, the Brazilian waitress frequently got her fair share of grateful embraces from people she hardly knew, which seemed only slightly less odd than those regular café goers who didn't acknowledge her at all.

'Hello again. It is Shelley from yesterday, yes?' Lucia said politely.

Hello again? Humphrey had been coming to this café for over two years and it was only last Christmas when Lucia started referring to him by name. The wrong one, usually.

'How is your house hunt yes?' continued Lucia. Bugger, thought Humphrey.

'Oh, still looking,' chirped Rob. 'I'll have a latte please.'

'Lovely area this, perfect for us,' added Shelley, her voice raised slightly. 'And I'll have a skinny cappuccino please.'

'Yes, of course,' said the waitress, trying to sound interested. She turned to Humphrey. 'Another latte for you, Hector?'

Humphrey paused, making a note to correct her at some future quieter moment. 'Best make it a decaf, Lucia. And in a cardboard cup, with a sleeve and lid please. Keeps it hot longer.'

Lucia slipped off, leaving Shelley smiling in her seat. 'So nice she remembered us,' said Shelley smugly, and opened up a local properties newspaper. Her curiosity soon had her glancing up and down the row of tables, and someone sat at the next table in a snowboarding jacket particularly caught her attention. *Hedley did the waitress say he was?* Shelley casually noted his dark brown brogues. With red trousers. Definitely a Type. *Didn't they all wear that kind of 'awkward posh-cool' round here?* Brogue-Boy was reading the same local property freebee as hers and appeared to be circling certain listings with a thick red marker pen. Question was, were they residential lettings or places for sale? She hoped the former. She took note of the distinctive turquoise estate agent banner at the top of the page he was on. She leafed through her own copy until she found the same page. Another eye flick. Brogue-Boy had circled a property on the second row down, third one in from left. She looked at her own copy. Assuming she'd triangulated correctly, he'd circled a two bedroom, luxury renovated Victorian apartment, six hundred and ten thousand pounds, share of freehold. Fourth row down, first and third pictures in. Three-bed terraced houses, both eight hundred and seventy thousand pounds freehold. So this guy had some cash then. She looked at his face. Probably some overpaid management consultant or something.

Humphrey crunched his biscotti, and made an undetectable peek back at Shelley's paper. Sure enough she was on the same page. The fish was on the hook.

'Putney Ferret remains the best long-term bet in South West London. Well that's what Kat was saying only last week,' she continued.

'Kat? As in Kat Rutherford you mean? She should wait. Prices will dip further' said Rob, sounding strained. 'They have to, with no-one able to get on the first rung, and besides she'd get a far better deal in Sheen or Acton than round here.'

Shelley scoffed. 'Acton's hardly on Kat's agenda. I mean, at least consider the right postcode.'

'Well, I'd happily consider it over Putney Ferret. We might actually swing a cat there.'

Once more, Humphrey began typing frantically.

@FerayNotFerret:
I do feel a bit sorry for a chap who has to cope with fiancée, esp if called Shelley #Aspirant

@FerayNotFerret:
Her permanent frown mark gives the Somerset town of Cheddar a run for its money as home to the UK's deepest gorge #needsbotox

Shelley laughed slightly. 'Always thinking like the humble barista that you are. I'm not going to live in Acton.' She tapped a picture on the page. It was of a property at least fifty thousand pounds more than the terrace houses she'd seen Brogue-Boy circle. 'Now, look at that place there, three streets away from here. Seven hundred and seventy thousand. We could stretch to that with the right lender, no problem.'

Humphrey winced at the prize imposter and continued typing.

@FerayNotFerret:
Public! Guy-next-to-me is a barista. A coffee-grinder! Wife-to-be is a faker contemplating Ferret! A farce: he's wearing a cardy!

@FerayNotFerret:
Even the most generous mortgage lender would turn some percolator-operator and his favourite horse away.

'Besides,' continued Shelley, 'Kat says renting for much longer is nonsense. Bricks and mortar and lots of it.'

Humphrey leant back. Funny, he'd made exactly the same point to a rather pleasant lady in a bar in Mayfair only two weeks ago. From memory she was called Kat too. Bloody place was littered with Kats.

'Damn it Shelley!' Rob slammed his mug down, sending latte froth up over the lip. He leant in, pausing to compose. 'This isn't the right time to move, or for that matter, to talk about it!'

It was time for Humphrey to do a little more stoking. He picked up his mobile, ensuring it was switched off, and then spoke into it.

'Hi Simon . . . yah, fine . . . yes I've been here for about . . .' Humphrey looked at his Breitling watch, which had only seventy-four more monthly payments remaining. 'Half an hour . . . I know, quite cold . . . okay, the house I'm after . . . well I'll do sealed bids and go ten percent above asking price . . . Best to you, too . . . bye.' Humphrey switched his phone back on. *Nothing worse than pretending to be talking into it and for it to ring.* He returned to his paper, and awaited a reaction from behind it. The silence was telling.

'Excuse me,' Shelley asked on cue. Humphrey kept a straight face. 'Excuse me,' she repeated. Eventually Humphrey lowered his paper.

'I'm sorry?' he replied graciously.

'Sorry for asking, but do you live round here?' Shelley enquired.

'Erm, yes.' Humphrey straightened in his seat. 'Right there actually.' He casually pointed to the white Victorian terraced house opposite. Shelley turned in her chair and glanced over her shoulder. Humphrey returned to his article. Past experience suggested it would only be a few seconds before Shelley might speak again.

'Sorry,' she started. Humphrey looked up again, deliberately giving off a feigned smile. 'Hope you don't mind, but a good place to live? Putney Ferret? Location and value-wise I mean.'

'Well yes, after all, the two kind of go together round here. Moved there in '06, and it's done very well.' Humphrey felt earnest. He leant in, resting crossed arms on the table. 'Practically doubled in value since then, even with the dip. But I can sympathise with anyone trying to get into the market nowadays.'

Rob dropped his newspaper down for a moment. 'You are a very lucky man, catching it at the right time. 'Great investment.' Humphrey sensed he meant it.

'Well, renting out a couple of the rooms always helps.' Humphrey raised his eyebrows, rocked back with all the confidence of a rare, thoroughbred Ferret property owner.

'Strange name though. Putney Ferrit I mean,' said Shelley.

'I hear it increasingly pronounced "ferray",' said Rob, momentarily distracted from an interesting article about the Tate Modern.

'Well of course and so it should,' Shelley scoffed, eyes trained on Humphrey. 'Never quite sure how to say it.'

'The pronounciation "ferray" is almost universally used now,' Humphrey said sternly. 'Only a few laggards insist on the furry animal pronunciation these days.' Something caught his eye. Opposite, Geoff was standing in the bay window and grinning. In Humphrey's experience, bad things tended to follow that grin and instantly his heart rate sped up, his torso began to burn like a furnace and his pile winced, leaving him cursing Geoff for having greater control of his bodily functions than he did. Definitely time to leave. As Humphrey began rifling for change, someone else joined the couple sat next to him. Although the new arrival's hair was styled a little differently to how he'd remembered it, her extraordinarily pretty side profile was unforgettable. Without her knowing, she sent Humphrey cowering behind his property newspaper, while he worked out what next to do. He'd have to say something. *But what?*

Kish had just returned from the kitchen and put two mugs of coffee down on the rattan-framed glass table.

'Funny thing,' said Geoff, his back to Kish.

'What is?'

'Just as some stunning brunette sits down at the next table—look,' Geoff said and guided Kish's line of sight along his arm toward his index finger, 'old Humpy-boy dives behind his paperwork! Not like him is it?'

Cornered behind his Sunday supplement, Humphrey tried to compose himself.

'I am so sorry for keeping you waiting,' Humphrey heard her say, presumably to Shelley. 'Train was running late.' Her voice was just like he remembered, plum-silk, clear and lively. Just like the night he'd met her. 'Anyway, it's lovely to see you again. How's the house hunting?'

'A few options,' Humphrey heard Shelley reply. 'Trying to target a few streets. But looking for a three-bed terrace, south-facing garden, and a ten-minute walk max to the station. You?'

'Hopeless. To live round here, I'm basically looking at one bedroom Victorian conversions. Studios even.' *That voice again.*

Lucia the waitress returned with a tray carrying the latest orders. Placing Humphrey's fifth latte on the table, she peered over his paper and said, 'Enjoy your coffee in there.'

But Humphrey couldn't leave right now.

Opposite, Geoff watched Humphrey carefully extended his hand round his upright newspaper to retrieve a cardboard coffee cup.

'What are you waiting for?' said Kish. 'He's seen us, you know. We're going to miss our chance.'

Geoff paused, then said, 'You don't think he actually knows her do you?'

'The cute one who just joined?' replied Kish. 'I'd be shocked if he does.'

'Added bonus if he does. Still, I guess there's only one way to find out.' Geoff then crouched down. 'Ready?'

'Ready.' replied Kish, as he put on some Bose noise reduction headphones.

Initiating Phase Three, Geoff pressed 'play' on his remote control, almost beside himself with gleeful anticipation.

THREE

Fucking grind us both, you fuck-of-a-bad-man!!!!!

The female's orders crackled from Geoff's Bose speakers into the early Sunday morning. Opposite, the large café windows shivered as her heavily accent slammed into them, while café-goers jolted involuntarily, switching their attention from somewhat quieter discourse on house prices toward the direction of the fierce outburst.

And just how do you wish me to grind you, madam?

. . . replied a man in Received English.

'Humphrey, comment on that!' Geoff yelled from below the window ledge, and then turned to Kish for a reaction. Digitally re-mastered to ensure a truly ringside experience, Geoff had teed up Cremed Swedes at the precise moment the hero of the movie, Dax Chiltern, a British telemark ski instructor engaged in what local residents of Putney Ferret were slowly concluding to be an overt 'three-way' on a chalet kitchen floor with two young ladies, who, according to the movie credits were Astrid Vulvo and her hayloft-wench lover, Bambi Strungg.

Kish just shrugged back. Wearing his Bose sound reduction headphones meant he was the only person located within a radius of fifty metres not to hear the unremitting and wholly unsubtle grunts and groans. Nonetheless, he couldn't fail to notice the reactions of those who'd not taken the precaution of wearing ear protection this morning. Take for starters the three bewildered old ladies passing by, fresh from early morning Mass at nearby St Lukes-on-the-Hill. Instantly reminded of a fallen world, even here on Putney Ferret, two of them shook involuntarily as they walked past the house, clasping frail hands on somewhat already deaf ears.

However, the third, the oldest, broke a smile as she recalled a hay field in Suffolk during the summer of 1944, and a long afternoon frottaging with two American GIs.

By now, Astrid and Bambi had admirably demonstrated their command of English as a second language to much of Putney Ferret, getting their mouths around several 'O' based sounds, courtesy one could assume, of Dax's imposing privates. At a café table opposite, not far from where Humphrey was sat, a little girl in a red hat was innocently processing the vaguely cuisine-related terms. Alas her mother had not cupped her daughter's ears tightly enough, as when she was asked 'Mummy, why does the noisy, not very nice man in that house over there want to eat a shaven pie,' the concerned parent was left cursing the day she betrayed her own better judgment and agreed with her selfish sod-of-a-husband to raise a family in a so-called affluent London neighbourhood. The mother seethed at the no-doubt childless arseholes who lived opposite, flagrantly advertising their sexual deviance by screwing each other with the aid of microphones, any which way possible, and damn what anyone else thought.

From behind a half-shut roman blind, Geoff saw it all, but did not flinch. It was Humphrey who he'd targeted and as far as he was concerned—the fretful mother with her innocent child, the three old biddies, local residents—were acceptable, if somewhat regrettable collateral damage.

For Humphrey C. Massey unapologetic social aspirant, perennial renting resident of Putney Ferret and vanguard for its correct pronunciation, the effect of the noise from his very own home was immediate and profound. The instant the words '*fucking grind us both*' hit him head-on, Humphrey spasmed more violently than anyone. His fingers straightened up like lightening rods, releasing his cup of hot coffee. As the cup fell, it clipped the right hand edge of his table, causing it to ricochet—its lid miraculously still attached—towards the feet of the very person he was trying to avoid: one Kat Rutherford, current resident, if he correctly recalled, of South Kensington, London. Humphrey braced himself for the almighty crash and splash. Luckily for Humphrey the sound of someone's buttocks being rapidly slapped with a kitchen utensil drowned out the noise of a cup exploding on impact with a hard pavement. He looked down, still shaking. Humphrey had frequently pondered how much coffee comprised a 'Grande Latte.' However, he'd never imagined using the interior of a fine, white linen Prada handbag as a unit of measurement. For now lying inside the wide-open handbag was his cup, half submerged in a pool of hot coffee. And as Columbian roast aromas floated up on rising steam, brown liquid began leaching through the Prada handbag's natural fibres. Meerkat-like, Humphrey jerked his head up to assess Kat's reaction, ready to blurt out a frenzied apology for transforming her bag into a brown, zip-lined, steaming horseturd-with-handle. He ducked back down again. Kat, like everyone else was fixated on the continued slapping noises from the house opposite.

Back cowering behind his local property newspaper, Humphrey suddenly experienced an additional violent pain across his stomach. The rubber water bottle he'd tucked under his top had chosen that very moment to start leaking its near-scalding contents. With his bladder just minutes from doing the same, there were simply no two ways about it. He had to relieve himself of the water bottle, escape inside, and relieve himself very shortly. Never the one to draw attention to himself, Humphrey carefully used his spare hand to unzip his top and grab the turgid rubber container through the neck of his jumper and with all the strength he could muster, pull it free. He hadn't noticed that at that precise moment, Lucia was stood right beside him, holding a tray of cups, and the momentum of the rubber bottle's release was such that it connected with the bridge of her unsuspecting nose, cracking it instantly. The hot water bottle then crashed violently through the tray of coffee cups, sending pieces everywhere, including part of a handle which connected with Kat's head.

With this added commotion, Kat and Shelley and several others span round to see Lucia bent double on the pavement and a healthy flow of blood emerge from a newly-shaped nose. Instinctively Kat rushed to help a shocked Lucia. Humphrey, in shock himself, tried to do the same, all the while trying to ignore his now near-exploding bladder and a haemorrhoid that had its own pulse.

'I am so, so sorry Lucia,' he burbled. 'Does it hurt? Don't answer that. You're in pain. I suppose that's obvious. Pinch your nose to stop the bleeding.'

Lucia wisely ignored him, and when she was finally capable of standing, she muttered a thank-you to Kat, and was led into the back of a colleague's car and taken to the local A&E.

Kat started staring at Humphrey. He looked awfully familiar, and then she recollected a recent conversation with a man about Syrah wines in a pub in Mayfair. She remembered some more. Rather posh, wine importer didn't he say? Lived in Ferret, and he had a funny name. Humboldt? No doubt in her mind—stood before her was the same guy who, a fortnight ago, laughed with her as they studied and swirled oversized glasses of northern Rhone Petite Syrah before swishing them confidently around their mouths. Back then he'd had a rather attractive demeanour. Which is why the current scene took some rationalizing.

Humphrey's mind also escaped to that evening in Mayfair a fortnight ago . . .

Flush with aspirant hope, Humphrey left for Mayfair around six o'clock, wearing a new suit he'd bought in the Gieves and Hawkes January sales. It served his posture well and somehow helped him appear a couple of vital inches taller than his stated five foot eleven height (and a half, if ever asked). He'd spent most of the afternoon helping two top drawer 'Yummies' select the wine for a dinner party that weekend, during which time they saw off a bottle of Seguin Per and Fils Pouilly Fume 2006 followed by a Lanzerac Estate Cabernet Sauvignon 2001. Humphrey had arranged to meet up for a drink with Jonny Norcliff, an old mate from university, and now a chartered surveyor who spent his time leasing office space in the City. Jonny, ebullient and effervescent, shared his early evenings in the company of fellow chartered surveyors, comparing cufflinks and advancing cirrhosis. Jonny had suggested one of his favourite haunts, The White Horse pub in Shepherds Market just off Piccadilly, easy enough for Humphrey to get to from Putney Station, via Vauxhall.

Jonny and Humphrey gelled well. Jonny was keen to improve his nose for wine through Humphrey, whereas Jonny, a great wingman, helped Humphrey on his search for the perfect woman. Provided he wasn't too drunk that is. By the time they met at around 6:45pm, Jonny was near the bar with three male colleagues, busy lining their stomachs with Spitfire Ale. Swiftly introduced by Jonny into the group as a 'great chap,' Jonny's surveyor friends insisted on buying Humphrey's ales. The conversation somehow got onto schooling, and Humphrey recounted his own school days at Pellerton College, a minor public school in Dorset that no-one knew about. It had closed its doors five years ago, which was no bad thing because Humphrey had never actually been there. By 8:00pm Jonny's colleagues had made for home, leaving Humphrey buzzing from five pints of ale on an empty stomach, and Jonny, who'd insisted on a tequila shot after every pint, minutes from collapsing altogether.

'S'cuse me chap, man-size slash required,' boomed Jonny through a deep, cheese and onion crisp-scented belch. Jonny then stumbled into the ladies' and was swiftly ushered outside by an altogether-too-considerate bar manager who'd kept a watchful eye on the suited hooligan.

Humphrey tried his best to placate the manager. 'Great guy, wouldn't hurt a fly you know.'

'In his present condition I suggest you just help him get a cab, sir. Best thing for him. You can come back in when you've sorted him out.'

Humphrey stood on the pavement propping Jonny up as naturally as he could. He admired Jonny for getting evicted so respectfully. When a cab finally approached, Jonny bared his backside at it. Unsurprisingly it chose not to stop. He performed a handstand for the next, which also drove on.

'Fella, if you want a cab, try not to behave like a pickled fart,' Humphrey pleaded.

Jonny checked himself, and sure enough the next cab drew up. 'Islington please,' said Humphrey as Jonny clambered in.

'He's okay isn't he?' said the cabbie, sounding moderately concerned.

'Of course I'm bloody okay, Mister Drive,' replied Jonny, imperiously. 'It's a school night. Garland Road, Islington, please. Off we go.'

As the taxi moved off, Jonny began telling the cabbie what a great mate Humphrey was. Their friendship had incubated within a loosely federated clique for the best part of three years at Uni, during which time they'd shared a countless number of experiences in the pubs and bars of Oxford, the memories of which were kept alive by the occasional beer together. Sadly their meetings ever since had rarely created any great new memories. What they now had was a safe, predictable and unchallenging friendship that meant they would remain in touch, if with ever-less frequency, for years to come.

Humphrey took a seat at the bar. Having finished apologising to the barman for his friend's behaviour, he noticed a lady for the first time, perched a couple of stools down.

'Can you recommend a good Australian red?' he heard the lady ask the barman.

'We've several good Syrahs,' replied the barman.

'If it's Australian, isn't it a Shiraz?' She responded, mischief in her voice. Humphrey's ears pricked up and the barman winked knowingly. 'I'll give one a crack anyway,' the lady continued. 'You choose.'

'Certainly,' the barman replied.

'Excuse me, but I would actually recommend Shelmerdine's Heathcote 2006?' interjected Humphrey. 'I think you'd like it.' Humphrey did not offer her eye contact; he chose to look at her through the mirrored back bar, a ploy he'd noted from several movies.

'Thanks' she replied, looking back at him via his reflection. 'Maybe the next one.'

'Fair enough.' Humphrey locked his eyes doggedly on a bottle of Bombay gin on the back bar shelf. It helped him remain composed. When the lady's wine arrived and she took a sip, it wasn't long before she was back onto the barman.

'Excuse me? Hi, sorry for being a pain, but this tastes well a bit odd—don't you think?' She held out the glass.

The barman sniffed it politely and nodded. 'Syrah or Shiraz, it's certainly off.'

'Tell you what,' she said, scanning the book-thick leather bound wine list, 'let me try the Shelmerdine Heathcote Shiraz instead please.'

The barman served up the replacement. In the ornate back-bar mirror's reflection, Humphrey watched the lady hold the glass up to the light, tilting the glass and rolling it one way and then the other. She then breathed it in, took a small sip, followed by a slightly larger one.

'Mr Barman, may I have the same please,' Humphrey asked. Glass soon in hand, he silently counted up to ten then turned, and silently raised his glass to the lady sat beside him, whilst struggling to focus correctly.

She raised hers back, and asked 'What do you see?'

"A room spinning uncontrollably" might have been one valid response. However, sensing she was referring to the wine, Humphrey composed himself then held his glass up toward the bar light. 'Let me see. Well, it's vibrant, almost purple.'

'Very.'

'But the light still cuts through its dark berry inkiness. Now over to you. What do you smell, what do you taste?' he asked. She inhaled, paused, and then sipped gently.

'It has berries, certainly, balanced with a subtle spice.'

'Rounded, gentle tannins, good phenolics, yep, it's opened up nicely.' Humphrey removed his nose from his glass, 'Apparently these guys' vines are grown in so-called Cambrian soils, basically very old dirt that helps produce fine Shiraz grapes.'

'It's delicious. You seem like you know your stuff,' she remarked.

'I have to. It's how I make a living.'

Immediately the lady swiveled ninety degrees and studied Humphrey properly for the first time. Humphrey's brain was on autopilot, his sole objective now was to remain in control, not say anything stupid. 'I'd love to know more about wines,' she replied. 'I am okayish on the whites, but it's these reds that leave me a little unsure.'

Through the fug, Humphrey established he was talking to Kat Rutherford, an analyst for an investment bank who had been decidedly stood up by her date. Kat had decided to sink a glass in any case, phone a friend to systematically vilify her idiot date and then go home.

'Live round here?'

'Not far, but moving a little further west soon.'

'Fantastic.' I live out in Putney Ferret myself.'

'Really? That's one of the places I am considering.'

For the next hour, with Kat looking at her rather nice watch with less and less frequency, she and Humphrey galvanised a mutual interest in new world wines. Twice she told him perhaps they could meet again?

The second time came with a touch on the forearm. But Humphrey could never read a sign. That was his perennial downfall. Finally she offered him her business card. He obliged by returning his. 'Just in case you ever want some advice or your company is doing some wine tasting.'

'Senior Wine Consultant, Royal Warrant. Well thank you, Humphrey,' she said, lingering a little. 'Perhaps I should go now. Early start tomorrow.'

Humphrey looked at his watch. 'Goodness. Yes, me too,' he lied. 'But let me get your tab.'

She initially protested but Humphrey would have none of it. 'Thank you so much. A real pleasure meeting you Humphrey,' she said. 'I meant what I said, I hope we'll bump into each other sometime.'

Humphrey was bursting. Give me a signal, he pleaded silently. Heart racing, finally he said, 'Sure, well you have my card. Feel free to call me.' Kat stood there silently. 'What I meant to say was, I hope you get home safely, and drink lots of water.'

Kat smiled nervously. 'Thank you—I will.'

Humphrey turned on his stool to watch her walk purposefully out of view. Strong, beautiful, elegant and he'd just about scratched the surface. Sighing he studied the bar tab. 'Good God! Hundred and twenty quid? She must have been sat here since yesterday lunchtime!' Fifteen minutes and a thirty quid taxi ride later, Humphrey walked gingerly into the Rutting Stag pub on Ferret Rise, whereupon he relaxed into a leather sofa and regaled his story to Geoff and Kish.

'So nothing happened then,' Geoff asked bluntly.

'Nah. She didn't show me a sign.'

Eight miles north, things were only just heating up for Jonny Norcliff. Having slipped into sub-consciousness, it took the cabbie ten minutes to shake Jonny awake and help him onto the kerb outside 32a Garland Road. For a moment Jonny considered sleeping there. A lovely quiet night after all. But sensibilities took hold and he walked up to his familiar front door. Jonny spent two minutes unsuccessfully trying to unlock the door, before conceding and calling his fiancée through the letterbox.

'Julie Woollie!' He shouted rather melodically, 'Open up sweetie. He-e-ere's Jonny!' He then began singing about a blackbird in a pie,

accompanied by anti-rhythmic bangs on the front door. Finally the door opened a few inches, its chain remaining attached.

'Who the hell are you?' said a male face, peeking at him.

Jonny looked back at the stranger. 'Who the hell am I? More like who the fucking hell are you!' Without warning, Jonny then put his entire weight behind his shoulder and rammed the front door open. About ten short, confusing seconds later, Jonny found himself clamped in a half nelson in the hallway, with one side of his face squashed down on parka flooring, staring sideways at the hall wall. Odd. They were a different colour to the mushroom grey he remembered. Come to think of it, that hallstand is new too.

'It's Mr Sommers isn't it? Hi, I'm Jonny Norcliff,' and the dreadful reality of the situation slowly dawned on him . . .

Following an uncomfortable night sobering up in an Islington Police Station cell, Jonny limped through a formal police interview. He was informed that Mr. Sommers would naturally be seeking compensation for a broken door, but would not be pressing criminal charges. As Jonny stepped out of the station, he wondered how the hell he'd managed to end up at the very flat he'd moved out of just three weeks before, rather than his new Wimbledon pad eleven miles south. Jonny had a shockingly porous short-term memory when drunk. Clearly, Humphrey's memory was just as bad—Jonny was sure he'd told Humphrey about his new place, yet despite this, he'd still sent him off in a cab in completely the wrong direction. Jonny wondered if all guy conversations lacked concentration like theirs did. Whatever, it was one heck of a tale for the boys at Contleys Surveyors, a company famed for rewarding character over competence. On this story alone, Jonny confidently predicted making Associate Director by June.

Two weeks since that encounter in the Mayfair pub, Humphrey found himself being stared at by the same Kat Rutherford. Shelley was glaring at him in the same sort of way Uri Geller does when mind-bending spoons. But it was Dax who made Humphrey truly snap to.

Damn it girls, that broccoli spear hurts!

'Excuse me,' Shelley sniped loudly at a dazed Humphrey. 'Your place opposite, right?'

As several café-goers speculated on the whereabouts of a particular brassica, Humphrey scrambled to construct his next, vital sentence. He cursed Shelley for being so interested in house prices earlier. *How on earth had he got into this insane situation?*

'Hi Kat, how nice to see you,' Humphrey shouted, leaned over the table and kissed a bemused Kat on both cheeks. Shelley looked at Kat then back at Humphrey, bemused. Kat gave an unsure smile, then perching back down.

'I said, that's your place?' Shelley's stare hardened, as Dax issued demands to his vegetable-wielding students.

'I—I rent it out,' he said finally. 'Renters. Awful.' Humphrey chose that moment to deflect attention from the noisy lovemaking. 'Kat, sorry but I rather carelessly spilt my coffee into your . . . bag.'

Kat followed his eyes down. 'Oh no!' she exclaimed and picked up her sodden bag. As Shelley watched on, jaw wide open, she carefully poured the coffee out of the bag onto the pavement behind her, then began picking out her sodden possessions. First to emerge was a dripping address book, then a once-pink silk purse, followed by some car keys and a waterlogged mobile telephone. Kat then produced what appeared to be an enormous oblong teabag, held by a string. 'Well. I won't be using that will I?' Kat said matter-of-factly. Humphrey leant forward and before he could stop himself, he prodded it. It swung back and forth.

'Dear God!' gasped Shelley, realising that Kat was in fact holding up a massively swollen tampon, with scraps of maize paper wrapping still clung to it.

'Goodness, the wrappers on those lady plugs don't hold up too well do they?' said Humphrey abruptly. Not getting the warm smile he'd expect from such a disarming comment, he tried again. This time, demonstrating his caring, empathetic side. 'I'm sure there's a vending machine in the café if you need-'

'No! But thank you,' Kat replied rapidly.

'Yes, of course.' Humphrey offered a deep, knowing nod. 'Discretion needed.' A point clearly lost on Bambi as she demanded through Bose speakers that Dax keep still like a good boy, then telling him that she has a mallet. That was quite enough for Humphrey. 'Time for me to end this. Landlord's prerogative.' He frantically dialed his mobile, tipping his head as low under the table as possible. The connection took an eternity.

'Yah?' Geoff said finally.

'Turn that ruddy thing off,' hissed Humphrey. 'Before all of Ferret actually believe they are witnessing a guy being harpooned up the bum in our lounge!'

'You'll have to turn it off mate, I'm not in.'

'What do you mean, you're not in? Turn it off! Geoff! . . . Geoff!' Humphrey looked up and watched helplessly as his two housemates strode out through the front door and down the hill. Humphrey frantically scooped up his Mac, hot water bottle, newspapers, and extracted himself from the table. Conscious of spectating Ferret residents, he tried to remain dignified as he hobbled across the road, narrowly avoiding being mown down by a freshly muddied mountain biker, himself somewhat distracted by the rumpus. Finding the front door key took Humphrey an eternity. When he finally burst in, the noise was unbearable. Bladder now approaching point of no return, he lunged into the lounge, then hurdled the sofa, before freezing in front of the TV screen. It displayed a naked man laid face down and spread-eagled on a flagstone kitchen floor, as two naked, buxom young women straddled him, each holding a sturdy root vegetable, and eyeing up his bare backside, a frozen broccoli poking out of it. Shuddering, he dived under the TV to switch the DVD off. To Humphrey's absolute horror, the DVD player was bound up with thick masking tape. It would take an eternity to rip apart. *The remote! Where's the sodding remote.* Of course Geoff had hidden it. *The plug! Shut it down at the mains.* With that, Humphrey dived left, just as Bambi carefully positioned a plump swede, then giving Astrid the signal to deftly thump it home with a tent mallet, presumably with the broccoli still in situ. As several cafégoers opposite flinched at the sound of Dax transforming from ski-instructor into a human vegetable larder, Humphrey grabbed the plug. Instantly two hundred and forty volts of electricity discharged through him, sending him flying halfway across the lounge. Sat in total silence beside the rattan coffee table,

Humphrey looked down and saw he was still holding the plug. In a rare cathartic moment, he noticed something odd about it. Neatly twisted around one of the prongs was a length of copper wire, the other end contoured around the plastic casing, precisely where one would naturally grip a plug. The TV screen was also blank. He'd tripped the entire downstairs electricals.

Geoff had truly excelled himself this time, even compared to last Sunday's effort when Humphrey was forced to scale the roof to retrieve the bright pink, two-foot long condom that Geoff had placed over their chimney. During Humphrey's descent, he had caught his snowboard jacket on a typically robust Victorian cast-iron gutter, and was left dangling in full view of his café-going public. 'Well, at least it broke your fall, chap. Small mercies and all that,' Geoff remarked at the time. Today it was comedy electrocution. Clearly, Geoff was trying to kill him. Humphrey calmly noted his bladder had involuntarily emptied itself.

After a few moments, Humphrey stumbled to his feet and peered towards the café opposite. Unfathomably, Geoff and Kish were sitting at the very same table he'd sat at just moments ago, and appeared engaged in amiable chitchat with Shelley, Kat and Rob. Humphrey's mobile rang. Geoff again.

'You total shit,' Humphrey said bluntly.

'Ahh, calm is restored. Take it you've defused the fusebox then?'

'No I didn't. I did find the plug though.'

There was a pause. 'You didn't actually touch it, did you? The plug I mean.'

'Funnily enough I did,' Humphrey continued calmly. 'Seemed like the only option, given the DVD player is hermetically sealed with tape.'

Humphrey heard Geoff hoot with laughter then relay the news to the table, before returning to the phone conversation. 'I thought you'd see the wire I'd rigged round it, maybe flap a little, and make for the fusebox?'

At which point, Humphrey lost it. 'Fusebox? Flap a little? Yes, I'd say I maybe flapped a fucking little!'

Across the road, Geoff raised his eyebrows. Humphrey very rarely swore. 'Look if it helps, Humpy, I really am terribly sorry.

Come on, you could probably do with a fresh coffee . . . to earth you.' Humphrey caught a couple of sniggers at the other end of the line. 'And come meet a very old mate of mine,' Geoff added. 'I didn't realise he was sat next to you. Bye-e.'

Humphrey placed the phone back in his jeans pocket, and began composing himself in front of the mantle-piece mirror. Receiving an unforced apology from Geoff was as rare as hen's teeth. The guy didn't 'do' guilt. Just then, a strange figure appeared behind him in the mirror's reflection. Humphrey jumped then spun round. Stood in the hall archway was a young woman. She was wearing one of his distinctly pink crew polo shirts. 'Who the hell are you?' he asked.

Lisa apologised and explained she was a friend of Geoff's. 'From . . . last night.'

Humphrey scratched his head. He didn't recall any noises, other than Elise and Kish having a barny that had resulted in Elise slamming the door behind her.

'I've been upstairs wondering who the hell was making all that racket. Didn't dare come down. Not you was it?'

'Not me personally, but entirely for my benefit. I'm Humphrey by the way. As for our mutual acquaintance Geoff, he's sat over the road. I'm just going to join him. Want to come too?'

Lisa looked through the bay window, then back at Humphrey, desperately trying to ignore the enormous wet patch on his trousers. 'No-no matter,' she replied swiftly, and began to rifle through her handbag. 'Just tell him to call me if he feels like it. I left my number by his bed. Make sure, yeh?' Lisa then thanked him for the loaned top and left the house, leaving Humphrey to quickly shower and get into a clean pair of undies and trousers. Ten minutes later, armed with a cheque for damages rendered, Humphrey sidled over to the café, and secreted himself between Kish and the café door.

'So what you been up to since then, Geoff?' asked Rob.

'Not a great deal. Been in London for the past four years, managing a wine store just down the road here, and am currently shacked up with these boys.' Geoff signalled towards Kish and Humphrey.

'And before that?' Rob continued.

'Let me see, Parents wanted me back on the farm, but it was the last thing I wanted. So spent a year in Africa. Botswana. Built a school.' Humphrey frowned at Kish.

'Turns out they were at school together,' Kish whispered to Humphrey.

'Is there anyone he hasn't met, shagged, or gone to school with?' Humphrey replied quietly.

'I think it's admirable to volunteer time to do some good for others,' said Kat. 'And not just go head long into some career for the next forty years after college, like the rest of us.'

Humphrey looked on in disbelief. Five minutes in Geoff's company and already Kat's perfect mascara-lined eyelashes were fluttering.

'Why thank you Kat,' said Geoff. 'It is important to give a little back. It seems everyone is just take, take, take these days.'

Humphrey now turned to Rob, and said 'In a city of ten million, you two bump into each other! I mean how coincidental is that?'

'Simple law of averages,' said Kish, putting down his mobile. He'd noticed a missed call from his mother—not a conversation he'd want to have this morning. 'True to say most people of our age who moved to London a few years ago tend to congregate around the same places, South West London's cafés being a prime example. And if you're friends at school sharing the same outlook on life, that sort of thing, at some point you'll bump into each other either via similar jobs, pastimes, bars, tube stops. If you haven't kept in touch via Facebook, be ready to bump into your past in person.' Kish smiled then returned to thumbing out a series of short emails over his phone.

'Incidentally Geoff,' said Humphrey, 'your latest one-night-stand got bored waiting for you, so left. Guess she felt a little neglected, funny that. Whatever, she asked me to get you to call.' The table silenced and looked a little uneasy.

'Not the Geoff I remember—too busy with his sport for the ladies was this one,' said Rob, 'and the best rugby player our school ever turned out. Come to think of it, practically made the big time.'

'Long time ago,' Geoff said. 'Rugby wasn't for me in the end. Nor farming. Or Africa. And now I am in London. And Humph, I don't think we need to burden these people with my pitiful private life.'

Kat was still frowning. 'Sorry to be a bit thick,' she started, 'but you all live together across the road, right? Where all that noise came from.' She pointed to Humphrey. 'And you're the one who owns it?' An awkward silence followed, the kind that only the weak willed tend to jump in and fill.

'Ahh, yes,' said Humphrey as Kish placed a firm hand on Humphrey's thigh and squeezed him to a halt. Borrowing from Dennis Healey, Kish whispered 'when you are in a hole, don't keep digging,' then addressed the table. 'Humphrey told you he owned the place opposite, what he really meant to say was that he rents it. He occupies the smallest room, very modest guy.'

As Humphrey tried to contain his bright rouge complexion, Geoff said, 'So Kat, you mentioned a few moments ago that Humphrey and you've met before, right?'

'Yes, a couple of weeks ago. A pub in Mayfair.' She looked at Humphrey, and remembered his eyes when they met. Kind eyes, hazel in colour, with a confident face and groomed hair. When she'd first met him she thought what good posture he had, before she snatched a quick look at his footwear. Black, formal, buffed and well made. He'd made for a good conversationalist. Today he looked and sounded very different. It wasn't his clothes, nor the flush face. It was his eyes. Today they were tired, self-conscious, darting. If she'd seen him for the first time today, she'd have walked past without a second glance. 'Yes Humphrey enlightened me on some fantastic wines,' she said politely. 'But, I'd expect that from a wine consultant with a Royal Warrant, right?'

'A royal what?' said Geoff, earning a kick in the shin from Humphrey.

Sensing Shelley's growing antipathy to the residents of No. 47 Ferret Rise, Rob cut in. 'Well, we've a lunch to go to. Geoff, thanks for the business card—I'll ping you.'

'Would you mind if I have one too?' Kat asked Geoff.

'But', started Humphrey.

Kish leant in and placed his hand on Humphrey's forearm again. 'Matey, stop whilst the going's good.'

The trio made their way back to the house, not before Humphrey rattled off a cheque to Kat to cover the costs of a new bag and phone, making a mental note to call the bank first thing Monday and confirm he could honour it. Geoff eyed up Kat's backside as it rode off in a pair of rather tight Diesel jeans. 'Very tidy indeed.'

One hundred miles west, Diana Reece put down her telephone and sat alone in her kitchen. It was the third message she'd left her son that morning. Was he okay? Why hadn't he returned the call. Diana then re-checked her appointment slip. Royal Edward Hospital, Bath, tomorrow at 10:00am. When Dr. Davey her consultant would be telling her how far it had spread.

Diana watched the steam puff up from her kettle. Behind the cloud, perched on the kitchen windowsill was a photo of her only son, taken many years before.

FOUR

Back at the house Humphrey continued his remonstration with Geoff. Geoff would have none of it.

'Not my fault that you pretend you own this house, then get caught out. Not my fault the guy sat next to you turned out to be an old college friend of mine. Not my fault that the very person you fed a line to a couple a weeks ago also turned up.'

Humphrey just huffed and logged onto Twitter to review his followers' reaction to his latest tweets.

@Piffle&Wiffle80: Barista? Ye gads. Does that qualify him as one of those front-line key worker jonny's?

@Possemoi: Is he Latvian?

Humphrey looked up at Geoff. 'Anyhow, it's them who pretend. Not me.'

'Pretend?'

'Yes, Shelley and her ilk. Pretend to be something they'd like to be. You should have heard her—of course, you couldn't possibly have because you were too busy tripwiring the lounge, as she banged on incessantly about buying a place here in Ferret, and getting her poor boyfriend in a sweat. Him a poorly paid coffee shop attendant and all that. Poor sod, I mean, serving lattes all day. Hardly Ferret material.'

Geoff chuckled. 'Not barista, Humph. Barrister. As in he represents people in court.'

Humphrey counted slowly to ten for the second time that day. 'Indeed, and he's a welcome addition to this parish. Clearly our sort. But her? The one they call Shell. My God! How'd she afford a place here, especially without her rich barrister suitor?'

'Unlike you, quite easily I'd imagine. She's flying high in the civil engineering game. Builds bridges, that sort of thing.'

Humphrey's stomach churned as he rocked back. 'Well, that explains a lot. Did you see her? Clearly spent too much time outdoors measuring up concrete pilings. Crow's feet, frown mark. Like chasms they were . . .' Humphrey paused for air. 'In fact it was her own snobbery that led her to assume I owned this place. I merely played along with it.'

'So in fact you acted.'

'No acting involved, chap. She assumed my social station, and with it the assumption I owned this place. Call it provenance.'

'Call it total bollocks,' retorted Geoff. 'You work on a till.'

'My day job doesn't define me.'

'Yet you defined Rob the "barista" by his.'

'Oh, forget Rob. I'd have had Kat in the bag until you two intervened.'

'Punching well above your weight with her,' added Kish, stopping briefly from tapping out emails on his Blackberry. 'No wonder you told her you're a royal wine-taster.'

'More a wine consultant. And before you continue, it was Elise who suggested it. Said it sounded more appropriate.'

'She was just being American,' said Kish. 'Yanks think you get class out of the cash machine.'

'Steady on,' replied Geoff. 'She is your girlfriend and all that. And besides, she's only half-American.'

'Quite right, which means I can have an opinion on her.'

Humphrey was determined to capture some higher ground, particularly from Geoff. 'Ignoring that for one moment, if I am going to get anywhere with the opposite sex, then the occasional off-white lie is necessary.'

'By telling them you are something you are not?' asked Kish.

'No, I simply use the present tense to describe my future occupation. Not so much a lie, more a timing error. No point hanging about for five years and only then tell her I'm a wine consultant. What lunacy!'

Geoff could hardly take any more. 'So in Humphrey's world, truth bends round time, rather like light does round strong gravitational fields. Sorry, this new field of physics is proving too much for my pounding head.' With the task of winding up Humphrey well and truly accomplished, and the one-night-stand having been sent on her prickly way, Geoff now only had his hangover to contend with. Work was certainly not the best remedy. As store manager of the Putney Ferret branch of Bacchus Braves Winestores Ltd, it was Geoff's decision not to open the store today, citing personal reasons. And who was Humphrey to complain.

Happily hidden behind roman blinds the boys settled into a typically agnostic, purpose-free Sunday.

Elise returned from her post-grad class around 8:30pm. She resisted Kish's placations over last night's heated exchange—something that had been on the cards for days, and instead sat listening to Geoff and Humphrey's amusing chit-chat. *I'll speak to him later. Yesterday wasn't the right opportunity.* For Geoff, the back-and-forth banter with Humphrey was a lighthearted distraction between less interesting chores. Conversely Humphrey regarded it as somewhat burdensome, a dull perpetual rear-guard action against the sod Geoff Fox who seemed to revel in poking him, but strangely compelling all the same.

'Humph, what do your parents think of your current job?'

'They have their opinions.' Humphrey knew his parents had wished more of him. In the absence of a credible job that gave some sort of lettered accreditation after his name, they'd progressively embellished him among their friends to the point where many folk operating in certain Hampshire social circles believed he was a major wine importer on the verge of receiving a Royal Warrant. 'And to your comment earlier, yes, I realise part of my job requires point-of-sale operational oversight, but without doubt I also conduct wine tasting. So, I'd say my parents are proud I work in a highly revered industry. You saw how impressed Kat was when she held our business cards. I mean, what did you say that Shelley person did?'

'Civil engineering,' Geoff replied.

'Well there you go. I occupy an industry superior to civil engineering.'

'Again, utter bollocks,' Geoff replied. Elise sat back. This would be fun.

'Okay, then explain why last month's Tatler's society pages covered Berry Bros Wines' annual charity bash, and not one thrown by some concrete bridge-builder or motorway-fixer? I'll tell you why. Caché my friend. Caché.'

Geoff looked up. 'You work in a wine store. Don't make it something it isn't.'

'Selling wine possesses a certain panache, which without doubt sounds better than saying your job is overseeing steel girders being welded together. It possesses a traditional 'establishment' feel. And, because I am established in something 'establishment', I need to ensure that what I do within it has caché, too. The job title 'wine consultant' gives off a specialised, more learned tone.'

'Almost professional in fact.' Geoff said wryly.

'Yes, an accreditation in wine imports would address that.'

'But Shelley already *is* a professional. She has an industry-recognised accreditation, you operate a till in a posh shop.'

'I'd hate to think what you think of me and my job,' Kish interjected.

Humphrey had a view but wouldn't air it, not tonight anyway. The most financially independent of the three, Kish had made a mint while still at LSE building an online dating service aimed at the foreign students wishing to connect with fellow countrymen and women across London's Universities. When he sold it to an established online dating firm, he apparently pocketed a tidy sum. Rather than use it to buy a house, Kish reinvested most of it into hi-tech stock, Apple and Google apparently. Humphrey curbed his envy by maintaining that Kish's wealth was brash and new, his job was selling software—in Humphrey's opinion an occupation barely one up from selling cars. For Humphrey selling software was not a real profession. Besides, what really got Humphrey's goat about Kish was his access to corporate-funded jollies. Take only last month. Kish had enjoyed Six Nation's Rugby hospitality at games held at Twickenham, Cardiff and Dublin, several theatre dinners, and a freebee skiing trip to Tignes. With a summer of events that comprised the British Season almost upon them, Kish's calendar would only get more busy with opportunities to quaff, network and generally enjoy life at the Boat Race, Ascot, Wimbledon, Henley . . . all at someone else's expense. Talking of Henley, how the heck did Kish continually gain entry into the Steward's Enclosure? Or entitlement to the pre-day showing at Chelsea Flower Show? For Humphrey it seemed the Season was becoming more a backdrop for corporate networking and less for discerning members of the public who valued it's true meaning, like himself. It was simply more appropriate someone like him was there. Kish and his type less so. *If only I could afford it though.* As Geoff got up to make a snack, Humphrey launched into his evening tweets:

@FerayNotFerret:
Evening Readers. The British Season is almost upon us, let us remind those who go for free, courtesy of their nannying corporations, that we don't like their sort.

@FerayNotFerret:
Would venture that the average 'Corporate Johnny' attending this year's Derby or Wimbledon wouldn't go if it cost them to do so.

@FerayNotFerret:
I vote all entrants to this year's Season events are means-tested for legitimacy.

@FerayNotFerret:
Selection based on industry they occupy. Prohibit anyone involved in IT. Then Civil Engineering. Followed by Lawyers #legalarses

Geoff had finished preparing a towering sandwich, and ran it through with a chopstick to prevent it toppling over. He licked the knife clean of mayonnaise then tossed it carelessly into a sink full of dirty cups, plates and cutlery. Clearly the others hadn't washed up for a couple of days.

'Damn it, we need a cleaner,' grunted Geoff, as he re-emerged in the lounge.

'And if we all just did our share, we'd not need one,' said Humphrey.

Geoff slumped into the armchair, and began demolishing his sandwich, dripping bits of it on him in the process. 'Elise, do you think we are messy?'

'I think all little boys are.'

Still sensing the chill from last night's row, Kish said, 'frankly, we're all relying too much on Elise's goodwill and hygiene standards. So yes, let's trial a cleaner. A couple of weeks, a month maybe.'

Geoff nodded, adding 'So Humpty, motion carried.'

Humphrey sighed. 'Okay, however I'll carry on cleaning my own room, so I expect to pay a proportional amount for the shared space only—that's the kitchen, upstairs bathroom, lounge, hallway and toilet.'

'Do stop being a twat,' said Geoff. 'It's one bill covering the entire house, split three ways.' Geoff concluded with a controlled belch and a thump to the chest. 'Buggering indigestion. Now, all this talk of cleaning has made me very thirsty.' He rounded the sofa and patted Kish and Elise on their shoulders. 'Who fancies going down the pub to sniff and swirl a pint?'

Kish turned to Elise. 'Just a quick pint? Fancy coming?'

Elise looked at her watch, and sighed. 'Really?'

'Just one, I promise.'

'You go. Please can you come back after just one pint?' She leant in. 'We really need to discuss things.' Elise had tried in vain to find the right time yesterday to break the news to Kish, it would need to be tonight.

'Absolutely,' said Kish as he kissed her. 'Coming Humph?'

'No, I'll stay in. Early start at the store tomorrow, Geoff. Don't forget.'

'Are you okay?' Humphrey asked Elise as soon as Kish and Geoff had left the house.

She sighed. 'You know as well as I do, Kish won't be back after just one. Geoff won't let him. I tell you, you two need to sort Geoff out. Or I will, believe me.' Elise stopped there. She couldn't recall Geoff sober on any single day since January.

On Sunday evenings, the Rutting Stag pub welcomed its usual bevy of patrons to relax in battered mocha leather sofas dotted across the well-worn wood floor. Surrounding them was a pronounced smell of roast lamb, rosemary and cinnamon candles, and the therapeutic sound of wine being poured into oversized glasses. Light background music selected by one of the six or so bar staff enhanced a mood of transition from an indulgent lounge-around weekend to the working week that paid for the next one. Kish and Geoff sat at its zinc bar swapping notes on work, a common discussion.

'So given both of us manage people, how do you keep their motivation high?' asked Geoff.

'My team you mean? First off, I give them plenty of cost-effective and justifiable praise. Congratulatory emails, copying in someone very important goes down very well with the rank-and-file. Some spot bonus for a particular activity. Personally I like doing quarterly awards in front of the rest of the team. Even better, the whole unit. That way, the act of recognition can be more stage managed.'

'So, not a salary rise then?' asked Geoff.

'I might up it a few percentage points each year. But that doesn't keep people motivated for the twelve months between. Plus giving public praise or some specific merit is beneficial to me too. Another mechanism to up my profile, and reminds people I have the power and authority to communicate others' good work. But that's just one part of creating the right reputation as a solid manager. Everyday, display predictable and consistent behaviour with your team and your stakeholders. Remain composed at all times, never ever be emotional or irreverent. Regularly communicate accomplishments. Every week show your boss and your team you know everyone's exact sales numbers and revenue to date. Every quarter, communicate results and be known for accomplishing one breakthrough activity—something your boss will remember you for—a bid deal, new process, something major. At selected moments in time also communicate your entire fiscal strategy as a three-to-five point plan. In short a reputation for delivering and having a safe pair of hands.' He held his palms out. 'These safe hands. I'm actually anticipating another promotion shortly. The big one to Director. I'll be the youngest with the title in the entire UK organization.'

Geoff cracked a smile. Whatever Kish had a reputation for, it certainly wasn't for being humble. 'Anyhow you must have pocketed enough to buy a place by now?'

'Yes, and the direct result of my gilt-edged reputation for success.' Kish pointed at his car keys laid out on the table. 'Along with the Merc, I've a larger disposable income than most my age, and financial security others yearn for.' He shook his wrist, allowing a loosely strapped Rolex to jangle. 'As for buying a house, I'll start looking in a few months. When I can pounce on someone desperate to sell up before they default on their mortgage payments.'

Geoff quietly sipped his pint, and wished Humphrey was here too. Humphrey inherently disliked Kish's public and overt mention of money, and often told Kish so. Humphrey hinted in public to his own personal fortune, the intention being to leave others to inflate it, which many fell for. Geoff played Kish differently, never rising to his crass commentary but instead waiting for a moment to bring Kish down a peg or two. Around two months back, Kish put a framed photocopy of his biggest-ever bonus cheque up on the bathroom wall, apparently to serve as a reminder of what to chase in life. Geoff brought it to the pub and had them hang it behind the bar for all to see. Kish received some acute public pillorying for that. 'Interesting,' Geoff said finally. 'And I thought one's reputation was defined by whatever people said about you behind your back.'

Kish didn't respond as quickly as usual.

Two hours had passed when Kish put down his fifth pint to read Elise's text.

One pint? Hurry back pls. Really need to see u

Kish smiled. A perfect cure for a bored guy on a Sunday evening. He texted her back.

With u in 5. xx

'Okay I really gotta get back. Coming?' said Kish.

'Nah, I'll stick around for one more.' Geoff motioned to the barman for another pint of London Pride.

Kish briefly scanned the interior of his favourite local pub. 'Well enjoy it. Life doesn't get much better than a decent chat with a mate over a pint.' He drained his glass and left. Back in the hallway, Kish noticed the answer machine's red light flashing away in the darkness. No point checking the messages. Bound to be for Humphrey or Geoff and besides with no pen handy, he'd be the poor sod lumbered with a message to pass on, which he'd only forget.

'Kish is that you?' came a whispering voice from the top of the stairs. *Elise.*

'Hi, hun. You just get yourself scrubbed and ready,' chuckled Kish up the staircase, 'I need some!'

'Sorry?' Elise whispered back. 'Some what?'

'You'll find out.' Kish strode across the lounge wooden floor and into the kitchen. He searched the fridge for something to snack on and made do with a large slice of Port Salut cheese, washed down with some orange juice.

Elise was sat on the bed sorting some knee-length rowing socks when Kish stepped into the bedroom, and without any warning dived onto her. 'You're breath stinks of beer,' she said, grappling with the duvet, then slapped his cheek as he tried to muzzle between her shoulder and neck. 'go brush your teeth.'

'Oh silly, silly,' Kish replied as he slowly pecked his way down her chest, stretching the neck of her top down with his chin. He stopped briefly then quickly dived under her top, blowing a raspberry on her belly. When he attempted to unbuckle her belt, her tone suddenly hardened.

'Kish, no! We need to talk.' It didn't immediately register with Kish, so she pushed his head away from under her. She stood up and moved away from the bed. Kish flopped onto his back and gently pushed his hand through his hair.

'Oy, oy, what's got into you then?' he protested. His eyes were vacant, which further annoyed Elise. No matter, this wouldn't keep another day.

'Kish! Quit being the asshole and look at me.' Slowly he hauled himself up and stared approximately at her. 'Kish, you know I told you I missed a period.'

'Of course,' lied Kish. Most likely one of those moments he was tapping out some email pretending to be interested.

'Well I . . . . think I'm pregnant.' She sat silent, face shivered slightly as she watched Kish rock back then begin grinning at her. She wanted to take in the smile. See if it went away. 'Suitably shocked then?' she eventually asked. She tried to smile again.

Kish's grin then disappeared, replaced by a frown, as he tried to get his mind working despite the gently numbing alcohol 'You're not joking are you? How do you know?'

'I did a home test on Friday. Well I did two.'

'Friday? As in two days ago Friday?'

'Yes.'

Kish saw her shaking. 'Come here darling, sit down. Why leave it 'til now?'

Elise at once felt guilty. *God, he's going to be a father. Of course he'd want to know as soon as possible.* 'I now know I should have told you sooner.' She smiled and squeezed his hand hard. 'Well? What do you think?' she said hopefully, her voice lifting a little. Inside she was bursting with a mixture of joy and apprehension. Kish would step up. He could do that. This was when she needed him to step up like never before.

'Talk about pouring cold water on passion,' Kish said gruffly, wrenching his hand away. 'It's practically bloody Monday, and you've known all weekend. You know how tense I get on a Sunday evening thinking about the week ahead. I don't need more hassle. Jesus Christ, Elise.'

Downstairs the front door slammed shut. Geoff, back home. Elise motioned to Kish to lower his voice.

'Still—' Kish said grinning.

'Still? Still what?' said Elise, hopefully. *Is he just winding me up?* It was the briefest of thoughts.

'Still, this!' and he jumped on her in exactly the same way he did when he first entered the room. This time he went straight for her breasts.

'Kish! Don't be so damned stupid! It's not appropriate right now!'

'What, given that news? Sure it is.'

'Kish, you don't know what you are saying, you're drunk.'

'Not drunk, just really horny.' Kish lowered his voice. 'Why don't you sort me out,' he asked blatantly, as his eyes glazed over. That final beer had entered the bloodstream.

Elise stood up. 'Did you not hear me?' she blasted loudly. 'We're pregnant! And you are a drunken asshole!'

Instantly overwhelmed by the loud commanding voice, Kish panicked and gripped Elise's forearms. 'Shush the fuck up!' he hissed. Elise froze. His eyes dilated and his breathing became faster, shallower. Kish felt the bedroom walls suddenly close in on him. His middle ear thumped with warm blood, diastolic pressure pulsed behind his eyes, and his forehead began to sweat. Without warning he flopped onto the pillow.

Elise had seen this many times before. Without much warning, Kish dropped like a stone and immediately fell into the intractable sleep that followed one of his anxiety attacks. 'You miserable, pig-headed, selfish bastard! How dare you simply fall asleep right now?' Sat on the bed next to him, Elise put her head in her hands. His bloody drinking again. All weekend, in her own nervousness, she'd imagined the moment she told Kish and his reaction to her news—a moment of shared excitement, some fear of course, but sealed with a bear hug that reaffirmed they were in it together. A reaffirmation of their love, their bond. Instead, she suddenly felt like a smashed bottle, her hopes spilled and her memory stained. Elise eventually took out a sleeping bag from the wardrobe and draped it over Kish, then slid herself under the duvet beside him. She'd sooner have gone back to her flat in Wandsworth if she wasn't so damn tired. Lying with her back to Kish, she looked around the softly lit bedroom. It was neat and ordered. Everything in his bedroom complied with his suffocating rules, everything doing what it was designed to do. Elise placed her watch, some loose change, some receipts, the pregnancy kit pack and her iPhone on the polished bedside table. She pondered her small messy pile of belongings—out of place and insignificant in a world of Kish's making. Elise's mum and dad were thousands of miles away in Seattle, and she now felt alone and very unsure. It would be another hour before she finally drifted off.

Diana Reece turned off her bedside light. *Perhaps he'll call tomorrow.*

An introduction to the neighbourhood of Putney Ferret, continued . . .

History: Putney Ferret's name goes back to AD 1072 when William the Conqueror granted Bishop Simon De Ferret land for the founding of a monastery (site long since built over).

Residents of Putney Ferret are well known for using various indicators of wealth and import to compare themselves with one another. One such indicator is how one wears his rugby shirt. Collars 'up' suggests 'the chap is one of us', a product of an elite university or public school, whereas 'down' implies the wearer received a state-funded education, and is unlikely to know his way round the more sought-after French ski resorts. Ferret residents new to parenting may find themselves scrutinising one another in the local Starbucks or Giraffe Café queue; it might be over one's choice of buggy, or name for 'baby': if the buggy cradles an Algernon or Olympia (in 2010, the most popular names in Ferret) you have true 'Ferret' demography.

Putney Ferret has a high concentration of gastropubs and cafés (at the last count there were 6 cafés along Ferret Rise, or 175 residents per café, where residents typically discuss the only matters that count: getting on the housing ladder (if renting), the value of property (if owning), and one's profession.

Little known fact: according to a recent survey, Putney Ferret has the highest per capita count of wearers of signet rings in the UK, at 1 ring for every 4.9 people.

FIVE

'Delays in the production of flu virus vaccinations contributed to approximately six hundred deaths across the country last winter. That is the conclusion of a report published today by the . . .'

Kish stretched across Elise and slapped his radio alarm's large snooze button. It was 6:15am and Radio 4's 'Today' programme would go off again in ten minutes. He rubbed his eyes. Elise was snoring peacefully on her back, and as Kish stroked her head her eyes slowly prized open. 'Morning lovely,' he whispered with a beer-loosened timbre. She stretched a little, then closed her eyes. Kish then heard the bathroom door unlock and instantly rushed out; he had work to go to and a full bladder. Passing Humphrey along the corridor, they exchanged the usual g'mornings. If there was one room in the house that Kish appreciated most, particularly on a cold morning, it was the bathroom. A disproportionate amount of the owner's renovation budget had been spent making the bathroom a corner of quality in the generally well-appointed house. It acted as a real sanctuary, save for the piss-splash that someone, most likely Geoff, had left on the warm tiled floor during the night. Kish made quick work showering and shaving, then returned to his room. Radio Four was back on. He settled for a non-iron shirt—on most Sundays, he'd have ironed five shirts for the week, and a suitable pair of dark trousers he'd forgotten to put in his Corby trouser press last night. Kish felt remarkably unprepared for work this morning. He cursed himself for taking Geoff up on his offer.

'Elise,' he asked. 'Elise? You seen my black shoes? The Oxfords?'

'No I haven't.' Elise kept her eyes closed.

'Bollocks. I'll have to wear my old Calvins then.' He tutted and put on the alternatives. 'Sure you haven't seen my Oxford's, or put them somewhere strange?' Elise didn't answer.

Despite working in an informal office environment, where jeans and fashion-cut shirts were perfectly acceptable, Kish deliberately chose to buck the trend. Dressing seriously meant being taken seriously. Kish's clothes reflected an ambitious nature and enhanced a nurtured reputation for success. That meant wearing highly polished shoes—settling for his Calvins today, plus a dark suit and a crisp open-neck shirt. Dressed, Kish sat on the bed and quickly scanned his inbox. Other than some 'catch up' meeting request from Mike Gribbin, one of his less favourable colleagues, nothing had been sent since checking in yesterday afternoon. The culture of the 'weekend email' was pretty much pervasive across management. Kish was no different, and regularly shot something relevant across the boughs of his boss, or even better, an FYI that justified a broader set of senior recipients, just to illustrate his dedication, even at weekends. Very rarely did he mail his team over the weekend. As far as he was concerned, they weren't the ones who got him promoted.

While pulling on his jacket, Kish noticed Elise looking silently up at him from her pillow. 'We'll talk later,' he said and kissed her forehead. 'You know, about last night. Okay?' Before Elise could offer a response, he'd exited and made for the front door.

Humphrey banged on Geoff's door for the second time. 'Fat lad! Get a move on!'

'Piss off. I'm ill.' A predictably blunt, muffled response.

'You need to open up with me. Stocktaking day today. Plus the delivery driver will be arriving in less than twenty minutes, and you are better dealing with his sort.' Humphrey had rarely felt predisposed to click with 'trade'. Unlike Geoff who could click with anyone. *Best not keep the delivery-jockey waiting though.* He didn't fancy hearing choice words come back at him from across his notional class divide.

Five minutes later, Humphrey walked into the Bacchus Braves store, located at the lower slope of Ferret Rise. He made straight for the office, turned on the PC, and an ancient version of Windows slowly booted up the home page. Oddly, the office wall clock read 6:50am. The clock on the PC monitor also read 6:50am. He looked at his watch. *8.20am.* No way his Breitling was at fault. 'Very odd,' he muttered. *Hadn't his alarm clock read 7:45am when he got up?*

And after thirty minutes of showering and dressing, hadn't the hall clock read 8.15am? So why the hell did every timepiece in the office insist it was still only 6:50am? He scratched his chin, and thought a little more. It had seemed odd to be up when Kish was, a very rare thing. Kish rarely ran late, too. And Ferret Rise had seemed unusually quiet this morning.

Then it dawned on him. Bloody Geoff up to his dumbarse practical jokes again.

Lying in bed with a cold wet flannel on his forehead, Geoff managed only a faint smirk as he imagined Humphrey right now. Last night, when it seemed like quite a fun thing to do, Geoff slunk unheard into Humphrey's bedroom and set his alarm clock back an hour and a half. Same for Humphrey's Breitling left on the bedside table. To ensure consistency, he'd also adjusted both the hall clock and the digital clock on the DVD in the lounge, before returning to an oversized whisky.

The obvious option for Geoff this morning was to remain bedbound and whimper quietly in darkness until noon. But today was different—today was a rare opportunity to share a few innocent moments with Elise in a completely empty house, and something not to be passed up, whatever the state of his head. In order to operate he first needed to rehydrate, and after three attempts he got to his feet and made his way downstairs. In the kitchen a beautiful, newborn light suffused through the blinds, and curiously enlivened, Geoff opened the patio door that led out to a small deck. A tannic smell of a freshly cut hedgerow filled the still air. 'The first spring-like whiffs,' he mumbled, slightly uneasy with his own whimsy. Excluding the various walk-of-shames back to the house following some Sunday-night binge and resulting hook-up, this was the first time in years he'd enjoyed fresh air so early on a Monday.

Any appreciation for a newborn light, or the scent of freshly cut hedgerows was lost on Kish. Today was simply the start of yet another processed week, predictably sliced and shaped, entirely dedicated to his single purpose of advancing his career. Come rain or shine, hangover or gym, he liked to be visible in the office before 8:00am, and always before Ruud, his boss. It was a short walk to the car from the house. *Forward planning.* By leaving work last

Friday around 3:30pm he generally beat other returning commuters to the best parking spots such as quiet St Leonard's Avenue. And he ensured he kept it by not using the car all weekend. Kish sat proudly in his three-week old Mercedes SLK roadster, his latest gift to himself. He buckled up and paused to look at the fancy houses along the avenue. One more year, two max and he'd get one of them. He fired up the engine and caught John Humphries concluding an interview on the Today Programme. Filling his lungs with the reassuring smell of new leather seats, Kish checked his reflection in the rear view mirror. A hint of southern European skin tone—a throwback his father used to say, stretched across the high cheekbones and forehead he'd inherited from his mother. *Not too shabby.* Kish had come to admire the onset of bags beginning to emerge under his eyes. No longer so young as to be patronised for having 'more potential than experience,' nor sufficiently old, greying and 'proven' to command universal credibility. At twenty-nine, Kish sat somewhat between both, yearning for his thirties and more success, and to hell with a few frown marks that might come with it. Wasting no more time thinking about things, he pulled out of St Leonard's Avenue onto Ferret Rise, continuing until he reached the Upper Richmond Road, where he accelerated west.

Kish had worked for Mironic Software Corporation for nearly eight years. Fresh out of London School of Economics, he'd beaten several hundred people to secure a place on the company's award-winning graduate scheme, designed to groom young, energetic recruits into tomorrow's leaders and business administrators. He had joined Mironic to get into sales and make some money, rather than due to a preoccupation for software per se. Leave that to the geeks and zealots. His passion was selling and seeing the resulting pay packet—giving the customer what they wanted, and not what unworldly software engineers assumed they should have. These days he found himself less able to work the insane hours he once did, opting instead to do fewer things better, saying the right thing, mimicking senior management behaviour and their various approaches in his own working day. Compiling his experience over time, he now possessed three simple golden rules on how to succeed at work, which he now exacted almost innately.

Kish's Rule # 1: *Always make yourself indispensible to your boss's success.* Kish had given every recent manager more success stories than his peers, taken on more dirty jobs, and made a point of never making him look like a dick in front of *his* manager. Result: trusted with increased responsibility.

Kish's Rule # 2: *Always use deliberate language, with emphasis on positive pronouns, and no suggestive nouns.* i.e. 'We must run two campaigns, one in October . . . ,' rather than 'We could run two campaigns, one say in October?' Result: A can-do, results-driven reputation.

Kish's Rule # 3: *Never smile unless absolutely necessary.* In Kish's view, smiling too frequently signalled weakness and irreverence, displaying deference to another's superiority. Generally speaking, people constantly needed affirmation, and that invariably meant seeking a smile from others. If it wasn't forthcoming, human nature dictated they'd work a little harder to receive one, ultimately remedying their own insecurities. For Kish 'smilers' tended to be nice people, who enjoyed similar company and genuinely believed that by being happy they somehow got stuff done. Fools. Cool bluntness got shit done. Kish concluded that smiling ultimately cost you respect, which in turn severely hampered promotion. This was reflected in the make-up of the company's organisation. Most smilers were confined to the rank and file; respected team-friendly individuals who shared accountability or helped on a task, rather than owned and drove it. The worrying consequence of this was that the bulk of the company was by its very nature, averse to taking ownership. He didn't complain: it meant fewer folk to compete with for the real jobs herding these well-intentioned tosspots around. By never smiling, Kish found others constantly working harder to gain his affirmation, irrespective of grade or function. It seemed self-confidence was a rare commodity in such a politically paranoid environment as Mironic's, and Kish milked it. A smile from Kish was rare, well earned, and thus respected. Yes, Rule # 3 was his core rule. It was also the only rule he'd come up with alone. If like all other things, rules didn't come in threes, he'd have a fourth: never be a victim. Nevertheless through his dogged use of these three simple maxims, Kish had secured management responsibilities, beating others possessing twice his ability, intellect or passion. To get the maximum execution from people, he was straight with them, never over-promised and always either over-delivered or gave his management the impression he could deliver. He was Chris 'Kish' Reece, self-styled 'doer,' the impresario of execution, and to hell with the blood trail he'd leave to see it done. And so what if sappy, self-righteous HR bleated on about 'values,' 'diversity,' 'appropriate conduct' and 'the right approach?' That was a laugh. He'd been invited to bed by two of them in the last year. *One at an office party.* Ruud had always sponsored him to bigger and better things. The healthy revenue he brought in every quarter, despite the dip in the UK economy, saw to that. It had been a great year so far and Kish had no doubt that at the end of the fiscal, which was little more than three months away, he would secure a bigger piece of the pie in the annual re-org. In the UK subsidiary of Mironic Corp, getting things done, and the money in was all that mattered. He was built for it, and he was going to use it to buy a pad in Putney Ferret whether it killed him. Nothing or no-one would distract him from this goal. Including Elise's news.

Traffic was getting progressively heavier as Kish turned off the M4 into Heston Services for fuel—tomorrow he'd use the train instead, work on ideas en route, save his new Mercedes from additional mileage, and if he could swing it, claim the train costs based upon some creative customer visit on his return home. As Kish filled the tank with enough petrol to last the week, he leant up against his polished pride and joy and considered the events of the previous evening. Very quickly he drew the conclusion that being a father by December simply could not happen. He didn't need the distraction from work, then there was his insomnia. *God, I'll have to move into some place with Elise.* Whereas their relationship seemed fine as it was, he'd never even for a moment considered if it was permanent or not, and a baby would force a decision. The prospect of a bloody sprog constantly needing a change or a suckle . . . *Jesus, talk about inconvenient.* And yet, despite all the negatives Kish knew there was something advantageous by being the family guy. Having a partner-cum-wife and kid carried certain credibility at work—grown up, secure, dependable . . . and at least the kid would turn out handsome. As Kish approached the Slough turn off, a thought suddenly occurred to him. *When the hell did the conception occur?*

Elise eyed the alarm clock across her pillow. She still felt the pain from the five-kilometre scull at competition speed just forty-eight hours ago. She was nowhere near as fit as she should be, so close to the start of the rowing season. Not that that mattered now her rowing season was over. Perhaps one more race though, and then be sensible, unlike her dumb-ass boyfriend. Suddenly reminded of last night's exchange with Kish, she wished she'd not passed him off this morning. There was a gentle knock on the bedroom door.

'Elise? You in there?' said Geoff.

Elise hesitated to compose herself. 'Sure, come in.'

Geoff peered round the door, holding a red mug. 'Mornin' me ducks,' he said mocking his own local accent. 'How's about a nice cuppa tea?' Despite having an English mother, Elise's American upbringing failed to note any East Midlands accent poke through. He handed her the mug, clocking a pregnancy kit package as he did. That confirmed what he thought he'd heard last night. He'd not *chosen* to overhear Kish and Elise's conversation while stumbling into his own room but it sounded very much like Kish wasn't happy with Elise's pretty profound news. Damn idiot. Geoff wound his way past the foot of the bed toward the window. 'It's a lovely morning,' he said. Kish's room overlooked the back of the house, and beneath him stood two rows of similar sized, high fenced patio gardens. Bare wisteria branches wove across trellis, whilst tubbed conifers and variegated shrubs sat in their funky-coloured glazed pots on patio slabs and wrought iron tables. Being south-facing, the room enjoyed good lighting, gently flooding eggshell blue walls, and bleaching the meringue-like fluffy duvet that lay ruffled over Elise.

'It's lovely tea too,' Elise replied. 'Want to sit down?'

'Sure. You doing much today?'

Elise huffed. 'Finishing my proposal for my Masters' thesis, which is due in tomorrow. About three thousand words.'

'Three thousand words? For a thesis proposal? Bugger, that's more than my actual thesis was.' What are you proposing to investigate?'

'I plan to research the impact of a strong sports curriculum on improving the profile and reputation of schools, and the knock on effect it has on pupils' longer term development. I'll compare the UK and US.'

'And?'

'Well, in the time I've been here I'm slowly concluding many UK state schools don't see the value of sport for most of its pupils beyond a weekly tick in the box. As many schools don't compete against one another in sport, kids don't get the opportunity to represent anything, and at the same time the school doesn't have a forum to show it's best side. Sport goes beyond keeping fit. At the personal level it's also about learning about yourself, discipline, commitment, self-confidence, team work, and actually representing something. At the institution level, it's about creating reputation and standing and contributing to a higher level of a nation's sporting achievement. In the US the school's sports team is the pride and joy of the local community, let alone the school. Big difference.'

Geoff prodded the bed. His own sporting youth had been an absolute pearl. He was always in a team, always part of his school's sporting inner circle. Must have influenced him somehow. Right up to his A-Levels he'd worked hard, not because he was the academic type, more because school had given him purpose, family had made him feel relevant and supported, plus he'd got into a routine, a discipline honed on the rugby pitch, and with it all the expectation of winning through hard graft and sacrifice. He honoured the school on the pitch and in return it honoured him off it. To that extent, he'd agree with Elise's hypothesis. His mother's family motto was 'Thole and think', with thole being some old English word meaning "to persevere under tough circumstances". Hardly the motto he lived by now. He'd be the first person to admit he'd coasted in the eight years since college, the low expectations he'd increasingly placed upon himself saw to that. When the credit crunch bit in 2009, he was stuck in a holding pattern, unable to change even if he wanted to. *In any case, what was the point in trying these days?* Geoff thought of his parents, financially worse off now than a decade or two ago when they'd comfortably paid for him and his sister to receive a private education in schools where sport was as important as sciences and humanities. His sporting prowess had failed to get him anywhere. Twenty-nine and still dependent on The Bank of Mum and Dad, because he could and always had, and despite everything he'd learned about having a 'lifestyle on loan', still not in control of his own financial security. *Yep, sport did bugger all in the end.*

Geoff looked at Elise and smiled again. Somehow her presence made everything more purposeful and unaffected. Considering the people in this household—an aspirant snob, an institutionalised corporate pragmatist, and a lazy, louche alcoh . . . Geoff stopped thinking. No need to reflect on such things so early in the day.

SIX

It must have been that 'RORO,' around three weeks ago, Kish concluded miserably, as he sat in slow traffic around the Windsor and Slough turnoffs. At the time, he'd thought that he was cutting the old coitus interruptus a bit fine, but never said anything to Elise. For some months now, 'Roll-On, Roll-Offs' or 'RORO's' as Kish quietly called them were by and large what intimacy had come to mean for him and Elise. Most evenings he'd come home thoroughly dulled by administrivial middle management, resulting in very little in the bedroom department. Very occasionally, perhaps once every week or two, what limited libido he did have was put to brief use. Affection basically consisted of a prolonged kiss during, but more often than not, after the 'action' took place along with some reassuring post-coital whispers. A few short minutes later he'd be asleep, unaware he'd left Elise looking up at the ceiling wondering if it was her fault. Romantic? Engaging? Not really, but it was a great tonic for his personal stress. And hell, Elise kept going on about needing some attention so he felt good he was doing her a favour. She often said all she wanted was a kiss and some assurance that came with it. Whatever, Kish knew she didn't put out like she used to. And this gave him a relatively clear conscience and excuse for the odd pursuit at work. Now wasn't the time to think about Elise. It was drive time, which meant listening to voice mails and contemplating his tactics to get him through the week ahead—key discussions he'd need to have, the points he'd be making, and above all the faces he needed to be in. Frankly, Elise and her predicament could wait until a quieter moment tonight. The traffic edging forward, Kish activated his mobile and dialed up his voicemail through his car's communication system. The first message was from his mum, apparently left sometime yesterday.

'Hi Chris, it's me.' His mother was the only person within friend and family circles who still called him by his real name. 'Sunday around midday but you're probably out. You didn't call last week, *perhaps you didn't get my message. See if you can call, I have something to tell you . . . oh, nice to know how you are and, anyway, sure your busy but I wanted to-'*

'Oh stop waffling woman!' mumbled Kish impatiently, not really listening. She sounded rough though. Another cold, another bout of flu. It's what came from languishing round in that oversized house of hers. Never bloody healthy, that woman. Then he suddenly remembered. *Her birthday on Sunday! The old dear is giving me the hint, yet again. No need to get overly concerned though.* He had a few days. Brownie points for him, her one and only. Kish smiled at the benefits of a love monopoly. As for getting a card, he'd get Elise to choose one. She knew what his mum would like card-wise. He impatiently pressed a button, cutting off his mother mid-flow, and skipped to the next message.

'*Morning Chris. Mike here.*' Mike Gribbin, his fatuous, kiss-arse colleague. Kish gritted his teeth as he listened to Gribbin's flappy message in that passive aggression-tinged tone of his. '*Wondering if you've seen my mails I sent yesterday evening regarding the data I need for next Monday. Hoping you can respond confirming you've got this message. Thanks for collaborating here!*'

Kish autodialled Gribbin's desk number and as hoped, went straight to Gribbin's voicemail. Gribbin was one of those people who set his voicemail daily. Not only that but the word was it was the first thing he did every morning, even before he'd kissed his wife good morning. An effective illusion that he was an early starter. *But you can't bullshit a bullshitter.*

'Mike hi, Chris Reece here. Monday morning, seven twenty-five. I got your message concerning the data ask. Really sorry but will have to push back on this one. You should have given me more notice. Given quarter-end, selling is a priority this week. Will discuss in the office later.' Click. 'Patronising twat,' Kish said and tossed the phone into the passenger seat. Kish didn't take orders from his peers, especially that brown-nosing toady. Gribbin was the Enterprise Group's Head of Sales Brilliance, a job designed to improve sales operations alongside selling. Good with spreadsheets but that was it. A more overvalued, bureaucratic toxin you'd be hard to find, and the personification of all that was going wrong with Mironic—too many folk spending too much time wrapped up on internal processes and business measurement and Mironic getting dangerously close to forgetting its customers altogether. Senior management needed Gribbin for his analytical skills and his old-school process-driven ways so they could provide over-baked reports to increasingly hamstrung, institutionalised bosses. Kish conceded Gribbin was someone you kept close, stood in your tent pissing out, but actually supported as little as possible.

By the time he passed Bracknell, Kish was back doing a respectable sixty-five mph or so. The GPS told him it was clear all the way to Reading where Mironic's UK HQ was located, sat in the same M4-M3 corridor stretching west from London that was the UK home to most of the world's software behemoths: Oracle, Microsoft, Fujitsu, IBM, SAP, Cisco, Unisys, CA, HP. And Mironic. All competing in the business software mire, or collaborating across it. Or doing both, by necessity.

Clearer headed now, Geoff found himself staring overtly at the pregnancy test kit resting on the bedside table. Elise had so far made no attempt at moving or hiding it.

'It's people like you who should be in this predicament. Not me,' Elise said plumping her pillow.

Geoff frowned. 'Sorry?'

Elise reached across to grab the small white packet. 'All your little conquests, with that cheeky smile of yours, and it's all so consequence free. Whereas I pee on this little thing and discover I'm pregnant. See what I mean?' She held up a cardboard paddle. 'It's blue.'

'Well I—' started Geoff, feeling somewhat railroaded.

'You know, it's not like Kish and I—well have sex that much.'

'Mind if I look at it? Geoff asked, his head busy computing the revelation.

'If you don't mind dried pee,' laughed Elise.

Geoff studied the small tester. 'You mean to say you train your piss on this thing?'

'Well, put coarsely, yes.'

'Nice one. I hope you were sitting comfortably.'

'Oh yes, I was quite alone in the loo back at my flat,' replied Elise conscious of Geoff's interesting take on empathy.

'Seriously, you've only just found out then?'

'Three days ago.'

'So this is like a first keepsake?' Geoff checked himself. 'Keepsake' might be a little premature. Then again he always went with his gut on most things. If not, a hope.

'I kept it to show Kish. He likes to see things with his own eyes. And just to reinforce reality.'

'And how did he take the news? If you don't mind me asking.'

'Well, let's just say he barked at me then fell into a deep sleep. Wasn't the reaction I was expecting. To be honest I feel a bit shellshocked this morning.'

Despite the camouflage of shapeless cotton pyjamas, it did not take much for Geoff to imagine the silhouette of Elise's frame hidden within. However, surely this was not the time to let his lusty thoughts on Elise take over. Her wondrous breasts and that bum. Geoff loved her bum. With the sort of tight buttocks you'd see airbrushed onto already gorgeous swimwear models, that gave way to strong toned legs, carved from the final killer metres of a five kilometre row, and perfect when displayed on a bar stool somewhere fancy, skirt riding up just a little. The 'feel' of Elise was something he'd never had, but which he'd often imagined, particularly when in bed, and often in the company of others. Like Lisa yesterday. *God's sake, she's pregnant. By your housemate!* Geoff stared at her face. It shone with a humility that seemed almost unearthly. 'Just do what's right for you. And stick to it. To hell with what other's think.' He kissed her on the forehead then held her face into his chest. Elise's eye's closed and her mind raced just a little less, and in that moment of silent reassurance she felt she could get some perspective. If only Kish would hug her right now like Geoff could, and was. Geoff gave her quick peck, this time on the cheek, got up and left the room. Ten minutes later, having skipped shaving and breakfast, he made the two hundred metres-or-so stroll, in Kish's Oxford shoes, to the Bacchus Braves store. *Bloody Kish. How the heck does someone so one-dimensional end up with a goddess like Elise?* thought Geoff. *Does he even realise how lucky he is?* Frustrated, Geoff kicked a large stone that nearly took out a glass door. He needed a full English breakfast before taking on the day, and Humphrey.

Fifty miles west, Kish finally turned into Reading's Thames Valley Business Park. His car's communication system screen lit up with Mike's name. He let it ring off, and nosed into Mironic's huge, empty car park. By the looks of things he was the second person in. If he'd have located his Oxfords sooner, he might have been first. By the time he'd parked, there was an instant message waiting for him on his smartphone.

Mike Gribbin: Chris, got your voicemail. Have u spoken to Ruud yet? Perhaps you should.

'Classic,' Kish smirked dryly. Any man who needed to reference another man, particularly their boss to defend his own request was a pathetic prick. Kish didn't need to speak to Ruud, his boss over some small matter of getting data in. He was a proven sales manager of a sizeable chunk of all UK Government sales, and Ruud, General Manager of UK Enterprise Sales loved him for getting customers signed and the revenue in. This being the final quarter, maximising sales time was all that mattered. Why should he care about Gribbin? After all, 're-org season' was upon them and it wouldn't be long before all the government sales teams would be consolidated beneath him. Ruud had practically spelt it out to him the previous week. Which meant a promotion to director, a pay rise, a speedier down payment on a place in Putney Ferret, and Gribbin back in his little box.

Kish's walk to the back entrance was barely ten metres. He liked his car parked as close to the entrance as possible. Everyone entering the building saw it, and Kish left no-one in any doubt as to who it belonged to. Once inside the building, Kish took the backstairs to the third floor where all UK Government sales resided. During the day, when the place was full, he opted for the exposed staircase that zigzagged up the side of the atrium. Keep the Kish image fresh in people's minds. Kish's open-plan desk was located close to the window as befitted his middle management rank, tucked behind a reasonably private divider. As with every morning, first he fired up his laptop. He entered his latest password '*1WinnerAmanda.*' Kish gave considerable thought to his choice of password. Convention dictates it's the first word typed into one's laptop every day, and therefore can be used as a powerful mechanism to frame the mind. So, '1Winner' seemed immediately fitting. The female name suffix represented the employee he'd be pursuing until his password expired in sixty day's time. His previous password was '*1WinnerFiona*,' which galvanised his concerted effort to bag one Fiona Matthews. Every time he needed to change his password, he changed his quarry. Which meant that right now it was Amanda Crabtree in HR. Like most of his other previous passwords, Fiona Matthews didn't speak much to him these days. No one likes hot and cold.

Kiss fired up his Outlook and while he waited for his emails to download off the server, he began on Job # 1: updating his calendar with new events. Many of them were mischievous, referencing important actions with important people, or simply marked 'private'. A bit of fun designed to confuse those nosey sods who thought they were onto something by dipping into other people's diaries. Between 1:00pm and 4:00pm tomorrow his diary now stated '*Update govt sales asks to JI, FO, & BG,*' the initials of three individuals easily recognisable as senior directors. Next he blocked out several hours across the week with must do's, making real the list of tasks he jotted down in his note pad, before others mugged him for his time, opinion and attention. On Wednesday, between 9:00am and 11:00am he was down to '*Organise 1-1 with Giles D.*' referring to the head of enterprise customer marketing, and finally on Friday he had '*1-1 with Liam F,*' the newish Director of Finance Operations who'd been given some extra responsibilities recently, and as such was worth sniffing out. Several more entries and he was done. A nicely planned set of communications spread across the week: all deliberate and utterly self-serving.

Job # 1 done, Kish embarked upon Job # 2: email admin. First he systematically cleared unimportant unread mails, starting with Gribbin's. Emails like those from Gribbin were the primary agents of ruin that leached into his workday. At Mironic as with most large companies, email was the primary method of communication, and in Kish's view its widespread misuse would spell its demise. First was the sheer amount of time everyone everywhere spent every day managing their inboxes, quite often at the expense of anything else. On several occasions, usually whilst taking his daily dose of venlafaxine in the Gent's, Kish tried to establish how much money the company lost through the collective distraction of two hundred emails per capita. Second was the idea that email got things 'done' efficiently. This was pure fallacy. Email had become a delegating tool for individuals (Gribbin being a case in point) attempting to shift problems and responsibility to un-accountable colleagues; shit scraped from one corner of the pigsty and dumped in another. And no-one to manage the sty. Just because someone with no authority over you sent you an email, it was expected of you to read the bloody thing, and bizarrely do something about it. Kish knew only too well the impact of this email shit-mix on his own business. Decisions now took longer to make because a) everyone used email to present their issues, but no one had time to read them, and b) no one had the authority to tell virtual teams what to do. *The perils of matrix organisations and shared accountabilities.* The latest version of email software helped Kish manage this vast in-flow of information, or at the least file it better: all emails from Ruud went into one inbox, those from his team went into another, anyone on his extended management group in yet another. Anything that thanked him or his team for good work was stored in another, ready for his end of year performance review. Only if he had the time would he wade through the rest. *'If it's urgent, call my mobile!'* was Kish's own auto-signature on the bottom of emails. Not that he picked up his phone that often.

Another instant message popped up from Gribbin, almost the same as before.

Mike Gribbin: Speak to Ruud?

Kish ignored it, and changed his online status to 'busy'. Gribbin was increasingly butting into his work and just about everyone else across the sales org. 'If I had my way, I'd restrict people to thirty messages a day and they prioritise their behaviour round it,' Kish had once muttered to Gribbin. He'd made his comments during a brainstorm on optimising sales face-time, ironically set up by Gribbin a week before quarter-end, and requiring the presence of twenty-three members of the sales team. Kish calculated it cost the business three hundred and ten thousand pounds in slipped deals.

'We need to prioritise all communication around the customer. If a conversation or mail or activity doesn't relate to a customer, then it's de-prioritised.' But any such radical idea had no place in Gribbin's world. How would he keep tabs of sales people doing sales face-time? Surely it needed measuring. Quite frankly the sooner people like Chris Reece were squeezed out of the organisation, the better for everyone.

Now feeling decidedly more pissed off than he should for this time of day, Kish stood up from his corner cubicle. It was time for Job # 3: cup of tea. Kish made the short walk across the floor to the nearest kitchen, passing the infamous 'Chicken Run': row-upon-row of hot-desks, used exclusively by the two hundred or so sales people whenever they passed through the office. 'Hot-desks' or 'hotelling' as his American HQ preferred to call the arrangement, made for a cramped, noisy sales environment in which to discuss difficult and often detailed issues with customers and partners. Perversely, the 'Chicken Run' delivered more revenue per square foot than any other part of the office, yet was afforded no frills. Unlike those creative marketing communications turds upstairs in their house-plant festooned desks, and more than the mid-management 'deadwood' scattered across various floors; old retainers who were steadily oxidising the business through their own risk-aversion, hunkered down in space-wasting offices systematically entrenching their roles, their younger passion supplanted by a smug entitlement to their annual Mironic stock vestments. Heaven forbid the company face a new computing paradigm, thought Kish. *We'd be thoroughly screwed.*

Just as the machine finished delivering hot Assam into a plastic cup beneath, Ruud Wankhuizen, Mironic UK's General Manager for Enterprise Sales and Kish's incredulously named half-Dutch boss, walked into the kitchen.

'Good morning Chris,' Ruud bellowed politely. Kish could almost feel the vibration of his voice, courtesy of an overextended epiglottis loosened with twenty years of cigarillo smoking. It was a timbre totally in proportion with his six foot, five inch frame.

Kish looked up. 'Morning Ruud. Great week ahead.'

'Yes. Certainly is. Chris, I need a moment with you?' he gargled, and together they walked into Ruud's office, a glass-fronted box at the end of the sales floor. 'I wanted to catch you before I make the formal announcement,' Ruud continued, closing the door behind them. 'The entire subsidiary is under great pressure to hit our target this year Chris. As you know I am still without a leader for the UK Government Sales Team, which is increasingly relied upon to offset a generally slow commercial sector business. All this brings with it greater scrutiny from HQ. Now you've been central to our security software selling and proved a vital presence in bringing forward next year's deals into this final quarter.'

Kish hid a smile as best he could. 'Sure Ruud. What's the plan?'

'Chris, frankly speaking I need a leader to bring all governments sales over the line. Someone who can bring people together. Which is why I'm not waiting until the end of the quarter to reorganise government sales.'

'Great,' replied Kish. *Here it comes.* Ruud had been without a sales manager for the entire UK government business for three months now, during which time he had directly managed the government sales team including Kish, alongside his other key industry sales directors across commercial space: retail, financial, services, and communications sectors. Kish leant back against the wall.

'With immediate effect, all government sales team managers, including you, will report to Mike Gribbin. He will be the new head of government sales, reporting directly to me.'

Kish computed the words, then finally said, 'Sorry you've asked Mike to do what exactly?'

'With immediate effect he will own all-up government sales across UK. It's a director position obviously. Now this has been a decision I agreed with the board on Friday, and I wanted to tell you directly. Mike's been informed naturally.' Kish remained quiet, determined not to revoke Rule # 1. Inside his guts were turning over like a fully loaded washing machine. Ruud continued. 'As my Head of Sales Brilliance for Enterprise, Mike has proved he possesses the necessary skills and visibility vital for building the processes we need for better selling, sales measurement, analysis and reporting, at the level of granularity required by me and HQ. Implementing more disciplined sales processes and scorecarding the business is a huge undertaking and something I feel Mike will do very effectively. Unlike point and press sales guys like me and you, eh Chris!' Kish nodded slightly, and Ruud continued. 'So, by having him interface between sales managers and me, we inform decisions more accurately. Better decisions, better selling. Better selling means more revenue. And you are all about revenue Chris, and that's why you are my number one sales guy!' Ruud slapped Kish on the shoulder. 'So, I think that's it. Oh before I forget, Mike will be contacting you over a new, more detailed way of reporting the business, one which I need you to prioritise around. As always Chris, I appreciate your focus and commitment. You are a great sales manager and someone I trust one hundred and ten percent.' Ruud opened the door for Kish and smiled. Meeting over.

Kish walked back to his desk with his tea and picked up his laptop, then made for his private office in then nearby Gent's. A few minutes ago, he was anticipating the title of Director at long last, and an accelerated bonus scheme that guaranteed enough cash to make that down-payment before the end of the year. Instead, he and his team had been moved under a trumped up bean-counter twat, someone younger than him, with no customer experience or personality.

At Bath's Royal Edward Hospital Cancer Unit, Dr Havey the oncology clinical specialist dealing with Diana Reece calmly delivered the results of the biopsy. The consulting room fell silent and Diana felt a sudden emptiness in her core and her arms and legs deaden. Dr Havey then invited Diana to ask any questions, but none came. She tried to give some reaction, some way of communicating back to him but couldn't, not now. She simply wanted to get out of there. The presiding nurse escorted her out of the consulting room grasping a pre-prepared folder full of advice and guidance on what someone in her situation should and could now do. Halfway down the glass walkway that straddled across one of the hospital's gardens, Diana stopped dead, and bowed her head.

'Mrs Reece?'

Diana creased her eyes, a teardrop fell from her eyelid. The nurse handed her a tissue. 'Thank you. Goodness me, it looks cold outside,' Diana said, and tried to smile. 'It's practically spring but you wouldn't know it by the weather.'

'Look there,' said the nurse, and pointed at some small cherry trees in a concrete clad quad. 'They look like they'll blossom soon. You just wait until you see the pink blossom.'

'Yes' replied Diana softly. 'I have one in my garden. It's lovely to sit under.' She checked herself.

The nurse stretched out and clenched Diana's hand, saying 'you'll sit under that tree and enjoy the shade soon enough. Now, you okay getting back home?' They began walking slowly to the main entrance and Diana scrabbled for her keys. 'I'll be fine.' She then turned to the nurse. 'It's all a bit of a shock, the news I mean.'

'We're here for you.' The nurse squeezed Diana's hand to emphasise her point and walked her out of the main entrance.

Sat in her car, making hard work of the seat belt, Diana began thinking how long it had been growing in her body. Doctor Havey had told her they'd caught it at Stage Two: the tumour was less than five centimetres, and no cancer cells in the lymph nodes in the armpit. *'It doesn't appear the cancer had spread. We can remove the lump surgically or do a course of radiotherapy.'*

She'd not noticed until a fortnight ago while half-watching some daft rom-com on the TV. At first she felt it over a wool sweater and thought it might be part of her bra. But it wasn't. All at once she panicked, pictured her son, Chris. *How on earth would she break the news to him? What would he say?* They'd not talked properly for a couple of months as it was. He hadn't called her back yesterday. Perhaps he would today, and she could tell him then. Diana turned the ignition on. What was the situation with her will? She'd need to sort that too. As if on cue her mobile lit up. *Chris maybe?*

The caller was not her son but someone else. Someone calling from many miles away. Someone who'd loved her unswervingly for the last nine or ten years. Diana fumbled the ignition off and barely able to hold back her tears, began to talk.

SEVEN

Aside from having to deal at close quarters with a cheery delivery driver who'd insisted on calling him 'matey', Humphrey had enjoyed his morning, spent in large part with several individuals representing his target demographic: selective, reserved, and with yacht, rugby or polo shirt collars definitely up. In keeping with his preferred customer type, he had spent a good hour repositioning a wine-tasting display, then completed some wine tasting notes before slipping into the office to tweet on the challenge of communicating simple instructions to people who made a living driving white vans.

Geoff's attendance record on Mondays was generally worse than other weekdays, due entirely to the fact that Sunday night was spent topping up his bloodstream with alcohol. But today was the final Monday of the month, which not only meant deliveries but also the monthly stock-take. The upcoming Saturday was month close, which meant every store was required to provide HQ with provisional numbers today. And in the case of the Putney branch that was Geoff's responsibility. So when Geoff finally rolled up at 10:00am, Humphrey was brusque to say the least.

'Unshaven and likely only half-washed. Hardly a surprise.'

Geoff ignored the remark, and helped himself to an Evian. 'Right, I'll be in the office doing the numbers.'

'Fine. Once you are done, please can you send a reminder to Karen that we still have that dodgy storeroom lock. And whilst you are on the subject of security, can you ask when we are going to get the video cameras fixed out the back? I noticed they were still on the blink when the delivery-jonny arrived this morning.'

'Good point, Humph. Head Office have done sweet-fanny-nothing about addressing our security. I feel like a vulnerable old lady working here. Anyhow, no interruptions for the next couple of hours, okay?' With that he closed the office door behind him. Geoff never involved Humphrey in the stock take, and Humphrey liked it that way.

At 1:00pm, Geoff re-emerged from the locked office and made his way over to Humphrey who was midway through a scatological poem, and trying to find a germane word rhyming with 'foal.'

'The preliminary stock check is complete and numbers squared,' Geoff informed Humphrey. 'Been a goodish month all round. High end wines in particular. Good up-selling. Good cross-selling. In fact both are twelve percent up year-on-year.'

'Not sure I understand all this criss-cross selling or whatever, but excellent all the same,' replied Humphrey. His wine-tasting afternoons obviously had something to do with this upward trend in sales. Not that he bothered asking how exactly, as that might invite a dull discussion on store finances. What did bother him slightly was that despite all these sales, the Putney Ferret branch of Bacchus Braves Winestores remained one of the company's least profitable stores.

Geoff celebrated the numbers with a can of Grolsch, on the house. 'The sophistication of crafting a beer amazes me,' Geoff said after the first long gulp. 'More so than wine sometimes.'

Humphrey inserted "toilet roll" into his rhyming poem, then looked up. 'How on earth can a can of lager possibly be more sophisticated than an alluring glass of wine? Wine is far more complex. Think of the range of notes it hits when thrown round your mouth.'

'Absolute toss,' retorted Geoff. 'Crafting a beer is more complex than making wine. Beer and wine both have ingredients, we agree on that. A wine grower however relies much more on external factors. Totally at the mercy of the sun, soil, location, aspect of the slope, etcetera.' He drained his Grolsch then opened a can of London Pride ale. 'Whereas the quality of a beer is almost entirely down to the honed skills of a master brewer, whose likely spent a lifetime selecting different hops and yeast varietals, the type and quality of barley, then deciding on the varying amounts used. He'll brew the required taste and gravity, time over time, developing small nuances over selected periods of time, its taste, aroma and colour all pivoting around the four same ingredients. Whereas your average plonk is in large part already determined the moment the grapes are cut. Beer's complexity is the true nature of sophistication, not who drinks it. And as the senior wine expert residing here, I think my opinion on wine is sufficiently objective, especially since my success in this latest chapter of my cosmic career depends on flogging the damned stuff.'

'Whatever,' said Humphrey. 'Wine is socially superior. That's why you have lager louts and not wine louts. And also why you get wine tasting, wine parties, wines paired and poured at sophisticated dinners.'

'An interesting observation Humph,' Geoff said between gulps. 'In my humble opinion, wine gets its sophistication not so much by what it is, a bunch of carefully fermented grapes, but by who chooses to drink it, and the rituals that surround it. In days of yore, beer was always a little less elitist than wine because of readily available ingredients, which made it cheap and accessible to more people, every day. A steadily colder British climate has meant English wine production has been practically non-existent for the past eight hundred years and has had to be imported, often at prices only the wealthy could afford. Volumes have increased, making it cheaper, but its image has stuck. So I might actually agree with the social stuff, but in terms of the drink's physical sophistication, where sophistication is marked by nuance and complexity then by true definition, beer wins the day.'

Thankfully for Humphrey's blood pressure the phone buzzed, concluding Geoff's pitch.

'Hello, Bacchus Braves.'

'Is that Geoff?' came the female voice. It did not sound like a customer Humphrey would enjoy serving.

'No this is Humphrey C. Massey, store-, deputy store manager,' replied Humphrey.

'Really?' the voice down the phone sounded confused. 'Didn't know we had deputies in our stores? No matter, it's Karen Williams calling.'

Humphrey's throat suddenly dried. He was speaking to his regional sales manager calling from Bacchus's HQ in Woking. 'How are you?

'Fine thanks. Now is Geoff there? I need to speak to him.' *Clearly in no mood for chitchat then.* Humphrey looked over to

Geoff, popping what looked like a couple of paracetamol into his mouth, and washing them down with his can of ale.

'He's actually out in the delivery bay, bit tied up. I'd be happy to pass on any message though?'

'No, go find him please. I'll hold.' There was silence. Humphrey muted the phone, then sped off after Geoff.

'Geoff! It's Karen Williams on the line. Wants to speak to you, and right now.'

'Oh Jesus. Okay—where did you say I was?'

'Out back in the delivery bay.'

'Good man. I'll pick the phone up from the office in . . . twenty seconds,' said Geoff.

'Important to gauge the walk time from the delivery bay.' At twenty, Geoff slammed the office door shut and picked up the phone. 'Hello Karen, Geoff here.'

'Hi Geoff, busy day?'

'Yes, it's been steady trickle all morning, lunchtime busy as usual and slowing this afternoon.' It was his standard patois. 'Incidentally before I forget Karen, I was wondering about the broken parking bay CCTV I reported several weeks ago. Given the stockroom has a very weak lock, we really need to address our store's poor security issues.'

'Yes, yes I am aware of both and as I told you before, I am personally onto it.' *Heard that before,* thought Geoff. 'Now to the reason I called,' Karen added indignantly. 'I'm putting you both on an assignment. Do you know Debrays?'

'Debrays? The upmarket hospitality event folk?'

'Near enough. Well, resulting from an exclusive partnering agreement I personally struck last Friday, Bacchus Braves will be the official supplier of fine wines to Debrays' Hospitality at a selection of key social events this year. Kicking off with the Oxford and Cambridge Boat Race, but also taking in the Badminton Horse Trials, Chelsea Flower Show, Ascot, the Derby, Henley, Windsor Horse Show, and probably finish off with Cowes Boat Festival or the Edinburgh Festival.'

'Wonderful. So how come you are talking to me about it?'

'You and Horace are going to deliver the required wines, and man their wine stand. Standard bar service stuff, nevertheless considering the magnitude of the events and the kudos factor teaming up with Debrays Hospitality, they specifically requested seasoned employees of Bacchus helping their show, which, at a stretch admittedly, qualifies you and Hubert.'

'He's called Humphrey by the way.'

'Humphrey then. I understand both of you know your way round a wine bottle?'

'And inside it,' joked Geoff. He paused at the silent reaction. 'So Karen, other stores are doing this too?'

'Of course. The guys at our Barnes and Richmond branches more than fit the bill. With a bit of a shuffle, the guys in the five other stores across South West London can make up the shortfall on the day all you guys are away. Now before you frown, we are there one day per event—a trial if you like. Make this a success and I—, we stand a very good chance of securing the entire Season next year. All clear so far?'

'Sure. Carry on.'

'By the end of this week, I'll want you to send me the names of the four events you want and can do. First come, first served. Once all's confirmed, you'll get details of what we need to do: timings, locations, and logistical whatnots. In the meantime the list of wines we're supplying is on its way to your inbox . . . oh, and I've sent them your CVs that we have on file. Debrays insisted they had some understanding of who you are. Your "fit" if you like. I am sure you two boys will more than fit in.' Geoff sensed the slight mockery. 'And before I forget you'll be supervised by a gentleman called Toby Sarber-Collins. Please don't cross him, or you'll have me sending a rocket northward up each of you. I'll mail you his details. Now, here is the full list of venues being covered by us. Got a pen?'

'Fire away,' replied Geoff, imagining Karen's self-aggrandising rockets. As soon as he'd replaced the receiver, Geoff opened the office door. Immediately he was met by a definitive 'hoohoo!' Humphrey had eavesdropped the whole conversation from the other line.

'And to think,' Geoff continued five minutes later, 'we'll be at our chosen events, free of charge, serving wine . . . who knows, even doing wine tastings. You will be in your element Humph!

We've just got to make sure that this store gets the best gigs and all the crappy ones go to those snotty twats at the Barnes and Richmond stores. In which case, we've little time to bag the events we want.' Geoff pointed at the computer screen. 'Here's the list of wines we're supplying. One or two I wouldn't mind just trying out before hand.'

Humphrey was ecstatic. At last, a chance for self-betterment had presented itself. An opportunity to do some fitting-in at last with decent, like-minded folk over a spot of equally decent wine, in the refined surrounds of a Debrays hospitality venue. On top of which, it wouldn't cost him a penny. 'The scene, the networking, the parade, the tradition, the atmosphere, the people watching.'

'The sport,' said Geoff, as he located the first bottle that topped the list sent through by Karen.

'Oh the sport, of course.'

'And the sex.'

Humphrey frowned. 'Not sure I understand.'

'Sex. The Season's sport and occasion feed off a deep, base sexual desire.'

'Well, it shouldn't,' stropped Humphrey. It was clearly necessary to educate his oaf of a housemate on finer points. Geoff's family might have a certain pedigree but Geoff himself was coarsely hewn and un-refined, someone who seemed to prefer endless pints of ale in a rowdy pub followed by a spicy kebab, to a saunter around Badminton Horse Trials. Heathen.

'Got to scoot,' said Geoff as he made for the door, wine bottle in hand. 'Delivery, so look after things, and if I'm not back by six, shut the place up?'

Humphrey watched Geoff crunch the van into first gear and nose into the traffic. He seemed to be doing a lot of deliveries right now. Still it meant Humphrey was in charge and accordingly he used the time to google Debrays Hospitality Ltd, then turn to Twitter to offer his own followers some insight:

@FerayNotFerret:
The Season, an integral part of British life for several hundred years, is upon us

@FerayNotFerret:
Promising a summer of wonderful social events for our delectation, with its appropriately arcane rules governing dress and etiquette
A picture of Kish entered his mind.

@FerayNotFerret:
BUT alas, the Season's now more accessible. Corporate hospitality dilutes the atmos with fakers

@FerayNotFerret:
If you seek sanctuary from company reps wooing or being wooed by other company reps, wine buffs Bacchus Braves will save you

@FerayNotFerret:
I hear they've teamed up with upmarket hospitality gurus Debrays to provide a haven of quality conversation over quality wines, for discerning guests

@FerayNotFerret:
And that Bacchus Braves' resident wine consultant (Ferret branch) will happily provide drinking pointers

Geoff parked up in St Leonard's Avenue, just around the corner from the house. His mind was also swirling with this Debrays gig. Only he was thinking about it from a financial point of view, specifically how he could make some money on the side before things got seriously bad for him. Exactly how would take some innovative planning.

Kish was perched on a warm toilet seat, safely locked away in his favorite cubicle, situated in one of Mironic's more remote bathrooms. It was here that Kish came when he needed to think, undisturbed With no-one else in the bathroom, he'd managed to participate briefly in a call with Natalie, muting his mobile phone when, still seated, he flushed the loo, and enjoying a gentle breeze beneath him. Sat there in silence, his laptop warming his naked white thighs, Kish had spent the last twenty minutes simply staring at his screen as one incredulous instant message after another popped up from Gribbin concerning the upcoming announcement, and now that Kish had been told the news, could he kindly accept the meeting request for this morning. Coming to terms with the inevitable and only course of action, Kish summoned all his strength and finally sent a short instant message back:

Thx, and congrats by the way. Yes, just accepted your 1-1 request, and looking at your report request as we speak.

Cursing quietly, Kish went into his deleted items folder and retrieved the mail from Gribbin entitled 'Planned Government Performance Scorecard'. Attached was an Excel spreadsheet, in which Gribbin had listed eighty 'key performance indicators' or KPIs, each with a target, the majority of which Kish had never seen before. Kish read Gribbin's instructions for completion. Of the eighty KPIs gauging the government teams' weekly business performance, Kish was responsible for reporting progress against thirty of them, each one presented as both an absolute total number and as a percentage variance against the target. Sixty numbers to calculate. Deadline for completion was 9:00am every Monday, at which point the spreadsheet was to be sent by Gribbin to the UK board and beyond. To make the damn thing easier for the execs to interpret, Gribbin had requested that the cells in which the numbers were inputted were to be filled with a specific colour denoting progress. Green meant 'job completed,' yellow 'in progress', and red meant 'not started' or 'major blocker.' Kish swallowed and read down the list of the thirty KPIs he was to report against.

KPI # 3: *Number of security sales engagements at 60% or more completion. Target: 45.*

KPI # 17: *Percentage attach rate of security product suite to productivity new business licenses. Target: 65%.*

KPI # 25: *Average license deal-size for security product suite with services attached vs. no services Target: $125,000 vs. $145,000.*

The other twenty-seven were even less fathomable.

In Kish's opinion, his job meant he should simply forecast the amount of revenue he'd bring in that month, and report against it every week. The last week of the month, he'd happily provide a daily update. This spreadsheet with all its required data went way beyond that. It effectively turned him from sales manager into business analyst. Clearly it had been designed by somebody (or bodies) who knew nothing about the basics of reporting sales, and clearly thought nothing of the financial consequences of removing a sales team from their customers to spend hours compiling a meaningless report that would take management another week to make sense of it. Indeed, once management got a handle on a new lens on the business, they'd take all this new information and pass down a revised set of actions that distracted the field's attention from the main goal: land deals and revenue. This spreadsheet was a worrying portent for bigger reasons. Everyone knew Mironic's growth was flatlining, these past eight quarters turning in low, single digit growth after a decade of stellar growth. When a company's innovation was no longer as potent as it once was, operational efficiency usually became a key focus. In the old world of driving strong sales against huge demand, people like Kish thrived. In a world of scrutinizing a growing number of problems through micro-management, Gribbin thrived. Kish shook his head.

Kish was still sat ruminating on his toilet seat thirty minutes later when Ruud's email came out. It said it all.

To: Mironic-UK-Enterprise; Mironic-UK-Government; Mironic-UK-Leadership-Extended; Worldwide-Enterprise-Leadership
CC: Mike Gribbin

Subject: Organisational Announcement—UK Government Sales Leadership

Government business revenue in Q4 and beyond is a key priority for the entire company. To succeed we don't just need strong field selling, we need greater focus and scrutiny of the business. To this end, I have asked Mike Gribbin to step up from his current role as Enterprise Sales Brilliance Manager to run all Government sales for Mironic UK, reporting to me. He will be ensuring no sales 'stone' is left unturned. Please join me in congratulating Mike on his new role, and a richly deserved promotion to Director level.

Thanks, Ruud.

Ruud Wankhuizen
GM, Enterprise Sales
Mironic (UK) Ltd

Within seconds a mail from Mike followed:

To: Mironic-UK-Enterprise; Mironic-UK-Government; Mironic-UK-Leadership-Extended; Worldwide-Enterprise-Leadership
CC: Ruud Wankhuizen

Subject: Re: Organisational Announcement—UK Government Sales Leadership

Following on from Ruud's mail, I am delighted to be taking up this challenge to drive us over the line in Q4 and into the next fiscal, working directly with sales, Ruud and HQ on this endeavor. Not wasting a moment, attached is a balanced scorecard that defines the way we will measure the business going forward. Finally, to my team, I will be setting up 1-to-1's with you all to ensure we establish a regular business rhythm.

Thank you and Good Selling!

Mike Gribbin, MSc
Director of Government Sales
Mironic (UK) Ltd

Kish noted the American spelling of 'endeavour'—clearly fawning to US overlords. *Moreover, what cretin mentions setting up meetings with his team (obviously) in a mail to a senior audience. And who says 'good selling' these days.* Whatever Kish's personal views on this unrelenting slimy moron, he knew he needed to up his game now. To gain anything out of this he'd need to keep his nose clean and over-deliver on both selling and presenting an efficient sales reporting operation. Kish took thirty minutes to complete an initial commentary on the scorecard, scrabbling around various reports and tools to assemble the data asked for. A few instant messages to various folk across the business later, he had managed to capture seventy percent of what was required, ready for his meeting. The rest he'd fill in later, pending data from his team. Kish studiously gave each cell the corresponding colour, many turning out red as his business only tended to go green in the last week. That was next week. These days, the UK execs only really cared about the reds, in reality because their paymasters at HQ did. It was the job of people like Gribbin to conspicuously report all weaknesses and then have Kish conspicuously eliminate them, in some relentless rearguard action. If anything, Kish was happy with the slightly negative tone of his initial draft. It presented a situation he knew he'd improve upon by quarter end. He then turned to a couple of mails that his new chinless manager, barely an hour into his new position, had already sent to the upper echelons, copying Kish on them and asking for Kish's immediate response to all on the to: line, including Ruud. In a work environment where 'how' you communicated often trumped what you actually said, he responded with one-line bullet points (no more than three bullets in a mail) reminding Ruud that Kish was to-the-point and cooperative.

Kish's laptop beeped telling him he had five minutes before his meeting with Gribbin. The fact he'd lost all feeling in his left leg told him he'd been sat on the loo long enough. He did a final flush, zipped up his trousers, and unlocked the toilet door. His left leg still leaden, he limped to the bathroom's row of granite sinks, where he rolled his shoulders and huffed at his reflection in the mirror. With his laptop tucked under his arm he then strode out of the bathroom, eyes front and centre, face stern, and towards the desk of his nemesis.

Mike Gribbin, Mironic UK's new Director of Government Sales and Kish's new direct manager was crouched over his laptop when Kish came by. He looked up and on seeing Kish, raised one finger as he typed on, and said 'with you momentarily'. Kish walked the few steps to his own desk and sat there. Seven minutes passed.

'Okay Chris, shall we?' Gribbin said finally.

'Kish grinned and stretched out his unwashed hand. 'Again, congratulations.'

'Thanks,' said Gribbin, shaking it limply. 'I've had quite a few congratulatory mails this morning. I'm sure I'll receive some more before the day's out. So, let's find a spot downstairs in the atrium.' Gribbin had few innate social skills, empathy included, and the majority of his behaviour at work came straight out of the pages of several self-help books, including one on hypnotism. Walking across the atrium Kish felt ambivalent at the assembled chatter. On the one hand, he embraced the company's willingness to have its own public 'commons,' a place for open dialogue and collaboration, a refreshing alternative for those forced to spend most of their day communicating through a fourteen-inch monitor, stuck behind a powder blue partition, with its pins, post-it notes and cables. The atrium was a place to gravitate toward, to meet to talk, to posture and wander. But that is precisely what jarred him about it. Here were managers, ordering espressos, catching each others' eye while pretending to discuss something half-cooked, sat alongside operations staff taking a breather from creating new processes, and clutches of admins happily ignoring their respective teams' requests to return to their desks and book a five-way conference call or chase a client. *Witness the contradictions of the modern workplace.* For whilst the company laid on a comfortable lounge area for its top-talent employees, with its soft music, waiter service, leather sofas and tropical plants, no-one ever appeared to be doing anything more productive than 'having a gas.' At least Kish was discreet about being work-shy. Hidden away in a toilet cubicle for hours on end. A far cry from his early years when raw energy was in the air and employees felt it their personal mission to get out there and sell the idea that every human interaction, be it talking, writing, calculating, having fun, observing, could be served through software, particularly Mironic's. If this morning's scene in the atrium was anything to go by, Mironic's workforce had got complacent.

Kish and Gribbin slumped into two leather armchairs facing each other.

'You know Chris,' said Gribbin, 'when it comes to making notes, you'd be far more efficient using Mironic's NoteJotty tool on your laptop, rather than using a pen and pad. Up to forty percent so, I read.'

Kish gritted his teeth. 'Quite so.'

'Give me a second,' started Gribbin drably. 'Just . . . trying . . . to . . . get my mobile to load up my NoteJotty app . . . it seems to have frozen.' In the five minutes it took for Gribbin to reboot, Kish found himself doodling a parachutist jumping from a plane with its engines on fire. Still fiddling with his supposedly smartphone, Gribbin asked in a flat, monotone voice, 'How was your weekend?'

Kish looked at him. Gribbin had never before enquired how his weekend had been. No doubt he'd reached the chapter entitled 'Creating trust with employees' in some management textbook he'd frantically read over the weekend. 'Very good thanks, tiring though. Had some friends round for dinner, fixed some shelving, then down the gym yesterday, caught up on some email. The usual,' he concluded dismissively. Aside from the email part, complete fabrication. Somehow, saying 'Actually got royally drunk a couple of times, found out I've sired a bastard, pissed off the missus, and played the soundtrack of a porn movie across a busy London street just to piss off a house mate' might test all but the most carefully constructed facade. Another of Kish's survival mechanisms was providing pre-formatted answers that complimented the personality of the inquirer. In front of Gribbin, Kish determined to portray himself as a safe, chino-clad conformist with attention to detail and an aversion to the irreverent.

'Good good,' drawled Gribbin unconvincingly, remaining crouched over his mobile and pressing his neatly manicured thumbs on virtual keys. 'Just checking how much time I've got . . . I should say time we've got. We'll have to keep this to thirty minutes. Got to see the other sales managers.' Kish actually didn't care. Gribbin finally looked up 'Now it's our first one-to-one in this new set-up, and I'd like to go over three things very quickly.'

'Sure, but I need to cover some items with you too.'

Gribbin looked at his watch. 'Okay, let me be quick then. First off, where are your guys on ABC Training?'

'Appropriate Business Conduct training?'

'Quite.' Privately regarded by Kish as yet another overcooked timesuck, Mironic's 'ABC' training had recently been launched with some fanfare. It consisted of a series of web videos featuring various scenarios of inappropriate behaviour, spanning sexual misconduct, fiddling expenses, and ethno-cultural diversity issues. After each scenario, acted out with skillful woodenness by aspiring TV commercial actors, the employee had to then answer multiple choice questions, like *'having overheard his manager's inappropriate language concerning his colleague Jane's physical characteristics, and his colleague's upset reaction, should Steve a) confide with another co-worker, b) laugh and enjoy a joke with his manager, or c) Go to HR in confidence?'*

As far as Kish was concerned, the answers were obvious to all but the grossly stupid, yet everyone knew the training was a mandate from on high. Two class action lawsuits were pending appeal in the US as well as another suit brought against Mironic's France operation, all of them to do with inappropriate behaviour in the office. Rumours circulated that one of the US cases was brought by a Puerto Rican woman whose male manager suggested at an office party that they 'get horizontal.' She was suing for defamation of character, racialist slurs, and sexual harassment, while he had produced a text allegedly sent from her offering 'hot latino pussy'. Needless to say, the company buried the issue quickly until others stepped forward and joined the suit against the manager. In France, if the rumours were to be believed, a female manager was charged with taking her male subordinate on several fully expensed 'business' trips. The manager's husband unearthed the truth and dobbed her in. The running joke was that if there were ever a place to get away with impropriety, the French subsidiary of Mironic would top the list, and that it would take something akin to a very public act of gross indecency with a chicken to stir HR into action. Publicly, Kish fully supported the training and never suggested anything to the contrary. The previous week, he'd sent an earnest email reminding his team to take the subject very seriously. Face to face, he promised to take them all for a team beer in the next few days if they got it done. The pub gave his team the forum for some controlled venting—the opportunity to bitch a little to a discreet manager who gave the impression he was on their side. Kish thrived on the insights that resulted from a pint or two . . . in vino veritas, and all that.

'Everyone's completed it,' he replied.

'Excellent,' said Gribbin, jotting a note on NoteJotty. 'Business conduct is uppermost in any business leader's mind.'

Kish leant in. 'Couldn't agree more. About time this company shows it doesn't tolerate bad behaviour in the work environment. Particularly fraternisation.' He continued to stare at Gribbin, not moving back an inch.

Gribbin slowly backed off, then smiled nervously. 'Quite . . . you saying you know someone who is?'

Kish continued to eyeball Gribbin, observing his face redden slightly. Perhaps there was something in those rumours about Gribbin being spotted with someone who looked nothing like his wife. Kish finally said, 'Nope, nothing I am aware of.'

'Good, good . . . second thing on the list is to quickly review where you are on filling the performance scorecard data. I'm sorry you said you couldn't do it, then you send me an IM confirming you'd do it after all. Important to be consistent.'

Kish swallowed. 'Happy to walk through my initial input now?'

Gribbin looked at his watch. 'No time now, but at first glance, I will need you to explain the negatives in more detail. I am sure we both want me presenting your business status in a favourable light. Nor do we want to be underplaying it. Sandbagging I mean.'

Kish tried to smile. Having Gribbin, someone who'd never carried a sales quota or in all probability never actually met a live Mironic customer, now suggest how to position his own business was a new low.

'I'm with Ruud Monday noon, Chris. Objective is to present each teams' status, but also discuss broader team development. Good opportunity to put you in a favourable light. So methinks you need to finish it and ensure you've provided more detail throughout.'

'And your third item for discussion, Mike?'

'I would like you to start considering Natalie for management in the next fiscal.'

Kish bit down. In role for an entire morning already critiquing his team. 'Natalie Watson? Ready for management?'

'Yes, I've gone through her last four performance reviews. You have reservations keeping a high flyer back?'

'Of course not,' said Kish, 'but she's not ready now, I think she'd do better with just one more year of sales experience under her belt.'

'On the contrary. I think she's someone you might consider to push sooner. She has a great future here. Everyone loves her style and she's giving me and other senior managers a run for our money.'

'But she has been in sales for only eighteen months,' said Kish. 'She is still quite young and inexperienced dealing with custo-'

'And she's also an MBA and has attended all HR's fast track management development courses, on top of which she has me as a personal mentor. I think she's competent and ready to manage a small team. Not worried about having to backfill her are you, Chris?'

'Of course not but—'

'Well that's sorted then.'

Kish knew when to leave it and take it in the nuts. Something just wasn't right here. Natalie's star was rising for sure but she was still inexperienced in the field. A bit of an innocent who thought the attention she was receiving from older, more senior and usually married men was solely due to her abilities. He'd heard a few mutterings around the office—her association with one or two senior managers, Gribbin being one of them, but nothing conclusive. For Kish ninety percent of office gossip was utter bullshit spawned from the admins gathering in their covens in the atrium. All the same . . . 'Sure Mike, will do.'

Gribbin studied his calendar. 'Okay, that's me done. Now you had some points?'

Kish looked at his watch. Three minutes left and his new manager had already checked out. 'I'll need a bit more time to do them justice. I'll schedule another half hour for later this week.'

'Well okay, if you think so,' said Gribbin. 'Time management, Chris. Key to getting into senior management. Sometimes we have to make use of what little time we have. At our next one-to-one, I'd also like to use the time to discuss your next career step.'

'Career step?' started Kish.

'I connected with HR this morning.' I am aware you were unsuccessful in your recent application for the Communications Director role over in Corporate Marketing?'

Kish sat back. This guy worked fast. Six months ago, Kish had made a wildcard application for a more senior role in another department, with Ruud's full knowledge and apparent support.

'I need to know who is going to be working for me next fiscal,' Gribbin continued. 'By late May you need to tell me whether you're committed to staying or off doing a new role. It's important Ruud gets the full picture.' Kish began to speak but was closed down. 'In the best interests of the business. I'm sorry but we have got a really big year to start planning around.'

'Okay, so what about Natalie? Do I include her in my succession planning. Assuming I am changing roles?'

'Oh not in the least,' Gribbin laughed dismissively. 'Getting her ready for management and me putting her into your job, I mean, should you decide to move on of course, are two entirely different things. Let's be clear on that.' Gribbin checked his watch. 'I must scoot. Senior HR briefing. You coming upstairs?'

'Actually, no,' said Kish deflectively, 'I need to visit the Tech Helpdesk. Catch you later.'

'So to wrap up then, I'd say a generally okay first meeting,' said Gribbin, now stood. 'But my manager feedback to you would be remaining mindful of other people's time, please? Touches on the company's Integrity and Courtesy values. The HR site has online refresher courses on both. I counsel you to go take a look.' Gribbin turned, leaving Kish to reflect on what the hell had just happened. His agenda hijacked, his aspirations questioned. More immediately however Kish had to get someone to update the scorecard, and ready for Monday. Natalie—she'll do it. Kish forwarded Gribbin's earlier note onto Natalie, copying in the team, requesting their full support. He then sent a separate instant message to Natalie.

Some changes afoot. Gribbin in driving seat (WTF!?) First job is to keep him sweet and fix this data sh*t. Monday deadline. Truly appreciated. Thx.

Kish then put a brief reminder in his diary to have a quick off-the-record conversation with Natalie. Advise her on a couple of things. With Gribbin now out of view, Kish exited the atrium, walked straight past the IT helpdesk, and headed up to HR section using the backstairs. Amanda Crabtree, a 'Workplace Consultant' did not react as he approached her desk.

'Hi Amanda,' he said loudly and clearly. 'I have my details, wondering if you could look at them.' Another office paradox: speak loudly and no one cares, speak softly and you arouse suspicion.

'I think we have a spare meeting room,' came Amanda's hasty yet audible reply, and she led him into a small windowless room used for on-the-spot, private conversations.

Kish shut the door behind them. 'I came on an important matter.'

Amanda's eyes widened. 'Me and you?' She sounded hopeful.

'That comes later. No, I'd like to know my position if I want to seek a new role but don't want to mention it to my manager just yet. I might need to act.' Over the next twenty minutes he confided in Amanda that he was now looking for another role outside Gribbin's group, and she advised him on how to proceed appropriately. 'So basically you are telling me I must record everything, cover my arse.'

'In your case, Chris Reece, absolutely.'

'Leave out the details about you and me.'

'Sensible. And what do I get in return for my advice?'

Kish smiled. 'Oh I could always prove a discrete distraction from your boyfriend.'

'Interesting proposition.' Amanda casually stroked his flank before they stepped out of the meeting room into the open office.

'Thanks for that Amanda, I appreciate it,' said Kish, noisily. He then spent the next three hours searching for relevant job openings posted on the company intranet. Nothing caught his eye. The Gribbin meeting was still unnerving him well into the afternoon, and at 3:00pm, Kish decided it best he left for the day.

Two miles past Maidenhead, a traffic alert cut in over Radio Four to confirm a pile-up had blocked two lanes, something Kish's GPS hadn't given him prior warning to. Stuck in traffic, Kish spent the next hour deep in petulant thought. How could that prize cretin Gribbin be promoted over him? Insane. Kish crept unawares past an emergency crew frantically working on concertinaed metalwork with their cutting equipment, while desperate paramedics fought to keep a middle-aged couple alive, every second counting. Kish thumped the steering wheel. 'Gribbin you prick!' Aside from the indignity of being his subordinate, Kish knew he'd been wrong-footed by a man perfectly adapted to, complicit to, a warped environment obsessed with data capture over action. A man who'd been quicker than he to realise the importance of owning the information chain, distilled into rows and columns on a neat spreadsheet and sent upward. Yet Kish knew that Gribbin was but a symptom of the general malaise that had altered him too. In the seven years since Kish had joined, the company's stock price had barely changed. Until today, his strategy to improve his own net worth had been to master his role to the point where he could do it in his sleep, keep hitting quota and get promoted every two years. Far better than pursue a job outside—that meant establishing new formal and informal networks, reading the new office politics and culture correctly. He'd calculated that in the past three years, fifty percent of his earnings at Mironic had resulted from self-promotion, twenty on things totally unrelated to work, and thirty percent on actually doing the job. A frank self-assessment. Always ensuring he folded the core objective of self-promotion into every daily task or duty. Anything that didn't offer the opportunity for self-promotion was cast aside. And for that reason, he was just like Gribbin. Yet Gribbin was a snake, someone who spent seventy-five percent of his time nosing his way up Ruud's arsepipe, and there was only space for one brown-noser at a time. It would be two years before he could expect a promotion in his current role.

Kish parked around the corner from No. 47. He had to get out from under Gribbin and get promoted. His mobile flashed up Elise's name as he walked through his frontdoor.

'Hi. How you been today?' said Elise, softly.

'Fucking shite. And I'm sorry about last night.'

'Last night is what I want to talk about.' Elise's voice sounded timid. 'My evening course finishes around eight tonight. Can I come round after?'

'Fine.'

'I just came off the phone with your mum. She apparently left you a message at home, and your mobile. She sounded pretty rough.'

Bollocks. 'Yes, I got her call this morning.' Kish paused. 'You didn't tell her about us did you?'

'Of course not. So are you okay then? With your mum?'

Kish frowned. 'Of course I'm okay.'

'Look, I'll see you in a few hours. And please be sober this time. Bye.' As far as Elise was concerned tonight Kish was going to speak with her *and* call his mother, *no* excuses.

Kish was in the kitchen when Elise arrived around 8:30pm. 'Once you've made your tea or whatever, we need to talk. I'll be upstairs,' she whispered to Kish, taking care not to let Geoff and Humphrey hear. Elise's phone call earlier with Kish's mother had left her feeling odd. All was not right with Kish's mum.

Upstairs, Kish girding himself and entered his bedroom. Without pausing he said, 'Elise, what I said last night about you being pregnant. Look I don't think-'

'Kish, shush. I want to talk about your mum first. You said you'd spoken to her. Yes?'

'Actually, she left a message. Sounded pretty crap. What with her birthday coming up I guess she was a bit down in the dumps,' He did not look at Elise, but wore a firm, sincere-looking frown nonetheless. 'Perhaps I should call her direct?'

'Yes. And do it right now. And then we can talk about us, right?'

Kish nodded and began retrieving his mum's number from his mobile's list of contacts, then waited for her to answer.

'Hello?' came a voice. Almost immediately Kish sensed weakness in her voice.

'Mum. It's Chris.'

'Hello darling. I was just about to try you again. How are you?' Elise pointed to the door and left Kish in private.

'Fine, listen, before you say anything, I'm sorry I will definitely see you get a birthday card before Sunday. Been absolutely manic.'

'That's very sweet of you. And I'm so sorry I left you such a burdensome message. The doctor's recommended some friendly faces right now. Of course if you can't pop down?'

'Sorry, I think I missed something. You said doctor?'

There was a pause. 'Chris, darling, I phoned you over the weekend to tell you I was off to see the specialist. This morning I went to the hospital for some results and well-,' Kish heard her voice crack, 'turns out I've got breast cancer, and I just—'

Kish's hand flopped from his ear to the bed. *Cut her message short on the way to work this morning. On top of those ignored missed calls.* 'Hang on, but why didn't you call me sooner?' There was panic in his voice.

Diana tried to talk while she wept 'I did try, dear, but I think you were very busy. Do you think you could come down soon?'

'Well of course I'll come down,' he said, stalling slightly as he fiddled with the tie again. 'How about this weekend?'

'I'd like that. Why not bring Elise too? It would be lovely to see her. I think I burdened her earlier.'

'You told her before you told me?'

'Of course not,' Diana replied softly, sensing a familiar defensive tone in her son's voice. 'We had a nice chat and I said I wanted to speak with you.'

A thought entered Kish's head, jogged by his time last night. 'Tell you what,' said Kish. 'How about I come down on Saturday evening? Say around teatime? I have a feeling Elise has some deadline for her course, so she's a bit wrapped up.'

'That's a shame about Elise, but how lovely you can make it. I shall look forward to it.'

'Take care, Mum.'

'And you darling. Love you. Bye.' The phone went dead.

Kish flopped across the bed, and tried to absorb the call. Breast cancer. And his own mum this time.

'She's only got me,' Kish said, recounting the discussion to Elise that evening. 'I mean, Dad's not going to lift a finger. Far too busy with his piece of skirt. So I'll stay over Saturday night, drive back Sunday. I'll do what I can to see she's coping with her condition.'

'Do you want me to come with you?' said Elise, holding his hand.

'No need. I think she'd prefer if I went alone.' He grasped Elise's hand. 'I would like to spend some time thinking about us too. Is that okay?'

'As long as you are sure.'

'Quite. Mum was always a bit of a hypochondriac, and besides I hear cancer is a thing of the past these days.'

Elise did not react. Irreverence after all was Kish's coping mechanism... *outside work.* However jarring. Kish silently pondered on his planned visit. He had not returned there for well over a year now and the last time was to pop in quickly at Christmas, when his mum had put on a massive spread for him and Elise; full of energy, and fussing on them the entire time. As he drifted off, Elise poked Kish in his back.

'What now, hun,' he replied.

'Now can we talk about our situation please?'

'Can we talk tomorrow,' said Kish. 'I feel very upset after that conversation with Mum. You don't mind do you?'

'No of course not.' Elise paused, then added 'But so you know, I'd like to keep it.'

Kish righted himself. 'And how do you think Mum would cope in her state if she found out she was going to be a grandmother?'

'Something exciting to live for perhaps?'

Kish swallowed. 'No, you don't know my mother like I do.' His mouth was dry, ears thumping. 'I need to go and make myself a drink.' Stood panting over the kitchen sink, Kish tried to make some sense of it all, finding a pattern that might help things through. A visit this weekend was timely—space from Elise, and demonstrated his concern for his mum. *How come she's got cancer? Is it hereditary?* His mind continued unchecked, subconsciously calculating his mother's finances. *Must be more than eight-hundred thousand wrapped up in that house. Would certainly help the down-payment...* Kish shook his head. He loathed himself sometimes.

Diana Reece sat quietly in the lounge of Gladstone villa, her Victorian home located up on Bath's Sion Hill. Other than the welcome phone call from her son it had been an uneventful evening, exactly as she had hoped. She'd spent most of the day cleaning, rearranging and polishing the already immaculate kitchen, lounge and bathrooms. Despite a warm log fire and an extra cardy, Diana still felt a chill from the northeasterly wind that had earlier canyoned through the hospital's concrete courtyard. With it came a cold, empty, and lonely feeling. This house is too big for just one person, she thought.

EIGHT

Like most Tuesdays, today's trade was slow at the store. When not serving the rare customer, Humphrey had spent much of the morning constructing a rhyming conversation between two turds lurking in a toilet bowl.

'I should put a sign outside advertising my wine tasting sessions. Drum up some customers that way,' Humphrey suggested when Geoff finally rocked up to the store at around 11:00am.

'Rather you didn't. Cricket's on.' Geoff set off toward the New Zealand section, located in a far corner of the expansive store, and there set about rearranging some Kim Crawford wine cases. Content with the boxes' new configuration, he switched on his radio and cricket highlights on Radio Five burst into life. He opened a can of ale and sat back into his stacked-box throne. The cardboard felt warm and comforting. A deep swig relaxed him even further and his hands ceased shaking.

Shortly there was a loud beep and their third customer of the day walked in. Humphrey recognised her and lit up. Chanel sunglasses perched on her scraped back blonde hair, skinny low-cut jeans, and a thin ribbed vest-top hugged her slender frame perfectly. Penny Miles, archetypal Putney 'demo'. Late thirties, a profoundly flirtatious personality, married to an older minted guy called Marcus Farthing. Reason enough she retained her maiden name. Humphrey put down his notepaper. 'Hi Penny,' he said enthusiastically, collars more erect than ever.

Penny stood and stared at him. 'Hi there . . . Huntley, is it?'

'Humphrey. A common mistake.'

'Humphrey, how embarrassing. Now, I've just come to collect the box of that Sonoma County which you recommended on Friday.'

'Certainly, let me find—'

'Come on England! Nice bowl Anderson!' Geoff screamed from the back of the store, immediately catching Penny's attention.

'As I was saying, let me find your Sonoma,' continued Humphrey, as he made his way sharply toward the source of the outburst.

'Keep up the pressure, Anderson my son! I'm dying here. Just get Simmons or Gayle out! Come on!'

Humphrey scampered round the corner to discover Geoff nested in the corner glowering at his radio.

'Geoff,' he hissed. 'Geoff!'

'What now?' Geoff replied ungraciously.

'I've got—actually we've got a customer here. Please can you keep it down? Or better still, help run the store?' Humphrey spun round, and in so doing, accidentally kicked over Geoff's freshly opened can, sending frothy ale across the floor.

'Typical. Now I'll have to account for another breakage,' said Geoff.

'Cans don't tend to break, Geoff.'

'More reason to record it then.' Geoff grabbing another can and knocked it back at such speed that he choked on it, propelling foam from both corners of his mouth down Humphrey's clean beige trousers.

'Oh for God's sake,' hissed Humphrey, brushing his groin frantically, then hollering over the eight foot stack of New World wines, 'back in a second with your wine, Penny.'

Humphrey re-emerged a moment later with a large box, held at groin height. 'Sorry about that. Here you go.' Humphrey placed the box on the counter, beside the handheld barcode reader.

A roar came from the back of the store, 'Yes! Off you go, de Villiers. Nice bowling Anderson. Pure class!'

Penny looked toward the noise, bemused. At this point Humphrey remembered HQ's guidance on 'customer cross-sell' and he spent the next few hopeful minutes showing Penny his favourites. 'And if you are interested, our new Italian range for the summer is in soon. I am doing some tasting evenings over the next few wee-'

'Oh Anderson you beauty!!! Duminy, off you go.'

Once again, Geoff had frustrated the opportunity for civil conversation—on Sunday it was his porn jape that did it; today it was via highlights of England's One Day International against South Africa in Chennai.

Geoff emerged from behind the stack. He strode toward Penny and Humphrey at the door. 'Su-flipping-perb,' he announced, his right fist clenched. 'Well hello Penny Miles. How are things?' He placed his hands on hips, rocking from side to side to ease his sciatica.

'Geoffrey!' Penny replied joyously, and promptly greeted him with a couple of well-aimed kisses.

'I was just telling Penny that I think she'd enjoy this broad-bodied Barbaresco . . .' said Humphrey.

Penny seemed more interested in another broad body. 'So Geoff, what's the cricket score?'

'South Africa are currently one hundred and twenty four for six.'

'Super,' said Penny and lowered her head, fixing her eyes on Geoff.

'I can't help it. These one-day internationals get me all heated up.' Geoff grabbed her box of wine. 'After you,' he said, signalling toward the door. On his way out he lifted a bottle of white from the small basket of specials at the entrance, and followed her to her Audi Q5 and chatted with Penny for a while, who from where Humphrey was standing seemed enamoured by Geoff's own brand of customer service. Predictably, Geoff crowed upon his return, 'I'm a winner. And you're a loser. And that's obvious.'

'Yes, Penny's really quite something?' Humphrey declared.

'Too right. Nice tight arse and loves cricket. Perfect woman in my book.

'Married of course.'

'Yes, Marcus is a bit up himself. Never around, always working, paying for the Ferret postcode. Plus he hates cricket so reason enough to dislike him.' Geoff strode over to Humphrey's wine tasting counter whereupon he poured two generous glasses from the Merlot Humphrey had left breathing for the past fifteen minutes. 'A toast to yummy mummies,' said Geoff, then took a sip, sucking air in over some wine loosely cupped in his dipped tongue. 'On the palate autumnal berries, will soften in a year or so. Nice choice Humphers. I'll give it a week before this Merlot needs restocking.'

'Without a doubt,' replied Humphrey before rummaging his tongue round the liquid. Geoff took his wine very seriously. Humphrey always admired that in Geoff.

'I'm going back to the match. I've probably missed hearing another wicket fall.' With that, Geoff handed the bottle back to Humphrey and returned to his nest. Humphrey tutted and wrote into his notepad:

Autumnal notes, will soften in a year or two . . .

He then re-positioned his polo shirt collars and made for the French Section. Perhaps it was less boredom and more his own view on how wines should be presented that compelled him to start rearranging some bottles, all the time idly swilling his Merlot.

Geoff yawned. 'I make it past five-thirty, and I want to get out of here. You can too, as soon as you correct that train crash I just saw in the French Section.'

'Not train crash, chap. New means of classification. I've rearranged them all by price point.

'So now we have reds and whites and varieties of all types all mixed up. Why on earth would you do that?'

'So I can gauge the customer better. Those with their beaks toward the right I can tell are worth talking to. Those to the left, chavs opting for the cheap stuff, and left alone.'

'Well put them back how they were, how they should be. By region and then grape variety.'

'But that'll take me hours.'

'True.' Geoff bagged up his empty tins and made for the door. 'I need to use the van for a delivery. Means you'll need to walk home.'

'But are you safe to drive?'

'Just chill bitch,' declared Geoff and he swanked out, whistling. He'd dump his empty cans at the first street bin, rather than adding it to Bacchus Brave's own refuse. Heaven forbid HQ thinking he was taking liberties with the store's stock.

By 6:50pm, Humphrey had corrected an entire afternoon's effort. He closed up just as the heavens opened. The short, if damp walk became all the more wearisome when he spotted the store van, parked not thirty metres from his front door down a side street, its distinct purple livery turned ink-black in the neon-yellow light. So Geoff could have given him a life home after all. Humphrey tried to rouse some anger inside, but it wasn't to be. He was more relieved Geoff had got back safely, and not wrapped around some traffic light.

Humphrey walked up the path to the front door, and the usual sounds of irreverence spilled through the open bay window. He entered just as Geoff bellowed, 'What complete and utter bollocks!' followed by unhindered, self-confident, haughty laughter. Humphrey smiled, before closing his eyes and shutting the door behind him. In the lounge, Geoff was crumpled down on the armchair, laptop on.

'No Elise and Kish?'

'They've gone over to Elise's. They started arguing here and then decided it best to continue in private.'

Humphrey leant in. He recognised the distinct banner of Twitter across the top of the screen.

'Ah, the trusty old parish mag.'

'Yes,' replied Geoff. 'I was just reading the reaction to FerayNotFerret's latest rant.'

'Really? What's being said?' asked Humphrey as innocently as possible. Geoff began reading the tweets aloud.

'Apparently, some of the older locals are still holding out and calling it Ferrit, complaining the place has been overrun by gentrifying incomers bent on poncing it up. Oh get this, someone has responded with "as a relatively recent incomer, Ferrit is not a word I can bear to associate with my new locale's aesthetic". And a few moments ago he got a response from someone called CompleteChief.'

Humphrey scanned his Twitter page.

@CompleteChief:
Ferretnotferay ponse, 2 reasons why this manor should be pronounced 'ferrit'

@CompleteChief:
First, unpretentious. no-one feels caught out. Second, house prices stay sane + fewer people squeezed out

Humphrey glowered. No one had countered his view before. 'Bloody Bolshevik. Transient obviously. Having a pop while he can with his alternative views.'

'You got to admit though,' said Geoff, 'a more social mix helps liven the place up. Fill the bars for one.' Up until last month, Geoff had prided his total disregard for this Twitter business as a reaction to Humphrey's evident love of it. Then he'd started to read the rants of FerayNotFerret. Amusing and incredulous. Two weeks ago he secretly began following FerayNotFerret anonymously as 'CompleteChief.' Like Humphrey, keeping his online identity secret from his housemates took some finesse.

Humphrey hadn't finished. 'Clearly this CompleteChief twit is getting right up this local hero FerayNotFerret's nostrils, and I quote, "Dear CompleteChief, for all the love in heaven, it was pronounced 'ferray' throughout the Victorian period", and "U hardly want to own a two-bed seven hundred thousand pound apartment somewhere called Ferrit".'

Seconds after Geoff had discreetly finished typing, Humphrey read CompleteChief's response.

@CompleteChief:
Comrade, I've moved in and starting a movement to mandate it being called Ferrit . . .

Humphrey checked Geoff who appeared uninterested then began typing quietly. Sure enough, a few retorts from FerayNotFerret popped up on Geoff's screen a few short minutes later:

@FerayNotFerret:
Complete and Utter Chief, whoever you are, you are clearly a walking recession

@FerayNotFerret:
Ugly place names dissuade incomers with cash. Gentrification begats gentrification

@FerayNotFerret:
It's no coincidence that Staines or Slough continue to wallow—they sound so dreadful

@FerayNotFerret:
Chalfont, Windsor, Virginia Water sound nicer, and attract the right sort

@FerayNotFerret:
If you start your movement, I shall start a counter-movement

Humphrey composed himself. 'Well, well, well. Seems our defender FerayNotFerret will champion a counter-movement to promote the right pronunciation. Frankly I'm all in favour, and will get right behind him. Or her.'

'Did you say you are supporting a movement? Very proud of you.'

'Meaning?'

'Well, you're turning your back on what I thought you stood for. Conformity, moaning but not rocking the boat and remaining boringly Middle England.'

'Nonsense. Middle England is the most politicised class in Britain today. Take this FerayNotFerret individual as a case in point. Besides, just because fellow readers of the Telegraph or Daily Mail don't go on strike or take up arms doesn't mean we don't take affirmative action. Last year many of us attended a march supporting the Countryside Alliance.'

'I know. I was there too, remember.'

'Marching shoulder to shoulder.'

'Well we walked along together but that's where any connection ended. I went because my family's livelihood depends on a thriving, working countryside that needs stronger help from the government, and not handouts from the EU. You were there because you wanted to try out your new Barbour jacket and be one of those daft bloodsport hanger-oners.'

'Nonsense.'

'Mingling alongside ten thousand others in similar gang colours, whose idea of rural life is seen from the window of their four-by-fours returning from a walk around a small section of Richmond Park in their Hunter wellies, or a weekend away in some converted barn their London accountant friend owns, giving them bragging rights in the office the following Monday. Less about keeping up with the Joneses, these days. More about beating the Joneses. Only they've now changed their name to Hamilton-Joneses.' Geoff finished his beer.

'Cynic and well, no,' spluttered Humphrey. 'Let me just say I am entitled to have a movement if I wish. And incidentally, if you must classify me, by any social definition I'm upper-middle.'

'I have no idea what classification you've gleaned from some society mag, but if you were a member of some elite sub-category, you'd not give a rat's arse what others think of you. Which you clearly do.'

'Frankly you've bored me now. I need my bed.' As Humphrey stomped off Geoff began on his second of several beers that evening, and another counter-rant on Twitter.

@CompleteChief:
Making this place more accessible means more late night drinking licenses in Ferret (pronounced ferrit)

@CompleteChief:
I won't need to go anywhere—save on my Oystercard, spend more on lager

Geoff glugged his beer and waited. Sure enough one minute later he faintly heard Humphrey say 'what a pleb' from upstairs. Winding Humphrey up through his own Twitter alter-ego was an ideal distraction from more pressing matters.

NINE

Geoff snored himself awake the following morning. He swallowed repeatedly to moisten the back of his baggy and beer-loosened throat. The alarm clock read 9:32am. Not too late for a Wednesday morning. He rolled over, and put his head in his pillow. Despite the thudding head, his mind was racing unusually fast, odd thoughts tripping over one another. Thoughts on being caught by angry husbands. Thoughts on Botswana. Thoughts on catching something nasty. Thoughts on his general physical condition, like these increasingly frequent night sweats, and pain behind the eyes. *What the heck is going on? Why these worries?* He rolled over and tried to drift back to sleep, but paranoid thoughts took over once more, like Karen Williams turning up today for the first time in two months and he wasn't there. Fear got him up. Passing Kish's bedroom en route to the bathroom, Geoff heard muffled a voice. Sounded like Kish on the phone. He must have come back from Elise's late last night. *Would Elise let on to Kish she'd told him about their situation? Unlikely. Should he admit it to Kish? Stupid idea.* Back in his room, Geoff took a nurofen with a swig of whisky from his bedside hipflask, and darting thoughts quickly dissipated. Geoff left the house around 11:00am, scrubbed and polished, if still bemused by his frame of mind when he awoke, spitting out worries like that. *Probably something I ate.* Smiling at his conclusion he approached the store feeling pretty self-assured. Even a new sign by the store entrance advertising wine tasting *'with our resident consultant, 2pm-6pm'*, didn't cause him much concern.

'Morning, wotcha up to?' asked Geoff, casually spying Humphrey fiddling with a trestle table in the front corner of the store. Humphrey was wearing a boating blazer.

'Oh, finally,' Humphrey replied, holding up a bottle of red. 'Setting up some trial wine tasting for this afternoon. Thought we could promote some of the newer lines.'

'Saw the sign. So who've you got coming as our resident consultant?' Geoff asked.

'Quote droll.'

'Well, provided I don't have anything to do with it, or with the additional customers, go make it your day Humphrey.'

Humphrey had spent the past hour mooching round the store, referencing the notes from his pad. After many a fraught moment, he selected six wines for tasting today. All were American, and represented the wine growing states of California, Oregon and Washington, and comprised a Chardonnay, a Riesling, a Shiraz, two Merlots, and a Rosé. He placed the Chardonnay, Riesling and the Rosé in the small stainless steel fridge sat on the countertop. Then he opened the Merlots and Shiraz. He put his pad to one side, placing his pen neatly alongside and feathered his collars up. Everything was set. Geoff's policy of zero involvement excluded sampling, eyeballing the Shiraz as he gamboled over. 'What do you think then?' replied Humphrey.

'A very good display.' Geoff poured a small glass.

'I wasn't asking you to taste them!'

'Can't comment unless I do. Cheers.' Geoff took a swig. 'Clement and dry, I'd say fixed in 2008, tropical fruit? Recommend immediate consumption.' Humphrey compared this assessment with his own notes from earlier: 'Dryish, taste buds flat at back, clean, mango-y.' Humphrey smiled, satisfied that his assessment was similar enough to Geoff's. Geoff took a mouthful of water from the tap, sloshed it round his teeth, throat and gums, then spat it out with some force into the sink.

'While we await the hordes of customers tapping into our resident consultant's expertise, how's about a blind test?' Geoff suggested. 'Got any white in that fridge of yours?'

Humphrey checked himself. 'Hang on. I can't have you drinking all my wine. Defeats the purpose if we have none for our customers.'

'Nonsense. Howsabout I get it wrong then I buy the house something decent for dinner. And do all the afternoon's deliveries.'

'Done.' Having Geoff buy dinner was too much for Humphrey to ignore. Taking care to hide the bottle's label, he poured Geoff a small amount and handed him the glass.

'Oh do come on. I can't evaluate vapours.' Reluctantly Humphrey added another half inch of wine. Geoff swirled it, and went through the motions, light, legs, tone, refraction, then swallowed it. Repeated then spat it out. 'Oh that's just fantastic. Top Burgundian Chardonnay. Well-integrated oaks; a sleek, dry finish. The French Chardonnay grape at it's best, courtesy of a master like, like something I had the other day. This is on the Debrays list, isn't it. It's—, it's Olivier Leflaive. If I'm not mistaken it's his Chablis Vaudesir Grand Cru 2007.'

'No, it's American, and you get dinner.'

Geoff took another swig, this time swallowing. 'American. American... Oh that is nice! Not overly oaky like many Californians, zesty lemon, lots of personality. And gluggable. Very balanced and look, it shines like a Chablis. No, this is quality reserve. And there are only a couple of wines like that. So if it's American, I'd say it has to be Hailla 2006, or possibly the 2009 batch from the Bridlewood Estate. Jeez Humph, whichever one it is, it's bloody top flight wine, with a price to match. I hope you are accounting for that wine somewhere in the books. How did I do?'

Humphrey quickly scribbled down Geoff's comments in his Aspall's brushed leather note pad. The carefully placed port stain over its top left corner added authenticity. 'It's from the US, Washington State.'

Geoff grabbed the bottle and studied the label. 'Chateau Ste. Rochelle?' He hesitated, 'I might have read about them once upon a time, but never tasted their stuff.'

'They're a winery somewhere near Seattle. Source their grapes largely from the Washington State's wine growing region further south-east. That one apparently got a Gold Medal at the Washington State Wine Competition.'

'I'm impressed.'

'And get this—we can source it at ten quid a bottle.'

'It tastes very similar to one of the wines on the list for the Debrays events I sampled a few days ago. The Olivier Leflaive's Vaudesir? And how much do we sell that for? Thirty-plus quid?'

Humphrey scanned the price list. 'Thirty-five fifty, actually.'

'So how long have we had this U.S. number in stock?'

'Came in just this week.'

'Where is it shown?'

'Over there,' said Humphrey, waggling his finger towards the New World section.

Geoff sauntered toward the New World. Sure enough, a tiny amount of shelf space had been marked 'The Pacific Northwest', and immediately Geoff thought of Elise. She was from that neck of the woods. And from her fond, often homesick-tinged description of its mountains, lakes, trees and Sasquatch legends, it sounded beautiful, wild, primaevel. Rather like a roll in the hay with Elise would be. Having located a clutch of ten boxes of Chateau Ste. Rochelle, he snuck a bottle in his rucksack. A little present for Elise later. Even if she was a little pregnant.

For two hours Kish had sat in his favourite cubicle reading The Times and comparing himself to Gribbin. Firstly, he had to be wealthier than Gribbin. The sale of his little start-up, plus several years of saving had seen to that. Secondly where he lived, far superior. He in Putney Ferret, whereas Gribbin lived in an exec estate puked up in the late Nineties on the outskirts of Reading. Third was lifestyle. A house-share gave Kish freedom, fun and self-indulgence while he saved his pennies through a period of house price volatility, or at least until lenders were once more offering mortgages on more favourable loan-to-value ratios. Gribbin had two young boys and a wife he rarely spoke of, along with a house worth ten-percent less than when he bought it five years back. Kish smiled as he thought back to three years ago, when he moved to Putney Ferret. A workmate had a friend keen to share, someone who might get on with Kish. Though poles apart, Kish and Geoff bonded quickly while advertising for a third housemate. A few weeks later, Humphrey came in, and re-defined the term 'poles apart.'

On the stroke of noon Kish re-entered the office area and scooted to his desk. Fatally, in the time he'd spent in the loo he'd not once checked his smartphone. Predictably, his calendar had been hijacked.

'Hi Chris. I was wondering where you were.' It was Natalie Watson, and a topic for discussion in Kish's one-to-one with Gribbin a couple of days ago. 'The confcall with the UK Environment Agency? Sorry, I set it up forty minutes ago, a bit last minute but assumed you'd be online to see it.'

Kish dumped his bag. Assumptions like that were getting more commonplace. Still on this occasion he didn't have much to stand on. 'Apologies, I only just got into the office. Had some domestic issues. Anyhow, got here in the nick of time.' Performance-wise Natalie was at the top end of his team, in her mid-twenties and altogether very pleasant to look at. She was like he was few years ago—never late, sharp as a tack and hungry. 'So who's confirmed on the call?' asked Kish. A nice general question that gave the impression he might know what he was talking about.

'Arthur Reach from The Environment Agency, plus Michael Atkins and one of his colleagues from ClearSteer Consulting. All set?'

Kish flicked a glance at his watch. 'Sure. Let's find a room.'

'No need. I secured Maui.'

Kish gathered his laptop and mobile and walked with Natalie into 'Maui.' Based on the advice of some 'work environment consultant', Mironic had taken the decision during the recent office refurb to 'theme' the meeting room names around warm sunny places. *Maui, Honolulu, Venice Beach, Capri* being some examples. Six minutes later and following several attempts, Natalie finally accessed the conference call, and put them on speaker.

'***You are the first caller to this call***' came the polite automated American voice. '***Please wait while others join you.***' The phone kicked off some music that Kish knew every sub-melody to, then made an announcement.

'***Now joining: Arthur Reach, Environment Agency.***'

'Hello Arthur,' started Kish 'Chris Reece here from Mironic's Public Sector team, along with Natalie Watson. Are you well and goo-'

'Now joining: Michael Atkins, Clear Consult.'

'Sorry Chris, what was that?' asked Arthur Reach.

Kish began again. 'I was just asking if you were well, and sounds like someone else joined the call? Hello? Did I hear Michael Atkins join?'

'No. This is Julian.'

'Julian who?'

'Julian Foster, sitting with Michael Atkins at ClearSteer Consulting. Michael's just left the room but he'll be back in a moment.'

Kish glanced at the clock on his laptop. *Nearly ten past.* 'Okay, we'll get started in a minute. Kish then pressed the mute button. 'Ever in your life had a perfect confcall?' he chuckled to Natalie.

'Yes I'm fine thank you Chris,' said Arthur. 'Is it okay however if we do a hard stop at twelve-thirty? I have to prepare a policy review meeting.'

'No problem,' said Kish, eyeing disappointment to Natalie.

'Hello-o?' said Arthur.

'Hello Arthur. Yes, that's fine,' responded Kish.

'Hello-o-o-o?'

'Yes Arthur I can hear you!' responded Kish. Suddenly, Kish heard

'Now leaving: Arthur Reach, Environment Agency'

'Oops,' said Natalie, 'we forgot to take you off mute.'

'Oh fuckadoodledoo,' started Kish, but not before Natalie had depressed the mute button.

'What was that?' came a voice.

'My apologies,' said Kish.

'Hi. It's Julian again. Do we have a crossline?'

'No still here, Julian.'

'Now joining: Arthur Reach, Environment Agency'

'Hi Arthur, Chris Reece here again. Just waiting for a few minutes for Michael at ClearSteer Consulting.'

'No problem,' replied Arthur. I am . . . today . . . poor network . . . If I drop off, I'll . . .'

'Now leaving: Arthur Reach, Environment Agency'

Kish pressed the mute button. 'Bollocks!' he shouted as he jumped up and walked round the room.

After a few seconds there came a 'hello?'

Kish depressed the mute button. 'Hi, is that Julian?'

'Yes, just wondering if the line was dead.'

'No, we're just on mute, until we get Michael back on. And Arthur now as it turns out.'

'Oh, Michael Atkins here. Sorry, I've actually been here for the past few minutes. Were you waiting for me?'

'Now joining: Arthur Reach, Environment Agency'

'Hi Arthur. Okay, we're all here so let's get started. To recap, I'm the UK security sales Manager for Mironic's Government Business Division. With me here is Natalie Watson, plus we have Michael Atkins and Julian Foster from ClearSteer Consulting and Arthur Reach from Environment Agency. It's twelve-seventeen and Arthur has now got a hard stop at half-past so I suggest we get into the thick of it . . . So, Arthur would you like to explain your situation at Environment Agency?'

'Of course. So as I was sayi . . .'

'Now leaving: Arthur Reach, Environment Agency'

'Arsecheeks!' shouted Kish, once again forgetting to mute. Thirteen frustrating minutes later, Kish emerged from the room hair moderately ruffled. 'So turns out Arthur Reach wasn't the right person to speak to.'

Kish spent the next hour catching up with Natalie, which proved more jarring than he'd expected. One thing was clear, Gribbin and her had been talking. He'd told her about keeping herself out of the gossip column by playing it straight with senior management, leaving her asking who might compromise her professionally and indignant that she'd be accused of anything inappropriate in the first place. Kish tried to calm her by talking about her career development; she told him it was her intention to go into management at the first opportunity and had accepted Gribbin's offer to mentor her personally to make it happen. Wondering what else Gribbin was doing without his knowledge, Kish backtracked on his earlier point about fraternising with senior management. Last thing he needed was Natalie naively relaying the conversation to her new mentor.

'I'm going through a bit of a rough patch this week, so sorry if I'm not myself. Domestic issue.' started Kish. He stared at Natalie. Sure enough she responded.

'Nothing too bad I hope, Chris?'

Kish paused for emphasis. No, honestly I keep my work life and my home life strictly separate.'

'We're a team. You can tell me.'

Count to six, look down, sigh, then look up. 'Mum—turns out she's a bit poorly.'

'I'm so sorry to hear that. I take it it's serious.'

'Yeh, breast cancer. Not sure how advanced it is.' Kish hung his head.

'Listen Chris, don't you worry about stuff at work. Surely you should go and see your mum.'

'You're right. I think I'll go this weekend. Thanks for the advice, think I needed the push from a woman who understands. Stupid me, getting a bit overwhelmed by the whole thing.' He paused and stood up. 'Thanks Nat. I've not let Mike know. Not his problem.' Kish left Natalie and took himself and his laptop off to his favourite cubicle.

Any hope of calm quickly vanished the moment Kish turned on his laptop to discover an email from Gribbin to the entire Government Sales team announcing that from next week all special approvals for key deals would have to go through him. Decision-making had traditionally been devolved down the organisation, and suddenly feeling emasculated, Kish set about approving every deal currently outstanding and which he was currently responsible for. Each one usually took considerable time to weigh up, today were approved with a simply push of a key. Then another email from Gribbin. Turned out HQ had reviewed the eighty metrics on Gribbin's scorecard and decided to change a significant number of them which meant everyone including Kish had to collate and submit new data. Kish's agitation grew the moment an instant message appeared from Gribbin requesting Kish prioritised accordingly. A further email from Gribbin broke the camel's back: Kish was to summarise his own personal performance as part of a 'sales manager performance instrumentation framework' Gribbin wished to pilot across the Government Unit, before rolling it out across the company in June. All that distraction a few days before quarter-end. *Pillock.*

Re-emerging from the store office, Geoff clapped his hands. The monumental price difference between two superb wines had needled Geoff and sure enough, by 3:30pm he had a moneymaking plan. Tomorrow he'd start on his contacts, find someone who could get their hands on some good wine, off the Bacchus books, which was miles cheaper than the stuff he'd be officially selling. The Boat Race was barely two weeks from now—he'd need to move fast. Satisfied he had the makings of a plan, Geoff pulled out a bottle of Aspall's cider from a fridge. He downed it in seconds, wiped his mouth and then threw the empty bottle into the bin behind the till.

Humphrey eyed the clock and tutted loudly. 'Starting already? Besides, probably best if you pay for that, chap?'

Geoff's initial reply was letting out a thunderous belch with quite remarkable resonance. 'Of course, chap. No cash on me though. I'll reconcile before next week's delivery to square up on the stock. Piece of piss.'

'Don't forget, chap,' said Humphrey keen to make a point. 'It was never simply one bottle of cider. I mean wastage and breakage is one thing but—'

'Quite right chap,' said Geoff, breaking open another Aspall's. 'I mean, our record this past year has been unforgivable.'

'Quite. Take that case of Chassangne Montrachet 2007 last year. Seven-hundred quid's worth, right there.'

'An entire case of wine found to be corked. Who'd have imagined it.'

Humphrey shook his head, recollecting the time Geoff told HQ an entire case of spoiled corked wine had then accidentally smashed all over the place as he'd loaded it up into the van—hence it couldn't be returned—and Humphrey noticing a case of perfectly fine Montrachet in their lounge a few days later.

Geoff took six huge gulps and discarded the cider bottle into a bin. 'Well I've got to go.'

'Don't tell me. Delivery?' asked Humphrey suspiciously.

'Yes, Penny Miles from yesterday. I dare say I'll need to keep an eye out for her predatory ways, but I'm a big boy.' Geoff then feigned a kiss to Humphrey. Before Humphrey could remonstrate, Geoff was out of the door armed with a crate of wine.

TEN

Geoff nosed into St Leonard's Avenue, situated directly off the top of Ferret Rise. The Avenue's proud, detached Edwardian houses were among the finest in the neighbourhood. Many were still single units, two—to three million a piece, their owners resisting the attractive prospect of carving them into sets of three, four, or five flats, as was largely the case along nearby streets. Penny and Marcus's place was No. 34, about three-quarters the way up the avenue. Same as yesterday, Geoff slowly pushed their wrought iron gate open and walked the up the red and tan tiled path that led up to a white porch. He rang the doorbell beside the large blue-lacquered oak door with stain glass slats. The bell echoed around a large lofty hallway. A short moment later, a blurred whitish image flicked between the small stained glass panes. Penny swung the door open, expectantly.

'Hi Penny,' said Geoff, more amplified than usual. 'You forgot to pick up your wine.'

'Why thank you,' said Penny, and then she whispered, 'Don't you worry, he's not back for a couple of hours, so why don't you come in and chuck them in the pantry.' Penny led him through the kitchen, past flush white cabinets with no visible handles, and a very large farmhouse dining table, over toward a built-in pantry. The kitchen alone must have been the size of Geoff's entire downstairs. 'Just in there. Wine racks are at the back, beyond the freezer.'

'Right,' said Geoff, as he flicked the light switch and headed into the small space. Just then Penny closed the pantry door behind her and turned the light off.

'Where are you,' she whispered. Geoff somehow sensed her feeling her way towards him. And just then he felt a hand brush across his stomach.

'Oh, Penny Miles!' started Geoff, chuckling nervously in the pitch black. He felt a hand placed on his chest, the other cup the back of his head and bring it down. Suddenly two glossed lips moved feverishly over his. He stretched his fingers into the nape of her neck, and pushed them up slowly through her hair, at the same time scooping her waist with his other arm and pulling her body up close to him.

'Oh Jesus, Geoff,' she responded breathily. Whatever he was doing, it was clearly having an effect. Geoff was pushing his fingertips across her scalp, and stooping a little, he then tilted his head down to kiss her collar bone, her throat and then the underside of her chin. Penny moved and swayed in step, shivering intensely as he began nibbling her under her ear, and gently clawing her hair.

'Geoff, oh I—'

'What's wrong?'

'The kids. They'll be home from school soon.'

'Save it for another day?'

'No—I think we're fine,' said Penny, fingering with his trouser belt. 'Just need to hurry things along so just relax and don't speak.' Geoff leant back against Penny's Whirlpool freezer. Trousers round his ankles, he wasn't there to preach parenting to a MILF like Penny. Her judgement. Her pantry. Her rules. All part of his own very special customer loyalty program. Part of the 'arrangement', as Penny called it. Just then the room lit up momentarily as Penny opened the freezer door, and grabbed a tub or some sort. Dark again, then Geoff heard a lid being prized open and sensed something very cold getting rubbed into his freshly sprung manhood. He blocked out the image of the door suddenly swinging open and some kid asking mummy why she was knelt nodding expertly into the icecream-covered crotch of a strange man. That tempering thought did little to stop his knees quivering though, and as Penny got more vigorous, he was fast approaching climaxing, quite possibly into the ice cream tub itself. For Penny, the moment was all about her and it felt good. Unfortunately for her, Geoff couldn't carry on much longer. The ice cream was transforming his scrotum into a rubberised walnut, which now required immediate resuscitation with warm water.

'I need the loo, Pen. I've lost all feeling down there.'

'Oh for goodness sake. Okay, you know where the downstairs cloakroom is. Hurry up though. And make sure you drop the childlock on the pantry door behind you.'

'You're not claustrophobic are you?'

'No, I'm a big girl now, but like I said, hurry!' Geoff did what he was told, pulled up his trousers and left the pantry, safely securing Penny for a moment in the darkness, a tub of vanilla ice cream her only company. 'Bloody insane, these Yummies,' he groaned into the bathroom mirror, his groin poised over the basin as he splashed lukewarm water over his still-shrivelled privates.

At 7:00pm, Humphrey left the shop happy and began his walk home up Ferret Rise. As a result of today's winetasting, he'd sold seven cases of the Washington wine, and had placed another order for several more cases. Humphrey loved his street. The uplights from Ferret Rise's small specialist shops, funky bars and boutiques twinkled in the cold calm night air, the product of an economic and social force that he was part of, yet about which he knew so little. Glowing orange just ahead was a shop called 'Chocolate Chowder' which sold nothing but chocolate-based drinks and food, including hot bowls of the stuff that required wooden dessert spoons. A sign on its window read 'Come try our Mint Choc Chip soup—the mint sourced from Putney Ferret Farmers' Market.' Continuing up the Rise, he picked out the bars he'd be visiting this week, places to dish wine diatribe to unassuming patrons, then calculating how much he'd need to fund such outings. Cash was a considerable pinch right now. He regularly talked-up his trust fund, in reality no more than a savings account set up by his Grandfather to see him through university and beyond, and now virtually run dry. The monthly rent dug the deepest hole, but moving to somewhere cheaper like Sheen or Earlsfield was a non-negotiable. As was leaving Bacchus Braves—he still lacked the experience needed to fledge as a real wine consultant, and couldn't comprehend doing anything in an office. *Cubicle factory.* Plus being the anonymous FerayNotFerret was an expensive pastime. A morning's worth of lattés set you back fifteen quid. Then there was the new snowboarding jacket, those Kenneth Cole Chelsea boots, the fortnightly haircut, and various activities through an increasing array of club—and society memberships.

This year alone, he'd added to his growing list the Ferret Outdoor Swimming Society, Salsa Ferret, and Friends of Ferret Trees. All courtesy of his regularly mugged visa cards. Yet he seemed to be making a favourable impression with the bank—only last week they wrote to tell him they'd extended his limit to a far more respectable ten thousand pounds. The new card that arrived was platinum in colour. Even more reason to have it more visible, paying for more things more often. He checked himself. The mere act of scrutinising one's personal income and outgoings like some company budget seemed awfully gauche. Humphrey strolled on, passing rows of small, prettied-up Victorian terraced homes stretching off the lower slopes of Ferret Rise. How long had people like him lived in these places? He'd seen these streets of Putney and Wandsworth in 'fifties film reels—when they were row upon row of uniform brick, the last vestiges of which you might just see in re-runs of 'seventies and 'eighties TV shows like The Sweeney and Minder. Where patio flower pots, 4x4's and soft-tops sat today, knock-kneed kids once played football and cricket. Incomers like him must therefore be a relatively recent phenomenon, he conceded; three decades max. For Humphrey there was no downside to this demographic change of South West London though. Quite the contrary, he was part of a revitalising force eager to man The Capital's exciting consumer and services-based economy, one person among legions of young educated folk drawn to London, armed with a value system borne of aspiration and disposable income, where friends replaced relations as one's extended family and truss. Humphrey was one of the renting minority of Putney Ferret, and increasingly sore of anyone his approximate age and sort who'd managed to buy a place in Ferret. Typically one of the smart two-bedroom terraced pads he'd just passed. It was the well-to-do families who'd renovated those larger, status-ridden Victorian carve-ups further up the hill. Humphrey's ability to join the ranks of the Ferret homeowner depended on either getting a very different job and saving hard for ten years, or taking up his parents' offer of a loan, albeit tied to unfathomable conditions where he'd effectively serve as a sitting tenant. Yet owning a place in Putney Ferret would say to the world, his world at least, that he'd made it. And owning a place on his measly salary would give the impression he was a man of private means, which meant even more social kudos. Humphrey looked about him. Yep, whatever the ridiculous conditions, he'd have to accept his parents' offer. 'Welcome to Ferret,' Humphrey concluded gleefully, this cold march evening. One hundred or so metres from the house, Humphrey noted the familiar purple store van parked outside the local deli. *So Geoff was making good on his promise and buying dinner.* Humphrey knew better than to pop in and help steer Geoff on his decision. Geoff would buy what the hell he wanted, irrespective of whether Humphrey helped or not. Moving on past Jaspers Florists, he briefly wondered if it was worth bringing something floral into the house. Would be lost on Geoff and Kish, but at the very least, might make Elise smile? She'd not looked herself for a couple of weeks. He stopped himself when he considered how much flak he'd get. Reluctantly he made his way up the garden path, and heard the usual dinner-making din coming through the lounge bay window, which was wide open as usual.

'Is that you Kish?' It was Elise shouting from the kitchen.

'No it's me,' replied Humphrey walking through the lounge toward her.

'Hi hun, pasta bake?'

'Rather. Although Geoff said he'd make dinner. Instead you are doing it.'

'Just helping out while he pops over to the deli.'

A few moments later, the front door slammed shut, louder than it might usually. Kish entered the lounge through the archway, dropped his bag and kicked it with the side of his foot across the wooden floor. 'Twat of a laptop.' Humphrey saw Elise's shoulders rise, tightening.

'Everything okay?' enquired Humphrey hopefully.

Kish walked into the kitchen and grabbed a beer from the fridge. 'Hi,' he muttered to Elise, choosing not to give her the usual kiss on the cheek. 'What a shite of a day. It's like polishing scaffolding.'

Humphrey looked on, saying nothing. Kish rarely got stroppy, but when he did it was either about work or money or Elise. Five minutes of awkward silence had passed when the front door slammed again. This time it was Geoff.

'It's bloody Siberia out there! Humph, I got this.' Geoff hurled a flat package toward him. With some effort, Humphrey just about caught it. 'Hot cherry pie. For dinner.' Geoff looked at the three individuals, none of whom were smiling. 'What's wrong with everyone? Come on, work's over!' Geoff slapped his hands together.

'Well I must say I did expect more from you tonight?' said Humphrey. 'You said you'd buy dinner.'

Geoff frowned. 'Don't think so chap. If I recall I said I'd pick up something for dinner. Something for dinner doesn't mean the whole shebang—it could mean starter, main or dessert. So I spoke to Elise and I sorted dessert.' Geoff put his large arm round Kish. 'What's wrong, grump?'

'He wants to become a scaffolder,' said Humphrey.

'No I don't!' snapped Kish. 'I was using scaffold as a metaphor for how my job is.'

'Well, I'm all ears,' said Geoff, nabbing Kish's beer bottle and taking a long swig from it, his arm still around him.

'I was saying that my work is scaffolding,' he continued.

'Told you so,' said Humphrey.

'For God's sake, shut up. Think about what scaffold is for. Its single purpose in life is to support the construction or maintenance of a building, right? But at my work we spend all our frigging time attending to the scaffolding, polishing it, telling people about it, working out how we can fine tune stupid, scaffolding when we aren't spending a moment actually looking after the building.'

'I sense a metaphor,' quipped Humphrey.

'Yes, I am talking metaphor, moron. All I do is see people spend time designing spreadsheets to report on the business, in other words, the scaffold, and no time actually working out how to fix the business, in other words, the building. This business is over-scaffolded. It's got so complex, everyone is spending more and more time tightening nuts on the scaffold and not enough time building the building.'

'You've clearly thought about this,' added Geoff.

'Speak the bleedin' obvious, Geoff!' replied Kish. 'It's over-engineered and over-resourced.'

'But you get paid for it.'

'Yes.'

'So stop being a ponce, and lighten up. You get paid a fortune. Lucky you. And instead of taking it out on us and sucking the life out of our evening, go vent it at work.'

Elise looked at Geoff, and thought about her time with Geoff earlier this morning. She smiled, then touched Kish's shoulder and said, 'Darling, Geoff is only saying it because he cares, you know.'

'Love, as far as I am concerned all you know is fuck all, so just drop it.' Elise pulled back her hand and looked at Geoff.

'I'll put that pie on,' Humphrey said hastily to the room.

Kish's acting, preposterous by even his own admission, had worked exactly as intended. Getting prickly with them all, Geoff included, meant there'd be zero chance of Elise bringing up the pregnancy conversation tonight.

Humphrey leant over the dessert packaging and quickly discovered it required total thawing before being baked, and the microwave was still on the blink. 'How about we save it for tomorrow night eh? We've got pasta bake on the go.'

'Superb,' added Geoff, opening a can of London Pride, imagining what it would be like to eat some warm pasta bake directly off Elise's thighs. And before he left he kitchen he leant into Humphrey, and quietly put an arm round him.

'And take no notice of that twat out there,' he said softly. If Kish had called him a prick Geoff might have slapped him. Whereas Humphrey tended to just withdraw.

Over dinner, Geoff remained thoughtful of Elise. It was as if Penny had heightened his appreciation for fantasies made real. Geoff couldn't muster much sympathy towards Kish and his situation at work, and didn't appreciate his attitude earlier. Kish's behaviour varied; he was great company when everything was going his way, but he could also suck the life and soul out of a situation in seconds if he wanted to. Geoff looked at Elise and thought about how she'd opened up to him recently. She worked hard on her relationship with Kish, and in Geoff's opinion, she wasn't getting much in return. Geoff also admired her discretion, and with discretion came the potential for duplicity . . . he stopped himself. Kish was his housemate and even Geoff had standards.

Besides, he knew Kish through a rugby mate who used to work with Kish and with one or two exceptions, anyone who liked rugby couldn't be all that bad.

'Kish, you ever happy?' garbled Geoff between mouthfuls of food. 'By the way Elise, this pasta is quite outstanding.'

'Of course I am. Anyhow, it's not about being happy.'

Geoff eyed Kish over a fork loaded up with pasta. 'Can't see what's the point if you're not.' There was a momentary silence. 'I'll make some coffee then,' said Elise, and she left the table.

Geoff lowered his voice and eyed Humphrey. 'Hey Humph, I think Penny Miles fancies me. Delivered her some wine today. Got the eye.' Geoff readjusted the crotch of his jeans.

'Lucky you. Elise that was wonderful,' said Humphrey as he left the table, making for upstairs. When it came to Geoff and his women, Humphrey remained ambivalent. He seemed to go through battalions of them with all the grace of a u-bend being un-blocked. He clearly enjoyed their company, and for the most part they seemed to enjoy his too. Even if it was momentary. It was Geoff's attitude to them afterwards that irked Humphrey. Geoff's time with that Lisa girl last Sunday was a classic case: all intimate fun and laughter one minute, then flakey and detached the next. Humphrey changed out of his work clothes and sat on his bed. There he quickly made some changes to the poem he'd been working on earlier in the store, finally settling on a word that rhymed with 'retention'. Placing his notepad back on his bedside table, he popped to the bathroom to brush his teeth.

'The bathroom is a bloody pigsty,' Humphrey announced indignantly when he returned downstairs. 'Got any further on sourcing a cleaner, Fox?'

'Yes, and I've spoken to Kish already too. I've lined up a few to pop round this week.'

'Jolly good to hear. Frankly this place is fast becoming a no-go zone for anyone with reasonable standards of hygiene. Imagine if my next date saw that upstairs loo.'

In the kitchen Elise gently nodded in agreement. Geoff grabbed the Telegraph off the coffee table and went straight to the back pages. It was time to compare his opinion of various sports results with those of the paper's well-prosed journalists. Kish settled down to a documentary on the Dordogne countryside and Humphrey googled Debrays, noting choice terms and facts pertaining to the British Social Season. Before long, Geoff had diverted his attention from an article on Leicestershire County Cricket Club's chances this season to Humphrey. 'Very starched, chap. Very starched.' Nose was still in his newspaper. 'Your rugby shirt collars. Very starched. Very upright. Very posh-h-h.'

Humphrey focussed hard on his screen. It was no use though. 'Something wrong with them?' Geoff didn't reply. Humphrey pressed him, 'what, you think they're odd?'

Geoff eventually lowered his paper. 'No, just saying I noticed how enormous they look on you. You look like you are wearing one of those massive conical collars a vet gives a dog to stop it scratching its infected ears. Still I see what you are getting at. Good one.'

'Meaning?'

Geoff paused. 'Very Ferray-y-y-y-y.' Another two minutes went by. 'When did you start wearing them like that?' Geoff finally chirped.

'What, my collars?'

'Huge, upturned collars.'

'What sort of question is that? I don't know when.'

'Okay, just asking.' Another silent minute passed, during which time Geoff read some more on the cricket selectors. 'Don't need to be defensive.'

'I'm not. Anyhow you wear them the same?' Humphrey's voice had risen noticeably.

'Do I?'

'Yes, except they usually collapse due to infrequent ironing and wear. Whatever, you never fold them over.'

'True. I prefer wearing them like that. Ironing is a faff. And my rugby shirts are both ancient and authentic having been worn in actual games. Besides my fat neck fills the collar. Your scrawny neck makes you look like a schoolboy at his first visit to Twickenham. Anyhow, I asked when you started wearing upturned collars.' Geoff looked at the badge on the shirt breast. 'And what the hell is "JW RFC 1st XV"?'

'I purchased it from Jack Wills in Richmond and given the look of my fellow clientele in there, it's a darn sight more fashionable than your Richmond Rugby Club shirt.'

'Which is who I once played for, a real rugby team and I still support them.' Geoff tried to remain lighthearted but Humphrey was sailing close. 'You bought your fraternity rugby wear in a shop frequented by seventeen-year-old boys and girls, and you think it'll impress the twenty-something la-di-da totty in the bars.'

'An utterly preposterous theory!' Humphrey was indignant. 'And besides, practically everyone else round here keeps their collars up, but I'm the one who gets a ribbing for it. No one wants to *not* fit in.' Humphrey recalled two recent tweets as part of his series "How to Spot a Not-The-Right-Sort".

@FerayNotFerret:
Face it Readers, collars 'up' means the chap is one of us

@FerayNotFerret:
Collars 'down' implies the wearer received state-funded schooling, & unfamiliar with more sought-after French ski resorts

Geoff sat up. 'I suppose it comes down to personal integrity.' Humphrey tried to feign disinterest. Unfortunately Geoff continued on unabated. 'In my book you might be a cock but so long as you are who you say you are, well that's fine with me.' Geoff meant it. Though the units of alcohol in his bloodstream largely determined his moral code, he remained consistent on one thing: do your own thing, and don't preach to others. Humphrey was mercurial, which Geoff disliked intensely and ridiculed remorselessly. Humphrey was something of a flaccid identity jockey, easily persuaded, easily provoked, easily sated by shiny things. And what was disturbing was that Humphrey fashioned his identity without any serious thought as to why it was so good. He just accepted it because it was consistent with the shiny well-spoken people of Ferret, the vast majority of whom Humphrey simply didn't know.

'Remind me again when did you ever play rugby?'

'At school. And Uni.'

'So, what position?'

'Inside centre at school. On the right wing at University.'

'How come? You must have been about eleven stone.

'Nearer twelve, actually. But injuries etcetera, you know how it is.'

'Finished you off? Yeh, I bet it was tough. Mixed touch rugby, I mean.'

'I shall ignore that remark,' said Humphrey as he casually folded down one collar. 'A compromise. Keeping the other collar up marks the fact that I used to play. A bit.'

Geoff exploded into laughter. 'Bless, little poppet.'

Humphrey stood up. 'Oh bugger the lot of you! I'll be in my room . . . door locked!'

'Oh buggery-bollocks!' Geoff stood bolt upright. He'd just remembered he'd left Penny Miles locked in her pantry.

ELEVEN

Today, Friday, was the deadline for Geoff and Humphrey to submit their chosen Season events, and everything Humphrey did in the store was conducted with heightened vim and pomp.

'Okay, you don't need to re-position that corner display yet again,' said Geoff as he tapped out yet another profoundly apologetic text in response to Penny's curt voice message left two nights ago. For reasons he could only put down to the light-headedness brought on by nut-thaw, on Wednesday he'd absentmindedly wafted out of Penny's place to the Deli, leaving Penny incarcerated in her pantry. Her voice message explained how she was stuck there for two hours. The kids were unable to work the childproof lock and it was her returning husband who finally unlocked the pantry door. Penny had no option but to blame the kids for the prank, and despite their teary protests were grounded for a fortnight. She did however hold her tongue when she found her husband helping himself to some vanilla ice cream. Geoff sat down in his nest and opened a can of ale. 'Ok, fire away Humphrey.'

'Well, the Boat Race is in two weeks and The Grand National is later in the month. May is Badminton Horse trials.'

'Boat Race, heh? Marvellous drinking opportunity. Grand National, a proper event. And mother loves Badminton.' Geoff leant back on the warm cardboard box, and closed his eyes. 'Carry on.'

'May is also Chelsea Flower Show.'

'Not my style. Full of retirees whose afternoon highpoint is watching Alan Titchmarch tickle folk with his interviewing technique. Let Richmond have that one.'

'And the start of Glyndebourne.'

'Opera is big no.'

'Duly noted. June is Royal Ascot.'

'Been a thousand times, and always enjoy it. Family will be there too.'

'You can bet mine will be there too,' replied Humphrey, raising his chin and throwing his voice in Geoff's direction. 'Next is Trooping the Colour.'

'That's part of the Season?'

'Apparently so. And June is also the beginning of Wimbledon.'

'I'd get bored not being able to see any of the games, and we'd be working late until light stops play.'

'And the Royal Academy Summer Exhibition.'

'Doesn't exactly inspire. I imagine a higher proportion of spectacle-wearers.'

'Well, July is Henley Royal Regatta, the Goodwood Festival of Speed, more opera at Glyndebourne . . . September rings in Goodwood Revival . . .'

'Yes to fast old cars, great fun.'

'And the Proms.'

'I resign if we get the Proms. Ghastly cymbals and half the home counties pouring into the Royal Albert Hall, waving flags to 'Rule Britannia' and mouthing the lines of 'Jerusalem' like stranded fish. Jerusalem! Seems you only hear it at weddings these days.'

Humphrey grunted. Hearing those sentiments grated him, especially coming from someone whose family has stewarded a part of the British countryside so finely it had inspired poets and composers. He recalled the last occasion he went to the Proms, five or six years ago now, with his parents and some family friends, all in fetching Dickensian get-up. For just a moment there in the store, Elgar throbbed up within him.

'What about Cowes?' Geoff asked.

'In all the excitement of being the only true patriot between us, I must have skipped August. Yes, Cowes Week and Edinburgh Fringe are both up for grabs.'

'Cowes. Outstanding. Full of dirty yachtie girlies.'

'Nice to hear these pukka events hold such appeal for all the right reasons,' replied Humphrey sharply.

'With the sense of occasion they bring, I think you'll make a great impression . . . drawing up in the purple wine delivery van.' Before Humphrey could protest, Geoff said, 'okay let's finalise our preferences: Boat Race, Ascot, Cowes and Goodwood Revival. Sound good?'

'They sound as good as any,' replied Humphrey.

'Though Edinburgh Fringe might be fun. I can heckle so-called humourists who infuse their monologues with the word "fuck" as a substitute for wit.' Geoff began tapping out an email to Karen to secure them before the morons at the Barnes and Richmond stores got first dibs. He'd then do the polite thing and contact this Toby Sarber-Collins fellow to make brief introductions before their first proposed event, the Boat Race. Geoff hit 'send' and made his way to a fridge. 'We need a toast. I might have a spare bottle of Voignier somewhere.'

'Breakage no doubt.'

'Absolutely.'

Kish spent most of his Friday sat in his toilet cubicle working on the revised Excel spreadsheet that comprised Gribbin's business scorecard, only coming out for a fresh cup of tea. No point trying to hunt down Gribbin for any pointers. He'd be somewhere on the campus, but precisely where was anyone's guess. Oddly, Gribbin hadn't responded to Kish's instant messages, and moreover, he'd not received a single email from Gribbin all day. Kish studied the scorecard's line items. It now appeared to focus less on activities already proving successful, focussing instead on the various areas doing poorly. He'd cancelled another four customer calls to complete the bloody thing. At 6:00pm Kish checked the scorecard then printed it out, placing it on Gribbin's desk. Gribbin looked like he was gone, so he'd see it first thing Monday. He was just about to email the document to Gribbin and UK Operations then he paused. Sending an email time-stamped at 6:05pm on a Friday was no longer exceptional so he reset the delivery time on his Microsoft Outlook to 11:40pm that night. Until then it would simply remain on some server somewhere.

Three miles away in a quiet pub in Caversham, Gribbin looked at Natalie over a glass of Pinot Grigio. The pub was not massively popular with Mironic folk, and being located the other side of Reading from his home, it suited him fine. It wasn't long before Gribbin related to Natalie his recent meeting with Chris. 'I've started to make him feel a little bit uncomfortable,' Gribbin said coldly. 'So we're on our way. Here, have another glass—I can't stay too long.'

'Mike, I thought you should know Chris is under a bit of a cloud at home. His mum's poorly.'

'Oh, and exactly what part of that revelation should concern me?' Consolidating his position under Ruud was Gribbin's priority right now. His plan was simple: aggressively demonstrate he could lead a diverse sales force and bring in the results. In order to do this effectively he'd need to get Chris Reece out of the picture. His strong relationship with Ruud was too much of a threat and Gribbin knew it. The person sat opposite him was a second reason for getting rid of Chris. With Chris gone, Gribbin could see Natalie got the promotion, and in return, Gribbin would get his weekends away with her.

Somehow Chris would need to slip up. Gribbin would make sure of it. And soon.

TWELVE

Despite her race this morning, Elise still hadn't forgotten that Kish was going to see his mother again later that day. 'I went onto the Cancer Research website which offers some wonderful advice and guidance,' she said then retrieved a plastic folder from her handbag. 'Printed these off for you to take down this afternoon. I picked up a couple of booklets too.'

'Thanks,' Kish replied and grabbed one published by Macmillan Cancer Support called The Cancer Guide. He scanned the titles of a couple of others published by Cancer Backup and Breast Cancer Care. *Nice touch.* His mum would be impressed he'd gone to such trouble.

Elise met Kish a good ten years ago, and had been serious these past couple of years. Ever since then she had struggled to understand Kish's pallid relation with his parents. Being the only child Kish hadn't had much family company growing up. Mother and father were career-focussed, his mother had been some top advisor on the Balkans, when she wasn't busy lecturing and tutoring at Bristol University. His father was until recently a senior civil servant in the MoD's Defense Equipment-and-Something-or-other, and spent equally long hours in the office. That was before he ran off with his young assistant several years ago. Divorce followed which, as far as Elise could make out, was the moment Kish distanced himself from both his parents. Elise knew Kish's relationship with his mother wasn't simple and Elise knew it was for this reason she cut him some slack. Even right now.

'And thanks for coming to see me row today. It means a lot to me.' said Elise. 'We boat in fifty minutes. Are the others up? We should go.'

Today was the earliest start to a Saturday Geoff had experienced for over a year, perhaps longer. But he'd promised to support Elise, and whatever the state of his head, a promise was a promise. Even if he had to endure Humphrey's inane questions to Elise the entire drive from Putney Ferret to Twickenham.

'So, what exactly is a crab, and where does the term come from? Any other colonial-cousin behemoths you know paddling at this year's Boat Race? I'm sure one or two. No doubt in their late twenties, on their second PhD or MA, and still growing. Like you Elise.' Geoff frowned. Elise frowned back. 'Growing as a woman, I mean,' said Humphrey. Elise frowned once more. 'What I really mean is growing as a woman rower. Stout new world stuff, cutting through all our silly old world fuddy-duddy, and just getting on with it.'

'Quite right,' Elise replied diplomatically. Stout New World stuff? Despite herself being half-british, she'd not grown up in the UK and as such Elise remained somewhat unclear on the purpose of such whimsical, occasionally lovable comments, which seemed perculiar to the English in particular. Presumably it was simply a jolly compliment. Maybe it was because some British guys loved to fill the place with idle talk. Irrespective, she didn't get hung up on the difference between Old and New, even if Humphrey thought the point was worth making light of. She'd been brought up in Seattle, a city borne of innovation, in a country where pragmatism, self-improvement and conviction still held; she dwelt in the positive. This had largely shaped her, made her into who and what she was today, and where she would, with no doubt, be tomorrow. In her world, what mattered was simply where you were going, not where you'd come from. Conversely it seemed Humphrey was bent on overplaying history's contribution to his own peculiar social status. It seemed that for many others living in Ferret, personal providence really mattered to them. She'd identified in her mind a particular, and not insignificant branch of British society which seemed comfortable merrily dining out on its past, quietly questioning its ability to change things for the better, its self-confidence knocked by a home-grown media bent on reinforcing an insurmountable gloom. Despite sharing similar economic peril, job cuts, repossessions, foreign debt and the crippling cost of conflict overseas, her American friends and family seemed to retain a greater self-belief.

The housemates dropped Elise off at the footbridge leading to Eel Pie Island, then made the short drive back along the Thames to Petersham. Geoff volunteered a choice word or two as he stepped out from Kish's warm Mercedes into the freezing morning air, and accompanied by Humphrey and Kish, they slowly made their way hunchbacked and shivering toward the cold flat water of the Thames. Behind them, cropped and frost-sheeted meadow grass stretched out and eventually disappeared beneath a dawn fog. Kish picked out a position about two hundred metres from the finish line. 'This is the best vantage point. We can jog up alongside the boats as they come through.' He studied Geoff's ashen complexion adding, 'I go through this unwelcome ritual more often than should be strictly necessary, you know.'

'And I was in bed thirty minutes ago.'

Dry reeds that lined the riverbank beneath them rustled as the three stood, each with their own reason for being there to see Eel Pie Women's Senior Firsts and Seconds race against each other. For Humphrey it was to observe and arm himself with the rowing vernacular required to sensibly converse with pretty spectator types at next week's Oxbridge Boat Race. For Kish it was about placating Elise. For Geoff, it was simply to watch Elise row. For Elise, it was her last row for many months. Geoff shivered, and wriggled his thick hands deeper into his tight trouser pockets, dug his chin into his neck, and chewing the zip of his fleece jacket. He'd noted the nine or so other spectators who had chosen the same vantage point to watch this head-to-head unfold. Most of them were male, shoulders hunched.

'All these guys standing around. Boyfriends like you Kish?'

'Some are. One or two from the club too, come to watch and encourage.'

'Nice,' remarked Geoff, pleasantly surprised by the quiet camaraderie.

'This lot are tight, whatever the weather.'

Geoff popped a couple of nurofen in his mouth and washed them down with some Glenfiddich from his hipflask. Steadying himself first, Geoff stared at the shallow calm water beneath him. In this soft, clear light, he looked worryingly unhealthy. He squinted, tightening the grey rucksack-sized bags under his eyes, his facial muscles extensively loosened by last night's excesses. 'I feel totally shot . . . need to get fit. Bloody awful state of affairs.'

'Don't worry, they'll be coming past in a couple of minutes, and you can go back to your bed,' Humphrey replied. 'Now is Elise at the front or the back of her ship?'

'Boat not ship,' replied Geoff, 'and she's at the back of it, the stern, although rowers face backwards so she's actually at the front! She's stroking so she sets the pace for others to snap to.'

Kish nodded and yawned simultaneously, leant his head back, and clicked his neck with a sharp wrench left. His eyes rested on Abi, another rower at Elise's club, stood nearby. He'd flirted with her once, and she'd walked off.

'Hi Kish,' she said politely, noticing him now staring at her flask. 'Have some coffee?' She held out her mug to him, and Kish grunted a thank you. 'Nice to see you out here. I'm sure Elise appreciates it.'

'Thanks. Any sign of them?'

Before Abi could answer, a single male voice further up the river could be heard, barking. Ten seconds later the tip of a thin white boat emerged from around a bend two hundred and fifty metres upstream, taking a line very close to the far bank.

'The girl in the bow seat. She's in yellow. That's Bella. It's the Seconds,' said Abi.

'Not the Firsts?' said Kish. 'Blimey, all that training and she still can't win,' he grumbled.

'Never quite that simple. Rowing on the inside of a bend means the Seconds have been pushed into a slower current and if you know your Thames like the First's cox does, he'll take the faster water in the centre.'

'Really?' Humphrey said. 'There's that much difference in river current ? Surely not.'

Abi glowered back. 'A race like this is won through consistent rhythm, speed, stamina . . . and always taking the best line.'

A hundred metres upstream, the race line straightened, revealing Elise's boat was at least a length and a half ahead. Just as Abi predicted, they'd used the faster current to propel themselves into the lead. Wellington-booted onlookers began to cheer and seconds later Elise's boat pushed past the Ferrets.

Put your backs into it ladies!' shouted Abi, and turned to Kish. 'Elise said they were aiming for about thirty-two strokes a minute in the final five hundred metres. I think they might be around that.'

'Row it like you stole it!' Geoff roared, eyes wide, then turned to his housemates and bellowed, 'see you numpties at the finishing line!' He slapped both on their backsides, and ignoring the path entirely thrashed his way through thicker, unkempt meadow-grass. Kish and Humphrey joined the chase along the bank towpath. For all the yells, there seemed to be no outward reaction from the girls in either boat. The rowers in Elise's boat appeared more stern and gritted, and their technical superiority and stamina began to show now. At every stroke, eight perfectly timed oars cleaved the water, picked the boat up and propelling it forward. The boat glided perfectly, and the cycle was repeated over again and again. Three boat lengths ahead now, each stroke edged them further away from the Seconds. Running at a pace that surprised him even, Geoff watched Elise's lats widen, driving her legs down and hauling the oar towards her, her left arm making a slightly more pronounced arc than her right, levering her body against the water and again propelling the boat forward. Again and again, eight oars cleared the water, followed each time by a short silence as the rowers slid forward in unison until their knees pushed up into their lower chests. A lesson in strength and balance, each rower committed to work as one with seven others and the run of the boat.

For Geoff, this was all proving to be quite wondrous an experience. Why didn't he do this every Saturday? Jogging faster than he might wish, he locked onto Elise's facial features: resolute and defined. Her eyes were wide, consternated, as she inflated her cheeks and let her perfectly tuned lungs expel an above-average volume of de-oxygenated air.

'Mouth like a howler monkey,' said Kish as he caught up with Geoff.

Wasted on Geoff though. For him this was pure art in motion. His eyes fixed on Elise's torso, his imagination drifted southward. Jogging had never been so edifying. This morning, it was as if he couldn't get enough of this pungent, perfect, real woman, capable of lifting his sense of wellbeing without knowing, while whipping the competition's arse. Pity it wasn't his arse, if only he could convince her to oblige. Running, senses heightened, the pristine condition of a spring dawn, the reed banks and timeless river beside a hawfrost meadow with its hovering cows breath. And in the middle of all this was Elise, radiating warmth, power and grace. He saw nothing, yet felt everything. Alive, and running blindly. So blindly in fact that he careered off the bank, and pancaked into the cold water a few metres behind Elise's boat. In that split second Elise's attention left the boat, she slightly mistimed the exit of her oar from the water. As the rest of her crew powered the boat forward her oar got stuck in the water, almost flipping her out of the boat with its pressure, the boat decelerated.

'Look!' cried Humphrey, 'Elise caught a crab thingy!'

The mistake gave the other boat a chance to close in. But Elise had managed to keep hold of the handle and quickly righted her oar. The Firsts knew the drill. They inhaled sharply, got in the set position. The cox' ordered a bout of higher rate strokes to get the boat back up to speed. There was no detectable panic as Elise obliged and the crew followed seamlessly. It would demand the near impossible from them all now.

Having scrambled back on the bank unaided and covered in mud and moorhen nest material, Geoff was more awake than he'd been in months. Oblivious of his cold drenched clothes, Geoff watched rower's legs pumping in unison. They were a delicious, raw pink, like fresh, uncooked sausages. He imagined grabbing Elise's pink thighs with his warm, generous hands. In the same moment, Kish looked at his girlfriend's determined expression. Her determination versus his stubbornness. Thoughts swiftly turned toward the likely state of her palms—rough and unladylike, the oar could well be ripping into raw skin by now. There were more cheers from the bank, more barked orders from the cox. Just eight more strokes to the finish line, rower's faces creased with the pain of exhausted muscles, their quads burning on the push over every stroke, legs dowsed by small splashes of the chilled water. Straining with every ounce of spare strength remaining, they pulled, their heads angled into their necks. Both Humphrey and Geoff were grimacing too, sensing the unbearable strain in the rower's forearms. Geoff's sciatica tinged as he imagined the collective back pain, and he faced the boat, clenched his fists and assumed a squat-like position guaranteed to ensure greatest volume. The message came out part-growl, a yell, all in one blurt.

'Come o-o-o-o-on!'

Huge cheers from the bank and a final triumphant bellow from the First's cox' signalled it was over. Elise's boat had crossed the line just as they jerked ahead on a stroke. Barely a bow-ball ahead.

The victory was all too much for Geoff. 'Su-*bloody*-perb! What a comeback! What a win! You see that? Brilliant! Woohoo!' he shrieked, shrugging off any possible mild hypothermia.

'Damn fine!' said Kish rather contained, as he received Geoff's handshake. 'Yep, she's a good-un.'

'Pretty close that,' said Humphrey.

'Quite so my boney-arsed friend, quite so,' replied an ebullient Geoff, not really up for a debate on the what-if's. 'The fact is they won. Superb, Cracking. And that was just a training race? Kish, your missus has opened my eyes to an entirely new demo.'

'And what demo would that be?'

'Arse-kicking, sweaty rowing girls. By the way, I'm freezing my balls off stood here.'

Back in the First boat, eight arse-kicking, sweaty rowing girls bent back and forth grasping for air, their boat still gently gliding on that winning stroke. The cox' again congratulated his team, before piloting the limp crew toward a well-worn landing stage on the nearside bank, where Humphrey and Geoff, now stripped to his underpants and wrapped in Humphrey's Barbour, stood clapping. Geoff ogled Elise's Lycra vest. Something to be said for the cold, he mulled. It would keep him buoyed all day at the store, which unfortunately opened in just over an hour.

Seeing her rowing just now, Kish felt lucky to have such a fine possession. All in all he felt good for making the effort this morning, especially before leaving for Bath. Hopefully it would serve to remind her he wasn't all take and no give.

Elise was lost in thought as the crew de-boated. Given her condition, she'd never intended to exert herself like that, and instantly she began to worry.

THIRTEEN

Over brunch Kish badgered Humphrey to post some mail he'd left on the lounge coffee table, before speaking briefly to a disconcertingly quiet Elise—'we'll sort through when I get back on Sunday,' then setting out westward to Bath. He snarled subconsciously as he drove past Junction 9 of the M4, the exit for Mironic's UK HQ. He relaxed though as he journeyed on through West Berkshire and eventually dipped into Wiltshire, before getting onto the A46 and traveling twelve short miles to Bath. He kept an eye on his speed—he couldn't afford further points on his license—while working on his game plan this weekend. *What to tell his mother if she asked after Elise, about work. Then again, need he really worry? Surely she'd want to discuss her own situation, which he could refer back to if she probed him too much.* As he wound his way up Sion Hill and into the avenue where he'd grown up, new questions came to him, questions he knew he'd have trouble asking. *Are you scared? What do you think your chances are?*

Kish nosed his car up towards one of two large bay windows flanking the centrally positioned front door. A newish white VW Golf was parked in the far corner, which he faintly recalled was his mother's recent purchase. He sighed deeply as he prepared for the doorstep greeting. He now realized he might actually have to talk about emotional, serious matters with his mother, someone to whom he bore some emotional attachment, but with whom he'd had very little experience discussing that sort of thing. It had been that way since his father's unexpected exit with his 'desk hand', as Mum had come to call her; when Kish basically went his own way inverting himself in the process. His own anger towards his father had rescinded in recent years, and at the same time he'd let his relationship with his mum coast a little. Nothing unique in that—work and London life had absorbed most of his time.

Kish pressed the doorbell beside the large oak door and steadied himself for an awkward hug. It opened to reveal his mother, beaming. She moved forward, lifted off her half-moon glasses, grabbed his head and kissed his cheek hard.

'Chris dear, come on in! Goodness it's been quite some time,' she said, briefly scanning her son. His skin was clear, and his eyes looked bright. Head held high too. Unaware of the instant assessment, Kish shuffled into the tiled hallway. His mother was one of the rare few who still called him Chris. Kish had always been his father's nickname for him.

'Nice to see you. How are you feeling?' he asked, trying his best to maintain eye contact. Christ, she looked terrible.

'Oh fine, considering.' Diana rested her specs on her nose. 'Come through, I'll get the kettle on, I'm sure you want a cup of tea. Or coffee maybe? Want a coffee instead?'

'Nope, tea's just fine.'

'Okay well we've got Darjeeling, Assam, and I think there's some Earl grey?'

'Darjeeling for me,' said Kish with a little forced pep. He was still surprised just how a person can alter physically in . . . Kish had to check himself. *Six months since I saw her last?*

'So nice to have you down here. Kettle won't take long.'

At 7:00pm, Geoff was back home and tucking into his second bottle of wine. With Kish down in Bath and Humphrey over the road happily tweeting, Geoff half-heartedly texted a few mates to see if any were free this evening. All were either off out with their other halves, or offered him alternatives in distant London parishes that required too much effort from Geoff. Perhaps he'd stay in for once. In any case he had important issues to think about, like the email he'd received from Karen earlier in the day informing him there would be a full audit of all store's accounts in late August, to comply with some financial reporting regulation. Big worry. For starters, far too soon. He'd planned to reconcile his little 'plan' after Goodwood Revival, which was September. He'd have to go back to Karen and swap Goodwood for some earlier event. Hopefully she'd let him. *But swap with what?* Geoff turned his attention to a backlog of unopened post. His particular favourite was the one from BuildLearn Botswana. Through this particular school-building charity, Geoff had been sponsoring a family in rural south Botswana since his little trip out there a few years ago. He opened this latest letter, identifiable by the charity's motif on the envelope. The family's latest news came from Tau, the eldest son who was now around thirteen years of age. He couldn't help admire Tau's academic achievements, considering he'd been head of the house since his father's death in 2009—one of the countless victims of the AIDS epidemic, and was looking after his bed-stricken mother and four siblings, and keeping a part-time manual job after school. School was a four-mile walk away across scrub and bush.

'Please write back to us soon, Geoff. You must be particularly busy as we have not received a word for some time,' Tau had concluded. Geoff looked at the thin, low quality paper and quietly conceded he would. It would be his first letter in over a year. Email would have been easier, but given all the other things they faced, PC's and email suddenly seemed almost incongruous. Geoff scanned the bookcase for a box containing last year's leftover Christmas cards. He selected a silver envelope and a card with three large snowflake prints on the front.

'That will do nicely,' he said to the empty room. He began by writing the address on the envelope, something he always did first. After twenty minutes, he read his note and tutted. *Far too rambling.* His second attempt was no better—*too sincere this time; too many questions.* It went in the bin. As did version three and four. Geoff conceded he was altogether useless at writing.

'If I had the guts, I'd write something like this . . .' he grumbled and he began scribbling.

After two hours of chatter and darjeeling, it was Kish who'd finally broke. 'So Mum, what's the situation, I mean, what's the doctor said?'

Diana sighed. She'd been waiting to hear that bloody question all evening, perhaps longer. Her son had expressly asked her and she could now start to unravel. For the next thirty minutes, Diana described the moments leading up to her diagnosis, and how she was beginning to accept the situation and its remedy.

'I'm learning quite a lot about it all as Doctor Havey takes me through the various procedures I face. They've already put me on these steroid pills that will shore me up when I finally start chemo. But that's a few weeks away.' Diana brandished her small biceps, hopefully. Kish sat and stared, Liver spots had set in, her skin tone inconsistent. He then studied her hairline. Diana was close enough to triangulate his gaze. 'It's a shame but the hair will be going soon. Not moulting yet though. I'll need to find a wig. Dreds perhaps. The eyebrows too, but that's what cosmetics are for.'

'No facial hair at all? Is that normal?'

'Well, about as normal as it can be given the situation! Chemo is powerful after all.'

Kish's hand limped slightly and a small amount of tea spilled over the lip of the cup. 'Oh shi—sorry I mean,' he corrected himself. 'I'll go get a cloth.' Diana motioned to get up. 'No, No,' said Kish, 'you stay there.' Kish strode into the kitchen. Picking up the green cloth by the sink, he noticed the framed photo of him perched on the windowsill. All skin and bones, the smiling little boy he'd once been, stood in the garden he'd grown up in. Stood beside was another photo in a plain-looking pine frame. Three people. He could make out his mother, stood alongside a young dark haired girl, beaming a huge smile and holding the hand of an oldish man, tanned and handsome looking. In the bottom right-hand corner were the words "With lots of love, Vilora. XXX". The picture quality was fuzzy. Kish shrugged and returned to the lounge to set about dabbing the spill.

Geoff chuckled as he read through it again:

Dear Family Mephemle,

First off, greetings from a rather too green and merry England. It's me, your Geoff Fox from London and I really want to apologise for the delay in writing to you. In honesty, partying got in the way. I hope you are well and this letter finds those of you still with us healthy and, above all, happy.

I hope weather is good—I imagine it's hot. I envy you, as it's been a bit rainy here . . . wet pretty much since December. And I am not sure how summer will turn out. At least a bit of rain will be good for the crops . . . if it was worth growing them. Funny thing is we're not allowed to—we actually get subsidized to grow less stuff. Don't you end up growing less food crop for yourselves and more shitty crap to export to us fatsos, and you wonder why your bill for imported food is so cripplingly high, right?

I hope you are all coping well despite the tragic loss of your father to the epidemic. Talking about poor old Dads, my poor old Dad isn't doing too well either. Not AIDs. No, gout, something you get from too much red meat, cheese and port in your diet. He is a farmer with a vast amount of fertile land, green and yellow as far as he can see, but all adding to this vast, gluttonous EU food mountain. You have too little, we have too much. Somehow it seems a bit unfair.

What do you do Saturday evenings? Stay in? I usually go out and spend approximately 20% of my weekly income on booze, talking bollocks just to get laid. You? It's different tonight as I am doing nothing (other than writing this letter). Come to think of it (and I'm thinking of you now Tau) at your age you don't have access to pubs to ease the monotony. Lucky blighter. You have sensible things like dusty football pitches and the BBC World Service to exercise your body and mind. I don't exercise either. Shagging a clever bird doesn't count. While I'm on the subject, use protection when eventually you do find someone. You gotta take care of yourself out there, buddy. You don't want to follow in your dad's footsteps now. He had responsibilities yet he still

couldn't help himself. Harsh to hear, but it could save your life.

Hope your mum is okay, and best to all the bro's and sis's. And Tau, don't forget to tell me how your new school is coming on! I helped built that remember! All the shoe leather you wear down on the walk there and back is worth it. Some fancy desk job in Gaberone surely beckons. Government administration seems to be the big employer there.

Lastly, on this cold slightly rainy march night, I hope the sun continues to shine where you are, and given I spent a lot of time choosing this card just for you all, please consider this a belated merry Christmas covering all the last six Christmases.

Use the forcey-force, love and kisses, Geoffrey Fox.

Geoff leant back. *Bit too irreverent? Try to write it properly tomorrow.* He tossed the envelope with the card enclosed on the coffee table, and nodded off. He did not stir when Humphrey nudged Geoff gently an hour later. Geoff had recently mandated that if ever he was found asleep on the sofa, he should be woken, whatever his protestations at the time. Apparently, waking up at 7:00am on the sofa was wearing thin for him. When Humphrey failed to wake him, Elise had a go. 'Honey, you get yourself up to bed.'

Geoff eventually groaned through his stupor, and slowly wobbled to his feet.

'This due to go out too Geoff?' Humphrey asked, waving a silver envelope above his head.

'Yeh whatever,' Geoff grunted as he tripped on the bottom stair.

'Pissed up again,' Elise whispered.

'Cirrhosis by thirty-five I imagine,' replied Humphrey. He sealed Geoff's festive note then placing it with Kish's letters into his bag. He'd send them all out with the office mail tomorrow.

Soon Humphrey was in his bed, fast asleep. He didn't hear the faint footsteps of Elise walking into Geoff's room.

Diana was surprised Kish had asked. She said, 'haven't you seen that photo before? That's Vilora from Kosovo. I spent time with her and her family when I was stationed out there. Don't you remember me saying?'

'Yes, I remember now,' Kish lied. *What bloody family? Who's Vilora?*

'She and I have kept in touch ever since. And it's only been a few years since her father died—he's the grey haired chap in the photo. I love that photo. I can remember when . . .'

Kish's mobile pinged. A meeting request from Gribbin.

Subject: Mike and Chris discussion
Date: Monday 22 March, 10:00am—10:30am
Location: the Kalua Meeting Room, Building 3, Floor 2

A meeting on Monday morning, but no explanation? Kish hit Accept, adding a short note: *'Happy to, what's the issue you wish to discuss?'*

'. . . but that was years ago now,' said Diana.

Kish re-engaged, oblivious. 'Wow, long time ago. Amazing,' he said. Maybe he did recall the occasional mention of Vilora, even if it was in passing. 'What's on TV?'

Elise was in the hallway when Kish got back on Sunday evening. 'How did it go?' she asked, offering him a hug.

'Fine, fine,' he replied dismissively, dumping his bag. He was far too preoccupied with Gribbin right now. *What in God's name was tomorrow's meeting about? And why had it been arranged so quickly?*

'Want a hand unpacking your stuff?' Elise asked. Get him somewhere more private to have a discussion.

'Later love, later.' Kish knew all too well she'd ask him endless questions. He hadn't any answers because he hadn't really come away from Bath with a clear view. Kish moved into the lounge to greet Humphrey and Geoff. He'd be safer there.

No sooner had Kish slumped into the armchair, the doorbell rang.

'Ignore it,' said Humphrey looking up from his latest Ferret tweet. 'Probably some badly-timed hawker from Grimsby offering frozen fish.' Humphrey made a note to tweet that later.

'Or maybe my little surprise for you two!' announced Geoff, as he made for the door. Geoff returned to the lounge with a young lady, early, to mid-twenties, wearing a large smile, and sending Humphrey to his feet like some jack-in-the-box. 'May I introduce Maria, our new cleaner. Maria is originally from Poland.'

'Hallo everyone,' said the arrival.

'A-ha, our Polish 'polish',' blurted Humphrey, a misguided attempt at relaxing a tense-looking Maria. Before Geoff could restrain him, Humphrey bowed slightly, shook her hand, and tried a second icebreaker. 'So Maria, you over here on gap year? Or holiday?'

'No, I am here to improve my English, and complete study in Business and Graphic Design. And of course earn money on the way.'

'So. You just over by yourself then?'

'My sister she moved to here three years before. She is now marry English guy, and is now a mother.'

'And where she live in England?' asked Humphrey, unconsciously mimicking her cracked English accent.

'Kingston. She looked after me for two weeks then I decide I work closer to college.

'Where are you studying?'

'At Roehampton. You know it?'

'Yes, of course,' added Humphrey, conscious that this was rapidly becoming the longest unbroken conversation with a female in weeks.

'Maria placed an advert in the Ferret Post Office window,' said Geoff. He'd arranged Maria to come over this evening. She had the most attractive, confident, swirly handwriting. No need to call the other two prospects now.

'Yes, I put in every news shop from Putney to Richmond.'

'And against lots of competition I think,' said Humphrey. 'Quite a proliferation of young Eastern European women—mainly Polish and Baltic—in and around Putney. For the past decade I'd say.'

'Yes, I have four girlfriends, all cleaners. All live with me too in very small flat. We all practically on top of each other,' she laughed. Geoff fidgeted slightly.

Elise coughed and Kish cut in. 'Instead of being interrogated Maria, why don't I show you the kitchen first off.'

Geoff remembered the appalling state of his own bedroom. 'Kish, I've just got to fetch something from upstairs. Can you quickly show Maria around the utility room—the vacuum and the cleaning stuff?'

Geoff bounded up the staircase thinking about several of Maria's non-cleaning qualities, and went into his room. First, he straightened the duvet and pillows, then collected up the bed-zone clutter—three FHMs, a hairbrush, some crumpled receipts, two used pairs of white cotton briefs, a wine glass slightly stained with purple rings, and a few suspect tissues scattered on the floor at his bedside—she'd never believe him if he said he was suffering from a cold—all of it went into a plastic bag. He straightened a rug out, opened the window, squirted his Calvin Klein cologne twice into the air, and finally draped a black jacket over the back of his armchair. Geoff quickly dusted the two pictures of his mum and dad and put them back under a side lamp by the table. He switched the lamp on then looked about him. His two-minute effort had transformed its ambience. *A nice place to spend time cleaning in. And wake up in . . .* Geoff recalled Maria mentioning the business course she was on. First, he darted into Kish's room and removed a guide to business management, and an introduction to business economics from his bookshelf. He returned to his own room, and put both in a small bookshelf where a sad row of pulp fiction sat. *Easily accessible.* He then grabbed the plastic bag full of his own detritus and made for Humphrey's room. Two short minutes later, Geoff scanned Humphrey's disheveled room, extremely satisfied with his handiwork. A large pad of paper perched on his bedside table caught his eye. He quickly sat down on Humphrey's now ruffled bed and began reading several sheets of what appeared to be short poems. *Humphrey? Poems? How very interesting.* They were funny, rude, quite lavatorial in fact. He carefully placed the pad back down where he found it then returned downstairs, wondering how he could fit Humphrey up with this fresh revelation.

When Geoff returned to the kitchen he found Humphrey demonstrating to Maria how marigold gloves operated. 'Okay Maria, I'll show you upstairs then,' said Geoff impatiently, then motioned to Humphrey, still wearing the marigold gloves, to remain precisely where he was.

'Oh dear,' said Maria politely as she walked into Humphrey's room. The central lightshade had been removed moments before, casting a harsh light on an unpleasant scene.

'I am so sorry about this. He is quite disgusting.' Geoff then pointed to a multitude of tissues around the floor near his bed. 'Some men prefer, you know, their own company. The lonely ones especially.'

'And all his drawers are pulled out?' she asked meekly.

'Yes, he is how you say, a complete pleb.' Geoff leaned in. 'Bit soft. Bit immature for his age. Needs to grow up and be a man.' Maria chuckled nervously. She'd definitely be wearing those marigolds in here. Geoff went on and concluded the upstairs tour with his own airy, atmospherically lit, and pleasantly scented room. 'Now just one minute,' he said leaning into his bookshelf. 'Here you go.' He handed her the two business books he'd found moments earlier. 'Borrow them if you want? Just give them back any time.'

'Thank you. So kind. Very expensive books yes.'

'If it helps you,' said Geoff. 'And here's the first payment. So see you Monday the twenty-ninth, right, say 10:00am? Okay let's go downstairs.'

'So she's round weekly, right?' said Humphrey after she'd left.

'Every Friday. Starts in a few weeks,' Geoff lied.

'Rather attractive I thought,' ventured Humphrey and slunk upstairs. What with Debrays plus the anticipation of a svelte cleaner rummaging in his room in a few days time, Humphrey needed to remain calm. Unfortunately he was anything but the moment he entered his bedroom and saw the extent of the mess wrought by Geoff.

'Right guys,' said Elise. 'I am off back to mine. Kish, are you coming?'

'Not tonight love. Bit of a kafuffle at work. But say hello to the girls, and see you tomorrow.'

Elise stared across the lounge at Kish, awaiting a further response. When it was clear none was forthcoming Elise silently closed front door behind her. Immediately Kish typed out a text to Elise:

Not right time to be discussing our sitch. Sorry. Talk tomorrow. Kxx

Seconds later he got a response from his girlfriend.

Do u know what a bastard you r being? What the hell r u playing at. We talk tomorrow eve or never. Somewhere quiet over dinner, like adults.

Kish made his way upstairs, leaving Geoff eyeing up an unopened bottle of whisky.

In the commuter town of Lower Earley, situated a convenient few moments drive from Mironic's offices, Gribbin sat watching his baby son sleeping soundly. He considered his strategy with Chris Reece tomorrow. It was time.

FOURTEEN

The following morning, 9:55am, Kish entered the Kalua meeting room to find Gribbin already there.

'Chris. Find a seat, let's begin. Now I want to talk to you about your personal performance.'

Kish sat down on a chair facing Gribbin. 'Personal performance?'

Gribbin looked down at his mobile then up at Kish. 'I will summarise the key issues facing you. Firstly, your team's morale. Feedback directly to me is that you are not supporting your reports with parity, nor providing them all the same resources with which to develop in their current roles.'

'Who said that?'

'Well, as you know any unsolicited feedback on one's manager remains anonymous.' Kish took a deep breath. 'Of course.' *Bullshit.* His team loved him. They told him.

Gribbin went straight onto point two. 'Secondly, I've spent the past week compiling direct feedback from my peers, yours too. The perception is that you are not working to the level expected of you. Coasting, one might put it. It's generally felt that you just don't, well, inspire leadership.'

'Inspire leadership? What do you mean by that?'

'The bottom line is that in my past week's assessment of you, I have concluded you don't show the way, and quite honestly, you lack the spirit of leadership. And thirdly,' Gribbin proceeded, glancing again at his mobile.

'Thirdly?'

'Yes, thirdly, and fittingly,' Gribbin continued with calculation in his voice, 'your irreverence. 'You're not seen to be taking things seriously. Frankly Chris, the general opinion is that you are well, bored. Checked out. Not hungry enough. I can't do with that Chris. And others won't either.'

'Others? What others? Me, checked out? Why?' Kish's responses were fractured, his mind scrambled.

'Your team's dip in performance is evident in the scorecard you gave me last week.'

'But I've given you my Q3 forecast. We're tracking at ninety-three percent with two weeks to go. I know we can come in over.'

Gribbin paused, then said 'Not convinced. And you've got a poor Q4 pipeline, which means—'

'But we've forecast that situation up to Ruud for months. The Environment Agency deal may slip, and all our local government contracts don't get renewed till May.'

'If I can finish. Which means, I need to make some changes to how we're running the team.'

'Meaning?'

'Meaning that essentially, your role might change, and with it your ability to fulfill its revised requirements.'

Kish remained silent for a few seconds then said, 'I'd have to re-apply for my job.'

'Yes, and I don't think you would be in pole position. In any case I would not support your application in any case. Particularly given you recently sought a role outside the government team. In my mind that indicates your preference to leave the team, something I will lend my fullest support to.'

'Are you telling me to find a new role?

'Yes, when it comes down to it. And by mid-May.'

'Mid-May? Mid quarter? The most important quarter of the year? And if I don't?'

'Mironic isn't a charity Chris.'

'Hang on, let's just slow down here. You know my application for that role in solution marketing was a wildcard, and something I did with Ruud's blessing!'

'That's neither here nor there. The situation has moved on.'

'May I say, you are being a little crass.'

'Don't let's get personal here, Chris. Some senior management advice for you before another rash, potentially regretful remark, a coaching moment as I like to put it. Remain professional at all times, and not just inside the office.'

Kish frowned. 'Sorry, what? Not just inside the office? I'm not following.'

'Just saying. With you hosting at all these jolly hospitality events I've been hearing about—Boat Race next week right? Well, I'd hate to hear more stories of you getting a little too merry. We must keep our heads on our shoulders at all times.'

'Mike, I've completely lost the thread here. What on earth are you going on about?'

'I think it wise we leave it there, Chris. Meeting over. You can leave now.'

Kish bit his tongue and stood up. He stared down at Gribbin who was hunched over his mobile. Seeing no reaction, Kish then left the room.

Back in the room, Gribbin smiled as he read the email he'd just sent to HR and Ruud. In his mind it pretty well summarised Chris Reece's latest display of unprofessionalism, his unchecked emotions, and wholesale resistance to constructive manager feedback. Only did Gribbin know he'd drafted it before the meeting.

Monday was proving far less fraught for the other two housemates. Conveniently, the store was closed due to a burst water pipe located above the office, courtesy of Geoff sabotaging it first thing that morning. The emergency plumber made it clear they couldn't fix it permanently for two days. Health and Safety Policy prohibited Geoff and Humphrey staying a moment longer. Elated, Humphrey spent his morning outside the Latte Pharté, with Geoff sat beside him, relaxing. Lucia the waitress approached with two coffees. She was wearing a large plaster over her nose from the incident with Humphrey two weekends ago. A patchy purple bruise sat just below her right eye. Humphrey took the drinks off her, thanking her. 'I am amazed she didn't sue me for loss of earnings, you know,' said Humphrey. 'Then again I come here all the time, valued customer and all that.'

Geoff just smiled. As a profoundly accomplished bee-charmer, he knew why. And one day he'd tell Humphrey just what considerable lengths he went to placate Lucia.

'Get's expensive though.' Humphrey stared momentarily at his small cup, then lifting his voice said 'I mean café-going practically requires re-mortgaging one's house these days.'

'Only you don't have a mortgage to re-mortgage,' said Geoff just as loudly. 'And you won't have one any time soon if you continue buying five expresso's every time you come here.'

'It's espressos, chap, with an 's', not an 'x'.'

Geoff put his Telegraph down. 'By the way, got a mail from Karen this morning. We are now doing hospitality at Glyndebourne Opera Festival instead of Goodwood.'

'Did she say why?'

'No idea. Logistics probably. You know how HQ are.' Geoff bit off a hangnail.

'Admittedly, it's really not my cup of tea is open-air opera. I mean, sitting in a field listening to classical music with legions of Nigels in brass-buttoned blazers. Would have much preferred Goodwood.'

'It's funny,' Humphrey said, 'how people like you seem to distance themselves from it all, by pretending to totally disregard class distinction. A mark of a higher class as t'were and the trademark that defines you.'

'You make me sound like I do it intentionally.'

'That's exactly what I'm saying,' said Humphrey emphatically, realising he could also apply the trait to himself.

'Well . . . say it then.'

Geoff was just about to phone HQ to update them on the plumbing situation, when it hit him. What to do with Humphrey's poems. 'Bloody great idea!' he said aloud, and instantly bounded back into the house, leaving Humphrey outside the café, none the wiser. Inside the house he ran upstairs, and grabbed the folder full of Humphrey's interesting poems, then put them carefully in his bag. A few moments later, he was back over the road with Humphrey.

'Expect me back about three. Emergency. Can't explain now. Plumbing. Involves toilets.' With that he headed for Putney Station. What he had in mind meant he'd need to rattle off some rough sketches en route. *Just how difficult was it to draw a lavatory?*

It had just gone 6:30pm when Kish emerged from his hidey-hole. He logged off the network, collected his bag and keys, and made for the exit. Most people, Gribbin included, were nowhere to be seen.

Somewhat slowed by contemplation, he quietly opened the door to the stairwell and slowly stepped down the carpeted stairs. Titters and, *were those feint groans coming from the top of the stairwell?* He stood there silently in the stairwell, One floor above where he stood, the groans grew more obvious. *Bloody hell.* By the sounds of it pretty flagrant violation of Appropriate Business Conduct. Kish then heard someone make a loud 'Shush' sound. Not in any mood to confront them, Kish slowly crept down the stairs, taking care not to tread on the noisier plastic trim, keeping instead to the carpeted section of each step. Once on the ground floor he gently opened the exit door to the atrium then walked briskly to the small office next to Reception. A sign at Reception read "If not attended, please pick up the phone to reach Mironic security".

'Security Department. John Carlton speaking,' came the monotone response.

'Could I have someone meet me here outside reception please. Rather urgent.'

'Who is this please?'

'Chris Reece from the Government team.'

Momentarily, a well-built guy in a black suit appeared. 'Mr. Reece?' he asked.

'Yes hi, listen, I'm sorry. I think there might be a potential breach in security. I heard something extremely suspicious up the top of the north stairwell leading up from the Atrium over there,' said Kish pointing.

'Top floor?'

'Yes, I think it could be people drinking or doing things they shouldn't be. I'm putting this in your hands as I know the procedure is to alert you guys, rather than investigate myself.'

'Certainly sir, I'll take a look.'

'Thank you,' and with that Kish picked up his bag and left. Within a few short minutes he was on the phone with Elise arranging their dinner and chat.

'I tell you, I heard something!' whispered the female, as she sat on the fourth floor stairwell, buttoning up.

'Nonsense,' replied Gribbin.

'I did. This is too dangerous.'

Gribbin heeded and straightened himself, then pulled his companion off the floor. They had walked down two floors when John from security met them on the stairs. He recognised Gribbin's face immediately.

'Everything okay Mr. Gribbin, sir?'

'Hi John, yes leaving now. Long day, sorting things out with my team. Problem?'

'Maybe. See anything unusual or a bit odd further up?'

'No why?'

'I'm just checking up on reports of potentially inappropriate behaviour on the stairwell.'

'Not seen anything.

'Well I'd best go have a look.'

'You do that.' Gribbin turned, then said, 'by the way, who called you?'

'The security guard looked at his notepad. 'Chris Reece.'

'Good old Chris. As diligent as ever.' Gribbin paused then continued. 'I'll make sure he and I catch up tomorrow. Thank you John.'

'Have a good evening Mr. Gribbin.'

By the time he'd nosed his Lexus out of the car park, Gribbin had made up his mind. Chris Reece had overheard him getting up to no good on company property. God only knew what he might do. No point taking chances, even if Reece didn't know it was him. Just one more reason to initiate Chris' removal, not just out of his team, but perhaps out of the company. That would need to be before the Manager Review process kicked off, preventing Chris from providing any negative feedback on Gribbin—accusations of constructive dismissal for instance, impropriety. Not only did his love life depend on getting rid of Chris, but potentially his own position. And that gave him only two weeks.

Kish and Elise drove the two miles to The Nude Tortoise, a small, highly commended restaurant in nearby East Sheen. Elise had been there a couple of times when visiting a friend who rowed out of nearby Mortlake, and had enjoyed its ambience. Hopefully it was the right choice and would help make tonight's chat with Kish both calm and amicable. Given his day, Kish arrived in no mood to discuss anything calmly and amicably. Knowing Elise wasn't going to leave it another day, he'd hear what she had to say on this wretched pregnancy issue, but he'd not budge an inch.

'I would have preferred if we discussed this in private,' said Kish, after ordering his starter and leaving it to Elise to decide whether she wanted one or not.

'And I would have preferred we discussed it sooner, period,' retorted Elise. She poured herself a glass of water. 'Private or not, do you realise how long you've refused to speak to me on it?' Kish kept silent. 'If you have nothing to say, let me kick off. For the past two weeks you have ignored both me and a situation that we are equally involved in. Do you know how upsetting that has been?'

'You're exaggerating as usual. We've been texting for starters.'

'I'll pretend you didn't say that. While you bury your head in the sand like a damn coward, yes a coward Kish, I've been thinking about this the whole damn time. I respect that you've got problems with your mum, I really do, but I simply don't have the strength to carry on waiting for you to tell me what you think.'

'About what again?'

'About me being pregnant!! For Godssake!'

'So what are you saying?' asked Kish, quietly hoping his strategy of gentle attrition was working.

'I plan to keep it. There you go.' She paused. 'And I'd like you to step up with me so we can work this through together.' Elise offered out her hand across the table, and placed her fingers on Kish's wrist. 'Kish, I really think this is the right thing to do. I can't have it any other way. And if we love each other—'

'So what you're saying is that despite the fact I don't want to do this, I've still got to go through with it. Bit one-sided really wouldn't you say?' Kish curled his lip and tipped the glass of wine down his neck as if to make his point.

Elise drew her hand back. 'No.' she started, her voice raised. 'I've never wanted to have to say this but I am going to have this child, whether you are involved in its life or not. And if you don't want to get involved, then, well that's the end of us.'

The waiter returned with their starters. Reading the body language he left quickly.

'Oh,' said Kish quietly now, 'So now you are saying basically I agree to support this, or we split up?'

'Don't turn this into an ultimatum Kish. I'm not some sort of silly business meeting. I am your girlfriend. Your pregnant girlfriend, Kish. And I guess it's not exactly ideal circumstances, but I think we have a strong enough relationship that can cope with this. And well, it's happened now, so we will deal with it.'

'Well clearly you've made your choice so I'll make mine,' said Kish obtusely. Elise seemed to shake a little, before steadying herself. Kish saw this and just carried on. 'First off, you're damn right it's bad timing. I don't think this is the right thing for me, not right now anyway. Second, well perhaps this relationship isn't as strong as you imagined.'

Elise took a folded napkin to her eye. Kish looked about him. 'Damn it. I knew we shouldn't have discussed this in public. I mean discussing something that upsets you in a restaurant of all places. Jesus, what were you thinking? Well I pray for the offspring's wit, that's all I can say.'

Without saying a word Elise bent down to retrieve her bag from beside her chair. Kish watched as she walked away from the table.

'Oh I see. You go and pop off to the loo, so we can't carry on.'

Elise didn't go towards the toilets; instead she made for the front door and walked out onto Upper Richmond Road.

Kish remained seated and poured another glass of wine, then gently sipped it down. He'd be buggered if he'd cause a scene over her. From that moment on, she could do whatever the hell she wanted. After all, that was her intention anyhow. Good luck to her.

A short walk away, Elise stood on the eastbound platform at Mortlake Station watching as the Waterloo-bound train slowed up. She'd skype her parents from her flat, tell them her news. Update them on her work and studies. She'd skip telling them she'd split with Kish. The asshole.

FIFTEEN

The morning of the 157th Oxford and Cambridge Boat Race found Humphrey in unbearably high spirits. Today was the Putney Ferret branch of Bacchus Braves' first official outing of the Season, courtesy of its partnership with Debrays Hospitality. Humphrey was determined today would go with a big splash. His first attempt at waking Geoff was by singing 'Row, row, row, your boat,' very loudly outside Geoff's bedroom door. It failed. 'Seize the day fatso!' he shouted with boyish exuberance.

'For Christ sake, get out of the house!' Kish yelled from along the corridor. He'd be there later, despite the lack of usual prompting to attend any rowing-related event. No contact with Elise for nearly a week.

To save time, Humphrey showered and shaved simultaneously, and when he stepped out onto the heated floor and glanced into the main bathroom mirror above the sink, he discovered he'd nicked himself in at least three places along his rather well edged chin, and had sliced opened a nicely flowing capillary in his nostril. Tutting at his misfortune, Humphrey strode out and along the corridor, towel-bound with several pieces of blood-stained tissues stuck to his face. Not thinking, he walked into Geoff's room. The rather unexpected sight of Geoff in a delicate pose with a naked stranger took him aback. Where Geoff got the "Police—Do Not Cross" tape wrapping his female companion's midriff was anyones guess. But still he pressed on. 'Just make sure you are down in ten!' Humphrey then turned to Geoff's guest. 'Very nice to meet you by the way.'

Downstairs Humphrey readjusted his collars up, down, then half up again, repeated, and once satisfied, placed the vacuum cleaner at the bottom of the stairs then turned it on. This particular cajoling tactic worked and within a few short minutes, Geoff swore as he passed Humphrey on his way out of the house, a violent waft of Humphrey's cologne following in his wake. *He hasn't showered again the stinking bastard.* Humphrey dashed back upstairs and into Geoff's room to grab the bottle back, while ensuring he apologised to a currently lady tucked up in Geoff's bed, whom he quickly established was one Amelia from Chiswick.

Amelia smiled at Humphrey and said, 'Geoff mentioned that once you've set up, he'll come back and drive me over to mine so I can quickly change, then get back to your little shindig near the finish line. Said he didn't want me embarrassed walking home in last night's clothes. Quite the gent.'

Humphrey smiled back and left. *Another vastly-inflated promise from Geoff.* He administered two squirts of cologne about his chin, screamed as the alcohol sunk into the razor cuts and instantly cauterised them, then left the house.

Geoff was sat in the driver's seat, over-revving the four-cylinder engine.

'Do you have to make that blasted racket?' Humphrey demanded as he slumped into the passenger seat.

'And off we go!' Geoff said, brushing him off as usual. 'Now remind me to call that young lady upstairs by eleven, okay? I can't forget this one. She's an absolute firecracker is Annabel!'

'You mean Amelia.'

'Exactly. Got a very good feeling about her. Won't last though. Now where are we off to?' Geoff tuned into BBC Radio Five Live's pre-race day discussion.

Humphrey studied the map and instructions he'd printed off the day before. 'We're making for Mortlake. The Ship Inn,' replied Humphrey, still reeling from Geoff's decision to load up the van last night and park it and its expensive contents outside the house—strictly against company policy. He studied the blurry map again. 'Looks like they've set up next door to the pub, right on the Thames Bank.'

'Spot-on vantage point. Close to the finish line.'

'You've watched the race from there before?' asked Humphrey as they wound down onto Lower Richmond Road.

'The last six occasions, I'd say.'

'Me too,' said Humphrey. 'Well, since last year.'

'I can't remember you coming down with me last year?' said Geoff, nosing his way down Thames Path.

'I didn't, I was with my ex-college friends.'

'Me too. I had a couple of friends at school that nearly made Goldie, Cambridge's reserve crew. Good rowers, really good, but to get even into the reserves takes something extraordinary. Physically and mentally.'

'But you never rowed, right?'

'Tried it once or twice at school—the early starts weren't for me. Also had a bad back. Sciatica.' Geoff motioned toward his right leg. 'Sharp pain goes all the way down from the depths of your buttock to the foot. Besides I always preferred rugby back then.' Geoff parked up. 'Right, let's get the van unloaded.'

Wedged into the overloaded Citroen Berlingo were five hundred bottles of various reds, whites and Champagnes. Geoff rifled through a pile of clothing that had slowly accumulated over time in the back of the van, and which probably represented almost half his wardrobe. Finally he pulled out his old school splash top, and gave it a brief shakedown.

'Nice tear down the side,' said Humphrey, scornfully.

'Pure character,' declared Geoff. It smelled characterful too.

A man around their age approached them as they entered the tent. 'You'll be Bacchus Braves,' he said with an air of unswerving authority.

Geoff stretched out a hand. 'Toby?'

'Toby Sarber-Collins, correct,' he replied over a firm handshake.

'Geoff Fox. We exchanged brief emails. Good to meet you.'

'And I'm Humphrey C. Massey,' said Geoff's sidekick, offering an over-cooked handshake and grin. It had only just dawned on Humphrey. Toby Sarber-Collins was none other than Mr Moleskin from the Latte Pharté a couple of weeks ago.

'So you are Humphrey. Always good to put a face to a name.' Sarber-Collins looked at them both. At least Geoff cut the mustard. But this Humphrey chump. All too eager. 'Well, good you are here, and if you don't mind I've got to get on, starting with talking to a couple of reporters covering us. I'll have a couple of our guys help you get the supplies in.'

'Interesting character,' said Humphrey, as Sarber-Collins strutted off.

'You recognise him?'

'Not really, forgetful face I thought.'

'Well, he's *the* Toby Sarber-Collins, heir to the Sarber Port dynasty. I think he lives up on Dysover Road, near the top of the Rise. One of those detatched Edwardian piles.'

Humphrey breathed slowly. It calmed him in these revolting situations. 'Must be hard still living with parents. I mean at his age too.'

'No, all his. The family pile's in Kent.'

Humphrey and Geoff made short work of unloading the bottles, coordinating Sarber-Collins' chain gang which stretched from the van to the back of the tent, occasionally looked on by Sarber-Collins.

'The van, Humph. Needs parking elsewhere and quickly,' said Geoff, taking a furtive swig from his hip flask.

Humphrey reluctantly made his way to the van. According to the written instructions accompanying his map, Humphrey was to park near the Debrays hospitality tent in 'Designated Parking'. Unfortunately a large, inconveniently located splodge obscured exactly where. Undeterred, Humphrey set off slowly eastward along Thames Path that ran parallel to the ink-smudged south bank of the Thames. *This must be it,* thought Humphrey, spotting a shingle slipway at the end of Thames Path. A couple of bright orange bollards were placed across it. *How thoughtful that Debrays had reserved such a prime spot.* 'This is how it should be,' he announced excitedly, and quickly put the bollards in the van for safe keeping, before carefully parking nose-first on the slipway. Before getting out, Humphrey grabbed a freshly laundered rugby shirt, and then put on a Jack Wills cap he'd deliberately left outside for a month. Not that it really needed the extra weathering—it already came artificially worn for instant authenticity. Although Humphrey had watched the Boat Race a couple of times, this was the first occasion he'd be participating in a more official capacity, rather than being some bystander. He put his Oxford University rugby top over his equally well-appointed Debrays polo shirt. Sporting a double set of upturned collars, Humphrey walked over to Geoff, who was holding two beers he'd purchased from the Ship Inn next door, along with two hot dogs wrapped in tissue.

'Pub opened nice and early,' said Geoff. 'We've a bit of time before we need to be back at the tent.' He noted Humphrey's rugby top. 'Oh yeh, I remember you saying you were at Oxford. Fancy that.'

'Meaning?'

'Nothing. Just that most of the folk I know who went there decided against till-work as their chosen career.' Before Humphrey could remonstrate, Geoff handed him a pint of Young's Special. 'Get this down you quickly, and don't let Toby see. We don't want to get off to a bad start do we? And by the way, twenty quid says Cambridge win today. What d'you say?'

In the relative calm, Geoff sipped beer from a plastic skiff and considered his own time in Higher Education. Calling himself a 'student' was mild hyperbole, given it implied being engaged in the act of studying, which he spent as little time as possible doing without failing to graduate. While enrolled on an undergraduate course in English and Sport Science at Loughborough, he dedicated almost all of his energies on his first love, rugby. Alongside playing some of the finest rugby the university had ever seen, he beat most rugby club drinking records, and following captaining Loughborough to win the British Universities Rugby Union championship at the tender age of twenty, he set his sights on his heroes down the road. Geoff left with a Third, which by his own admission was a miracle.

Two pints later Geoff and Humphrey returned to the tent. Their job, issued by Sarber-Collins was simple: keep the bottles coming, un-cork, serve and smile at the guests. 'We're running a well oiled machine today, chaps,' said Sarber-Collins. 'Keep it—and our hospitality punters well oiled, please.' Sarber-Collins then re-joined a couple of guests he knew from his old TA Regiment.

Geoff hadn't bothered to form an opinion of Sarber-Collins. Whereas Humphrey could think of nothing else. Disliking him seemed counter intuitive, so did acting with deference toward him. The family dynasty, the money, the background, Mr. Moleskin himself. Humphrey found himself dithering between the two, and felt even less the man for it.

On the whole, the morning progressed rather nicely for Humphrey and Geoff. Their location proved a great place to watch the action while providing a variety of corporate and private guests the level of service befitting the Debrays Hospitality experience. For Geoff this included striking up subtle conversations about the woes of local cleaners, and where he got a bite, oddly dropping the name of a local great company he knew. The lane slowly filled with race-watchers, piling in and out of the Ship Inn. Minutes before the race was due to start, Kish also turned up with a few others, presumably clients.

'Hey old bean,' hollered Geoff, signalling him over. 'No matter that you and your guests are technically my valued guests, don't forget you're still my sodding housemate.' Geoff chose not to ask after Elise. She'd already shared with him her torment, his arm around her as she spoke quietly in a café near her rented Wandsworth flat the day before.

'Doing some wine tasting today?' came a warm voice to Humphrey's right. It was Kat.

'Hi! Well yes and no,' he said nervously, before embracing Kat on both cheeks.

'Kat!' said Geoff, 'Glad you got my voice mail. Did your company get hospitality with Debrays in the end?'

'No, but a friend with some spare tickets did. They are on their way.'

While Geoff sorted Kat a glass of bubbly, Kish asked Humphrey, 'when ever did you start introducing yourself by kissing people on both cheeks?'

'Oh, since time immemorial.'

'You mean when you saw certain people doing it. Unofficially I heard the use of two-kisses as an introduction, not to be mistaken with the more pervasive two-kiss greeting actually took off in Kings Road around 1995,' said Kish wryly. 'It got exceedingly popular around Chelsea, Mayfair and Kensington circles before spreading like a contagion wherever young aspirants met for the first time in socially pressured surroundings.'

'Utter rot,' replied Humphrey.

Kish continued, 'Yes, the increasingly pervasive use of the 'two kiss' as a greeting among aspirant types, rather than the traditional, simple 'one kiss', is apparently largely down to fear—many now simply do it as a precaution, particularly when faced with acquaintances wearing pashmina or a corduroy jacket. I heard that offering just one kiss is now regarded as a social faux-pas in Thameside neighbourhoods from Chelsea all the way to Richmond. I'd not be surprised if Barnes have actually banned it, with stiff penalties.

'Offering two kisses due to fear, how preposterous!' Humphrey retorted, secretly adding it to his growing list of socio-economic indicators.

'Really?' Kish replied. 'Then here's the acid test: anyone who greets their London friends with a two-kiss, but uses just one kiss for family members, is guilty. Period.' Humphrey considered the way he'd greeted Kat; someone he'd only known a few short weeks, compared to the single kiss with which he typically greeted his female cousins, aunts and his own mother. Come to think of it, his mother had recently started double-kissing her friends too.'

One of Kish's team from work, Natalie Watson had sidled across to him, resulting in Humphrey eagerly introducing himself, with two kisses. Having overcome an awkward moment or two that followed, she spoke into Kish's ear then passed him his drink.

'I got to watch out,' Kish replied to Natalie. 'Gribbin's probably got it in his head I've drunk too much already.'

'Go on. It's a wonderful Chablis.'

'Okay, just this one, but you got to look after me if I start saying dumb things to our customers. I've already had a few.' Kish then made his apologies to Humphrey, but sensed the need to join his guests who were still sat at the back of the tent, along with his new boss, who Humphrey had just learned from their conversation, was a bit of an emotionless prick. Humphrey watched as Kish joined the huddle: dull, listless, introspective and severe-looking. Most of them seemed bent on fiddling with their mobile phones at the same time holding having group conversation. Humphrey sighed. The Boat Race's élan was being eroded faster than a denuded riverbank.

Barely a mile away, Amelia, Geoff's conquest from the previous evening, paid the cabbie and stormed into her flat in Chiswick. She felt very raw, having waited all morning at Geoff's for him to return. *Who the hell did he think he was anyway?* She looked at her watch. There was just enough time to join her friends at the finish line, then locate Geoff and tell him as publicly as possible that he was a selfish bastard.

No sooner had the announcer signalled the start of the race, the sky brightened and fuelled with Champagne and expectation, Humphrey began discussing course tactics with several guests, specifically what the cox might do at the Chiswick Eyot bend. When Kat sauntered over, Humphrey made his excuses and joined her outside the tent once more. 'Ah Kat, all this takes me back.'

'You rowed?' she asked, eyes still focussed downstream.

'Used to. Club rowing really,' started Humphrey, determined to appear non-plussed. He'd read somewhere that women like Kat loved modesty. 'At just under six foot, too short I think, well that and a rather unfortunate injury.' He pointed to his leg, even though she wasn't looking in his direction. 'Sciatica.'

'Nasty,' Kat replied, remaining focussed on the river.

Several seconds of silence passed before he gave it another go. 'Yes, I enjoyed my time at Oxford,' he volunteered. 'Spent most of it arriving late for lectures and getting into the usual trouble.'

'Oh? Which college?'

'Magdalen.'

Kat looked back at him for the first time. 'Beautiful. I was at Somerville.'

'Small world,' Humphrey replied meekly, hoping she wouldn't ask him when he was there.

'Oxford commanding a sizeable lead now,' said the race official over the PA system.

Humphrey stared upstream from his position behind the tent bar. No sign of the boats rounding the wide bend. He noticed that everyone was looking past him, down river. He looked at his watch, then said to Kat, 'Downstream already? Surely they don't travel that damn quickly do they? Couldn't have passed already?' He peered upstream once more.

Kat broke her fixation. 'Humphrey, they're there,' she said pointing downstream at two boats charging up toward them.

'Must have bloody changed direction since I last was here,' Humphrey slurred loudly.

'That would have been 1863,' Kat replied. 'The last time they rowed downstream.'

'Come on Oxford!' bleated Humphrey, determined to forget himself in the wave of cheers that rolled along the bank in unison with the boats, and towards the finishing line at Chiswick Bridge.

'And it's Oxford by four lengths!'

The news sent an exuberant Humphrey skyward. When he finally calmed down, Geoff sidled up to him and smiled. 'Making a bit of a point there?' he said then thrust twenty pounds into Humphrey's hand. 'You won the bet. Can't say you deserve it, but spend it wisely.'

Another hour of serving passed, helped along by wine and rowing vernacular delivered from a well-oiled Humphrey. Then a brief shuffle. The swirling, crammed crowd slowly got noisier as more people saw the three tall men walk into the tent, beaming. Geoff frowned. Surely the crews would be in the enclosure getting their fill of reporters and debriefs. 'It's the Dark Blue Seconds!' someone chimed. Free now to enjoy the afternoon, the rowers from the reserve boat made their way to hospitality. Everyone who they squeezed past tapped them, hugged them, slapped them, and generally hurrahed them as they made their way into the tent as guests of Debrays.

'Geoff Fox! Well fancy seeing you here!' said one rower as he launched a vast arm past Humphrey's head, narrowly avoiding certain injury, towards Geoff.

'Well bugger me! Hello young Joel!' A powerful hug promptly convened beside Humphrey, who in turn sighed at it all.

'I just saw the Worksop College Rowing on your kagoule,' said Joel, a tall, athletic young man with an equally healthy grin.

Geoff said, 'Humph, meet Joel, younger brother of Gregor, a contemporary of mine at school. Jesus Joel, you're a bloody giant these days.'

'Stopped growing two years ago, thank God. Buying new clothes all the time gets expensive.'

'Well, bloody well done on the Oxford win. Super job,' said Geoff.

'They did great. Cheers,' Joel replied, gratefully accepting a glass of fizz from Geoff. 'So you get a chance to go out on the water these days, Geoff?'

'Me? Lord, no. Stopped years ago.' He then gestured at the bottles beside him. 'Got into the wine trade.'

Joel turned to Humphrey. 'You know he was an excellent sculler, one of the best our school ever had. Before he dedicated himself to rugby.'

'Whatever. Now did you bring any spraffing little coxons with you?'

'Sure did. Meet Ems, my girlfriend.' Joel stepped back.

Before Geoff could introduce himself, Humphrey tapped his glass loudly. Geoff knew what was coming and closed his eyes. Humphrey bellowed, 'Ladies and Gentlefolk. A toast!' Geoff ran his hand through his hair and bowed his head. 'To Varsity rowing champions Oxford and their fearless Seconds, cheers!' As glasses were raised and clunked together, Geoff wondered if there were any occasion that Humphrey wouldn't raise a toast to. He'd toast the arrival of a gas bill through the letterbox if he'd half a chance.

Presently, Joel was joined by his goliath parents and it was only after a few moments into the discussion that Humphrey had decided they were definitely his sort. Joel's mother—Humphrey had missed her first name—was a tour de force, and to his absolute pleasure, she sported an enormous signet ring.

'A wonderful day, full of laughter, excitement and occasion,' she remarked as Geoff handed her a glass of Champagne. 'Isn't everyone here so fit-looking,' she added, ribbing her towering son.

'Selective breeding,' said Humphrey resolutely. Geoff coughed as she frowned, as if a little thrown by the comment. Oblivious, Humphrey scanned her face. Her features were extremely striking if well-travelled; hers was the product of several decades-worth of exotic holidaying, a life spent embracing the outdoors. She was lightly made up, with some delicate earrings flicking against some upturned rugger collars. Humphrey was so transfixed on the moment that he didn't notice the crowd congregating around a distinctly purple van parked on a slipway. Joel pointed to

Humphrey's rugby shirt. 'By the way, thanks for coming down and supporting us,' he said. 'Which college?'

'I . . . Magdalen actually.'

'Magdalen College. Really Humphrey?' It was a loud, cutting voice, one that spun heads. Sarber-Collins had appeared from nowhere, then continued, 'I may be confused on my universities but I'm sure your CV mentioned you were at Oxford Brookes University, not *the* Oxford University, therefore not at any of its colleges?'

Humphrey froze and his face took on a colour one shade off pure scarlet.

'So . . . not Magdalen then?' asked Joel.

'Not quite,' Humphrey muttered, conscious that quite a few people were now listening with interest. His head began spinning. 'Well that's to say I applied, in fact I got in, but then decided otherwise at the last moment. Felt I needed a more vocational degree offered by a more progressive university. A course that would truly prepare me for the modern workplace.'

Joel looked Humphrey up and down. 'Well no worries, good to see wider support.'

'Bit sad,' said Sarber-Collins pointedly. Geoff simply raised his pint in response. *Reap what you sow, Humphrey old mate.* Indeed, Humphrey was still inert with embarrassment when a voice came over the PA system.

'*Could the driver of the Bacchus Braves Winestores van please attend to their vehicle. That's the driver of a purple Citroen Berlingo van that's parked on the Thames Path slip.*'

Humphrey casually looked out towards the towpath. He could just about make out the outline of the van roof—the rest of it was obscured by the mass of folk streaming left and right. *What tosh. The van is hardly in anyone's way* 'Geoff, I wonder why—' said Humphrey, turning back round. 'Geoff?' His housemate had disappeared.

Unknown to Humphrey, Geoff was hiding under a nearby table. Bad knee or no bad knee, he'd just clocked Amelia, *or was it Annabel*—whomever, the lady who stayed over last night and who he'd completely forgotten about until five seconds ago. Her expression suggested she had vengeance on her mind and on her arm, a large handbag with which to dish it out.

The same stern voice as before crackled over the PA system, this time pleading for the owner of a very purple van to move it immediately. Humphrey began to sweat. *Can't possibly be seen driving a van. Not here, not today!*

'Popular stretch of footpath all of a sudden,' Humphrey said to Joel nervously, noticing the recent surge in race-watchers milling outside.

'No wonder,' Joel replied. 'Biggest spring tide I've ever seen. Water is starting to lap over Thames Path, right up to the grass bank beneath this tent we're in. And that's not all—a purple delivery van is slowly disappearing under the Thames, which is getting some attention. Its idiot driver actually parked it on the slip to the river. I wouldn't be surprised if it floated off shortly.'

Humphrey laughed haughtily then drew breath. 'Do excuse me for a sec, need to make a phone call.' Turning, he dropped his smile like a stone and weaved anxiously through corporate hospitality ticket holders. Several folk happily marooned on the Thames Path wall were pointing and laughing at the half-submerged van. Wading beside it was a thoroughly irritated-looking policeman, busy with his radio and flanked by two course officials. Humphrey bit his tongue and proceeded to meet the mob.

It was Sarber-Collins who kicked off the roar of applause as Humphrey approached the van. 'Funny, I could have sworn he said he was a wine consultant, not a delivery man,' he chortled with his personal guests.

Stood outside the tent, Kat watched Humphrey flap as several authority figures remonstrated with him. Later on her bus ride home to South Ken, she would wonder what Humphrey was all about. Evidently not quite as self-assured as she'd originally thought. Not like Geoff, who seemed blessed with confidence. Humphrey was different, but she couldn't work out what it was. Perhaps she should have stayed and offered to help him, she thought. *Might that embarrass him further though? Male pride and all that.* By Earl's Court she thought no more of it.

By 6:30pm, the crowd that had joshed with Humphrey had dissipated. Nearby Kish was clearly enjoying the attention of Natalie Watson, large red wine in his hand, while his clients were taken care of by other members of his team. Having given Amelia the slip, Geoff signed off a very productive day with Sarber-Collins. While Humphrey exchanged words with a wading police officer who had been sorely tempted to charge the little berk for illegal parking, and send him a dry cleaning bill, Geoff quickly filled several large refuse bags with the empty wine bottles and quietly discarded them in a recycling bin located up a small side passage.

'Sign here sir,' the towman said. Having positioned his recovery truck with some skill he slowly winched the sopping van from the water, a muddy line marking high tide along the windows and paintwork. The entire engine compartment had been submerged, and if the towman's suspicions were correct, there'd be untold water damage under the floorpan.

'. . . which is where all your electrics are see,' the towman explained, pointing to a section of the van Humphrey had no understanding of. Humphrey duly tried the remote locks, and frowned when nothing happened. 'Like I just said, the electrics,' said the towman wearily. 'Need a lift back to the garage?'

'No thank you my good man, I need to get home.' The thought of suffering further intellectual side-swipes from a mechanic didn't appeal to Humphrey.

'Okay, sir. Garage will contact you on the number you gave.' The towman handed him some documentation, checked he'd secured the van on his truck, and then moved off slowly down towards Chiswick and a chuckle with the late shift.

Humphrey dialled his home number and waited. Hopefully Geoff or Kish would be in by now. An odd response greeted him: *'You've reached Ethnic Cleansers—award winning local quality cleaners serving the bachelor community of South West London.'* Humphrey hung up, tried again. Same message. Cold and now confused, Humphrey called Geoff's mobile. His mobile was bleeping, signalling a critically low battery.

'Hello?' replied Geoff.

'Hi, it's Humphrey.'

'Hey Humpers, mate, where are you?'

'Where I parked the van. By the river.'

'Well sort yourself out and come and join us. I'm with Kish and a few of his IT customers and colleagues. His company have hired a space at a bar over in Chiswick called Nec . . .' *Bleepbleep.* Humphrey looked down limply at his lifeless mobile. He drew a long breath, and made his first step in the wrong direction to the nearest train station, just as the rain that had held off all day held off no more. As the downpour intensified into a small monsoon, Humphrey recalled his sense of exuberance that morning. Today was intended to be a big splash. Instead it had turned out more a damp squib.

SIXTEEN

A large hot chocolate then bed, Humphrey thought as he walked through the door. He then spied Elise in the lounge, finishing up packing a holdall. 'Hi stranger, how you been?' Best to play safe—according to Geoff things were a little fraught between her and Kish.

'Hi,' replied Elise softly. 'Sorting through a few things . . . no matter. Oh and by the way some guys came round to speak to you earlier. About four o'clock.'

'Me?'

'Well I guessed it was you because they asked to speak to Mr. Massey, resident owner and donator to the campaign.'

'Campaign? Rather intriguing. Which one?' It could be any number that Humphrey had signed up to: the awareness campaign to promote Putney Ferret's correct pronunciation, the campaign for the extension of Putney Ferret Farmers' Market opening times, or the street lamp. His fears that it was in fact the latter were swiftly confirmed.

'Something about street lights and collecting the contribution from this house. They were very grateful and asked I remind you to settle up on your pledged donation as soon as possible. Here, they gave me this.' Elise handed him a letter, and picked up her holdall.

Humphrey gulped. 'So . . . you off?'

Elise stuttered. 'I'm not going to be staying here on the odd night anymore. Kish and I have decided to spend some space apart.'

The Nectar bar was situated near Chiswick Green. As the latest new place, its short-term appeal was assured, just like all the bars before it that had promised some novel concept for drinking alcoholic beverages. Its décor was modern—geometric yet sumptuous with hints of traditional, its seating dark and its bar luminous. It might become a permanent fixture, or more likely follow a predictable path: in the first year it would doggedly pursue some self-proclaimed exclusivity, but as profits missed their ambitious projections after year one, management would need to drum up new business. That meant more people—counter-intuitive to the exclusivity mantle. The lifecycle of such bars were similar to a mayfly's: metamorphic and finite. For the pedants, a Buddhist mayfly: regularly re-incarnated with a new theme or feel. But for now, Nectar had hit the button.

While some of Kish's team held court with Mironic clients, Kish sauntered off to a nearby sofa with Geoff. 'And if anyone asks, you are with some bloody government agency nobody's heard of. And I'm an excellent host.' Kish looked up and eyeballed Natalie Watson on his team, who winked back. He then pointed her out to Geoff. 'I've told that girl to calm down. She has a certain power over sad arses like me.'

Geoff nodded. 'Any case, where were we? I think you were saying that work frustrates you almost as much as your boss does.'

Kish nodded halfheartedly as he sank deeper into the rich leather, his mind flitting between potent and depressed. 'Two years of career progression dashed by a new level of hierarchy. Don't think the support's there for me like it used to be.'

'But is it right for you? Mironic I mean.'

'Course it's still right. One of the most successful companies on the planet.'

'Doesn't mean it's best for you. Just means you can show off at parties to others who think similar to you.'

Kish took a swig from the bottle of strong beer he'd been handed by Natalie moments ago. 'I hear what you are saying but, I mean, your job hardly fills you with enthusiasm does it?'

'Well, I work less, for less,' replied Geoff. 'I set my sights low, expect little, and come in generally contented.'

'Any aspirations?' asked Kish.

'Not these days. At least, none that can be fulfilled by some better paid job. I guess I'm not one of those people who define themselves by their job title and employer.' Geoff leant in, eyeballing him. 'I suppose when you put so much effort into one thing, like you do, where your job is everything, you have to constantly assure yourself you've done the right thing. Jobwise I mean.' Kish smiled wryly. Point firmly made, Geoff lightened, saying 'If you want misguided aspiration, then Humphrey genuinely believes that being part of the wine import and sales industry carries some caché. He's proud of it, therefore works harder. As his manager, I know this, harness it and in turn he makes me look good.'

'Ultimately his goal is to somehow be respected?'

'Yes, but he's a walking contradiction. He says he detests people with new money even though he is a product of it, he hates aspirants but he would kill to own an address in Ferret, and picks holes in anyone who dresses like he does. I think the universal truth that governs us all is that you have to define your own success and not be told by someone else. I guess for you lot in the corporate bear-pit, you are told what's success, and in return for being looked after, you follow the rules. If you accept it, fine. Just stop whining.'

'I suppose that last comment is directed at me.'

'At you or me, Humphrey, Elise, at anyone. Humphrey likes to distinguish himself from others, more outside work than in it. I get the impression you do it the other way round, more in work than outside. But here's the thing about him. He's settled for a company with a good reputation, like you have, but what he's singularly failed to find is the reason he's been put on this planet. He's creative. Great writer, whatever you think of the content. He could re-train and pull in triple what he earns right now. But that's too hard. So he rests on a company's caché.'

'I know. But bills don't get paid by caché.'

'Well yours might. But yes, hence his poor credit card. If aspiration is a disease, then credit is the world's most powerful, available drug to ease it.' Geoff rocked back and took a mouthful of beer. He could distill Humphrey down, Kish and Elise too, and anyone else for that matter. Except himself. He didn't have the nerve to.

'So with all this aspiration, why's he not scrambled over you and told you what to do?' Kish asked.

'Simple. He lacks focus and conviction in himself, because he's so caught up chasing other people. He's a bit of a passenger is our

Humph, happily avoids the decision-making. And when HQ see me and Humphrey together, the dynamic between us, I win out.'

'Insightful,' said Kish. Geoff had snagged a nerve inside Kish. Something hideously similar to Humphrey was driving him too.

'Now, in Mironic, I imagine there's no place for passengers.'

'You're joking, right? Mironic's bloated full of them. Two types of passenger you see, Type A and Type B. Passengers Type A are wannabe managers who fail to beat the others to a smaller number of driving seats, so are forced against their will into prolonged existence as a so called 'individual contributor', a term created to provide some corporate definition to those not in power, and who spend all day and most nights fighting for any small nugget of differentiation and recognition in front of the boss. And fuck does it look pathetic. But it's a fearsome energy readily exploited by the drivers. Then there's Passenger Type B: Passengers doing well despite doing basically very little, coasting on well-honed brown nose skills. Hired in the good times, and as long as the business maintains it's growth, somehow tolerated and quietly acknowledged as decision-averse deadwood. Once there's a downturn in fortunes, the COO orders the cull. They are the first to get knifed.'

'And what about the managers or individual contribu-thingummies who actually do work hard?'

'They are the rare good guys. They either elect to stay because they genuinely love it or wake up one day realising that Mironic isn't the best thing for them, so they leave.'

'But not you?'

'Frustrated, but I can't see myself leaving just yet. I'm at that 'scrambling up the pole' stage, blinded by an Excel spreadsheet we all build that maps out what I could earn if I see it through these next few years.'

Shortly, Natalie approached Kish and Geoff, asking if they wanted another drink.

Kish crossed his arms and leant forward to speak to her. 'Two Vodka Redbulls please.' His head was now whirring. 'Natalie meet Geoff my housemate, Geoff, this is Natalie.'

'She's gorgeous,' whispered Geoff as Natalie walked off.

'Hands off.' Geoff sensed him slur a little. 'Boy this beer's strong. Off to the lav.'

Kish made for a cubicle and before returning splashed his face at the sink and began on a text message. Natalie was stood at the bar when he returned.

'Hi, you might want to read my text when you have a mo,' he whispered.

She jumped a little, conscious of a rich bile odour, and said quietly, 'Chris, take it easy.' A few moments passed, something more was said, Kish then winked, and made his way back to Geoff, nodding to a couple of Mironic colleagues. Mike Gribbin just stared at him.

A waiter came over a few moments later to Kish and Geoff. 'Sorry gents, time to settle up the bill please.'

Smiling, Kish waved his mobile at Gribbin and Natalie, stood next to each other at the bar. As he left, he couldn't quite read her expression but Gribbin was smirking.

Geoff and Kish returned home twenty minutes later. Humphrey's letter was the first thing Geoff saw as he settled into his favourite sofa.

'Now it's not what you think it is,' said Humphrey nervously, as he watched Geoff scan a signed donation form pledging an eight hundred pound payment from the residents of No. 47, Ferret Rise, Chris Reece, Geoff Fox, and Humphrey C. Massey.

'Not likely,' snorted Geoff.

'No, well yes, well think about it. A sweet investment considering it'll illuminate the house as a honey magnet. Eight hundred pounds split three ways, that's nothing.'

'Sorry,' started Geoff, 'but you don't pledge things on my behalf, particularly Victorian cast iron lamps. If you want the lamppost, you pay. Besides, what idiot would rent a house but buy a street lamp outside it?'

'I'm sure Kish is with me here. Kish?' said Humphrey. Kish was rocking back and forth trying to fill a glass with water. 'Even if you owned the house, it would still be a waste of money' he slurred.

'How, and please go slow with me, did you get wrapped up in this latest cock-up?' asked Geoff.

Humphrey was looking visibly concerned. 'Well, these very respectable gents from the Putney Ferret Residents Association came around, a couple of weeks ago in fact. I got a little kind of involved in the moment. Next thing I knew I told them that we all co-owned so naturally I found myself registering our commitment.'

'Co-owned?'

'Well you know, bought together. We got talking about keeping Putney Ferret special, and I agreed that the installation of renovated wrought iron streetware was the way to go. I was planning on telling you, but I guess it just slipped my mind.'

'But why would we invest, if we rent for heaven's sake?'

'Well, I thought if we considered buying the Victorian lamppost then other's in the community might praise us for our contribution to the community's upkeep. And think we were well, permanent. Oh and I signed us all up as Community Association members.' Humphrey added. Admittedly I forked out thirty pounds for that. But don't worry, you can both pay me back when you feel like it.'

Geoff craned his neck toward Humphrey. 'You bloody-well need a girlfriend. Get to the end of the Debrays gig and land one and I'm almost tempted to buy your sodding lamppost outright.'

'Child,' said Humphrey. 'But, okay.'

Geoff threw Humphrey a tightly crumpled ten pound note. 'Your turn to get the food. Extra large peperoni, all the trimmings please.'

When Humphrey returned, Geoff was slobbed out lengthways along the sofa, beer in hand, watching The Bourne Conspiracy for the sixth time.

'Here you go,' said Humphrey, handing him the pizza.

Three large bites into his pizza, Geoff started to nod off, mumbling as he did about sabotaging Humphrey's efforts to find a woman. Humphrey left him there to sleep it off. Tomorrow, Sunday, he'd be manning the store alone, again.

SEVENTEEN

Kish awoke with a jolt the following Monday morning, instantly regretting a full-on weekend. His temples thudded with every heartbeat and his tongue was stuck dry to the inside of his cheek. It was late for Kish, almost 8:40am, and panicking he simply ducked his head under the shower, and skipped a shave. He sprayed himself thoroughly with deodorant before putting on a thick jumper to hide the unironed shirt beneath. Humphrey stood by the fridge sipping some Darjeeling as Kish came through. 'Morning. Feeling shit I trust.' Kish grunted in return as he slowly dropped two Alka-Seltzers into a glass of orange juice. Ghastly taste but it would give him the kick needed to make the train station. On his way out, he noticed a pair of large feet poke over the arm of the sofa. Geoff was a vision Kish could do without.

Kish spent most of the train journey to Reading dozing, and ignoring several calls and instant messages from Gribbin. Clearly trying to get him to do something menial. As he approached Reading, he began thinking about Elise's note. Gone for good. He called her, and it went straight to voicemail. He didn't leave a message. At Reading Station, Kish walked slowly to the free bus laid on by Mironic and other businesses based out of the same business park. He would keep a very low profile today—straight up to his desk, make everything look like he was there for the day—bag displayed prominently next to desk, folders out, monitor on, then retire to his favourite cubicle, hack through some unread emails and delegate requests to eager members of his team. His mobile phone rang—Gribbin again. No point ignoring it, Kish answered. 'Hello Mike.'

'Oh finally.' There was no warmth in his voice. 'I've been trying to call you for over an hour.'

'Sorry about that—been on the phone with my mother since before seven. Bit sick right now and—'

'Chris. Not now. I'll come straight out with it. There's been a serious complaint made against you. I'm upstairs with HR right now.'

'Complaint? What complaint about me?'

'Just get up here. Rachael Frears' office. And I wouldn't keep her waiting any longer.' The phone went dead.

Rachael Frears was fierce with a capital 'F'. As Mironic UK's head of HR, she'd only get directly involved in the most serious matters. And from the instant he entered her office, Kish knew things were not going to be pleasant.

'Good morning, take a seat,' said Rachael. She barely gave him time to sit before continuing. Gribbin was also present, and a little taken aback, although gleeful about Kish's unusually disheveled appearance. Sitting close by, he was also instantly aware of the smell of stale beer. 'Chris, were you present at Mironic's event at a London bar called Nectar on Saturday night?'

Kish frowned and smiled simultaneously. 'Yes, I was. Nice bar. How can I help you?' he chimed flippantly, remaining composed. Fiona was holding what looked like an email.

'At ten past eight this morning, Mike informed me that one of your team, Natalie Watson has made a complaint regarding your behaviour toward her on Saturday evening. The complaint has now been formally taken up by HR.'

Gribbin chipped in. 'To be precise, Natalie informed me she was upset by certain comments, comments of a sexual nature, made by you while you were inebriated. I was there myself and clearly recollect you having had far too much to drink.'

Kish's neck began to sweat as he tried to recollect his exchange with Natalie. He sat on his hands as he began to realise they were shaking. His wrists were already sweating and the thick jumper was not helping. Nor was the dehydrated state of his body.

'Rachael,' started Gribbin. 'I did try my best to discuss the situation first thing this morning but he did not respond to any of my several calls.' Gribbin leant back, smug and happy that for the first time he'd got some mileage from an unresponsive Kish. 'I think I tried seven times.'

It was five times, you wanker. But Kish might agree that was a moot point.

Rachael handed Kish Natalie's statement. His eyes skated across sentences containing "inappropriate and suggestive comments of a sexual nature", "deeply upsetting", and "trust you will take appropriate action".

'Quite a statement, wouldn't you agree?' Gribbin said smugly. He saw a cornered and exhausted animal, ready to be brought down. The smell stale beer wafting up from under Kish's collar was telling.

Kish remained limp in his chair, his head ducked as perspiration spread down his back and across his hot, adrenalin-knotted stomach. The accusation was serious enough. Gribbin now had him where he wanted him, and Kish knew the trouble he was in. Not exactly the retirement plan he'd envisaged.

'But I'm sure I did nothing wrong. I mean I was a bit merry but Natalie didn't give me the impression she was offended at the point we talked?'

Rachael interjected. 'Chris, I need you to understand we take such accusations seriously, particularly in situations where an employee's activities compromise the welfare of a fellow employee, particularly when it comes to sexual misconduct. In front of Mironic customers it serves to further compound an already very serious situation. Given Mike felt strongly enough to have contacted me directly on Natalie's behalf, I'll handle the matter personally. Chris, I would like a statement from you, and Mike a full list of names who were also there.'

'Is this a resignation situation?' asked Kish flatly.

'Not yet,' replied Rachael categorically.

Gribbin looked confused. 'But Natalie clearly states that Chris blatantly—'

'Natalie has accused a fellow employee of serious misconduct, which needs substantiating.' Rachael's legal training then kicked in, and she turned to Kish. 'Chris, in the interests of the company and your standing in it, I am instructing you to take a period of paid leave. Be sure that in any investigation like this, your personal record will also be taken into account. I do ask that we requisition your laptop and all company property.'

Call it what you liked, thought Kish, it amounted to the same thing: Part One of a two-part story on getting fucked out of the company. Kish then leant forward and vomited over his own shoes.

'What the hell!' Gribbin gasped, then looking frantically toward Rachael for affirmation. 'I'm so sorry,' Kish gurgled, wiping his mouth with his woollen sleeve. He jumped up. 'Rachael, excuse me, but I think . . . I'm going to . . . be sick again,' then rushed for the office door. He flew across the open plan office of HR staff, and out onto the gantry.

'Want to go check he's okay?' said Rachael calmly. She'd seen a lot of human emotion in this office.

Gribbin shook his head. 'I'll go in a sec. Sadly Rachael, it's been a long time coming.'

'Nonetheless, given Chris's pretty clean record, let's assume innocence until any guilt is proven. Last thing I want is this turning into an unfair dismissal case. The instant Chris returns from the restroom, he is to be formally escorted to his desk to gather his personal items, and then out of the building.'

Gribbin didn't respond. He just wanted the guy out permanently. Getting a list of customers present at Nectar would be his priority. Hopefully one of them he could tug a little.

Instead of making for the lavatories, Kish ducked down some stairs and sprinted along the connecting corridor to Building Three, wiping any remaining vomit from his mouth. He had less than ten minutes before they'd get suspicious.

Geoff studied the bold green signage above the office entrance. Just a week before, he had paid an initial visit to the very same Haggard Cards Ltd, leaving Humphrey's poems and some accompanying sketches he himself had done, for their consideration. Geoff had clearly caught someone at precisely the right time because now, barely a week later, Haggard wanted to meet and move forward.

A man greeted him in reception. 'Mr. Fox! Great to meet you. I'm Des Orr, Sales Director for Haggard Cards.' Geoff shook his hand nervously. 'Rude poems about people sat on the toilet. Told through their own turds floating beneath. Genius!'

'Thank you.'

'So let's tootle upstairs and discuss next steps.'

EIGHTEEN

In Rachael Frears' office, Gribbin was still ruminating. 'You know, if encouraged, I think there may be female colleagues in the company who might just be inclined to come forward with similar stories to Natalie's?'

'Mike, if you have any reason to suspect wider inappropriate behaviour, you have an obligation.'

'No, I mean to say you hear rumours, office rumours, tittle-tattle in the corridors. I also heard it might be why he's tried to apply for other roles outside my team.'

Rachael sat back. 'Well, there could be plenty of reasons for a career move Mike, but duly noted. I'd also be extremely careful you don't get accused of using a situation. That's all I'll say.'

In an instant, Rachael reminded Gribbin who really ran the company. Gribbin looked at his watch. 'Maybe I'll just go check Chris is okay. See you in a second.'

Rachael watched on as Gribbin zipped across the office and toward the bathrooms. In recent years she'd become increasingly wary of a certain mindset afflicting the company's mid-management, usually male, who seemed a little cocksure of their own intellect and abilities, and perhaps not beyond some quiet scheming against other males around them.

Gribbin flung open the door to the gent's loos. Other than some bald guy taking a piss it was empty. Then he remembered Rachael comment on confiscating Reece's laptop, and cursed his own stupidity.

Puking up in Rachael's office had provided the distraction Kish needed. Wasting no time, Kish had left Rachael's office and sprinted back to his desk in the adjoining building. There he logged onto his laptop. *Five minutes to purge it. Ten, max.* Kish had heard stories like this before, a single incident that had led to some deeper investigation that in turn unearthed something far more serious.

And Kish was no angel. Although his own emails tended to be pretty clean and his flirtations restricted to shortlived texts, he'd retained plenty of questionable material over the years, reposited in various locations across his hard drive. And which were now being sent in bulk to the recycle bin. Next, his 'temp folders', which revealed several hundred internet downloads of saucy, comic or soft-pornographic footage and pictures he'd have considered quite hilarious on any other occasion. Nothing illegal in a court of law—that wasn't Kish, nonetheless deep into non-compliant territory as far as Mironic was concerned. Faced with so many files, he now began deleting any 'wav', 'jpg' or 'gif' file ever received or sent, probably including hundreds of credible, useful images. Next he made a swift call into Rachael's office. Amazingly she answered. 'Rachael, it's Chris Reece. I am so sorry I had to leave like that—I've returned to my desk to dump off my jumper given the mess, and if you want, collect my laptop and bring it over.'

'Chris, we haven't finished our meeting. You have ten minutes to return, or I will escalate this. And by the way, Mike is looking for you.' The phone went dead.

Next, Kish went into his personal folders on his hard drive, and indiscriminately deleted their entire content. Documents across four years, business plans, employee reviews, vital password reminders, select emails of congratulations, all of it sent to the recycle bin. Kish then fired up an application. Being in Government Security Sales meant he'd seen, heard and in this case early access to particular enhancements to Mironic's security software line up. The beta application codenamed "Creambun" was the company's latest hard drive wipe offering, due for launch in a year or so. With a special 'backdoor' step Kish was privy to that prevented Administrator override, the user could irreversibly delete all files off their hard drive via the Windows recycle bin. As soon as he was prompted, Kish hit 'delete contents'. The screen hung for a moment before a pop-up informed him the files sent to the hard drive were permanently deleted. Any reference to their existence in the hard drive had gone, too. He sat back staring at his screen.

'I'll take that please!' A puce-faced Gribbin scooped up Kish's laptop.

'No need,' replied Kish. 'I just called Rachael, told her I'll bring it up to her.'

'Bullshit,' Gribbin spat, sending out small globs of spit from the corner of his mouth. Across the immediate office people nudged each other—witnessing a public confrontation between two managers was rare, and fun. 'That room. Now!'

Kish was sufficiently clear of mind to weigh up his options. He could simply refuse Gribbin's invitation to join him in a 'quiet room'—deliberately sound insulated, no phone, no windows, and instead simply make his way to Rachael's. Alternatively he could stand his ground, have it out in the open. Or he could heed Gribbin and go into the room. 'Okay Mike, let's discuss sensibly.' Kish casually picked up his mobile, gently sliding it into his back pocket, then walked into the meeting room. Gribbin followed, and closed the door behind him. Gribbin knew his adversary had a temper, which he needed to taunt out of him, and with any luck irreversibly seal his miserable fate once and for all.

Gribbin started. 'You really think you're getting away with this?' Kish stared back, forcing down his heartbeat as he slowly put his hands into his back pockets. Gribbin continued. 'It's so clear now. You are neither motivated nor interested in motivating others. Why else would you be drifting in on a Monday morning, clearly still drunk from the weekend?'

Kish carefully flipped open his phone. It was on silent, no ring, no vibration. He speed-dialed his office telephone number. Just a few seconds until he'd be diverted to his own voicemail . . .

Gribbin smiled. 'Incidentally, I'll have your mobile please. The one you are probably dialing right now?'

Kish aborted the call and handed it over. 'Sorry, just letting my next meeting know I'll be late.'

Gribbin didn't react, and placed Kish's only lifeline on a chair beside him. 'Now, perhaps we can have a more frank chat?'

'I think I should see Rachael,' replied Kish.

Gribbin stood, hands on hips. 'Rachael can wait. Right now it's just you and me pal.'

Kish slumped in his chair, resigned. He pushed his hands deeper into his front pockets. His right felt something. He paused as he realised his luck as he gently pulled his Bluetooth earpiece out of his pocket, hiding it in his clenched fist. When Gribbin sat down, Kish activated the call button. 'So Chris, going AWOL during an HR meeting? Doesn't exactly look professional does it?'

'I was sick and embarrassed. I cleaned myself up, do us all a favour and quickly collect my laptop. Called Rachael to tell her that. She's expecting me. And you.'

'First off, fuck Rachael Frears!' Gribbin snarled. 'And second, Natalie's accusation is just the tip of the iceberg.' Gribbin patted Kish's laptop. 'A serious accusation that warrants further investigation, not just of the incident, but of you and your deeply flawed character. And why I'm confiscating your laptop right now. Just in case you fancied doing something silly and start deleting emails. We don't want that do we? And even if you do, the email server always backs up. You should know that.' Gribbin saw Kish clenching his right fist. With just a little more incitement, he might just lash out.

'And if something doesn't turn up?' started Kish. He was holding the Bluetooth earpiece very tightly now. Kish knew that deleting email files was more or less fruitless, but at least the data on his hard drive was gone. The local office IT administrators wouldn't yet know much about Cremebun, and even if they did, the arrogant wankers would never suspect some dumb sales guy knew about it.

'I'm pretty sure I can find something or someone. There are people who can corroborate Natalie's story.'

'Namely?'

'Oh, other than me?'

'So you are actually constructing grounds for my dismissal,' Kish smiled straight at Gribbin and winked. Come on you shite, say something stupid, thought Kish.

Gribbin leant uncomfortably close to Kish. Kish steadied his nerve, squeezing his fist harder. 'Well let it be a lesson for you, for working too late.'

'You're penalising me just because I work late, Mike?'

Gribbin stalled. *Did Kish know that it was me and Natalie frolicking in the stairwell?* 'I'll say no more on the matter. But I will say this. You have been highly offensive in this private session. Be sure,

I'll be telling Rachael I have felt my personal safety compromised. Personally I'd consider a resignation. Avoid the embarrassment.'

'Utter crap Gribbin! That's your word against mine! Just like Natalie and me on Saturday.'

'Now do you see the pathetic situation you are in?' Gribbin smiled unconvincingly. 'Meeting over. Time to conclude our chat with HR. Pick up your phone on the way out.'

Gribbin didn't notice Kish press *End Call* as he did.

Geoff exited Haggard Cards trying to make sense of the letter of intent and list of next steps. Subtle refinement to his sketches this week, Copywriters next week, graphic designer early May, publication and distribution mid-July. For a second he contemplated calling Humphrey. Not a good idea right now. Instead, feeling lightheaded, he called Elise. 'I'm in your neck of the woods. Don't s'pose I can come round for a cup of tea and a flirt?'

The pretty closes and executive homes of Wokingham, Ascot, and Sunningdale flitted by in the spring sunshine. They appeared peaceful, secure and established. As Kish leant back into the train seat, he was feeling anything but. The formal issuance of extended leave, the desk clearance, the hasty exit, the avoiding eyes. Trying to recount his interaction with Natalie on Saturday night. He needed Elise. Of all the times to leave him—she probably called it necessary. He called it bloody selfish. Kish began picking his way through his confrontation earlier with Gribbin. Then he remembered the call he'd attempted to make via his Bluetooth earpiece. It would have gone through to the last person he'd called before his altercation with Gribbin. But who? Kish stared at the list of recent calls.

At the top was Elise.

Kish sat there and let it sink in. *Of course.* He'd tried calling Elise earlier, 9:22am, from the train, and it had gone straight to voicemail. Kish checked: the last call he'd placed to Elise, the one via his Bluetooth, was just over three minutes. She'd either listened in, or it had gone to voicemail. Kish sat back. Either way it was no use—Elise would let him hang.

Feeling deflated Kish dialled Geoff, who promptly answered. 'Mate, I've got to talk to you. It's about that Mironic event on

Saturday after the Boat Race. Basically work received a complaint about me harassing a female colleague.'

'Go on?'

'I don't think I should talk much more about it right now.' Call it self-preservationist paranoia, thought Kish.

'Okay, meet you at the Stag around eight-ish.' Geoff replied. 'I've got some stuff to work on. Store accounts. Humph might be back a little earlier.'

'Stag sounds fine. You haven't heard from Elise by the way?'

'Nope. So she's not been in contact?'

'No.' Kish put down the phone. Thirty minutes later, he walked up Ferret Rise from Putney train station and considered his situation. *Not a good time to lose a job. Who'd employ me if I end up getting the boot?* Kish had about a hundred and thirty thousand in savings but needed another sixty at least to secure the £350,000 mortgage required for the sort of pad he wanted. *How would he ever secure that mortgage without a well-paid job like the one he had right now?* He pulled back his shirtsleeve and looked at his Rolex. It provided little succour.

Kish's bedroom looked very bare without Elise's stuff everywhere. The large holdall that had sat on top of his wardrobe, the few garments, manuals on rowing, her study books, all gone. Kish felt very much alone as he read her farewell note once more.

'Who was that you were speaking to earlier?' Elise asked Geoff as she came back into her small studio lounge.

'Your bloke. He's worried for you.'

Elise dropped down onto the sofa next to Geoff. 'I think he left me a message this morning. Frankly, I can't stomach listening to him.'

Without prompting Geoff put a large arm round her and drew her close. 'Deep breaths, darling. Deep breaths. When's the scan?'

NINETEEN

Perched on a barstool, Kish relayed his latest news to Geoff over several pints of London Pride.

'Paid leave? Elise has left? Your mum? It's all happening to you,' Geoff replied. He did not question Kish on his priorities, and as far as Kish was concerned, Geoff knew nothing of Elise's predicament. 'What are you going to do?'

'Get myself out of London for starters. Go stay at Mum's down in Bath.'

'Sounds like a good plan.' Geoff rarely heard Kish speak of his mum, other than apparently he was made executor of her will recently, and that she was still doing the odd guest lecture. Geoff knew a little bit about the circumstances of Kish's father's departure, but not really how Mrs. Reece had coped in the years since. She was not someone Geoff knew that well. His own parents regularly swung by Putney Ferret, and in due course had come to know Humphrey and Kish quite well. But Mrs. Reece? Very rarely seen, and relatively unknown. One of those equivocal situations you just didn't pry into, particularly if you were Geoff.

'I thought I had it all sorted.'

'Sorted? With your mum?' Geoff suggested.

'No, I mean sorted at work. I had clear rules of engagement, I had my fun, and I had my ways. I was well in with senior management, the ones who up til today supported me.' Kish stopped briefly to wipe his mouth with his sleeve. 'Allowed me into their conversations up the pub, a fond respect if you like. But I was wrong on two counts. Wrong because my new boss, someone regularly lambasted in those pub chats, was promoted over me. And wrong because their support evaporated the instant the shit hit the fan. Accusations of misconduct, harassment whatever, it scares them witless, especially given all this business conduct training crap we're doing. And as if those fuckers are totally clean.

Which is why they're thankful for someone to scapegoat—someone displaying the same, bad behaviour you see in yourself.'

'That's deep, fella,' said Geoff, thinking of ways to lift the atmosphere.

'Whatever, can't take any more work bullshit tonight. I guess a couple of weeks with mother dear will help sort me out, and we'll see what happens.'

'Plus, I imagine your mum'll be pleased to have you there too.'

'True. And no matter what I contributed at work, I'm dirt right now. All because someone on my own team dreams up some bullshit complaint. Eight years down the drain.'

Geoff reluctantly continued the conversation. 'So no truth in it then?

'What!?'

'Sorry', that was wrong of me.' Geoff moved swiftly on. 'But the point is they recognised your efforts those eight years and paid you for it.'

'Future looks shoddy though. And yes, I got the bonuses, but never got much public recognition beyond some maybe paltry pat on the back email or some engraved crystal plaque. But even that they're pulling the plug on that. Now it's a perspex plaque and a certificate on flimsy A4.'

'Do people seriously get motivated by getting a plaque?'

'Curiously yes.'

'Is the plaque worth much?'

'No. It's made of perspex.'

'I mean in terms of recognition value.'

'Bollocks, no. In fact, ever heard me come home and tell you I was an award winner?'

'Nope. You've come home showing off your tax bill though.'

'Yes, that's obvious, because cash is king. Whereas engraved glass or perspex plaques are simply platitudes. No one, other than the most naive entry-level trainee, or total idiots with no life outside work would, in any seriousness, believe the hype. But as a good corporate citizen I learn to show my appreciation by exhibiting my various awards on my corner cubicle desk. Show I'm grateful for the recognition from on high, grateful for the chicken bone thrown from the feudal lord's table. And you know why they are double bullshit?'

'No.'

'Because senior management never get plaques. They get real trinkets. Real stock, real salary, real bonus, alongside a bone fide career path, with projected earnings hardwired in. Not some shelf-filler that's been knocked up in some sweatshop in China that has about as much use as a monk's cock. So it makes you start thinking, hey if your boss isn't getting one, then it can't mean all that much you getting one.' Kish's voice began to waiver as he realised the seriousness of his situation. 'I thought I was on my way up, I really did. In reality, I was really just a foolish fuckwit, on a slightly higher grade than the other fuckwits, all the while fighting for those rare, meaningless chicken bones tossed our way.' Geoff sat back. The subject matter might be totally alien to Geoff but Kish was quite the eloquent ranter nonetheless. 'Little wonder we seek some welcome distraction to awaken us from the daily numbing, patronising stupor. And if that includes flirting with a colleague just because she's giving you the come-ons, then so be it.'

'Well, this could be the luckiest day of your life. You could be free of it all,' Geoff replied. 'Come and work at the winestore. We're off to Ascot in a few weeks—you could provide tasting notes to all the IT folk there on some corporate junket.' Geoff liked pub talk, but always made sure it was never too deep, never too confrontational, and never caused him to think too much. Spoiled the fun. Geoff waved to the barman to pour two more pints of London Pride.

'I'll make sure I polish my CV while I'm down at Mum's,' Kish replied sarcastically. The respite had allowed Kish a moment's reflection. 'But I still get drawn to IT and software—it's a massively important thing. It's just that so many people who don't work in it think it has no . . . caché. If an IT mainframe goes down in a government ministry, or a bank, then a chunk of the UK's operation halts and a minister or Chief Exec is hauled over the coals. Or when three hundred thousand pension funds go awry, or your credit card doesn't work the moment you are paying for dinner, or if it's a security breach, with some hacker rummaging around your hard drive, livelihoods are at risk. Yet IT is still some spotty, ginger-haired step-child of the more traditional professions.'

'Still, it makes you over a hundred grand a year.'

'And the rest,' Kish replied ungraciously. 'Which is another thing. I can't even impress some people with the only thing that I do well, making money. Mother for example.'

And there it was. After ten minutes of ramble, the parent approval thing finally came out. Geoff asked, 'are your parents not proud then?'

'Not really. Mum doesn't even get the bits that do some good. Like the project to provide secure online patient advice. She thought we were replacing doctors.'

'And were you?'

'Not really, it's a tool to improve diagnosis. We were managing the operation out of Hyderabad. Like any diagnosis, diagnosing a health problem is a series of carefully tabled binary questions, asked one after the other and eventually narrowing down the options toward a final, accurate assessment. A building full of people with some nursing qualifications sat on a phoneline twenty four hours a day, firing questions created by the software and then providing a non-binding diagnosis at the end.'

'So you outsourced the work of a GP to Hyderabad.'

'Well, more like a GP's cyber assistant, helping GP's get closer to identifying the ailment and cutting down on waiting time. You'd have thought people would like the idea.'

Geoff changed tack between sips. 'So, do you keep the Merc?'

'For now. The laptop is back with them though. And the company phone. Geoff's eyes widened. 'I deleted everything rude you sent me, and that I sent you too. I'm sure it's on a server somewhere. Not that I'd be worried.'

'Why?'

'Because in the event of any legal action with me, they'd get rid of anything before any emails got subpoenaed, because so many others were on the to:line or cc:line or sent from. Beneath the polished surface of HR rules and carefully constructed internal and external PR, the place is rife with bored schoolboy crudeness—I'd bring countless souls down with me. No, they'd let me go, possibly with a nice chunk of gagging money.' Kish smiled. 'See how twisted it is. Stuff them, because tomorrow I'll be in Bath, feet up, no email, Mum's cakes. Wonderful.' Kish looked at his watch. *Nearly 10.00pm.* 'Pizza on the way home?'

'I've kind of gone off pizza recently,' Geoff winced as he remembered waking on the sofa late yesterday morning, covered in one. 'How about a doner kebab?'

When they returned, Humphrey berated Geoff for his no-show at the store, that day, while Geoff slobbed out lengthways along the sofa, opened a beer and tucking into The Bourne Ultimatum. Making short work of his kebab, Kish snuck off sharpish.

'Is Kish okay?' Humphrey asked Geoff a minute or two later.

'Elise has left him and he's been suspended. Can I concentrate in peace please?'

'You've seen this film eighty-four times. Maybe I should ask if I can do anything?'

'For God's sake, Humph! Look, he'll work it out. He's off to see his mum tomorrow, so you and me can spend quality time together. By the way, I'll work late tomorrow if you can go in early.'

Really? Works for me. Van's being delivered at eight. All cleaned up.'

After three more bites into his kebab Geoff nodded off while mumbling, 'what's wrong with not trying in life? At least you don't get disappointed.'

Humphrey finished his cocoa, turned off the TV and the lights and quietly left Geoff sprawled across the sofa, a half-eaten kebab resting precariously on his chest. *Nice touch*, thought Humphrey.

TWENTY

It was around 10:00am the next morning when Maria, brand new marigold gloves in hand, arrived to discover a large man lying face up on the sofa with his underpants round his ankles, snoring heavily. Had Humphrey followed Geoff's strict instructions and shooed him from the sofa and up to his room last night, or if Kish had at least given him a nudge before leaving for his mother's this morning, Geoff's intended flirt with Maria the new cleaner this morning might just have played out as planned. With Kish and Humphrey leaving nice and early, Geoff had *planned* to scrub up for a casual yet choreographed opener—*Maria would let herself in and make her way into the lounge. She'd see him relaxing in the armchair, crisply groomed with a hot cup of coffee and a note pad. 'Good morning,' he'd say. 'I do hope you don't mind me being here this morning—I'm just going through some rather boring paperwork. But please allow me to make you a cup of tea before you start.' She'd smile and feel instantly relaxed in front of such a charming gent.*

Geoff couldn't have been less prepared. Through the course of the night, his subconscious tricking him into believing he was sprawled on his large double bed, he had successfully undone his own belt, wriggled his trousers to his ankles and his underwear down around his knees. In reality the only thing covering his half-naked body were congealed kebab meat pieces and scraps of red cabbage.

Maria was a woman who usually took people as she found them. But she'd never found a man who'd covered his erect penis with takeaway food. Distinctly unsettled, Maria considered leaving quietly and returning some other time. It was then she remembered she'd already been paid for this first session, so she quietly made for the kitchen, reminding herself that if she worked efficiently, she'd be out in ninety minutes flat. Despite her best efforts to wash up in silence, a clanking of cereal bowls jolted Geoff from his sleep.

'Uhh? Humph?' he blurbed, making out a blurry figure in the kitchen. As the figure walked toward him, he slowly focussed on her nervous smile. Approximately two-thirds operational, Geoff straightened his arms then turned his torso, sending a collection of damp pita bread, cold lamb cuts and shredded red cabbage off his groin and into Humphrey's unfortunately-located Kenneth Cole Chelsea boots. Geoff sat upright and looked up, scratching the top of his head. The same woman that had knocked him senseless a week ago was standing less than five foot away.

'Maria?'

'Geoff? Is that really you? Sorry, I did not know you to be in. I hope you did not mind me here?'

Geoff swivelled and stood up before realising he was naked from the waist down. He hauled up his trousers and undies, his kneecap clicking. He chewed down on a swear word, then edged round the coffee table, scraping his leg hard on its cut glass edge and mouthing another of his more choice expletives, finished buckling his belt then held his hand out, smiling. Conscious of where it had just been, she politely clasped his fingertips, marigolds on.

'I thought you were due around ten.'

'Yes, as it is now. I can come back?' volunteered Maria.

'No! You've come all this way to clean, and clean you shall!' Geoff slapped his hands together. 'A cup of tea.' He then walked right past Maria and into the downstairs loo. She stood there, staring at the closed door. It then swung open again.

'I'm not actually making tea in here, just got to do my business first, with you in sec.'

I put kettle on,' replied Maria. Even in the kitchen she heard Geoff's groan accompany a minute-long stream of urine strike water with considerable pressure. Once done, Geoff scooted upstairs and began wrecking Humphrey's room.

'Before you start on upstairs, let's have a quick break to enjoy that tea.'

'Yes thank you.' Maria smiled at the strange man.

His mother's kitchen was decorated very differently these days. For starters, it had artwork, far more photos than Kish ever remembered, with a certain orderliness about it that threw him. At least that table, with all its scratches and dents, gave some familiar comfort. While his mother busied around the place, throwing out anecdote after anecdote on extended family members and her friends he barely knew, he accessed his personal Gmail account through his private iPhone. First thing he saw was a mail from Frank, a drinking buddy in the technical sales team, who by the looks of things had received Gribbin's mail thirdhand, and had the foresight to forward it on to Kish's private account.

'Mate,' he'd written, 'I got this, forwarding just in case you haven't seen—wassup?' Good old Frank, thought Kish.

From: Mike Gribbin
Subject: Extended Leave of Absence—Chris Reece

For personal reasons, Chris Reece is on an extended leave of absence until further notice. In the interim, Natalie Watson will assume management responsibilities for the Government Security Sales team, reporting to me. As we enter our final quarter, I recognise we have a lot to do over the coming weeks, and I ask we all rally together behind Natalie, and focus on closing key deals. I appreciate your efforts and understanding.

Mike.

How bloody convenient, though Kish. All it took was a department reorganisation and his role would be redundant, simple as that. Which probably meant they'd keep him away until at least June and the end of the quarter. Even longer maybe.

'Another cup of tea, dear?' said Diana, avoiding eye contact as she made a beeline towards the kettle.

'Yes, that'd be great.' Kish continued watching his mum busying about the place, not relaxing. Her appearance had noticeably worsened since his last visit. Face less toned, almost bloated. He'd not been one to pry, she was not one for letting on how she felt.

Kish's mobile beeped. It was a text from Amanda Crabtree in HR. Kish smirked as he tapped a response:

Thx, under the circs, feel a bit odd. HR have the knives out for me, so I guess you'd be wise not getting involved.

'It's nice to see how you are keeping,' said Diana facing him. Kish put down the phone.

'Likewise.'

'And a little rest and recuperation from work doesn't hurt anyone. So long as you are sure you don't want to spend your Easter holiday somewhere more fun.'

'Yep, this is just right. In fact I was wondering if I can stay a little longer? I've just found out my application for a sabbatical has been successful. I can start it straight away.'

Diana paused before answering. 'Of course, but are you sure you don't have to be anywhere else?'

'No, why would I want to?' Kish stared at his watch impatiently. 'Mum, I'd quite like to pop down the pub. Want to come?'

'Oh, goodness me no! Not really a pub-goer these days. Which one are you thinking of dropping in to?'

'The Eagle I think. It's still there, yeh?'

'Well, it's been there for a couple of centuries, though I dare say that's no guarantee,' Diana countered reverently.

'I'd best go help save the local pub then.'

Kish walked down the quiet avenue that snaked down Sion Hill, marked by fine Victorian villas and Georgian terraces. In diffused moonlight, this particular Bath suburb, on the surface at least, seemed to be enjoying life. Houses looked neat, their roofs well maintained, with pristine brick and stonework, clipped front gardens and a fair share of 4x4's parked alongside. Another couple of roads later, houses and cars got a little smaller; he passed a couple of cul-de-sacs left and right where rows of small, 1970's detached family homes still looked as respectable as possible. After another few minutes, he approached the pub, one of several haunts during his sixth form days in Bath. It hummed gently as he approached with the odd cackle of laughter rising above quiet background music. As he entered he was engulfed by a guff of warm, steamy air. It was the first time he's been back in there in seven years. Maybe longer. While he waited for his pint of

Bellringer Ale to pour, he casually clocked several familiar faces. One or two twitched in half-recognition, another volunteered a smile; Kish nodded in return. Old faces from his primary school days, at eleven he was the one who'd been sent off to private school the other side of Bath, resulting in thinned connections with those he'd once built sand castles with. It was only in the sixth form and down the pub he'd begun talking to them again.

Feeling a little flush, Kish peeled his Arran jumper over his head. Beneath was a t-shirt with some innocuous American fifties branding. Immediately he felt a little more in keeping.

'Scuse me, are you Chris Reece,' came a voice.

Kish held out his hand to a stocky man, while trying to recall his name. He'd competed against him in sack race at primary school twenty years ago. Saw him again during 'A' Levels—that was about the sum of it. 'John, right?'

'That's right, mate. Long time and all that. So what brings you back here then?' John said in his thick west-country accent.

'I'm down visiting my mum.'

'Your mum, she's Diana right?' Kish nodded back. 'Yeh, I like your mum. Always smiles when she comes into my hardware store.'

'You know her then?'

'Too right. Especially after she was in the local news once. Something about doing some work with, I forget now, the United Nations was it? Always smiling, your mum. Always says hello. Yeh nice place she has there, popped round once delivering a bunch of fire guards. So where you living now?'

'London.' Kish responded.

John nodded. 'Didn't you go work for some big IT company or something like that?'

'Yeh, Mironic. Dull but it pays the bills.'

'I'm sure it does.' John scanned the designer jeans and t-shirt that must have cost a bomb. 'Back home for long?'

'A few days, you know relax, get away from the high life.' said Kish irreverently.

There was a pause, consciously filled by nursing a long sip of beer. 'Well, I'd best be back over there. With the missus and her old man. Tell your mum John Ellis says hello.' John raised his pint again before turning and getting back to a convivial table in the corner.

Kish watched John plonk down and resume the chatter with his wife who he now recognised. She'd packed a few extra pounds these days, and was full of laughter lines. She briefly looked up at Kish without reacting. Kish dragged a bar stool underneath him and remained at the bar, inviting conversation from the barman or regulars nearby who only smiled in return. But his comments failed to hook, so Kish made swift work of his second pint, and soon headed for the exit. Only John half-noticed him leave.

Diana was in the kitchen when Kish returned. 'Nothing changes round here does it?' said Kish tongue in cheek.

Diana just smiled. 'Well, depends on your viewpoint.' Kish sensed some hesitation. 'Now I had something I meant to tell you earlier. You remember Vilora, the little girl from Kosovo?'

'The one from Pristina was it?'

'That's right. Only she's not so little. She's nearly nineteen! Goodness. Anyway, she's coming to stay in a couple of weeks. It's her first ever visit abroad.' Kish flicked a glance at the photo on the windowsill. The one he'd seen a couple of weekends ago. 'Mum, I'm sorry I didn't get the message sooner. About your news and all.'

'Oh don't be silly. You're here now. And that's all that matters.' Diana moved round the breakfast table and tentatively squeezed his shoulder, then touched his head. 'It is lovely to see you.' Diana walked off into the hallway. 'CSI Miami is starting. You coming through to watch?'

As deflective as ever, thought Kish as he joined his mother in the lounge for an hour's decent cop drama, punctuated by a few more texts and emails from closer colleagues. The rumour-mill was at full crank.

When Kish emerged downstairs the following morning, his mother was wrapping herself in a thin overcoat and headscarf.

'Morning dear. Popping into Bath. Have to see the consultant for a quick chat.'

'Do you want me to come with you?'

'Oh no need. All a bit boring. Next time maybe. Now you put your feet up, and I'll be back before lunch. Perhaps we can do something together. Drive over to Clifton maybe?' Diana then kissed him on the cheek and left.

While waiting for the kettle to boil, Kish scanned his private iPhone for new mails. No messages from nosey colleagues, nothing from Elise. He was still waiting for her to make the first move. Next he scanned the latest banal Facebook entries from various folk he'd met along the way. Kish went to the fridge. No proper milk from cows, only rice milk, which he reluctantly poured into his tea, giving it a thin opaque quality. Sipping as he sauntered round the kitchen, he paused to study the fridge door. Postcards held up with magnets, a bright wooden sunflower magnet, and two quotes. One was by Freud on the ego. The other was more interesting. By someone called Brasher:

Perpetual devotion to what a man calls his business is only to be sustained by the perpetual neglect of other things.

As far as Kish was concerned, 'fridge magnet philosophising' was designed specifically for the insufferably pompous and self-righteous, living in quiet frustration. *She, of all people, criticising those who sacrificed for their life pursuit? Bloody hypocrite.* His mum's long work days meant he'd hardly known her when he was growing up. At the time he believed that attending all those after-school activities provided through an expensive private education was entirely for his personal growth and benefit. Looking back he now felt somewhat conned. Not that his father was around much either—that rat had spent his evenings getting frisky behind his locked office door. Kish wandered into his mother's book-lined study. Nothing immediately jumped out that might interest him: not a business management book or Lee Childs or James Patterson in sight. Just row upon row of geopolitical tomes, the history of this, the explanation to that. Kish plonked himself down at his mother's desk. One half of it was covered by an unruly pile of bills, postcards and magazines, the other half bare, but for a new-looking Dell laptop in the middle. He wondered how much the Dell had set her back. *Why the hell hadn't she phoned him to get* his opinion—heck he might have been able to get her a discount? Kish spun around in the desk chair and faced an old bureau, nicely veneered in walnut. He remembered a time when he'd sit doing his drawings there, alongside either one of his bookish parents on those Sunday afternoons while they prepared for their workweek. On top of the bureau sat photos of him during his younger life, and two framed photos of the Vilora girl. Above the bureau were several packed shelves that ran along the entire wall. Kish spied the bookshelf a little closer. At one end were nine folders, neatly arranged and bright red in colour. Each one was marked with a year, beginning with 2002, continuing to 2011. He stretched up to grab the one marked '2002', the thinnest of the nine. In it was a bunch of handmade cards, plus a large brown envelope marked "FD—EU, Kosovo" with some sheets of paper inside. *Mother's boring EU work. FD, must be some dull do-goody department.* Kish turned his attention to the cards. *Far more interesting.* The card on top of the shallow pile depicted a fine pencil drawing of an angel, its wings draped elegantly down its flanks. Written beneath it, in very soft pencil were the words "Diana, by Vilora, age 10", and dated September 30th, 2002. Pretty good for a ten-year-old, thought Kish. Towards the back of the folder were two postcards from him. The writing was scruffy and slanted down the page, the words abnormally large. Filling the postcard with large letters meant he could get away with writing less.

Hi Mum,

Hope you're well. In Pattaya, located in South Thailand. Met a ton of people from UK, all of us going a bright pink in muggy sunshine. The geography, the landscape . . . great relief here. Trees right down to the beach, which is stunning. Big skies at night. Keeping well, hope you are too. Will try to email you soon (need to find an email connection) Cx

'Great relief here,' he chuckled, recalling the illicit 'happy endings' he got on the beach from a lady, who it turned out was a man. He shuddered then read the next card.

Hi Mum,

As promised another card. A day north of Chiang Mai, top end of Thailand with some folk I met a few weeks ago in Pattaya. Got a bit of a rash from the sun so lying low for a few days in the forests. Chance to catch up on some reading and the natural history. Beautiful people, great food, wonderful atmos. Working hard on local project. So much to write—will email when I get a connection in our next big city. Cx

He studied his writing. The pen work said 'disengaged', 'uninspired'. He cast his mind back to September 2002. A bit of a haze then, let alone now. Going travelling rather than spending his summer break at home had been a straightforward decision. At the time. things had blown up at home between his parents. Kish sifted through the folder, and a homemade card with a bright yellow flower on the front caught his eye. Inside, written in poor ink:

Auntie Diana,

Thank you so much for being with us yesterday afternoon. I love you.

Lots of love and God's blesses, Vilora x x x.'

The handwriting attentive, every word cared for. Kish leafed through. More letters and several printed emails addressed to his mother.

Auntie Diana, Thank you so much for coming to our school on Friday . . .

Thank you so much for helping us get the spare food from the soldiers yesterday . . .

Thank you for helping us in our small vegetable garden today . . .

Thank you for the lovely pink dress. Papa says I look very pretty.

Clearly she hadn't spent all her time twiddling her thumbs behind some desk then. The warms word, affirmation of what warmth his mother could evoke. Right at the back of the folder were two handwritten letters, kept in their original envelopes. Clearly written by someone older, mature, educated. He picked one and began reading.

My dear Diana, it is barely a week since you left Pristina . . .

Kish went straight to the last of four pages, and read the bottom.

. . . My love to you as always, Your Fadim.

He then scanned the content. References to a chance meeting last month, along with comments on the conflict, limited electricity and water, that fateful NATO bombing, relief from the local UN post and '*my little Vilora*', '*Prayers for her mother and brothers, now safe in Heaven*'. Kish scratched his head. 2002 wasn't just the year he was in Thailand. It was also the year that Dad pissed off. Next, Kish pulled down the folder marked '2003', then '2004', then '2005'. Over the course of the next hour, a story began to emerge; his mother was chummy with this Fadim bloke, the girl Vilora's father—that seemed clear enough, and through which a young girl's relationship with Diana had deepened over the years, an innocent's gratitude to 'Auntie Diana', who'd nurtured young eyes to see the world beyond racial and religious persecution, and who like her father Fadim, had opened her heart to forgive those who'd taken her mother away from her. *Who'd taken Vilora's mother away though?* Didn't sound like it was Social Services.

Kish placed the letter back in its folder. Admittedly, correspondence from Vilora and this Fadim character was proving quite interesting. Yet far more interesting would have been the correspondence from his mother back to her. He might even get a mention. Pity, Vilora or Fadim must have those letters. Five minutes later and armed with a cheese and pickle sandwich, Kish slunk off into the lounge and slumped in front of the TV. Sat on his mother's sofa, Kish's mind drifted back to his mother's red folders and the correspondence contained within them. His mum had clearly spent her time in Kosovo knitting her way, saviour-like, into some poor disadvantaged family. Itself a bit odd. The sheer width of the folders meant there must have been almost constant chit chat between the UK and the Balkans; the commentary to a life his mother had enjoyed yet he knew practically nothing about, its existence confirmed only through a few photos, and the most brief of conversations he'd had with her on the matter down the years. *Did I miss something? Something more meaningful?* It was times like this he wished he was a better listener on those infrequent phone calls with his mother.

Back in Putney Ferret, Geoff was in his room when his mobile phone rang. It was Elise. 'Are you discreet?' she asked.

TWENTY-ONE

Over the next two weeks, day-to-day management of the Ferret branch of Bacchus Braves Winestores Ltd proved even more lackadaisical than usual. Humphrey had spent considerable time finessing a small poem concerning a lady called Jen who was troubled by piles, a subject he knew all too well. Geoff had his distractions too, such as domestic cleaning, as Humphrey discovered one morning.

'Here we go,' Geoff said rather excitedly as his mobile rang. 'Eva. Yes, hi—, you go to Thurlow Avenue with Nikki tonight, and that should mean you are done by six. Then go to the other place afterwards . . . yes, with gloves and hotpants . . . Bye.' Geoff concluded and shut his phone, triumphantly. 'Smashing!'

'Do explain,' asked Humphrey half-knowingly.

'Terrific new concept in cleaning. Cute Eastern Europeans who specialise in cleaning batchelor houseshares, and who don't mind you watching them clean in hotpants when you're a bit hungover. No touching. Just a pleasant view. Just a sideline, mind. I got Maria involved.'

'Is that legal, let alone ethical?'

'Watching a pretty girl push a Vileda Supermop round the floor? Course it's legal. Turns cleaning into the most anticipated activity in the week. We can do evenings. Whatever.

'And dare I ask what you've called this novel enterprise?'

'Well I've narrowed it down to three. 'Cleanski's and 'Vladette's.'

'And the third?'

'Ethnic Cleansers.'

Humphrey choked on his coffee. 'You are bloody kidding right?'

'No. Why?'

'Ethnic Cleansers? That's an awful name, and you'll get roasted for it. Besides the whole thing sounds a bit risky to me.'

'A risk now and then is good for a man.'

'I wasn't talking about you. I was referring to the girls.'

'Ah. Now that is why I have drawn this up,' said Geoff, pulling a slightly mauled sheet of A4 from a pile of paperwork. A full contract for cleaning, with a non-harassment policy wrapped in.'

'You are insufferable. It's outright pimping.'

'It's legal. It's not a front for escorting or whatever. It's what it is. Bit like Hooters only with a bottle of cleaner, not beer. More broom dancing than pole dancing. Besides, beats selling wine.'

'Cleaning beats wine? Tosh!'

'Whatever,' said Geoff.

With no news from work or Elise, Kish had neither reason nor desire to go back to Ferret just yet, and for two weeks now he had busied himself on chores here and there, fixing a loose bracket on a kitchen cupboard door, sorting a bed leg that needed tightening, giving the lawn a decent mow, then popping down the pub for lunch or for a few beers in the evening. Every other day or so he would pop into the study to read some more Kosovo correspondence, taking care to brush his tracks. The pamphlets that Elise had given him had been truly appreciated by his mother; he knew she'd read them when he noticed them piled up beside her bed when he brought her a cup of tea one morning. There'd not been a peep from work, apart from a couple of updates from the odd colleague. Current rumours were that he'd disgraced himself in a nightclub by flopping his tackle out in front of a senior government customer.

Diana's house was silent this particular afternoon, save the ticking of the grandfather clock echoing along the hollow hallway. Not like Ferret Rise, with its ambient traffic hum, or the frequent groan of a plane overhead, as it made its final decent into nearby Heathrow. Taking a break from reading the Dean Kootz novel he'd brought with him, Kish walked around the lounge munching on his roughly made cheese and onion sandwich. He studied the framed photos on the large imposing fireplace. A couple of pictures of himself and several of this Vilora person. Different ages, different backgrounds. But the same smile in each. He picked out one of her sat on an old bench with a book and he brought it closer, under better light. Written in silver pen in the bottom right corner were a few simple words.

With all my love in the world to my Auntie Diana, Vilora. X January 2005

Having not seen his mother all afternoon, Kish wandered through to the study, where his mother was at her laptop. 'I thought I'd see if you needed anything.'

Diana took off her glasses and looked up to him. 'Goodness is it that time already? You must be hungry, you hardly ate at lunch.'

'I'm fine. Need to slim a little.'

'Actually darling, I wanted to catch you before tomorrow. Before Vilora arrives. I hope it wont be too much of a hassle for you sharing the house with a complete stranger?'

'Of course not.'

'She's very keen to go onto higher education.' Kish considered whether Kosovo actually had a university. 'She missed at least two years of learning because of all the fighting and disruption. Exceptionally bright though. I will help her with her applications.'

'You've been kind of looking out for her, right?

Diana seemed to perk up. 'Yes. Nine years or so.'

Kish tried to recollect any lengthy conversation about Vilora. He hadn't committed much to memory truth be known. He had to be careful—he knew more than perhaps he should from reading the folders. '2002? I was at Uni, right? Think I remember you saying she lost her mother?'

'Yes, in 1999, toward the end of the Kosovo war. Many family members were killed; a few who survived were treated very badly. Nasty things went on. I kept in touch with her father and her though, mostly letters at first, and thanks to internet and email access in Kosovo, we've had a wonderful correspondence in more recent years. I print the longer emails. That way they're more tangible.'

'Still got the postcards from me too I see,' said Kish, pointing at one he'd sent from Thailand that sat right next to a picture of him with their old dog, a terrier called Sniff.

'Ahh yes, all a long time ago now.'

Kish just nodded. It also crossed his mind to ask her if she printed out his emails to her, then he considered just how rare his emails ever were. And brief, and dull. He yawned. 'Well if you need me to come with you to the airport, just let me know first thing. Right, a quick walk into Bath sounds quite good right now. Fancy coming?'

'Things to do for tomorrow I'm afraid.' Diana tried to grin and put her glasses back on her nose.

As Kish made himself scarce elsewhere in the house, Diana shut down her laptop, terrified at the prospect of the doctor's appointment first thing tomorrow morning.

It was the phone ringing in the hallway that stirred Kish the following morning. *Eleven AM!* He'd overslept. He grabbed his dressing gown and sped downstairs to answer it. It rang off, and tutting he went into the kitchen. There he saw a note from Diana on the kitchen table:

9am—Off to my appointment. Will go on and pick up Vilora straight after from Lulsgate. Mum xx.

Kish frowned. *Surely there was no mention of an appointment yesterday? What appointment? A hospital appointment? A nail appointment?* The phone in the hall then rang again.

'Hello?'

'Hallo . . . Is Diana Reece there please?' A young woman's voice.

'No, this is Kish, err Chris Reece, her son . . . who's this?'

'Chris? Hello at last Chris! This is Vilora! So pleased to hear you! Is Diana there?'

'No, actually, but I think she's coming to fetch you?'

'I got earlier connecting flight two hours before. Visa check was quick. She said she would pick me up after her doctor appointment. But I can wait for her here.'

'Don't worry, I'll let Mum know and come fetch you myself,' said Kish, still wondering what this appointment was all about.

'I will wait outside main exit yes? What car are you driving?'

'A black Mercedes, probably needs a wash though,' Kish replied, not entirely sure what he was babbling on about. He spelled out his registration number, just in case.

'Okay. You are so kind—just like your mother.'

Forty minutes later, Kish ground to a halt outside the main exit to Bristol International Airport, still known to locals as Lulsgate. A stunning-looking young woman with silky dark hair was stood next to two large cases, peering at him. Kish didn't need to second-guess, and as he stepped out to meet her, the young lady stepped forward and hugged him. *I could get used to this*, he thought, aware of one or two envious onlookers.

Bags in the boot, Vilora jumped into the car, and sat smiling at Kish.

'Right, so first off, a big welcome to England! You know where my mum is?' he asked.

'Yes, another chemo appointment this morning.' Vilora replied checking a notepad. She said she finish there and was to come collect me. I hope everything is okay? We drive straight to the hospital I think?'

Kish caught himself frowning. 'Of course. Silly me, forgot. Which hospital again?' he asked.

'Why, the Royal Edward Hospital in Bath of course.'

One hour later Kish strode up to the hospital's central reception desk. 'Excuse me, hi, looking for a patient called Diana Reece. I'm her son.'

'One minute,' replied the receptionist as he searched through the hospital appointments system. 'Yes, she's still being seen. You can always sit and wait for her here.'

'Do you think everything is okay?' asked Vilora, unfolding a sheet of paper. 'Dr. Davey seems to be a nice man, don't you think?' Kish nodded slowly. 'Here is Diana's schedule. Yes, this is the fourth session. And Diana say the medical staff are the best for her type of condition so she in good hands, I am sure of this.'

Mr Davey? Schedule? Vilora appeared to know exactly what was going on. 'Perhaps we both find out together,' Kish responded diplomatically. He needn't have waited much longer. He spotted his mother walking towards the reception, flanked by a large man who Kish presumed to be her consultant. Kish studied her stride. It was timid, unsure. Her torso appeared to stoop slightly, shoulders sagging, her face tilted slightly downward, and as she got closer, he saw a worried expression, and in her eyes, pain.

'Nënë!' Vilora shrieked as she lunged forward and wrapped her arms tightly around Kish's mother, both women instantly tearful.

'Vilora, darling. You got here! I'm afraid my phone died. Hello, Chris dear.'

'Vilora arrived early. Called me from the airport,' said Kish, feeling his chest instantly tighten.

'Sorry for being a bit teary,' said Diana as she grabbed a tissue from her blouse cuff. 'Chemo was a little too rough on me this morning.'

'Oh Mum,' mumbled Kish, 'Why didn't you tell me where you were going this morning. What happened?'

'I thought I did? Last night? Didn't you see the note on the table?'

'Yes but—'

'Diana said weakly, 'I thought it would be good to get it out of the way and enjoy some time with you both. But you see,' she paused, 'the results from the last round of chemo aren't so good. Looks like the cancer has gone a bit further than we thought, and my wonderful consultant here, Dr. Havey here knew better than to sugar coat the facts. Might be heading into some lymph nodes.'

Kish watched his mother's eyes well up, forcing a tear down her very pale cheek. Vilora was now fighting back tears himself, and avoiding any eye contact with Kish. Kish was more frustrated than tearful. He couldn't stop himself thinking about why Vilora knew and he didn't . . .

Having received the nod from Diana, Doctor Havey then took it on himself to explain the situation clearly. 'Diana's cancer is at what we call Stage Three. We subdivide Stage Three, but essentially her tumour is greater than five centimetres, and the lymph nodes in the armpit contain cancer cells. We're monitoring very closely for further spread but she now requires stronger treatment and we will be agreeing very shortly on what that is. She needs her family around her right now.'

'Mum, I wish you would have told me the extent of all this,' said Kish. As he spoke, Vilora's tears fell gently onto his mother's tightly-grasped hand.

TWENTY-TWO

Vilora had been with them for over a week now, and was reminding Kish what youthful exuberance really meant. For starters, she was up every morning before six, done jogging around Victoria Park by seven. By eight, she'd dressed for the day and was putting the finishing touches to breakfast, which she ferried upstairs to Diana unfailingly. A bowl of Alpen, a pot of tea with a small pot of extra milk alongside, and a glass of orange juice. Before serving it up on a tray, Vilora would draw back Diana's curtains, plump up her pillow and sit with her for a few minutes before leaving her in peace with a copy of The Independent and setting off for Bath Central Library. On other days she'd be found sitting with Diana for hours on end discussing new stronger treatment options she should now take, or the implications of a lumpectomy and post-surgery chemotherapy. Kish would join in when he could be bothered, usually referencing information from the advice booklets he'd brought with him.

Today, they sat out on the sandstone patio. Kish quietly sipped his beer while Vilora dipped into her bag and produced a small package, wrapped in silver paper. With Diana's situation she had waited for the right moment, nerves and tact playing against her natural wish to show gratitude. 'For you with many, many kisses, yes.'

Diana took it and carefully unwrapped it. 'Oh sweetheart, thank you,' she said, holding a small antique silver photo frame.

'Father would want you to have it. It is old family belonging.'

'Oh let's see,' said Kish, intrigued at its potential value as a future heirloom.

'Vilora, your father was a very kind and handsome man. He also knew your dad, Chris.'

Kish rocked back. 'How come?'

'University. That's where we all met.' The mild, late afternoon air was a further comfort for Diana, helping her forget the constant pain. 'I need to stretch a little,' she said finally. 'Come on, I'll

202

show you both something I've become very proud of these last few years—my clematis collection.'

'What is clematis?' Vilora enquired enthusiastically. Kish was glad she asked—other than knowing it to be some sort of plant, he didn't have a clue what a clematis was either, nor that his mother had made a point of growing them. Probably a plant with big fronds and small flowers, or maybe the other way round. Maybe it was a bush.

'It's a beautiful plant with large colourful flowers, which climb up walls. I have grown several varieties.'

'The flowers in the photos you sent?'

'That's right. Now bear in mind they are only just beginning to bud,' said Diana getting up, causing Vilora to stand up quickly too. Kish remained seated, and found himself staring at the young lady's slim jeans a couple of feet away. She possessed a classic young Eastern European frame—long legs, a thin waist, defined hips, and slim, toned arms. Would make a perfect model. Kish glanced at his mum, who looked back at him, and immediately he found himself staring at his knees.

'Come on Chris, bring your beer with you,' Diana said. 'I'll show you some real plants, unlike those overgrown weeds you don't do anything about on your patio back in London. She turned to Vilora. 'Could be such a lovely space. Honestly, I don't think he inherited a single green finger from me.'

'A little unfair,' replied Kish with a slight smile, trying desperately to keep his eyes from wandering where they apparently shouldn't. 'We keep a basil plant in the kitchen.'

Vilora giggled at his light heartedness and they made their way down some steps to the lawn which stretched about eighty feet, and walked towards a small coppice of young birch trees. Vilora extended her arm toward Diana. Diana grabbed it and then curled hers around it, before continuing on the walk. 'I think I know where we going, yes?' said Vilora, 'I remember from all the pictures I have in my head. We go round here yes?'

'You're absolutely right,' Diana exclaimed enthusiastically. Kish followed slowly behind, taking in the shapes and form of the garden he'd played in as a child. The jasmine shrubs that still grew wildly, and next to them, African grasses that gently swayed in large terracotta tubs that bordered the path to a raised shrubbery area full of heathers, and behind it a long wall, half in the sunlight, half partially shaded.

'Here we are,' said Diana. Along the whitewashed stone face, a myriad of stems were carefully pinned and trellised, one or two trailing early buds in all directions. Some more bush like. 'My clematis collection starts here and moves around the garden,' Diana announced proudly. 'We're in a bit of a microclimate because the cooler wind coming down from Lansdown simply doesn't get round here. The garden's enclosed quite well.'

'Hardly any of them in bloom though?' said Kish gruffly, still trying to remember when all this clematis-chicanery began.

'Not yet dear, it's been a cool spring. But in a few weeks, all along this wall will be vibrant colours splashing and unfurling.'

Vilora gasped. Kish quite liked the sound. 'I think it is beautiful now,' she said, the photos and her own imagination coming alive in front of her. 'Now I know and not just think I love England. And your beautiful garden—it has your heart in it everywhere I see.'

Diana smiled. 'That is a very sweet thing to say.'

Kish imagined Vilora bare all. In the garden. At night, on cool wet grass. Silent and hidden and . . .

'That one there enjoying the sun is a variety called Armandii, which has a lovely smell. And that one there is Tangutica, which was always a favourite, and will start flowering in late May. I have twenty in the collection, many are cultivars, others from seed. A joy to have. Now, the one I'm most excited about right now is this one.' She knelt down at a leafless specimen.

'It's a bit spindly?' said Kish curtly.

'It was cultivated as a hybrid, and this is its first year planted out. Produces the most dazzlingly bright sunburst-yellow flowers in late august, early September even. Delicate but resilient, it will make a strong but graceful climber.'

'You make new type of flower?' asked Vilora.

'Well a new variety, yes. And I should get round to naming it. It'll come to me soon.'

'It is truly magical.'

Kish stooped to take a closer look. As he did, he could not help peeking at Vilora. In his view she was the best exhibit in the garden.

He scanned his mother. She was wearing tan cotton trousers, which did not flatter her. The weight of the secateurs sat in the left thigh pocket pulled the hem down and made her appear a little lopsided. Above the overtightened belt sat a notable midriff.

'Mum, you put on weight?' asked Kish bluntly.

Diana looked up at the sky, smiling nervously as she did. She then looked round but with her eyes closed. On another occasion she might show a little more pique. But she knew her son, she knew his crassness. The point was he was there with her. Diana looked back at Vilora, affectionately. 'It is the medicine I must take, steroids. They do funny things to your body, and can make you put on a tiny bit of weight.'

'Just kidding,' said Kish hopefully. He'd read up on Stage Three cancer. Apparently, around fifty percent of women diagnosed at that stage lived for more than five years and forty percent lived for more than ten years. 'And nothing like a spot of gardening to burn off calories. She's a good gardener, Vilora.'

Vilora smiled at Diana and said, 'I think you in a garden, is what makes it so beautiful. More than flowers and clem-' Vilora paused.

'Clem-a-tis,' said Diana softly. 'Derived from the Greek word 'Klema', meaning 'vine branch or 'vine-like'.' Vilora squeezed Diana's hand, and Kish clenched his jaw hard, wondering when the hell he last extended his hand to his mother. Or she him for that matter. High time he snuck off with his beer, and well away from all this sisterhood bonding guff.

TWENTY-THREE

It was now June, one day to go before Ascot. Business was slow this morning, so Humphrey found himself tweeting more than usual. It hadn't escaped Geoff, either.

'Our friends FerayNotFerret and CompleteChief are back butting heads,' he exclaimed, tucked away at the back of the store with his mobile.

'No doubt that defective CompleteChief will pose something preposterously militant to our local hero,' Humphrey replied.

'He sure will,' said Geoff as he began to write. What Humphrey saw appear on his screen a short time later both shocked and delighted him. He'd clearly hit a raw nerve in this CompleteChief miscreant.

CompleteChief:
@FerretnotFeray, it's folk like you who've completely re-shaped the countryside's personality . . .

CompleteChief:
What with your misguided notions of a rural idyll and your Postman Pat-cum-Miss Marple arcadia

@FerayNotFerret:
That's right—go insult millions of folk sat in the higher tax bracket

@CompleteChief:
You and your fellow masses pour out from your urban executive class avenues for the odd weekend in a pub B&B armed only with Hunter wellies

@CompleteChief:
Or commute in from a village you've killed because you don't want development or you've priced out everyone who doesn't commute themselves.

@CompleteChief:
Ferrit, understand the countryside is not simply a clipped village green, a church and a pub in aspic

@FerayNotFerret:
Ah the good old village-green pub. Pop in for a pint of real ale, and a wild boar with chutney sausage sandwich. Bliss.

@CompleteChief:
Replanting the hedgerows we paid farmers to grub out in the seventies & who r now paid vast amounts to put back in

@FerayNotFerret:
Yes, preserved for generations thanks to the determination and support of commuting incomers

@CompleteChief:
And some slowly poisoned songbirds . . . may look nice but it's at breaking point

@FerayNotFerret:
Looks healthy to me . . . sunken lanes and thatched cottages still prevail in many parts of the Home Counties

@CompleteChief:
Countryside is becoming no more than a food source and recreation facility for an urban-biased population. It doesn't sustain itself

@CompleteChief:
Doesn't even sound or smell like it should these days

@FerayNotFerret:
Tosh! anyone armed with a good nose and driving with the roof down knows the countryside is rich with all sorts of countrysidey smells

@CompleteChief:
So you urban sybarites return back to your homes, clogging the M4 & M40 on a Sunday evening

@CompleteChief:
Determined to support the countryside you've dipped into via some future trip to the farmer's market

@CompleteChief:
Where the cheese packaging alone looks so-o-o much better served to approving friends at suppahh.

@FerayNotFerret:
True, I do seek out a few brunch provisions on a Saturday morning in Putney Ferret's farmers' market

@FerayNotFerret:
And in so doing reinforce our allegiance to you, rural custodian

@CompleteChief:
Farmers Markets = weeny % of how people buy. Remaining 99.9% via supergrocers. Tiny margins on tiny revenues

@CompleteChief:
Result: pathetic, subsidised agricultural economy wearily rides through another growing season

@CompleteChief:
Propped up by a bunch of bean counters in Brussels, and an influx of cheap labour

@CompleteChief:
Never mind we get screwed overproducing it, over fertilizing it, over sanitising it, or underpricing

@CompleteChief:
So long as excessively packed shelves entice you to buy, not caring that 1/3 of it is wasted

'Geoff, are you still reading this rant between the Ferret hero and this Chief moron?' hollered Humphrey across the empty store.

'Certainly am. Love following this Chief dude, sideswiping that poncey twat FerretnotFeray.'

'Other way round, oik. He's called FerayNotFerret.' Clearly the ingrate Geoff had mutinied from the honourable ranks of landed producer to subversive town-dwelling consumer.

Geoff scrunched the empty beer between his two palms can and toe-punted it toward the aluminium bin near the office. *Farming. Who'd do it.* It was time to re-work more interesting stock entries for the past few weeks. Questionable breakages and his new wine substitution operation—successfully tested at the Boat Race, could be fully reconciled after the Season events he'd deliberately selected, and way before the annual store audit in October. His plans for tomorrow were even more ambitious than the Boat Race.

'Humph, I'll load the van for tomorrow. You go home,' Geoff said, just as his phone rang. He'd have preferred to take the call later but the person on the other end was too important to ignore. Geoff acknowledged the instructions with brief responses, mindful that Humphrey was nearby. 'Nine-thirty, Monday . . . no problem, should I wear a suit? . . . sure, looking forward to it . . . bye.'

'Who was that?' asked Humphrey nosily.

'Oh, the dentist.'

Humphrey gone, Geoff set about working out which fizz to load up in the van. Ascot would be fun, a chance even to see his parents enjoying themselves on a very rare day off. Following a visit from Elise to the empty store office, Geoff returned home a happy man.

TWENTY-FOUR

'Geronimo!' Geoff stormed Humphrey's room at 6:00am dead, grabbed Humphrey's bed frame then tipped it and the mattress on its end, sending Humphrey flying off towards the bedroom wall. 'We leave for Ascot in thirty minutes!' said Geoff, and left Humphrey muffling obscenities from behind his upturned mattress. Fifty-five minutes later, Humphrey emerged out front fully dressed, bar one of his shoes, which was tucked under his arm. Geoff over-revved the engine in annoyance.

'Stop that!' Humphrey hissed. 'People will think we're right plebs.'

Geoff was in no mood. 'Just get in. You can finish off dressing up in the back.'

'Me? Sit in the back?'

'Quite.'

'Hello boys,' said Elise in her calm pronounced way, stopping Humphrey in his tracks. 'Any objections me joining you?'

Geoff scanned her thoroughly, and his feet went cold. She stood in a eucalyptus satin dress, with a sloping hem that waved across her smooth toned thighs. He looked at her tummy, just like he did every day since she'd told him. Still barely showing. Before Humphrey could perform the role of house gent, Geoff was out of the van and escorting her over to the passenger door.

'I thought I'd give up that front seat for you,' Humphrey stuttered hopefully. 'You're very kind,' Elise replied. 'I'll look after your jacket if you'd like, keep it from creasing.' Elise smiled at Geoff, and arrested him once more. She gently flattened her dress around her hips before curving herself into the passenger seat.

'Doesn't quite match being chauffeured around in Kish's Merc, but still fun eh?' asked Humphrey.

'Thank you all the same,' replied Elise, ignoring the Kish comment. 'It'll be lovely to catch up with some old girlfriends who are there today, and of course, interesting to see you two in action!'

While Humphrey settled himself in a battered old armchair, wedged secure between stacked crates marked with the Pol Roger crest, Elise gently stretched her arm and squeezed Geoff's hand sat on the gearstick.

'Turning up in a van. The shame of it,' Humphrey mumbled, checking the crates for their sturdiness. 'And no insane speeding up there!'

Heavy traffic made their progress far slower than expected, despite Geoff making allowances for a calmer drive to accommodate Elise's condition. Geoff silently cursed himself for not having chivvied Elise or Humphrey earlier. It could reasonably be said that they operated on their own standard time, approximately twenty minutes behind Greenwich Meantime.

Around one hour in, as they neared Sunningdale, Geoff and Humphrey began to discuss logistics. 'Humph can you do a quick recount of the Pol Roger crates?'

'Thirty cases on the nose', Humphrey replied. At approximately six glasses per bottle and twelve bottles per crate, there'd be less than three thousand servings. 'Is that enough?'

'Those are the remaining few cases that make up the required inventory. Don't worry the rest are already there. We'll be manning two Debrays hospitality stands. One next to the Paddock Enclosure, one accessing the Royal Enclosure. Got a preference?' asked Geoff.

'Given my attire, isn't it obvious? I'll take the Royal.'

Geoff wasn't going to argue. Frankly, having access to the Royal Enclosure offered fewer opportunities to wander off and have a punt or two; it meant serving drinks rather than consuming them. Conversely being housed in the Royal Enclosure removed a significant problem for Humphrey, namely not running into his parents, who in recent years had made Ascot an annual event and typically settled for passes to the slightly less grandiose Paddock Enclosure—'*one up from the Silver Ring, but one up all the same,*' apparently. Avoiding them meant avoiding their awkward habit of offering views to unsuspecting strangers whose only crime was standing in earshot. His father droning on about the trappings of being a senior executive, his mother's bombast when it came to subjects she held dear: anything from preserving rural England, to her son's wonderful career. Humphrey had seen this peculiarity grow in recent years.

It was a further twenty minutes of stop-start before finally entering the town of Ascot, and already an early morning crowd were trickling out from the car park and toward the main entrance. For Geoff, plenty of presentable, tightly contained backsides to gawp at. For Humphrey it was the occasion that had him smiling, as he spotted several racegoers in their well-fitted morning suits and hat's, superbly fashioned shoes and fob-watches. Then Humphrey's heart sank, as if to rudely remind him of the realities of more inclusive times. 'There goes the corporate brigade emerging from their corporate-subsidised cars, dressed in well-pressed lounge suits and slim oxfords. My God. Place is littered with them. Oh, that new Range Rover over there, that's what Dad's got.'

'Does he drive off-road to work?' asked Geoff.

'Actually they live in Thrubsham, not Andover. And no he uses the M3 but yes, they plan to go travelling further afield in it.'

'Where? The Yukon?'

'Devon, actually.'

While Geoff tried to stop erupting into hysterical laughter, Humphrey focused on a group by the entrance, and said 'Good Lord, look at 'em. Square-built chavs who've foregone this week's shop at IKEA followed by a drive-through McDonalds to come here, I see sporting this year's provincial high-street fashion.' Humphrey paused, hoping for a response. 'And what is it about shoewear and some people? The large knot ties is bad enough, but tan-coloured footwear with dark suits? Ye Gads! This is Ascot for God's sake, not some wedding reception held at some village football club.

Elise was not in the least bit swayed by Humphrey's unique socio-economic commentary. She gazed admiringly at women of all ages, backgrounds, shapes and sizes, uniting with them in their determination to have a damned good day out. Today she also couldn't help but smile as small, smartly dressed children were gently shepherded by kitten-heeled mothers.

Geoff made a sudden swerve and abruptly reared up on the pavement by the main entrance, instantly attracting the attention of several well-dressed passers-by.

'What on earth are you doing?' wailed Humphrey. 'Our entrance is further down! Keep going!'

'Calm down, and get Elise's door will you. She needs to be presented.'

'What? I can't get out here!' Humphrey exclaimed.

Geoff turned to him. 'Get out!'

'I can't!'

'Twat! I'll do it then!' growled Geoff, unbuckling then scooting round to Elise's side.

Elise emerged laughing, straightening her dress. 'Enjoy the day, Humphrey,' she said, replacing her fascinator. She turned to Geoff. 'Thank you handsome, such an understanding gentleman. I'll call you if we can get into your enclosure otherwise me and the girls will just have our own fun, and see you around five o'clock. And don't go too hard on Humphrey. He'd be distraught if he knew my condition.'

'Hey, Mister Chivalrous,' said Geoff, now back in the van. 'Why don't you sit up here.'

'Rather not. Might be seen.'

Geoff rolled his eyes, gripped the steering wheel, and seeing the road was clear, dropped the clutch. The van catapulted off the kerb, tossing an unbuckled Humphrey violently across the interior, denting his top hat. A minute later Geoff slowly navigated the van to the services parking area. He walked round the back of the van, and motioned two stewards over. With great aplomb, he then swung both van doors back.

Humphrey's emergence from the rear of a purple van proved quite something. Dressed according to the strict code of the Royal Enclosure—full morning suit with grey-striped trousers, and set off by a light blue Gieves and Hawkes shirt, plus top hat, Humphrey was looking extremely sharp.

Geoff made a deep bow and remained so, not through deference but through doubling up in laughter.

'Peasant,' Humphrey scoffed. 'You look like you were sired in a Leicestershire field. That suit looks like it was last used as a manure bag, and by the amusing way it clings to you, very likely purchased several hundred kebabs ago.'

No use. Geoff was in hysterics. 'Just seeing Lord Pomphrey . . . arrive in a van.' He blurted before creasing up again.

Humphrey eyed the two bemused stewards beside Geoff, then said, 'I'm so sorry. He is a little retarded. Care in the Community.'

'Retarded? That word's a bit out of place these days, sir,' said the older of the two stewards dryly. 'My son is in a special school, so I take a bit of an exception to anyone referring to others as being retarded.'

'Certainly,' croaked Humphrey and his throat dried up.

'Jesus!' wailed Geoff. 'You refuse to help a lady out of a car, slag off innocent race-goers from the van, then call people retarded. So much for class. And as for my fine jacket,' continued Geoff, just about managing to stand straight now. 'Fond memories stain its weave.'

'Figuratively and literally I imagine,' gasped Humphrey.

'Practically a genetic extension of me.'

'How utterly charming. On that note shall we unload?'

An hour later the Bacchus Braves cargo was fully installed and chilling nicely behind the Debrays hospitality stands. Geoff said, 'Humph, you go find out where the hell Toby Sarber-doo-dah is, I'll do a quick re-count, then get a couple of guys to bring them your share up to you.'

With Humphrey gone, Geoff removed a bottle. It was Pol Roger all right. Not exactly the Blanc de Blancs vintage advertised on the boxes, but the less expensive Brut reserve. At several pounds a bottle difference, multiplied by three hundred and sixty bottles, it was a nice little earner. 'Perfect,' he mused. Ten short minutes later he'd flattened the boxes and had the younger of the two stewards from earlier obliviously bin the evidence before someone discovered that the box labels were at odds with their content. 'Want to do something more interesting today, like serve pretty ladies wine?' he asked the young man, who turned out to be called Kyle. Kyle seemed only too keen. 'Then point me to your boss.' The ensuing discussion with the Operations Manager was easy enough. 'We're with Debrays and we're one man down,' Geoff lied. Ten minutes later, he returned and threw the lad his own Debrays polo shirt.

'Kyle, you've been promoted. You'll be sharing shifts with me on with Debray clients in the Paddock enclosure. First I need you to shift all these bottles here of Champagne to the well-dressed chap by some brightly coloured umbrellas in the Royal enclosure. He is a Lord so you must address His Lordship as Your Lordship. Clear on that?'

'Crystal clear,' came the enthusiastic response.

'And ignore him if he insists you call him something less formal. While you're doing that, I'll shift the other half of these bottles to the Paddock, and meet you there when you're done. Help me man the bar, you keep your tips. Deal?'

'Deal,' Kyle replied. He shook Geoff's hand, and made off towards His Lordship.

While a couple of temporarily requisitioned stewards shifted his stock Paddock-ward, Geoff spent the next hour reading the Racing Post and addressing the tirade of texts and calls from Humphrey, demanding to know Geoff's whereabouts, that Sarber-Collins was checking up progress at the Royal Enclosure and had made him put on his Debrays shirt, which by the way was utterly impertinent and frankly didn't go with his topper, and lastly who the heck was this Kyle character who doggedly addressed him as Your Lordship in front of everyone. Geoff turned his phone off and set about placing a series of bets with the Tote. Analysing the horse's form was proving difficult to do, given the other kind of form walking by. Geoff had enjoyed horseracing for many years, his extensive knowledge very much down to the tutelage of his nag-mad dad, and visits to Nottingham, Market Rasen and Leicester Races, just about whenever Geoff wasn't playing rugby for his school and county. And today, the Paddock crackled with promise of a great meeting. Geoff felt good. And regardless of what Humphrey said, he knew he looked good, too. Despite one or two extra pounds, his height and square shoulders allowed him to carry any suit well. Geoff could wear a dining chair and still cut an impressive dash.

Just then, there was a stark 'Yoohoo Geoffrey!' It was a very familiar woman's voice, embodying the very essence of life itself.

TWENTY-FIVE

Geoff span around, along with several others. Striding towards him at considerable speed was a tent-sized cream and plum jam-coloured silk dress, housing a generously proportioned thoroughbred English Countrywoman. Geraldine Fox, or 'Gerri' as she was universally known had been the cornerstone of Oakridge Hall for the past thirty-one years. Every one of the four hundred acres surrounding the Georgian manor house, was her husband Teddy Fox's responsibility. The farmhouse itself and its immediate garden was Gerri's domain. Within that perimeter, she was CEO, Head of Finance and Administration, Chief of Operations, and majority shareholder. Her husband's responsibilities, the loamy soil, the farm employees, farm animals, animal smells, oily implements and course language, all of it stopped dead at the boot room door accessed via the stable yard—heaven forbid Teddy or anyone else working on the farm enter from the front during working hours. The boot room acted as an airlock between two repelling environments, and was governed by Gerri under strict laboratory conditions. This is where retriever's paws were towelled thoroughly before being allowed to proceed further into the home. Here, insulated gloves were removed, along with mud-caked wellies and all other shoes (with no exceptions). Here, musty and ancient Barbour jackets were hung up to dry off by the ancient boiler, overalls were thrown into the enormous washing machine that rotated day and night, and shooting sticks were propped up. Mess strictly contained, the sanctity (and quite possible sanity) of a beautifully presented and maintained home beyond was assured. Every one of its seven sash-windowed bedrooms, its neatly managed farm office, its quiet yet imposing library, its four bathrooms of varying size and grandeur, its drawing room, sitting room, lounge (out of bounds except on Sundays and for special visitors), and of course the room she was most proud of—the perennially-set dining room, dominated by a four-panel mahogany table that comfortably accommodated fourteen well-built people, and over which lifelong bonds had been forged, tested, and reinforced. The large hallway and the open curved staircase that drew the eye up towards darkened oil paintings of local vista's and one or two distinguished, and now extinguished, family members. Among all of this, Gerri had weaned, nurtured and supported the lives of one hardworking husband, two adored children, and an ever-welcome army of extended family and friends. And not forgetting the (sadly decreasing) number of people who worked on the farm, and their spouses, quite happy to sit down for a quick cup of tea between daily tasks, and natter with Gerri on this and that, which usually included gently ribbing Mr. Fox, who in turn had spent most of his adult life shoring up the economic wellbeing of the farm. Not that Gerri didn't contribute to the farm's finances. She was in her eighth year operating a small, but nonetheless growing chutney-making business. This allowed her to employ a couple of retired friends part-time, and to travel around the East Midlands on Thursdays and Sundays, selling it in the farmers' markets she was so passionate about.

Geoff braced himself as his mum enveloped him, her big loving arms wrapping tightly around him. 'Hi mother,' he said through a slightly contorted smile.

Gerri kissed her son purposefully on both cheeks, then gave him one last squeeze before releasing him, allowing Geoff to breathe and study her in her finery. 'You could set up home in all that whicker,' said Geoff, pointing to her hat. Its feathers suggested a large flightless bird might have already moved in. She chortled and hugged her not-so-little treasure once more. Geoff looked beyond her shoulder, and through the feathered ensemble, spied his approaching father. Teddy was roughly the same height as his son, but notably slimmer these days, sporting his trusted morning suit of twenty years. An active lifestyle always kept the pounds at bay, and despite his love of Gerri's unrivalled cooking he politely requested smaller portions these days.

'Put the poor boy down, Gerri,' said his father. He had an irrepressible twinkle in his eye, reserved only for his inseparable wife and a good joke over dinner.

'Hi Dad,' said Geoff, vigorously shaking his father's large worn hand.

'Geoffrey. How are you, old chap?'

'Isn't that obvious, Teddy?' Gerri snapped mildly at her husband, and looking back to her firstborn said, 'you're looking so pale and ill. I saw an item on the BBC about it—in the house or outside, you are breathing all sorts of dangerous things in nasty old London. Chemicals and carcinogens, that sort of thing.'

Geoff chose not to remind his mother of the untold volume of man-made chemicals she plied daily to keep her own home artificially free from a single bacterium.

'Gerri, do stop bothering the lad. You're embarrassing him,' Teddy volunteered.

'Well, I'm fully entitled to worry. It's my job to worry, and I can't stop worrying if I don't ever see you living and eating properly. Goodness, I shudder to think just how you young city boys manage to cope looking after yourselves.' Gerri paused and smiled, squeezing Geoff's hand. 'Well we're just so looking forward to spending some time with you today. I can happily go fetch you some food for starters. And we have a small picnic in the car for later.'

Geoff smiled. There'd be nothing particularly small about one of his mother's epic picnics. It typically comprised several kilos of crumbed ham, topside beef, porkpie and scotch eggs, a monumental salad, generously filled sandwiches and fruit of all varieties. Not to mention the whole roast chicken that usually accompanied it all, and more than enough liquid to wash it all down. Geoff looked at his watch. He knew his mother would only become more impatient for some decent time with him. She'd feel her love was unreciprocated, and Geoff simply couldn't have that. It would play on him all day, week even. 'Tell you what, let's have that saunter now, before things get busy.' They linked arms and made the short walk through the gates and toward the Royal Enclosure. 'Humphrey's up there too. So you get twice for your money.'

'Oh how lovely,' said Gerri. 'I hope you're looking after him. Now he is someone who needs feeding up. Far too thin. Does he have a girlfriend yet?'

'No. And before you ask, neither do I.'

'We'll get to you in a moment,' Gerri replied and the Fox family entered Ascot's finest Enclosure.

Once Sarber-Collins had left the immediate vicinity, Humphrey had removed the offending Debrays polo shirt, and spent the next hour working on his pose amongst the backdrop of several yellow Debrays umbrellas that flanked the Debrays stand. *Appear welcoming without appearing humble, confident without appearing officious.* Just at the point when Humphrey had settled into a conversation with his first guest, a like-minded individual with strong opinions on last year's Bordeaux harvest, a horribly familiar face caught his attention. He made a short-lived, self-conscious smile, and it attempted something similar, hand clamped down on what appeared to be a lace-enshrouded beret, pinned at a slight angle to neat curls of mousey hair, and doing a very good impression of a very large ice hockey puck. A cold wind had entered the Royal Enclosure, and carrying with it his mother, Rosalind Massey.

Bollocks, thought Humphrey.

A somewhat attractive woman of fifty-eight, Rosalind Massey shared the same well-appointed nose, piano-friendly fingers and narrow-gauge eyes as her son Humphrey. Rosalind scanned him. Well turned out, which was a nice reflection on her after all. Groomed and looking very respectable. She determined she'd have to ask him about his career progression during a quieter moment later. Working for an upmarket wine company was passable, though she'd prefer if he'd extended himself just a little more beyond store management. Certainly within an industry respected by fellow members of the parish council, and preferably within a company people knew.

Humphrey straightened up, just like he did before being handed a neatly packed lunch and a wave off to prep school. 'Hi, Mum,' he said dryly.

'Hello, dear,' started Rosalind.

'How was the drive here?' Humphrey asked.

'Pleasant trip up through Hampshire, though the traffic around Ascot was dreadful.'

Having moved to the quaint Hampshire village of Thrubsham many years ago, in most part to improve Paul's commute to the company's head office in Basingstoke, Rosalind was an established player on her village's parish council. She was also an increasingly vociferous critic of the local district council's sustainable rural economic development plan, particularly its apparently bloated section on rural residential planning. For Rosalind, her own residential planning policy was simple: no more new homes in her village. In 2008 she successfully prevented a former village hall from being demolished to make way for some much needed affordable housing, whose advocates saw as vital to the long term economic vibrancy of a village and surrounding small industry and services. Following this victory, she then spearheaded the 'Cherish Thrubsham' campaign that successfully halted the development of thirty new executive homes, their design almost exactly the same as the Massey's home but which were doomed for failure the moment planning documents revealed they would be built in a field overlooked by one Mrs. Massey's kitchen window. Her support was drawn mainly from the ranks of well-educated, solvent and politicised residents of Thrubsham whose occupancy of key positions across the village's various institutions now wielded considerable influence over the absolute protection of *their* rural idyll. Not to mention the value of their properties. Rosalind Massey gave a new meaning to the term 'Not In My Back Yard', and her triumphs earned her the title 'Lady NIMBY' among battle-scarred county, district, and local council planners.

Approaching her from behind and fiddling with his Blackberry was Humphrey's father, Paul Massey. To the average onlooker including Humphrey, Paul appeared somewhat detached today—impersonal eyes, detached expression, looking somewhat self-conscious in his hired get-up. Neither parent noticed Humphrey hastily unclip his Bacchus Braves badge and slip it into his trouser pocket, his heart beating faster now.

'Hello Humphrey,' Paul said some five foot away, causing Humphrey to lean in to shake his own father's hand. Their exchange was restrained, mindful of their surroundings and watcher-ons.

'Fancy seeing you both here, of all places,' Humphrey said nervously, hoping for some more hospitality guests to arrive and need serving.

'Oh, wheels within wheels,' said Paul dismissively. 'A bit of hospitality.'

'Let me guess, courtesy of Debrays?'

'Yes,' continued Rosalind, 'Our dear friends the Page-Aitchisons offered us some complimentary tickets. Mr Page-Aichison is big in tax accountancy apparently. We know them through the Rookwood School Governors Association.'

Humphrey scratched his head. He couldn't recall knowing any Page-Aitchisons, nor any connection with some school called Rookwood. But given they'd moved to Thrubsham after he left home, the social circles within which they now operated was anyone's guess. Nonetheless, nice to hear his mother had a few hyphenated surnames in the personal address book.

'Wotcha folks,' said Geoff amiably, appearing by the Debrays area.

Rosalind turned around to see Geoff standing beside an older couple. 'Hello Geoff, how good to see you,' she said. Geoff politely leant in and she kissed him on both cheeks. Something she'd recently started doing, and increasingly expected in others. She smiled disingenuously at the stains scattered across his shoddy suit trousers, and the creased Debrays polo shirt. Friend or no friend of her son, Humphrey clearly wasn't managing his employees with the necessary rigour. Rosalind and Paul had met Geoff a few times over the course of the past few years, usually when they were up in town meeting friends, or on those equally rare occasions when Humphrey invited his housemates to flank him at some Sunday lunch or barbeque down at his parents' place. In her view Geoff was something of a spoilt lay-about, not to mention a questionable influence on Humphrey.

'Rosalind, may I introduce you to my parents, Gerri and Edward. And this is Rosalind Craven, Humphrey's mum.'

'Sorry, I should have introduced you both . . .' started Humphrey diffidently.

'Very pleased to meet you. Well I must say don't you . . . look the part,' said Rosalind, eyes resting on the lapels of Geoff's suit which was clearly second-hand.

Gerri nodded, and turned to Humphrey, adding quietly 'though I think you'd look even more handsome taking your top hat off when inside, dear.' Rosalind glowered at her son as he quickly removed the offending headwear. Conscious of Gerri's discretely delivered advice, nonetheless she'd ensure in no uncertain terms he understood the Ascot rules of etiquette at that quiet moment planned for later.

'And hello, I'm Paul Massey,' Humphrey's father bowed forward.

'Ah, of course,' started Humphrey, 'my . . .'

'Humphrey's father,' Paul added sternly.

Watching as Paul and Teddy shook hands, Rosalind was struck by Teddy's impeccable dress, his high forehead, elegantly swept grey hair, and a ruddy complexion that comes only by working outside all your life. *Clearly upstanding rural stock. Squirearchy, certainly worth galvanising their acquaintance. Particularly if the Page-Aitchisons are looking on.* 'By the way Paul, did you sort out the valet parking?' she added, pointedly.

Paul shuffled nervously. 'All taken care of, dear.'

Rosalind then announced to the group, 'If I ever park I'll most likely crash the silly thing. Still getting used to a longer bonnet and a rather powerful engine.'

'You are all of a tizzy my dear,' came Paul's rather pompous response, before turning to the others, adding 'still excited over our . . . small investment.' Paul rocked back, tilting his chin ever so slightly upward.

'Oh I'm sure Teddy and Gerri aren't interested in our little purchase,' replied Rosalind. She didn't wait for confirmation one way or another. 'Yes, we took the plunge and bought a horse.'

'Really?' said Humphrey, instantly pumped by this wonderful enhancement to the Massey caché. He handed over four glasses of Pol Roger.

'Thank you, Humphrey,' said Paul, who continued, 'bought a small share as part of a syndicate. Great bloodlines, and racing today at two thirty-five. Frank Discussion is his name. Obviously didn't come cheap but let's just say, a present to ourselves.'

'Now we're mortgage free,' added Rosalind. Her comment got people silently studying their wine glasses.

While Humphrey set about advising a guest on choice of Champagne and Geoff checked on the inventory, Paul said, 'I must say, I do love how our sons' employer gives them scope to grow. I mean Humphrey can pursue his management talents, and at the same time bring his entrepreneurial flair to the store with a new wine tasting sideline.'

'I agree,' said Gerri earnestly. 'Though I think Geoff just gets his head down, does the stocktake, and keep customers happy.'

'I wouldn't worry,' replied Rosalind. 'Humphrey is, I am sure, a very good manager for Geoff and the others in the store. And with his winetasting operation taking off, maybe a management opening for Geoff soon?'

Teddy frowned. 'I thought Geoff already manages something or other right now?'

'Perhaps he's managing a section of the store maybe? Or possibly the till?' Paul suggested.

Teddy said, 'No, I am sure it's the entire sto-,'

No-one saw Gerri jab Teddy. 'Yes, I'm sure you are right,' she said. 'To be honest we rarely know what he's up to.'

Humphrey finished proferring Champagne and against his better judgement sidled up to the group. His mother instantly said, 'darling, I was trying to explain your expansion plans for the store. Do tell us about them—how you are turning the place around, making it a roaring success.'

'Well I suppose I . . .' Humphrey started, before being interrupted by the announcer: only ten minutes left to the next race.

'Geoff, not gone crazy working for young Humphrey?' chuckled Paul.

'Actually I—,' said Humphrey. *Here it comes.*

'No real problem at all,' said Geoff. 'Good manager to work for. Fantastic sales numbers. You should be proud of him.'

Paul gave Gerri and Teddy a nod, then said, 'and I imagine a Hardy-esque Gabriel Oak-type such as your son is certainly helping to broaden those narrow shoulders of his. Before you get a little too urbane, eh Humphrey? I mean, running a winestore is all very good but-'

'Boutique winestore, darling,' added Rosalind.

'Quite,' continued Paul, 'but one imagines a stint in the countryside doing honest graft might have done him more good. Farmwork, that sort of thing.'

'You farm?' asked Teddy.

'Not personally. Though it never left the blood. And we live in a village that's very agricultural.'

'Understanding the state of British farming is never a bad thing Paul,' said Teddy. 'You'll concede, I'm sure, that farming's definitely a hard way of life, and not without its problems,' he added philosophically.

'I hear you, Teddy. I do feel connected somewhat to the soil. So much so, I'm working on bagging a barn conversion opportunity. Farmer is prepared to sell off several outbuildings as he moves toward retirement. Farm's not doing too well. His children have decided not to take over the family business. Frankly the countryside's not what it used to be.' Geoff winced.

'Certainly got a point somewhere in there,' suggested Teddy, taking another mouth of Champagne and not taking his eyes off Paul. 'Without EU subsidies, we'd certainly struggle to continue. In my father's day the farm was better off, but even then you could see things were changing. Estate management is a very different beast nowadays.'

'Ever thought about diversifying?' Paul asked. 'I hear a lot about farms and estates doing other things these days. Bed and breakfast, alpaca wool, emu rides, golf courses even?'

'Other than stewardship schemes, we've done holiday lets for thirty years now, pioneered rapeseed production in the area in the late seventies, and we've a small chutney and fruit preserves production going which is Gerri's brainchild. 'But it's a family business we're in, and it's both a passion and a full-time job. It's a way of life we try to preserve.'

'Must be so hard,' added Rosalind sympathetically. *Poor dears up against the wall. Old Money's not all it's cracked up to be.*

'Farming certainly is. However our stud farm helps.'

Rosalind coughed.

'Quite, be your own man, I say,' said Paul, also computing the stud farm comment. 'Which is precisely what Humphrey needs to discover. Find his way. Plough a straight furrow. Now I'm not saying farming is his calling. Goodness me no, but I keep telling him how he could do something bigger with his life, beyond managing a small wine store. Never listens to anyone does our Humphrey.' Paul clunked flutes and sent a mouth of Pol Roger down the hatch. 'Anyhow, cheers.'

Having been probed on his own profession, Teddy thought it only polite to ask Paul what he did. After all, Paul seemed the type of chap who liked to talk about himself.

'Yes, I'm the Finance Director for a major British manufacturer, and one of Hampshire's top employers,' replied Paul proudly.

Rosalind intervened. 'Come now, don't be modest. Chief Financial Officer, you mean.'

'Which company?' asked Teddy, as Rosalind sunk her nose into her Champagne flute.

'Jollygurgle,' replied Paul.

'Not sure I know them,' Teddy replied politely.

'The nappy people,' said Paul.

'Ah, got you.'

'Not just nappies, darling,' Rosalind added quickly. 'An array of leading baby hygiene products and solutions.'

For the second time in an hour an uncomfortable silence followed, during which time Geoff saw his mother pinch her own thigh. She often did that to fend off the giggles.

Paul finally broke. 'Rosalind, time we squeezed a bet in.' Turning to Geoff, Gerri and Teddy, he mustered a grimace-like smile, shook everyone's hands then bustled himself and Rosalind away from the Debrays bar. Teddy watched Paul and his wife disappear into a growing crowd, then grabbed Gerri's hand, said goodbye to Geoff and walking off in the other direction. Geoff shrugged, grabbed a glass of bubbly and slipped off to find Elise, who'd texted him to join her.

Humphrey could relax once more. His parents had not delivered today's dose of condescension as privately as he'd hoped, but he'd survived nonetheless.

The first outing of their horse, Frank Discussion had not gone quite as planned for its part owners, Rosalind and Paul Massey. It was a point not lost on Rosalind who made her frustrations clear early into their drive back home to Hampshire. 'I told the Page-Aitchisons to bet on our horse, and it practically limped the entire race. Thoroughbred? I ask you!'

'Well these things take time, and . . .'

'And as for meeting the Foxes. You just had to talk about your company. Next time, I suggest you make something up. The nappy people? Goodness me!'

'I did mention the barn conversion plan?'

Rosalind conceded that it went some way to recover their position. 'Next time perhaps mention we're investing in a place in Putney Ferret. That would have gone down particularly well.'

'Next time?' asked Paul.

'Given the circles we're increasingly in, I'm sure we'll run into them again. I'll speak to Humphrey about it. The Foxes are an acquaintance we must nurture, dear.'

Having said her piece, Rosalind began to nod off. Despite Paul's ill-preparation, it had proved quite a nice day out nonetheless. Shame though not to have caught up with the Page-Aitchisons, despite Rosalind calling them several times. Still, she'd make a point of updating them about their dear friends the Foxes at the next Rookwood School Governor's Association dinner.

Back in Ascot, Geoff grabbed Kyle and slipped him an extra twenty pound note. 'Thanks for your time today. One last favour. Can you get rid of all the Champagne and wine bottles?'

It was Humphrey who ended up driving the van back to Putney, with Geoff sat in the back gently swigging from a chilled bottle of Pol Roger, and Elise quietly reflected on a great day in the sole company of sympathetic girlfriends. Later that evening, sat in their lounge, Humphrey casually thanked Geoff 'for not letting on to Mum and Dad. About the situation at work, I mean.'

'Anytime fella.' Geoff had learned more than a thing or two about Humphrey today. 'If it's any consolation, I often get it in the neck from my dad.'

'About your job?'

Geoff stalled as he studied a text from Elise thanking him for the day out and helping her these past few weeks. 'Sort of. Silly stuff from years ago. He still gets upset I didn't try hard enough. Rugby. I just wasn't cut out for it.'

Humphrey nodded. 'I sometimes wonder what I'm truly cut out for. Until then, I suppose I make do and embellish. Not take the initiative.'

Geoff remembered his phone conversation with his "dentist" earlier that day. A salutary lesson on seizing an opportunity. *Well, seizing another's opportunity.* 'I'm turning in. Night chap', he said, and went upstairs, excited about his appointment on Monday with Haggard Cards. He was determined to use all of tomorrow to prepare.

TWENTY-SIX

Having made cursory preparations on Sunday evening, Geoff was up early the next morning. *Not always the play-worn slacker,* he thought as he knotted his tie and put on the less worn of his two suit jackets. At 9:00am he quietly exited from No. 47—before Humphrey could start asking questions, and walked down to Putney train station. A little over thirty minutes later, Geoff was stood in the boardroom of Haggard Greeting Cards Ltd, surrounded by several sales, production and marketing folk. Des Orr, the company's sales director who'd signed the deal on Haggard's behalf and who was leading today's meeting quipped that Geoff looked 'flushed . . . and bloody right too.' A few of those assembled laughed.

Stood beside Des Orr near the presentation wall, Geoff re-read his notes: *confirmed distribution across all major UK greetings card and stationary stores. To think, an opportunistic meeting just a few weeks ago led to all this.*

'Okay everyone, I want to finally introduce you to Geoff Fox, originator of our new line in greeting cards, Suzie's Toozies,' Orr announced. Bemused applause followed. 'Suzie's Toozies is a series of what I term Urbane-Lavatorial poems, aimed at the sixteen-to-thirty year-old female demographic, open to laughing at themselves and up for a bit of toilet humour.' Orr turned to Geoff, whispering 'you go sit yourself down at the back. Enjoy the show.'

'That's right,' Orr continued, his north London, second-generation Irish bluster taming the room. Suzie's Toozies—a themed series of cards disclosing a discussion in a toilet bowl, "caught between two stools".' Chuckling alongside frowns. 'After twenty-one years in the business, I know a winner when I see one,' Orr said, focussing his stare on one of the frowners, then he picked up the first oversized mock-up, a giant card measuring five by seven feet, made of white reinforced board. 'Jimbo, please pass around the smaller samples in that pile in front of you.' Jim Pallot, Head of Distribution for South East Region duly passed around the packs to the audience. Orr pointed to the large mock-up. 'On the front of each greetings card is one of Geoff's simple drawing of a toilet. Simple lines, ink pen on what will be rough, slightly off-white paper.' Geoff smiled contentedly at the professional rendition of his hastily sketched latrine. 'Now you'll see two speech bubbles coming out of the toilet bowl. A rhyming conversation taking place by two stools residing within.'

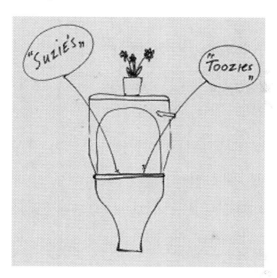

Orr then flipped his man-high card open. 'And inside you get the same picture with two speech bubbles finishing the poem off. 'In this first example card, Poo Number One kicks off and says to Poo Number Two: 'Jen's cheeks dug into the edge of the seat, as she sunk deeper into the bowl'. And Poo Number Two replies: 'Her buttocks acquired a circular red mark' and, the poem ends, 'as ripe piles popped out of her hole'.'

Geoff froze in the prolonged silence that followed.

'Comments?' a perspiring Orr asked finally.

It was Jim Pallot who piped up, 'These cards are branded Suzie's Toozies. So we're intending the author to appear to be female, right?'

'Correct!' said Orr, energised. 'A head-on admission that even the ladies need to go to the small room. When in fact Mr. Fox back is our Suzie.'

Another said, 'Just coming to terms with a card that references haemorrhoids. Does our brand wish to be associated with haemorrhoids? Do young women, our target audience associate with haemorrhoids?'

'Well I do, occasionally,' replied a young sat woman opposite.

Orr placed the oversized haemorrhoid-themed greeting card on the ground and picked up another giant card propped up beside him, then quoted the card.

'Sue peered back into the bowl,
Proud of her latest production,
It just shows that a high fibre diet,
... Results in mass weight reduction.'

'Is there a niche for female lavatory humour?' asked another reviewer.

'Certainly. And let me read this one off.' Orr repeated the process.

'Pushing like a horse in foal,
Milly dripped in sweat,
Not only was there no toilet roll,
... But even worse, no vet.'

Orr now had the room's fullest attention. 'Warming to the theme?' he said, and delivered the next one.

'Jess was skiing in Val d'Isere,
When she suddenly got the shits
So she perched behind a well-place tree,
... And thanked God she'd got her mitts.'

And another:

'When Emma pushed, it was painful,
She suffered from anal retention,
So she dabbed her rear with muscle relaxant,
... And removed some pent-up tension.'

Lastly:

'Liz worked for the local baker,
Who asked, "What's that smell on you?"
"Well I got a little confused" said she,
. . . "And I just kneaded a poo."'

Orr had finished his presentation. All eyes were on him.

'How many of these do we plan to sell?' asked one of the reviewers, leaning hard on his elbows.

'We'll launch these seven first and do a run of three and a half thousand each. Personally I could see these babies selling out by autumn and us doing a second run through winter.' Geoff did the maths. *That's near enough twenty-five thousand cards. With the agreed royalty fee, that means nearly three grand.* 'And we've got another five being worked on by our creative genius there at the back.'

Geoff had forgotten about that. The mantle of Creative Genius belonged to someone else.

Despite one or two personal reservations, those assembled generally agreed that this production had potential, and now wanted to get the launch date confirmed. For some, so they could be miles away when it did. It was thus decided that they'd launch on July 25th—just under a month away.

After everyone filed out, Orr turned to Geoff and shook his hand. 'Flawless, Geoff, flawless. Now you get ready to be a publicly acclaimed greetings card artiste, my friend. And start on the others. Meantime, we must get you over to our commercial team. They have your copies of the contract waiting, and that upfront payment of yours. Follow me!'

Half an hour later, as Des Orr discussed summer holidays over the phone with his wife, a very happy Geoff headed back to the train station, contract and banker's draft in hand. Geoff had taken a huge risk and apparently pulled off a whopper. Now he had to get over to the store and prepare his wine-swap operation for the Glyndebourne Opera Festival. It had worked like a dream at the Boat Race and Ascot. No reason it couldn't work even better in the peaceful East Sussex countryside.

TWENTY-SEVEN

Just like June and May, and several months preceding them, July saw no change in the manner by which the housemates handled life. Humphrey stubbornly chose to drift in and out of his workday, happy in his distorted version of reality. By taking hoodwinking chances all the time—calculated ones when sober—Geoff had made some personal gain these past several weeks, but with it came an increasing, annoying guilt. Based on recent events, Kish's continued calculation hadn't exactly helped him. Bloody-mindedness and naïve self-denial had left him sat pondering on Kosovo for hours in his mother's study while awaiting news from work. It didn't stop there. Elise's parents, delighted by their daughter's pregnancy news, had offered to come over to London, only to be politely discouraged by Elise. Regarding the collapse of Kish and her relationship, she was not doing very well skirting the issue over Skype. Heaven forbid how she'd cope face-to-face. 'Really love to see you but please just give me a few more weeks, Pop. Doing a degree part-time on top of a full work week is proving tougher than I imagined.'

Geoff and Humphrey emerged bleary-eyed from No. 47 just before 6:00am into what promised to be a beautiful, warm day. Humphrey quickly requisitioned the driving seat, and readjusted a cravatte he'd tucked into his polo shirt.

'No dawdling Humph,' said Geoff biting his lip. 'Fifty miles to Glyndebourne and we have only got an hour to get there and we need to get over to the store first to pick up the wine.'

Debrays' hospitality wine tastings at Glyndebourne had been shoehorned into a few short days across this all-summer festival and by all accounts was anticipated as a particular highlight on the hospitality gig calendar. 'Don't fuss,' replied Humphrey predictably. 'We'll be there with plenty of time to spare.'

Two-and-a-half hours later, the purple delivery van pulled into the festival grounds. Several factors contributed to their delayed arrival: it had taken a full thirty minutes to load up the van, with Geoff doing much of the donkeywork, he having spent the previous evening carefully packing the boxes and not wanting to leave anything to chance, not least prying housemates asking awkward questions. Secondly, Humphrey chose a distinctly novel route. Given Glyndebourne was located due south from Putney Ferret, it was unfathomable to Geoff that Humphrey elected to exit London via Richmond Park to the west, then continue out of the Capital for several miles in that same westerly direction.

'Why not just go south via Croydon?' asked an exasperated Geoff.

'Hardly a suitable build-up for the final refinement of Glyndebourne,' came the warped response. Thirdly, at their breakfast stop en route, Humphrey insisted eating in situ. 'I must digest my breakfast slowly and thoughtfully, and I flatly refuse to step back in the van until I've finished; we can't afford to arrive covered in McMuffin.' Lastly was Humphrey's somewhat pedestrian driving speed. 'If we ever get there, you can do all the social mixing you want, just get a move on!' Geoff barked, rubbing his chest. 'Giving me bloody heartburn here.'

'Hush there. A gentleman never rushes, even for more discerning guests.'

'Gentleman? Oh, meaning you?'

'Quite. And an upper-middle one at that.'

'You mentioned that before, and I meant to ask you . . . what exactly *is* upper-middle class?'

'It is a mantle afforded to those who can distinguish themselves from the vulgarity of the social aspirant middling masses. Those with that little bit of extra provenance that gives you the edge.'

'And assuming somewhere hidden you have this, this extra provenance, you think it simply existed since time immemorial?'

'Centuries at least. Scottish royalty. Aristocratic landowning types were-, are the Masseys.'

'So it's your assertion that you are a direct descendent of someone important enough for you to assume some latter-day social superiority over the rest of us?

'Fact, chap. Not assertion. Fact.'

'And you don't think that even the Masseys had humble origins?

'Can't see how.'

'All families who've had power over the centuries have won it from somewhere or someone, which means they had to start out somewhere less, well fortunate. For every one of them it simply took some determined Norman ancestor to win in some ancient incident requiring someone else's disemboweling, reinforcing it through decades of feudalism where successive generations saw to the family's economic and political ascendency through taxation and suppression of the mass of peasants who lived under their lordship's gaze, peasants whose descendents went on to become urban peasants when the Industrial Revolution sucked them in to the Empire's manufacturing machinery, owned in large part by the ancestors of that Norman landowner. And only then did a tiny-weeny minority get lucky by inventing something or diversifying into something new. And those few who got wealthy were only rejected and considered vulgar! Honestly Hump, and I thought the class system was dead.'

Humphrey paused then said, 'the class system may be dead but class consciousness and social differentiation are alive and well in this country. You yourself have just proved it.'

'I'd certainly agree that today, people are more able to set themselves apart than centuries ago,' Geoff replied. 'Usually through a greater array of ways to make money, reinforce their wealth through shares and bricks and mortar, and spend conspicuously to underline their status. Usually beyond their means. That last part is something you do very well.'

'I hardly need a credit card to send the right message.'

'Bullshit. You're a banker's wet dream, the amount you spend on utter crap and then have to pay interest back on.'

'You forget I have a trust fund chap. Trust fund. Small, but there all the same.'

'Oh dear God!' Geoff would wedge him there and then if it didn't mean causing Humphrey to crash into the motorway hard shoulder. Instead he looked at the speedometer. Exasperatingly, they'd gone back down to fifty mph.

'Like I said, a gentleman never rushes.'

Geoff scanned the deserted parking area that stretched out before him. It was a flat, freshly mown field of several hectares, surrounded by several hundred hectares of farmland stretching into the hazy distance. He half-hoped they'd arrive to find the place packed and with Karen Williams his area manager, or even better, Sarber-Collins from Debrays, stood waiting to give his sanctimonious housemate a damn good public dressing down.

'You see Geoff, no need for panic. I got us here nice and early,' crowed Humphrey.

'Shut up and park up.'

Following a quick stretch in the cool morning air, Geoff opened his coffee flask and poured its contents into two mugs. He and Humphrey leant against the bonnet and gazed across still green wheat fields toward the woods and a hazed sunrise beyond. To their right, where a field had been left to fallow, a hawk swooped down onto some unassuming rodent. 'A glorious morning, when nature's at its best,' said Geoff. 'A wonderful time generally to consider life at its most raw, its most base, most unpasteurized, most . . . wild.'

'Here we go,' said Humphrey.

'No hear me out. Suppose we were on the run from the authorities, how would you survive in the countryside, hidden away?'

'Well,' started Humphrey reluctantly, 'I suppose you'd expect me to be grubbing up roots and scrumping apples. Instead, I'd be booking myself into some pub B&B under a false name and wearing a false nose, fresh from busking my keep at the nearest market town square.'

Geoff laughed. 'You're missing the point. In this scenario, we're on the run. That means no pub. Just our survival instincts, and nature's platter. So wotcha going to do? Starting with a good source of protein.'

Humphrey began to think. 'I suppose if it was autumn I could count on mushrooms, but not much protein in mushrooms. Unless the plan was to eat about four kilos-worth, after which you'd probably inform me they were highly poisonous.'

'You are right to raise concerns over mushrooms,' responded Geoff. 'Seasonal, a poor source of protein, and risky. Now roadkill, there's another option. Pheasant, rabbits, other small mammals.'

'I suppose lightly fricasséd with some parsley and some wild garlic?' Humphrey said sarcastically.

Geoff ignored him. 'I'd probably opt for snaring something. I'd need to kill it myself to know it was fresh.'

Slowly warming to this totally hypothetical scenario, Humphrey offered a couple of his rules. 'Okay, now let's just say we have matches or a lighter in this situation, for fire. And a knife.'

'In which case, and if I had the patience, I'd tickle out a trout in the local stream,' said Geoff. 'Did it when I was a kid. Now, blackbird eggs have potential because you can generally reach them in hedgerows. Mixed up with earthworms and you have a wholesome omelette.

'So now you have a frying pan handy,' said Humphrey. 'And what about shelter?'

'We'd find shelter in a thicket or hedge.'

'Little cover from the elements I'd imagine,' suggested Humphrey. 'Easily spotted too.'

Geoff rubbed his chin, thinking. 'You look in any hedgerow and chances are you'll stumble across some old piece of corrugated steel, or a fertilizer bag at some point.'

Humphrey knew the conversation to be yet another pointless one, yet he too had seen Bear Grylls surviving in the wilderness on the Discovery Channel. Compelling stuff, and watched from the comfort of a warm sofa, it had registered in a fallowed corner of his consciousness, that one day he too might be thrown into a similarly terrifying scenario. *Humphrey Versus Wild.* Set down in the shires of southern England, and armed with nothing but an ordnance survey map, warm clothes, cash, well marked paths and a village pub, should he need a cottage pie and a pint of ale to recover after a twenty minutes collecting blackberries. *If that's what nature threw at me, bring it on I say.* Unlike Geoff, thought Humphrey, who would go feral in Belgravia if given half the chance.

'An alternative to a hedge,' continued Geoff 'is a field of sweetcorn. Well-drained soil, so it's not boggy underfoot. And plenty of cover. I'd probably find the highest point in the field and nest myself there beneath the crop line. In my corrugated iron and fertilizer bag hut.'

'Why highest part of the field?'

'Aspect. So the farmer doesn't see down into some big hole in the crop from his bedroom window. Also better drainage.' Geoff offered up his hip flask. 'Fancy some Glenlivet?'

'Why not,' replied Humphrey. 'Who'd not have a nip at nine in the morning?'

'Horse sperm,' came a brisk-sounding voice from behind them.

Someone had been listening to them.

TWENTY-EIGHT

The Ferrets span round. Appearing from apparently nowhere was an older-looking man in his early sixties and sporting an old, if well-maintained wax jacket. The gent's face was almost thickset, yet his thin hands betrayed thinner, more proportioned days, and a bald head that reflected the rising sun rather well. All in all, he struck an amiable appearance. At his feet sat a young King Charles spaniel, panting and alert.

'I'm sorry?' Humphrey blurted incredulously.

'I said horse sperm. An excellent source of protein, if you were really up against it,' the man said.

Humphrey flashed a rather embarrassed glance at Geoff, then stared at the old gent. 'Any pointers on how you'd extract your equine-based supper?' Clearly the old dotard was off his rocker.

'Simply bring him off and be done with it. Enough zinc and amino acids for a fortnight, I'd imagine.'

'I don't suppose you actually have horses of your own?' added Humphrey, hoping to God he and Geoff hadn't just unearthed something warranting the immediate attention of the local constabulary.

'Practically brought up with 'em. But for the record, should any young vagabond or fugitive do that to mine, whether on death's door or not, I'd bloody lynch him on the spot. Bloody animal harassment, that. Illegal and quite frankly disgusting.'

Geoff extended his hand. 'In any case, good morning. I'm Geoff Fox, Bacchus Braves Winestores Ltd.'

'Good morning to you too, Mr. Fox. Yes, Roger Ashton, Facilities Director for Debrays Hospitality. Was just taking the dog for his morning dump and saw you two pull up. Rather obtrusive colour isn't it?' Ashton wagged a finger at the van's bright livery. 'More mauve wouldn't you say, than your true red wine colour, what?'

'And I'm Humphrey Massey, also from Bacchus.'

'Welcome, welcome,' Ashton said, providing a hand for Humphrey to shake. 'It's going to be a fine day today. And, I take it the goods are all present and correct?' he noted with a rather camp flourish, somewhat incongruous with his more stoic demeanour. Ashton rifled deep inside one of the larger pockets about his poacher-cut Barbour jacket.

'Should be,' said Humphrey. 'I loaded the cases up myself.'

'Okay, well you're quite fine parking up here. What we'll do is get your load transferred into the large van and we'll then take it all down to the site, and prepare it for Debrays.'

'Driving down's no trouble.' Geoff tried to interject.

'Not to worry, it's all sorted,' said Ashton, reassuringly. He stared blankly at the grass beneath him. 'Anyone seen my spaniel?' he asked.

'He went off sniffing up there,' said Humphrey.

'I'll come back with our van in just a jiffy, once I find the hound.' Off Ashton stalked, roughly northward toward the other end of the field, yelling 'Gideon! Gideon!' and 'where are you, you bloody arse,' before catching his heel on a large clod of soil and stumbling into long grass. Humphrey and Geoff watched as he picked himself up, and continue in a more deliberate fashion up over a stile and eventually out of view.

Humphrey then turned to Geoff. 'Don't we need to liaise with Debrays directly?'

'No need. I'm sure this Ashton chap'll take care of it.'

With Gideon suitably retrieved, Ashton returned soon enough in a large white Mercedes van with his errant dog and two assistants, who promptly helped Humphrey and Geoff transfer the cases to the back of their van. Done, Ashton made his way up into the passenger seat. 'See you in an hour or so.' The van jerked off toward the main buildings, and the place fell quiet again.

In the distance, visitors in their cars were being stewarded toward the bottom of the field nearest the main festival area, in a field that could comfortably house six hundred. Geoff checked his watch. *9:30am.* The sky was losing its translucence to a deeper, noble blue. 'The beauty of it all,' he said in a relaxed voice, unscrewing the coffee flask again. A couple of wood pigeons cooed from a hazel tree that stuck out from a rather unkempt hedgerow. Some sparrows chattered in the dust lining the lane behind it. 'Once the work's done, one deserves to be idle. It keeps you youthful.'

'But fella, you're not some teenager whose done his homework and has the weekend free. You're touching thirty. You have responsibilities. If not to others, then yourself.'

'Thirty is the new twenty, which is near enough teenage, and I'm practically no different to when I was twenty. And I'll work very hard to make sure that continues.'

'How?'

'Through the continued hard work of others.'

'Other like me, you mean.'

'Yes, like you, Humphers. Between us we have established a mutually favourable division of labour at home and in the store. You are officially classified as a labour-saving device.'

'I'm not some bloody washing machine or toaster,' Humphrey replied, adding a small shot of whisky from Geoff's hipflask into his coffee, then lifted himself to his feet. 'Besides, we actually have work to do. Come on, let's find the Debrays tent.'

Shortly, Humphrey was surveying the space that would be his kingdom for a day. Tent didn't really describe it. Fine marquee more like, with an assortment of chairs inside and a long bar for serving and presenting wine tastings. Meantime, Geoff concluded a brief chat on his mobile.

'Humph, that was that Ashton guy again. Apparently the Debrays team are one man down in the delivery bay. I need to just pop round and help out. Back later.'

Geoff's walk took him through a series of fine Victorian brick out-buildings to Ashton's white Mercedes van, just as he'd been told, hidden away from view by a tall long garden wall, well away from the delivery bay. Ashton was busy offloading wine boxes when he saw Geoff.

'Geoff. Sorry 'bout callin' you just now. I needed to know how much bleedin' wine I'm taking away with me.' Roger seemed to have lost his refined tones.

'Like I told you yesterday, you take away the twenty-five cases in my van which have "special" written on them, and you fill the tent with the unmarked ones from my van, plus the ones I told you to bring.'

'Got it,' Roger replied, opening up one of the marked cases. His eyes lit up. 'Some very nice wines you got here, a few bottles of Rauzan-Ségle, some Trimbach . . . Very nice indeed.' Ashton then re-sealed the box, and said 'Oh by the way, I got my hands on some rather posh sarnies for lunch. Fancy a couple?'

'Nice. Just stick them all in my van when you have a mo, and let's get the cases to Debrays. Horse sperm, honestly!'

'I was getting into role.'

Back in the Debrays tent, Humphrey was busy checking his reflection in one of several ornately framed mirrors lining the back bar. 'Massey, you handsome devil,' he proclaimed, ensuring his Debrays polo shirt collars were at peak erection. Just then, someone behind him piped up with a polite question.

'Excuse me, sir.'

Humphrey turned and faced a middle-aged man and his wife. 'Sorry about that—I was just checking the mirrors were clean.'

'Of course. I understand Debrays are offering its guests wine tasting master classes?' The man waived his hospitality pass.

As if on cue, Geoff came bounding in with the first of several cases of wine, and a fitting response. 'Good morning, I see you have met our resident wine expert? We begin wine tasting in exactly ten minutes time. Some French and Italian classics and some exceptionally rare wines from Washington State. Exciting discoveries your friends won't have ever tasted nor even know about.'

Humphrey looked at his watch, flummoxed. It was 10:35am. *Don't we kick off at noon?*

'Nice early start. We'll just hang around here. By the way, I'm Roger Keeting and this is my wife, Harriet.'

'Humphrey C. Massey,' Humphrey replied, wondering if there was a small band of well-spoken Rogers running about this Season. Even the ruddy Champagne was called Roger.

While Roger and Harriet studied the list, Geoff strolled over to Humphrey. 'All the whites are back in the cooler, and the reds are in the pantry boxes, temperature eleven-point-five degrees. In other words, I'm done.' Geoff pressed four twenties into Humphrey's palm, and made for the exit. 'It's what I owe you to cover my shift. Back in a few hours.'

'I can't do tastings on my own!' said Humphrey, horrified.

'Ready to crack on, Humbolt?' hollered Roger Keeting with a grin.

At least ten Debray Hospitality guests had now ambled in and begun huddling round the wine tasting counter. Humphrey collected himself. He had a duty to perform and as a Massey, perform he surely would. 'Absolutely. By the way, it's Humphrey. A common mistake.'

From the moment he was thrown headfirst into the morass by that workshy shit Geoff, right up until the final cork-pull by late afternoon, Humphrey performed non-stop. Wine taster, advisor, and convivial companion. And they loved him. He'd enjoyed the odd glass himself, and as his confidence grew, so did his exotic verbosity. By 12:00pm he could be heard describing a Pouilly Fume as 'limes crushed, the taste having the same closure as a billiard ball thunking into a far pocket'; by 1:00pm, 'the smell of a Saturday morning bike ride in a village near Ludlow.' Around 2:00pm he would be telling a rather bemused old Major's wife, 'Now slowly hum a resonant tune around the Rauzan-Ségla 2005,' he'd told 'That's right. Actually hum a song into it. It will sing back to you in calm, round Baccarach tones, imagine the melody while skipping as a young lady might among birch trees in cool autumn, russet apples wet, and beech leaves, crushed and muddied beneath stout walking shoe. And then . . .' he paused and closed his eyes, his voice now a whisper '. . . heed the slow rise of nature's must . . . pear-like?' Humphrey opened his eyes and stared at the now infatuated Major's wife, who winked at him. He instantly summoned some composure. 'Yes, a great Burgundy, a little young for its age, 2004.' By mid-afternoon, as his guests siphoned bottle after bottle, Humphrey did a quick stock check. Surely he couldn't have got through all the Rauzan-Ségla 2005? Come to that, supplies of Trimbach 2004, the Vaudesir Grand Cru 2007, and the Pio Cesare Barolo 2000 had already run desperately low. But most noticeably there seemed an awful lot of the Washington State wines left, despite an overwhelming request from guests for something very novel._Humphrey simply shrugged away his concern, in the same way he'd regularly shrugged off the sight of Geoff waltzing dandy-like about the marquee entrance for most of the afternoon. Indeed, if Geoff was trying to annoy Humphrey, it wasn't working. This tent had become Humphrey's niche environment, his true domain, his manor, his people. Out there, beyond the tent entrance, lay the savage, unapologetically hostile and competitive wilds of the Glyndebourne lawns. Who knows how long he'd survive out there. Especially with Geoff out there, poised to arse things up for him.

TWENTY-NINE

Geoff was far from simply 'waltzing dandy-like'. He was busy keeping tabs on the Debrays hospitality tent. So far, he'd estimated nearly three or four hundred guests, the majority returning several times for a refill. He'd scrutinised Humphrey's reaction each time he'd opened a new bottle and proffered his opinion. So what if Humphrey guessed the inventory had a few bottles of something different. What mattered was quality. Geoff knew Humphrey was getting better and better at sniffing out 'suitability' and if the wine didn't fit the occasion, it was only then that alarm bells might sound. Humphrey was good at sniffing out a badly fitting wine, and so Geoff had to be even better choosing one that fitted. Today it appeared he'd pulled it off. In the run up to Glyndebourne, Geoff had spent several days formulating a selection that punched way above their price tag, and scaled up the operation of substituted wines. At the Boat Race and Ascot, his substitute wines constituted no more than fifteen percent of the total, a ratio easy to bury in the overall list, provided he diligently removed all the empty bottles afterwards. For Glyndebourne, just over half the total inventory was not on the original order. This meant collaborating with someone who could first source cheaper wine for him, thus keeping it off Bacchus's order books, and second, had the means to sell on the wine Debrays had originally ordered, at a reasonable price that kept them in profit. Both transactions had required one Roger Ashton.

The absence of Debrays officialdom sniffing had also left Geoff feeling good. Sarber-Collins had been forced to spend the afternoon dealing with the guys from the Belgique Bier Bazaar, tasked with supplying beer to the Debrays hospitality area but who'd got paralytic (apparently on their own delivery earlier), then inflicted several injuries on one another whilst playing jousting knights with several of Debrays' parasols on hand to shade-seeking clients. With the likes of Sarber-Collins distracted elsewhere, who the hell could check the inventory chit for discrepancies in the odd vintage or producer? Or indeed the sheer number of empty Washington-labeled bottles bagged up at the back of the hospitality tent, ready to be disposed of later by Ashton. Just to be sure on quality control however, Geoff still needed to taste them himself. Enlisting two new acquaintances called Rosie and Polly to give the impression he was simply showing off, he returned to the bar where Humphrey gladly poured a Bolivinas Valley 2005 Chardonnay for Geoff and the Chateau Ste Rochelle Sauv Blanc for his two companions.

'Pity you're not single,' Rosie had remarked to Geoff, before taking a sip and gazing at him through a wine-legged glass.

Listening and watching, Humphrey groaned. He'd seen this scene played out on countless occasions. Geoff's standard tack with a new attractive female acquaintance was to state he was taken. Counter-intuitive to the standard male practice of denying any existing romantic attachment whatsoever, He believed his approach played on the appeal of 'the unobtainable' for a woman. He'd remain controlled in these pursuit situations—mildly flirtatious, lucid and above all, disarming to the point where women, single or otherwise, felt at total ease in his company and were found pondering on snagging *him*. 'Like tickling trout,' he'd often say. Conversely, if he'd said he was single, true or not, then it was assumed to be his responsibility to pursue her, and with that came a higher chance of being snubbed. As Geoff always said 'snubbing single blokes is a favourite leisure activity among women. Most of them don't believe you are single anyhow.'

Geoff took a sip of Rosie's Sauv Blanc. 'Exceptional,' he muttered, satisfied both Washington wines surpassed the grade. Emptying his glass, Geoff waved goodbye to Humphrey, before reminding Rosie and Polly not to stray too far, then casually moseyed off towards the delivery bay. Ashton had just one more thing to do, and that was to get rid of all the wine bottles at the end.

Geoff returned to the tent at 5:30pm, along with the salmon sandwiches he'd retrieved from the van. Ashton followed him in with Gideon wagging at his side. 'Take a couple each guys, you must be starving,' said Geoff.

'Wonderful', said Ashton devouring his immediately.

'Humphrey, you've been a star,' added Geoff. All nineteen grand's worth of wine sunk.'

Humphrey nodded appreciatively, unaware that almost half of what he'd ended up serving wasn't strictly what Debrays had originally ordered. He rolled off his apron, and stepped outside the marquee for the first time that day. A hundred and fifty pounds in tips and the double shifts meant he'd made nearly three hundred pounds today. *Just by talking wine.* He'd certainly had his fill too, and the heat made the sensation of mild inebriation rather more potent. As he polished off his slightly warm salmon sandwich, he surveyed the hundreds of people relaxing on picnic rugs and collapsible chairs, stretching towards the formal seating and the imposing stage where tonight's performance would be shown. Beyond, the South Down's rolled away in the hazy warm English summer sun.

'What stunning scenery,' said Humphrey to Geoff, who'd sidled up to him. 'Looked after by good solid folk who treat her like the gentle beauty that she is.'

'Not all of the countryside is like this, you know, all manicured,' added Geoff.

'Well it jolly well should be. All cleaned up, old untidy hedges trimmed, old barns turned into desirable residences. Nice, polite people in it, and running it. Idyllic.'

'Idyllic like your parent's cul-de-sac, you mean?' said Geoff. 'And I bet the exclusive development they live in has quite a charming title?'

'Yes, Buttercup Meadows.'

'Don't you think it a bit odd naming a housing development after the very thing it's been built over and destroyed forever?' asked Geoff.

Humphrey just grinned, inanely.

The sun arced, and Humphrey and Geoff sat with their backs to the tent, their glasses charged, and watched the beautiful countryside cool off. It was a scene that clearly meant very different things to each of them.

THIRTY

Sat on the patio, Kish finished his second glass of wine of the evening and sent a text to Humphrey and Geoff.

In garden celebrating Miss Kosovo's birthday, Mum is chaperone. Visuals to die for

Still no texts from Elise. In fact she hadn't texted, mailed or called since he'd arrived at his mother's. He was about to pour himself another wine when Diana returned from the kitchen and placed a tea tray down on the table.

'Are you any good with barbeques, dear?'

Kish eyed-up the purpose-built brick affair stood in a corner of the patio. 'I'd say exceedingly average, but I'll have a go.'

'Well that's wonderful. I'll make up a large salad. We've got some chicken that I marinated this morning, and Vilora would love to try some genuine English sausages on her nineteenth birthday.'

Kish twitched involuntarily, then said, 'sure, I'll go freshen up first.' *No news from Elise, so why not give Vilora a crack*, he thought as he made his way to his bedroom. His was ensuite, and first things first, he set to work on three day-old stubble. He was thankful for a blisteringly hot shower, it distracted him from having a quick one off the wrist, this not being his home and all that, but thoughts of Vilora nearly got the better of this unwritten courtesy. Towelling vigorously further took his mind off his desires, he then ruffled his hair up with some wax, and jumped into a loose linen shirt, some DKNY jeans and leather beach sandals. He perched his Gucci sunglasses carefully on his head, turned back to the ceramic-surround mirror on the wall, readjusted his hair, snapped his fingers magnanimously to a smug reflection, and exited. He walked along the corridor, pausing at Vilora's closed door, before continuing downstairs.

In East Sussex, the air was heavy with the wild garlic and cow parsley lining the hedgerow. At the top of the field, Geoff and Humphrey stepped out of their van sporting fresh clothing, and made their way back down for tonight's performance, Monteverdi's L'incoronazione di Poppea, *The Coronation of Poppea*. Only in the final scene before the first interval did Humph realise how Geoff had secured those front row seats. The briefest of smiles from Ottavia, apparently played by one Christina Minas, gave it away. Up until then the soprano had captivated Humphrey throughout the entire performance. Shortly after the final curtain, an usher approached Geoff. 'Mr. Fox, Miss Christina would be delighted to receive you and your friend backstage.' Elated, Humphrey stood up. In an instant he felt his head spin and his stomach instantly cramp up. He smiled nervously and began following the usher. After just ten worrying seconds he felt liquid course through his lower colon, and the floor of his throat rising. He grabbed a large vase of flowers, one of several lining the edge of the pathway, wrenched out the attractive blooms and then vomited violently into the vessel. *Find sanctuary, and fast.* With no time to dwell on formalities now that his lower gut muscles were contracting and rippling violently, he left Geoff and the bemused usher and buttocks clenched, tight-legged his way across a lawn toward some bushes, feigning a smile when needed. Eventually reaching a quiet stand of mature rhododendrons, he frantically dropped his trousers, whereupon he lost his balance and fell deep into the vegetation, and instantly evacuated his bowels with considerable and explosive gusto.

'What the fu-!' gargled a smothered voice from under Humphrey. Being violently and unexpectedly defecated face-on by a complete stranger somewhat put the dampeners on a romantic moment for a young chap and his equally horrified partner. Such an experience might either galvanise the couple forever, or end the relationship pretty much there. Not keen to find out one way or the other, Humphrey desperately scrambled off the freshly-manured pair, and made off down the pathway, trousers wrapped round his ankles, and into the field beyond. Guts gurgling fiercely, he slalomed left and right through the field of cars, in the rough direction of the van. The very moment he reached it, he vomited over the bonnet. Three minutes of continued groaning passed, violent reverse peristalsis making his whole body rock up and down. Then, his throat burning, he fell backwards and lay sweating in the cool grass. Empty at last.

The next thing Humphrey remembered was a bright light and the roar of a car exhaust close by. A female voice registered somewhere. 'Oh dear me. Are you okay?' Humphrey slowly rolled his head and looked up at a young woman peering down at him from the cockpit of a blue convertible sports car. 'Want some water?' she continued.

Humphrey could not muster a response. Then his phone rang. He ignored it. It rang again. This time, he summoned the strength to reach into his pocket. 'Hello' he said in a dull, scorched voice.

'You okay?' asked Geoff. 'It's been nearly two hours since you ran off.'

'I had an unfortunate experience and need to die.'

'Well if you plan to die, just don't do it near the van. Those girls, Rosie and Polly we met earlier? Well I told them to park near us. When I told them we had a van, got the distinct impression they were up for some fun in the back. Told them you were often mistaken for a pony in the dark.'

'Whatever.'

'Well if you do go up to the van, look out for a blue open top Maserati.'

Humphrey clicked off. His face throbbed, fine blood vessels round his had nose bust open, his eyelids sweating. He couldn't care less for Geoff's plans, and soon he was asleep in long grass beside the van.

The barbeque was still glowing when Diana stepped onto the patio holding a small cake and singing Happy Birthday. Kish joined in after which Vilora thanked them both and blew out her candles.

'So tell me more about the place you live Kish? Putney Furry?' Vilora asked, gently brushing some crumbs from her bottom lip.

'Putney Ferret. In South West London. But spelt like Ferret, you know, the little animal?'

'No.'

'Hang on,' chuckled Diana, 'I wonder if I can find it in the dictionary here.'

'Okay well Putney Ferret is kind of, how can I put it, posh . . . posh yeh?'

Diana interjected, 'A lot of wealthy people.'

'Yes, a real cool place these days for young wealthy people to live.'

'And do it so conspicuously,' chipped in Diana.

'Quite,' added Kish, taking it as a semi-compliment. 'And it's getting so popular, its houses are becoming expensive. Owning a home there is sheer fantasy for most people until they are even older than me, and I am nearly thirty and doing well.' Kish had wanted to weave his age in at some point. He studied Vilora for a reaction. She did not baulk, but just smiled on, which pleased him.

'And you rent a big house?'

'Yes, with two other guys.'

'And you have a very nice car I see,' said Vilora.

'Well I need it for my work.' Vilora smiled and tried to keep up, and Diana looked up from her dictionary.

'By the way, I think the Albanian for ferret is qelbës.'

'Qelbës,' said Vilora. 'A funny name for a place to live.'

Kish wondered if Vilora's choice of clothing this evening was intended for him. Why else would she be wearing such a gorgeous figure-hugging knitted top which sat just above her navel, and a flannel skirt, that ended at mid thigh? Her legs were brown and toned. Kish looked to see if the temperature was having any effect of Vilora's nipples. To his delight, it most definitely had, leaving him wishing he'd knocked one out earlier. Perhaps Vilora hadn't got a clue of her power over him. Or worse, very clearly did. He needed to think about something else. His mother's ailment. Now that was a worthy, even convenient distraction.

'So Mum, how do you feel?'

'Oh dear, tonight is not about me. It's about Vilora. Here you go Vilora,' said Diana, passing her a lap rug. 'Don't want you catching your death of cold. Chris, you need one too?'

'I'm fine thanks.'

Diana reached beneath the table. 'A few gifts. And one for you Chris, to say thank you for being here too.'

Kish looked down. His hands had already pulled much of the wrapping paper away, revealing a backgammon board. 'Thanks, that's terrific.' Kish leant to kiss Diana quickly on the cheek, before shrinking back to his chair. He looked at a board again and curled his lip. *Something for eBay.* Diana caught his non-plussed expression from the corner of his eye. The anti-depressants that came with her course of pills had made her less sensitive, and besides she was much more interested in Vilora opening hers. Vilora peeled the sellotape carefully and then unfolded it open. She placed the paper neatly to one side and took the box. Inside was a set of books.

'For your upcoming adventure,' said Diana.

From the other side of the table, Kish studied the upside down titles across the large paperbacks—a skill that had served him well when selling to clients sat the other side of any desk.

'"How To Survive University", eh?' said Kish, trying to think if he knew any Balkan universities. *Probably one in Sarajevo.*

'Yes and "The History of Great Britain", "The Lonely Planet Guide to Great Britain", and "Selected British Poetry". I don't know what to say! I cannot thank you too much,' said Vilora.

'Oh don't be silly, it is a privilege that you'll be living here.'

'Living here?' questioned Kish, putting down his wine.

'Yes . . . I am working to help get her into a University over here.'

'Perhaps in London with any luck,' added Vilora.

'You'll need it. Tuition fees these days.'

'I'm sure we'll work out that side of things,' Diana chipped in graciously. 'Meanwhile, who's for a cup of coffee inside?'

Kish stared at Vilora pensively. He could accept his mother helping her find higher education back home in Kosovo. He'd not considered she'd be vying for a place on his own doorstep. A faded memory of his own application process for LSE emerged after over ten years . . . no recollection of either his mother or father helping him with any application. Come to think of it he struggled to recall his parents helping him much with coursework, homework, or in fact much else in those years preparing for higher education. Kish felt his temples thump.

'Yes, let's go in, it's getting chilly,' replied Kish. Then his phone rang, flashing up *Natalie Watson—mobile.*

'Going to get that, dear?'

'Nah, its just work. Sabbatical's drawing to an end, I bet they just want to discuss my re-start date.' Kish collected a stack of plates and made for the kitchen, then briefly stepped out into the hallway to listen to the voice message. It was Natalie asking how he was and could they speak. *Bloody two-faced cheek.*

Shortly after 6:30am the following morning, Geoff prodded Humphrey with his foot, causing him to stir. 'What a bloody state.' His housemate laid facedown beside the van, stained shirt hanging out over the seat of his trousers, salmon-pink vomit beside him which, judging by Humphrey's hair, had been rolled into at some point during the night.

Humphrey turned over and looked up at Geoff. 'Where am I? And where've you been?'

'Following my lovely chat with Christina the ballerina, I wandered back here to find Rosie and Polly. You must have scared them off, as I couldn't find them. 'So there I was, at a loose end, desperate for a piss. I wandered off and well, you'd not believe it I chanced upon a young lady who'd turns out had mislaid her car. Carla her name was. I think.'

'Need I guess what happened next?'

'Well would you know, we found ourselves in the back of the van.'

'A pleasant image,' whimpered Humphrey. 'And all the while you were happily at it, you left me lying here? I could have died of exposure.'

'In July? I doubt it. Any case, I checked on you, gave you a blanket from the back of the van. Enough jibber-jabber, our work here is done.' With a feigned grimace, Geoff extended a hand and Humphrey slowly wobbled to his feet, groaning as he felt the cool dew that had seeped through his clothing. One of his eyes had gummed up, and his neck glistened with the shimmery trail of a slug that had journeyed over him at some point.

'I tell you, Geoff,' said Humphrey steadying himself, 'it was that ruddy sandwich. It nearly killed me.'

'Stop quibbling and get in,' Geoff replied harshly and turned the ignition on. 'And wind down your window. You stink.' *Okay, so I kept a couple of salmon sandwiches in the van on a warm day. But only for a few hours max?* More importantly Geoff still badly needed word from Ashton that he'd disposed of all the substitute wine bottles they'd used during the day, just as Geoff had done following the Boat Race and Ascot. Geoff smirked as he recalled last night's opera, The Coronation of Poppea. From what he could make out, the main thrust of it was that virtue is punished and greed is rewarded. Given the margin he made on the Debrays wine order, Monteverdi might just have got it right.

As they joined the M25 on the journey home, Humphrey craned his neck round, then calmly turned to Geoff, who was whistling obliviously to the radio, and groaned, 'did you forget something last night?'

'Uhh?'

'That girl you copped off with last night.'

'Carla, lovely girl. What about it?'

'Look's like she's just woken up in the back.'

THIRTY-ONE

Around 11:00am the next morning, Humphrey left the house feeling much better, and even more so as he passed Geoff snoring on the sofa, a brandy bottle slumped beside him. Despite leaving several messages all day yesterday, Geoff had not heard from Ashton, hence the several Convoisiers to calm himself.

Humphrey arrived at the winestore entrance and was met by Karen Williams, Bacchus' regional sales manager, her gleaming BMW 3-Series coupe parked alongside. From her expression, Humphrey could tell all was not right.

'You are over one hour late. Straight through to the office please,' she growled in her usual estuary English. Karen Williams had spent her life repping for several companies in the hospitality and beverages sectors, and was as tough as her shockproof laptop case. She possessed little finesse, simply a desire to win in her chosen profession, and never miss her monthly target. She was going to enjoy drubbing this couple of silverspoons. After all, it was she who drove the Beamer, not them, had worked her arse off for it, along with the apartment in Chiswick. *Who the hell did these lazy toffy-nosed sods think they were, lounging round all day, while she tried to run a profitable business?* Karen led Humphrey into the small room, which unfortunately for Humphrey still looked ramshackled since Geoff's burst water pipe incident.

'Jesus Christ! Just look at this place!' she yelled staring round the office. 'It's unacceptable!'

'A good morning to you, Karen,' said Humphrey pointedly. He'd not drop his standards of civility, even for blunt instruments like her. 'So what can I do for you?'

'Save the fluffy talk. Where's Geoff?'

Humphrey's brain engaged, 'I think he is on his way in. But I'm sure he mentioned that he had something he had to do at home, but—'

'Stop driveling—I want him here now, understand? You make me wait much longer and I promise to make this even harder for both of you. Starting with me calling the police.'

'Calling the police for being late? Surely that's a little extreme?'

'For God's sake, you think I'd be wasting my time on account of you being bloody late? Well don't just stand there. Get Geoff in here. Now!'

With that, Humphrey grabbed his mobile and ran out to the back of the store, dialling frantically. Despite the chronic hangover, the word 'police' had Geoff leap from the sofa and within minutes he bolted into the store office.

Karen did not waste any time laying into him. 'Geoff, as store manager, you are unacceptably late for work, the office is a mess and where the hell is your Bacchus Braves Polo?'

'Hi Karen, yes sorry, had a domestic issue. And I didn't have a clean Bacchus polo shirt so wore this red one as a best attempt at a substitute. And good morning by the way.' Geoff extended a hand. Karen didn't oblige him.

'You reek of alcohol,' she snapped.

'I'm afraid I didn't have time to shower when I got the urgent call from Humphrey.'

'So you usually turn up at this time?'

'Only when there's an unforeseen domestic issue,' Geoff replied sharply, somewhat misreading the situation. 'Can we get on with this please?'

'Don't give me that tone, and sit down!' screamed Karen. Geoff sat down.

'You were both at Glyndebourne on Saturday with Debrays. Both of you working behind the bar?'

There was a pause as Humphrey looked at Geoff then said. 'No, it was just me. Geoff was checking up on . . . guests.'

Geoff added, 'Karen if it's a case of me not pulling my weight I assure you I was working between the tent and the facility-'

Karen held her hand up to Geoff, silencing him, then squared up to Humphrey. 'Is this true? You were the only one serving?'

'Yes, Karen.'

'At seven-thirty this morning I received an official complaint from Toby Sarber-Collins at Debrays. He asserts that much of the wine you served on behalf of Debrays was not what Debrays paid us for.' Karen paused. 'If it's found that you swapped in and sold cheaper wine without Debrays or Bacchus' prior knowledge, you are officially in shit.'

'I don't understand,' volunteered Humphrey. His voice wobbled like it always did in the presence of an accusing authority. 'We checked-off all the wines with the Facilities Director that morning. A chap called Ashton.'

'Who?' snapped Karen.

'Roger Ashton, Debrays' Facilities Director.'

'Please don't feed me crap. The only person you liaise with is Toby.'

'I'm telling you Karen, I checked all the cases off against the list Ashton had. The cases were correctly labelled, and the quantity was spot on. Once done, this Ashton chap took them away.'

'So why would you not simply unpack them yourselves and store them in the Debrays tent, ready for Toby to check off?'

Humphrey paused. Karen had a good point. 'Because he and his helpers did it for us. We offloaded them to him first so he could sort through, then he delivered them to us in the tent. I swear it's true,' continued Humphrey shaking more now. 'Mr. Ashton came to see us by the van more or less as soon as we arrived. With his spaniel, Gideon I think.' Karen glowered at him. 'Karen, what I mean is he must be the one you need to track. Mr. Ashton that is, of course, not Gideon.' Humphrey paused again. *Just how much of that significantly cheaper Bolivinas Valley Chardonnay 2005 and Chateau Ste. Rochelle Sauvignon Blanc 2006 did we actually get through? From memory, a heck of a lot—far more than ten crates which was marked on the inventory. More like fifty or sixty. And the Trimbach and Barolo which all went so quickly, considering we were supposedly delivering twenty-five cases of each.* Humphrey began to flush.

'So basically you are saying arrived at the event, and someone who wasn't Toby took the wine off you, then delivered it back to your tent a short while later?'

'Yes,' said Humphrey. 'But now I think about it, it does appear a little overly bureaucratic. We just did as we were told.'

'Well until we've checked things out, such as Toby's evidence, you Humphrey are officially on suspension, pending potential disciplinary action. Please leave the premises immediately, and you will not return to this store until further notice. I have no more to say to you.'

'But I know that Roger Ash-' blurted Humphrey. Geoff gently squashed Humphrey's foot with his heel, stopping him. Humphrey shook his head then left the office, head bowed.

Alone with Geoff now, Karen looked at her watch, saying 'consider this your first and final warning. Toby has made a list of all the wine bottles he and his team collected afterwards, which I'll receive later today. I'm sending over a store auditor this Wednesday to check that the store inventory matches the books. If they don't match up down to the last sodding cork, you're out!' Karen didn't wait for acknowledgement and made her way to the store's entrance. Geoff followed.

'I can assure you that actually Humphrey—'

'Save it.' Karen stopped at the doorway. 'Just get cleaned up and run this fucking store. And wipe the van bonnet. Someone's been sick on it.'

As Karen tore off up Ferret Rise, Geoff locked the store door, turned off the store lights and walked to his nest at the rear. He perched on his warm box, eyeballing the insignia on his beer can. *I got greedy, thought I could push my luck. Got that Ashton sod involved.* Twenty-four hours until the store audit would unearth the true extent of his handiwork. *God knows what else they'd turn up.* He'd been deceitful and cowardly to his friend. He closed his eyes and tears squeezed through his eyelids. As his shoulders dropped, he began to sob for the first time in years.

At a small Italian café two doors down from the store, Humphrey was nursing his second hot chocolate, trying to make sense of it all. He looked down at his left shoe. The toe was scuffed where Geoff had twisted his leather heel down hard. *Why did he do that? Could Ashton have somehow duped Geoff on the wines, somehow swapping the original list for some cheaper alternatives?* That made no sense though: the wine was all good quality and that Washington State drop was exemplary. He'd seen it all named on the list for sure, yet just how much of it was anyone's guess.

'I fancied a change of scene too.' Humphrey looked up. Geoff was stood over him. His eyes were red.

'What the heck are you doing here? Karen will roast you if she finds out you've left the store.'

'Don't you worry about that. We need to talk.' Geoff collected a small cappuccino, and quietly retrieved his hipflask. Today was not a good day to give up alcohol.

'Hell we do. I'm not going down for this Ashton guy. Geoff, I swear to you, I did nothing. He's the issue here. I'm sure of it.' Humphrey was shaking.

'Calm down. I know you had nothing to do with it.' Geoff paused to pour some whisky into his drink then said, 'basically, the wine. A lot of it was swapped.'

'That sod Ashton! We must tell Karen.' Humphrey began to search the contact list on his mobile.'

Geoff clasped Humphrey's hand. 'Actually it was me who swapped them.'

'What do you mean?'

Geoff took a swig of his fortified cappuccino. 'Remember we did that silly blind test a couple of months ago, you know, as a bet for who got dinner? And I guessed it wrong?'

'Yes, but what's that got to do with it?'

'Well it got me thinking. You know we have latitude to swap in similar wines if we can't get the exact wine specified.'

'Up to ten percent of the order, wines of similar or greater value, at no further cost to the client.'

'So what if we substituted part of the total order with a box or two of wine that's of similar quality, but is actually much cheaper for us to supply?'

'Don't really know.'

'Well, I did just that. And Debrays still paid the original amount. Take the Boat Race. Debrays paid twenty grand for Champagne and wines and got a similar quality worth a total of nineteen and a half. I'd noticed at the Boat Race Toby seemed more interested in other things than to check every bottle against the original order, so at Ascot I took a risk. I increased the number of cases of cheaper wine. Twenty percent of the Champagne inventory alone was Pol Roger Brut Reserve, cheaper than the Pol Roger Blanc des Blancs which was the original version ordered. And at Glyndebourne I got more greedy and again increased the amount of cheaper wine I swapped in.'

'How much was swapped at Glyndebourne?'

'About half of it. But that's not the point. At the Boat Race and Ascot, I was the one who got rid of the bottles so there was no evidence I'd swapped in alternative wine. At Glyndebourne, Ashton was supposed to get rid of the empties, and Debrays would be none the wiser. Instead it turns out he went home early when he fell ill eating one of those sodding salmon sandwiches. Toby or one of his henchmen stumbled across the empties, did a cross-check with the order, found a disproportionately high number of empty bottles of unordered wine, and a very low number of bottles of wine they'd thought they ordered in, did a rough cost estimate and fancied they'd been sold short. Then the alarm bells went off.'

Humphrey looked at his hot chocolate. 'Suddenly I need something stronger.' Geoff obliged by tipping a generous slug of whisky into Humphrey's drink. 'What happened to the expensive stuff that presumably Debrays paid Bacchus HQ for, got delivered here but never made it to Ascot or whatever?'

'I sold it on the side, my special home deliveries etcetera, and used part of the profits to buy up the cheaper Washington wine directly off a supplier I know, off the accounts, and sell them via the Debrays gigs, but at an inflated price.'

'The supplier . . . it wasn't Ashton wasn't it?'

Geoff nodded. 'And at Glyndebourne he not only supplied me, but he bought from me the expensive wines I'd originally ordered and sold them on. So now God knows how it all stacks up but I've got until Wednesday to fix it.'

'Why?'

'Because on Wednesday, the store's stock is audited, and I need to account for four hundred-or-so bottles of specific wine that Toby believes never got to Glyndebourne. If I magicked them up, I'd get fired for gross incompetence, and if I can't locate them, I get fired anyhow and then get arrested for company theft. Anyhow chap, I plan to call Karen tomorrow and explain you're innocent in all this. All I ask is you bear with me until then.'

Humphrey was shaking. 'You know they'll throw the book at you.'

'Not relevant to this conversation. I just want to let you know I'm just very sorry. It wasn't ever my intention to get you involved, you know, if shit happened.'

Humphrey sat stunned. He was living with a common criminal. *In Putney Ferret of all places.* The odd bottle of breakage is one thing, but this was a whole new level.

'But why, Geoff?

Geoff drew his breath. 'I'm in debt Humph, worse than you know. Horrible, horrible debt.'

'I don't understand. How come?'

'I suppose I buy quite a few more beers a week than I admit, plus all the socializing . . . it soon adds up. Even excluding the beers and wine that come courtesy of fake breakages. So I had to dream up something else. This Debrays gig gave me the opportunity I needed to supplement the income and feed the beast.'

Humphrey bowed his head. He'd heard enough. 'If you don't mind, I think I'll stay here for a bit. Your toxic sandwich, along with all this latest bullshit has aged me.'

'Sure. Meet you outside the store at six. I'll drive you home.'

Geoff left Humphrey and returned to the store to consider his situation. He was in trouble. Real trouble. The order said he'd supplied among other things, ten cases each of Rauzan-Ségla 2005, Trimbach 2004, Vaudesir Grand Cru 2007, and Pio Cesare Barolo 2000. Which never got there. They weren't at the store either.

First things first, Geoff needed a stiff drink. He'd quit the booze tomorrow. *Well, cut back tomorrow. Next week at the latest.*

At 6:00pm, Geoff drove the back-up van down the store's side access lane. It was an ancient Ford Transit, and had barely scraped through its M.O.T. test last year. Its exhaust, clutch, fan belt, alternator, and windscreen wiper motor needed replacing very soon. Beneath the two years of accumulated dirt, it was apparently white. Humphrey hated that van. Less back-up, more last-resort.

'Humph, we need to take this one. The purple grape's virtually out of petrol.'

'Humphrey looked about him. 'Do we really need to get in that thing?'

'Yes. I can park an acceptable distance from the house. Do you mind if you drive? I'm way over the limit.'

Humphrey hesitated. 'Okay, move over,' he said, feeling far from okay himself. He wound down the squeaking window for some air, saying nothing, and nosed the van out onto Ferret Rise. It was several years older and far less easy to drive than the purple Citroen Berlingo, and being substantially wider he found himself driving close to the kerb to avoid any oncoming vehicle. As he made his way up Ferret Rise, his thoughts slowly turned toward possible lawyers, court, fines and-

'Watch out!' shrieked Geoff. There were two large bangs as something crunched into the van's left side, followed by a yell.

'What the fu-!' screeched Humphrey.

'Shit! I think you just hit someone!' gasped Geoff.

Humphrey checked his left wing mirror. It was missing.

Geoff craned his neck out of his window. 'Oh shite!' Geoff gasped. Forty metres back, a policeman was rapidly re-mounting his bicycle, and fumbling for his radio. 'You twatted a copper with your wing mirror!'

'What?! I must stop!' Humphrey signalled left and began to slow down.

Geoff turned to Humphrey face on. 'Listen to me. If you don't want to get fired, let alone breath-tested, you do as I say. Now!'

'I should stop. I'm sure I'm not over the limit!'

'You are at the very least on it, and yes you will be fired, you will be in court too.' Geoff scanned the scene behind them. 'He's peddling after you so put your foot down, and make a right!'

'But it's a built up area! It's still light! And this is hit-and-run!' Humphrey pleaded as he began to press down on the accelerator then make a rapid right.

'Good. Another right. All the way down then left on Upper Richmond Road. Faster! Get through those traffic lights before they go red!' Humphrey gripped the steering wheel and hurled the van left at the Putney Bridge lights just as they changed. Geoff barked,

'Now keep going!' Four minutes later they'd passed Barnes and were approaching East Sheen. 'Damn four stroke engine!' Geoff said, willing the van on. 'Now take the next left . . . there, and forty seconds later, 'Slower now, keep calm and take the next left. Then more slowly.' While Geoff desperately worked out their options, the van turned sharply into Vicarage Road in East Sheen.

'Oh Lord, what are we doing?' Humphrey cried.

'Pipe down. I'd say we have about three minutes before we get a patrol car on our arse. Turn right just up ahead at this triangle. Drive slowly alongside the park. We've got to time this perfectly.' Geoff ducked his head out of the window. Allotments to the right, and a bank of trees and a thick hedge to the left. *No houses. No police cyclist. No blue lights chasing them.* Geoff jumped over the back of his seat into the back of the van and removed the van's fire extinguisher that was clipped above a rear wheel arch. Geoff then said, 'Now lean away as far as you can from my side.'

'What? Why?' asked Humphrey.

'Just do it, and keep driving straight!' Geoff pulled the handle positioned above the slide-door behind the passenger seat, and slid open the van's side door. Checking his footing first, Geoff leant out, a strong wind buffered him, then he punched the fire extinguisher through the front passenger window, sending small grit-sized pieces of glass over the front passenger seat and floor.

'What the hell are you doing?' shrieked Humphrey, jerking left and sending Geoff swinging off the slide-door handle, his feet dangling madly outside the van.

'Just watch the road!' Geoff shrieked back, frantically pulling himself and the fire extinguisher back into the van. Seconds later Geoff said, 'drive right up to the end.'

'You've sent us down a bloody cul-de-sac! We're screwed? What now?'

'Calm down, this is perfect. Now just park up. Easy does it.' Humphrey parked behind an empty car, and turned off the engine. *No one around.* Geoff exhaled, then fumbled for his mobile. 'Hi, can I order a taxi please? Thanks . . . outside the Furrow Inn, East Sheen. Twenty minutes . . . great. Please don't be late.' Geoff put down his phone.

'What you doing?' asked Humphrey, ashen-faced.

'Saving your arse and mine. Now listen very carefully. Give me the keys, put this kagoule on to cover your Bacchus shirt.' Humphrey did exactly as he was told, and Geoff then said, 'I need you to walk across that small park behind us, towards the tennis courts. To the left of them is a small footpath. It connects with Stonehill Road, at which point you walk straight up. At the end of, turn right and walk along Sheen Lane 'til you get to Christchurch Avenue on the left. Go up Christchurch Avenue. The Furrow Inn is on the right hand side another two hundred metres up. When you get there, just sit outside on one of their benches. Don't go in, don't order a pint, don't take your kagoule off, don't say anything to anyone, understood?'

'Across to the footpath, up the road, then right, then left. Sit outside The Furrow, and do nothing. Okay got it.' Humphrey turned and walked rather awkwardly across the small park.

Despite the alcohol, Geoff thought clearly and worked quickly. First he clipped the fire extinguisher back in place, then rifled through the glove box and found himself a pack of tissues. He turned on the windscreen spray and soaked the tissues with wiper fluid. He meticulously rubbed the door handles, steering wheel, indicators, windscreen wiper switch, handbrake, seat belt buckle and housing, clipped the extinguisher back in its housing, wiped it and the latch down, the plastic surround by Humphrey's chair, and the interior door lock. Geoff ripped the plastic housing from around the ignition system and using brute force serrated the ignition wires with his door key, then he wiped the plastic ignition surround. He jumped out, leaving the driver door wide open, and placed the keys in his pocket. He grabbed a large, empty cardboard coffee cup wedged in the door pocket and used it to scoop up the shattered glass from the front passenger seat, then carefully placed the cup of glass upright into his jacket pocket, and made his way up the same pathway as Humphrey. He looked at his watch. He'd wiped down the van in twelve minutes flat. Which meant he'd got eight minutes to get to the Furrow pub and the taxi.

Geoff found Humphrey perched on a wooden garden bench outside the Furrow, and in the brief moment before the taxi turned up, he gave Humphrey further instructions. Humphrey said nothing during the ten-minute taxi ride back to Putney. About four hundred metres short of their house, Geoff signalled the driver to stop. 'Just here is absolutely fine thank you,' he said in a peculiar Scottish accent, prodded Humphrey and said. 'See you soon, Billy.' As agreed, "Billy" said nothing. 'On to Hyde Road,' Geoff instructed the driver.

From Hyde Road, a quiet street comprising small, charming Victorian cottages with extortionate price tags, Geoff walked back on himself to the store. There, he deactivated the alarm, put the van keys on their hook on the office wall, and made for the back exit, and passed under the broken CCTV camera. In the store's rear car park, he retrieved the cup full of glass from his pocket and tipped glass shards on the ground, roughly where the van's passenger window would have been barely forty minutes before. *Thank God for Karen's cutbacks*, thought Geoff. His watch said it was 7:15pm. He locked up behind him and returned to the office, keeping the lights on. While he waited for the police to arrive he completed the store receipts and made a couple of traceable phone calls and a fax to HQ concerning an upcoming German wine promotion. Working diligently, following Karen's harsh warning.

At 7:35pm, while Geoff was pushing round a broom at the front of the store, two police officers knocked on the glass frontage. He walked nervously to the entrance and opened up. He knew exactly what to say. 'Evening officers,' he started politely. Everything okay?'

'Excuse me, sir,' said the older-looking of the two policemen. 'Is this store the owner of a white Ford Transit van?' He read out the registration.

'Why yes. It's parked just behind the building. What's wrong with it?'

'We've found it parked about three miles away in East Sheen, with its window smashed in. Hotwired too, by the look of it. More to the point, we believe it was involved in a hit-and-run incident earlier this evening where a police officer was knocked off is bike. Mercifully, he was only slightly injured but it's a grave situation nonetheless,' said the younger officer.

'Goodness me!' Geoff exclaimed. 'That's awful.'

'Quite. Now would you show us to where you had it parked sir?' said the older officer. 'Certainly. Please follow me.'

Once out at the back, Geoff feigned total shock that the van was missing. 'Well this is where it was parked just hours ago,' he said vehemently.

The younger police officer tipped his torch down onto the ground. 'Look there, sir.' Geoff bent down. Glass fragments glinted under the torch's beam. 'Rest of the glass is on the van seat and footwell. But you still get some fall outside when the door opens. I'll get this photographed.'

'I just can't believe it got stolen from under my nose,' added Geoff. 'And in any case why not nab the nicer purple van there?'

'It's newer, better security. The old one's much easy to hotwire.'

'Was there anything in the stolen van?' added the older police officer.

Geoff paused. He was about to say no, when a thunderbolt hit him. *Humphrey I love you,* he thought.

THIRTY-TWO

'Yes, there was.' Geoff's mind was racing at the possible implications. 'Approximately three hundred bottles of high quality wine. Twenty-five boxes. I put them in there last week because—' Geoff paused. His second inspiration of the day flashed before him. *Of course!* '-because I couldn't keep them in storage. The lock to our storage room is very temperamental. Look.' Geoff grabbed the door handle. With two firm yanks and the door broke open. 'I've been onto HQ about it for weeks. And the broken video surveillance.' Geoff pointed up at a camera. The younger police officer made some notes and took some more pictures.

The older officer pulled back slightly. 'Have you been away from the shop at all today?'

'Me? No. Well I did step out for a few minutes at lunch and I know the van was there then. But I haven't been out back all afternoon truth be known and I wouldn't be able to hear a thing from in the office.'

'And you are sure your other van is secure, sir?'

'Yes, quite secure.'

'Good. Well depending on investigations this evening, we'll either have your transit van impounded or have it brought round later after we've examined it further at the scene. Could you remain here until we contact you later tonight?'

'Of course. I'll email our HQ too and let them know. Please follow me to the office. The van keys are there.'

Having exchanged pleasantries and waved the police off, Geoff walked back into the office and fired off an email to Karen summarising the evening's events. Insurance would have a field day with her, and he and Humphrey might actually be off the hook. Feeling more in control now, Geoff locked up behind him.

By 10:00pm, Geoff was back home with a glass of wine in his hand, recounting his conversations with the police to Humphrey. 'No prints at all. Police said the van had been wiped down.

Professional job by all accounts. Reckoned they hotwired the van, whoever they were and took it somewhere quiet to unload all that wine we'd been forced to leave in the back on account of the unsecure storeroom. No frigging camera working to film the scallywags either. Bloody Karen's incompetence saw to that.' Geoff began flicking through his post. 'I told HQ that I worked all day and you have been doing your own thing.' Humphrey said nothing. One letter had *BuildLearn Botswana* written across the top in red letters. 'God what do they need now?' said Geoff aloud. 'No doubt writing to tell me I'm forgetting about young thingummy.'

'What are you talking about?' said Humphrey, jarred by Geoff's show of fickleness.

'Oh, an African family I got sponsoring a few years back. This is a letter from the charity who funds the programme. Probably want me to renew my subscription. On a day like today, it's highly unlikely they'll get the most philanthropic version of Geoff Fox, I can tell you.'

Humphrey watch Geoff open the letter, and see his happy expression vanish slowly vanish. 'I'm off to bed. Night,' said Geoff, curtly.

'Night then,' said Humphrey emptily.

Geoff flopped on his bed and re-read the letter. Just as he thought he might be in the clear on one thing, something else had to come along. He unscrewed his hipflask and took a large swig.

Over coffee, Kish had been half-listening to his mother and Vilora discussing life at university. He'd chipped in here and there, offering his views on the carnage of Fresher's week, where to get a cheap laptop with all the right pre-installed software, and the best cure for a hangover.

'I don't drink, it doesn't interest me,' Vilora said. 'Even if I was allowed, I still would not,' she added. 'No need.'

Tiring slightly, Kish took off to bed early. Drifting off, he heard a small creak out on the landing. *Vilora making her way to her own room further down the corridor.* 11:00pm. He went back to sleep.

Kish turned his bedside light on. His iPhone now said 2:34am. Vilora's presence in the house was frustrating him on several levels now. His mother's connection with her, brought alive by those folders downstairs. *That Fadim bloke . . .* Kish rolled over, and tried to get back to sleep. It proved pointless, so he put on a dressing gown and went downstairs.

The study was cool, which helped Kish think more clearly. He began by choosing a red folder at random, it turned out to be the one marked "2007". The first thing he saw inside was a greetings card with a yellow bouquet on it, and the words 'Happy Mother's Day' printed beneath. *At last, something from me.* Smiling, he opened it up to read his comments. It was from someone else.

Dear Mother Diana, I am just getting used to calling you that. I think of father everyday . . .

Kish drew a heavy breath. He re-read Vilora's words before stuffing the card clumsily back into the folder. Something was missing still. *Vilora's father, Fadim. When did that correspondence start?* Sensibly he picked out the first folder on the shelf—the one dated 2002. This time he ignored the colourful handmade cards and focused on the large innocuous brown envelope with 'FD—EU, Kosovo' written on it. Contained inside wasn't boring work notes, but three handwritten letters. Each one of them was signed off with '*my love forever, Fadim*'.

> **Dear Mother Diana,**
>
> **You are so fortunate to have a son who travels doing so many great things. I dream of similar happiness for my Vilora as she grows so that she too can see a world beyond the troubles and pain she saw here. Unknowingly so many others are very grateful to you to have as a mother, for your kindness clearly extends through his work in Thailand and Laos to help people less fortunate than he . . .**

What the hell had she been saying? Him, helping people? Not exactly the images Kish recalled of his time in Thailand. Certainly the odd payment here and there, and always on his own terms. The next letter immediately piqued his interest.

> **My dear Diana, do you remember those times we sat together in St James' Park? After lectures when it was sunny. In our last call, you asked for a copy of the photo I've kept since my time in London. Please treasure it. After our last call it means more to me now than ever. My love for you now is as strong as it was then . . .**

Photo? What photo? He sifted through the collection of cards and letters. No photo though. He looked around the room. No picture though. No nothing.

'Chris? Are you down there?' His mother's voice, whispering from halfway up the stairs, made Kish jump. Kish stuffed the folder and its contents back among the others, grabbed the nearest book and left the study. His mother was leaning over the banister in her nightgown.

'Sorry, couldn't sleep,' Kish whispered. 'Needed a book to read. You go onto bed. I'll keep quiet.'

Kish gave his mother a few minutes to get back to bed and settle before he went back to his room. The best place for him right now was bed.

THIRTY-THREE

Humphrey was asleep when Geoff barged into his bedroom. Geoff had been up for two hours, reading the BuildLearn Botswana letter over and over, with a bottle of Amstel for company, and a dull buzzing feeling across his body. Another odd symptom to add to the others.

'Morning Humph. I need you to put your thinking cap on. I got a bad, bad letter.' Geoff leant his back against a bedroom wall as Humphrey rubbed his eyes and sat up. 'The family I sponsored . . . their eldest son, Tau . . . BuildLearn Botswana wouldn't tell me much, except that they don't want my money anymore because of a letter I wrote which arrived shortly after . . . after Tau died. Tau's dead. They say that my letter distressed the family . . . it was in exceptional bad taste on all levels . . . particularly hurtful given the years I've known them. The family thank me for my sponsorship up 'til now, but don't wish to hear from me again.' Geoff sagged and shook his head in his hands, white fingertips pushing through his greasy scalp. 'I need to ask, did you ever post a letter of mine?'

'You mean a letter several weeks ago to BuildLearn Botswana, in a silvery envelope? Yes, you told me to.'

Geoff lurched forward. 'I did?'

'Yes, you did. You were in the room but your brain was toast.'

'Oh shite.' Geoff flopped down on the floor, shaking his head. After a few moments he spoke. 'It all started by accident, if I'm honest. The charity connection. Fell in love with one of the local organisers when I was out in Botswana, building that bush school.'

'Did anything happen to you and the teacher?'

'Nope, but I wanted it to. I came home, back to the farm. She was all set to visit, me paying for her flight and all that. Then I got the worst letter I'd ever received.'

'And?'

Geoff pinched the bridge of his nose. 'She'd contracted HIV somehow. Never ever saw her again.'

'You never even wrote to each other?'

'She did at first. I didn't. I couldn't come to terms with it. So I just pottered round the farm for a summer, and then moved down to London. But I kept thinking about her, determined to remember her somehow. So I got in touch with BuildLearn Botswana when I got back and start sponsoring a family whose kids would use her school. That poor woman, it could so easily have been me, not her. Given the amount of times I've been round the block, just seems unfair. Who knows, if I keep carrying on chalking up one night stands perhaps, well . . . life's a lottery, chap.'

After pausing for thought, Humphrey said, 'Okay, first thing you do is calm down, and then you write to apologise for sending such a thoughtless letter.'

'Good idea. I suppose I could say it was my nephew or niece who wrote it, not me, but here's some money to go towards whatever you choose.'

Humphrey remained calm. 'No, you say it was you, and plead with them it was not intended to be sent and here's two hundred pounds to show you mean it.'

'So not say fifty then?'

'No.'

Geoff nodded then bounded downstairs. He found some plain white paper he'd removed for personal use from the store printer, and sat beside the coffee table. For the first time ever, Geoff was heeding Humphrey's advice, almost without question. He'd post the letter at lunchtime. Meantime, he needed to get ready and open up the store, early for once.

Elise walked into the store around 10.30am. She seemed tearful, and Geoff put the kettle on without a thought.

'I have my scan later today. Would you mind coming with me?'

Geoff hugged her. If he had a girlfriend like Elise, he thought, someone who just cared and loved him, he'd change everything that was wrong with him. Anything. Just for her.

Kish woke up, and instantly felt resentful. *How come this Fadim guy was sending his mother photos? And what exactly was Vilora up to with this "Dear Mother" nonsense?* Both questions stuck firmly in his mind throughout breakfast. Indeed he was in no mood for polite chatter much later as they drove to Salisbury for lunch. At least with him driving, it provided him the excuse for limited engagement. 'Sorry if I'm a little quiet, still getting used to your car, Mum.' He also remained distant over lunch in Salisbury Cathedral's refectory restaurant. On the return journey to Bath, Diana let Vilora try her hand at driving, magnetic 'L' plates on. 'Don't worry, Chris. I've already seen to it she's insured.' It was when Diana insisted they stop for a brief walk in the Wylye Valley, that Kish changed tack. A provisional hug with his mother seemed to make Vilora smile more. And this wasn't lost on Kish, who hugged his mother a little more than he might normally. He got more smiles.

Kish made quick work of a light evening meal prepared by Diana and Vilora, then made his excuses and spent the remainder of the evening sat at his mother's PC. He downed a glass of red then scanned his personal Gmail—nothing much of interest from anyone, and nothing from Elise which riled him. *As if it's for me to mail HER.* He then set about flicking through Linkedin, seeing who'd checked his profile, and onto Facebook. Elise's Facebook page had not been updated in over a month. He poured himself another glass of wine, and necked half of it. Next he googled "Kosovo war pristina". Over the past week, he'd spent several hours reading articles concerning Kosovo in the late 'nineties, the massacres, the alleged war crimes that continued to be investigated. This evening he focussed on the capitulation of Pristina in 1999, and articles on the waves of refugees forced to trudge across to neighbouring Albania.

Diana made it to about 9:00pm before popping her head round the door, bidding her son good night through a yawn. No sooner had he heard his mum's door close, Kish went tactical. *This is it,* he thought. He logged off and then made for the lounge, carrying two glasses and a freshly opened bottle of Rioja. Sure enough, Vilora was curled up on the sofa, busy reading her university guidebook.

'Mind if I join you?' Kish asked, smiling.

'But of course.'

We've both experienced life's problems, he reasoned. *Who said losing family members through armed conflict was any worse a wrench than him not speaking to his father who was still alive yet practically estranged?* Just like her, he'd encountered problems. Like her, his life had been spoiled by power-crazed bullies. For him, it was Gribbin. Her, a bunch of heavily armed Serb paramilitaries. *And yet they shared the same familiar, common denominator. His mother.* Kish stood beside the sofa and looked once more down at Vilora, who flicked unawares through her guidebook. Kish gawped at her frame, causing his toes to curl involuntarily. She had the most unbelievable midriff and hips. Her outfit showed them off so well. *She probably calls it fashion,* thought Kish. He called it willful seduction. *Time to test the water.* Kish took a swig of wine, which warmed his gullet and before he knew it, he'd sat down next to her. Kish began by asking knowing questions about Kosovo. Questions about the town of Pristina, and what it looked like. She answered the questions in a considered way, mirroring the manner in which he asked them, and all the while, he pondered whether his attraction to her was genuine, or simply a matter of seducing the enemy. Once or twice he remembered Elise and placed her firmly at the back of his mind. It would interfere less there. He then poured a small glasses of wine and handed it to Vilora.

'Thank you Kish, but you know I am not liking alcohol.'

'Of course. Stupid me. Forgot.' Kish poured her glass into his. His mother must be asleep by now, so he moved the conversation on as discreetly as he could. 'Your life has certainly been rather full. I feel very privileged to hear more about you.' He smiled gently. Vilora smiled back. Yes, he was a warm and caring person, just like in his mother's emails. Kish kept smiling sweetly, then said, 'This is very embarrassing.' He perched himself back beside her.

'What is?' Vilora enquired innocently.

Kish ducked his head, looking upward. He smiled. 'I find you very beautiful person.'

Vilora remained seated. 'Thank you. And you are very polite man.'

'Yes, but I want to be very rude.'

'Excuse me?'

Kish sighed. 'Sorry, I have . . . how do you say, naughty thoughts.' He smiled. 'Would you let me kiss you?'

Vilora moved back a little, suddenly feeling less relaxed. *Wasn't he in a long-term relationship with his American girlfriend?* Even though he had said very little about her, Diana had told Vilora about Elise on several occasions, and always with affection. 'So, do you not have girlfriend then?' said Vilora as she casually picked up her glass and held it. Her father had always told her that holding a full glass of liquid was a good thing when talking to a man. Just in case.

Kish considered her response. She hadn't refused him. 'Elise has left me,' he replied. That was true enough, even if it was temporary. 'We have', he paused deliberately, 'problems that we cannot fix.'

Vilora wanted to ask him more questions, at least offer an ear. He looked so sad. He was certainly attractive, even if a little older. But still it wasn't worth thinking about. Since her youth, she'd imagined him more a distant family relation, so she simply smiled and held his hand in sympathy.

Kish reached out and took her glass. 'Just kiss me,' he whispered.

Vilora kept a firm grip of the glass, and giggled nervously. 'No, but goodnight hug. Like cousin,' she replied.

'Oh don't say things like that,' replied Kish. Vilora felt him cup the back of her head and push his lips against hers. She let out a nervous chuckle from the side of her mouth, and now tried to tilt her head left, away from him, all the while trying to balance her glass of wine.

'Now Kish, be good, let us talk first,' she managed to say, contorting her mouth as his lips followed her. Just then, she then felt a gentle brush against her right breast. It was not the first time a boy had tried to touch her, but that was silly playground stuff with little boys her own age. Kish was different. She was different, older now. And he was older than her. He was bigger too, far stronger than she. Her heart pounded with all the uncertainty of the world, as Kish weaved his fingers under the knitted top and upwards.

In his fug, Kish reckoned at best she was letting him proceed, teasing him at worst. *Capitulation imminent.*

Vilora tried to pull herself away from him. Nigh impossible now that his hand was under her head and his weight more fully on her. Kish pushed his head down toward hers, much harder now to kiss her as passionately as he could. He made a small groan as he did. And suddenly Vilora thought about his mother upstairs. She thought about everything she'd been taught. *This isn't right.*

Upstairs a door slammed harder than usual, briefly distracting Kish and providing Vilora with instant resolve. She wriggled to her right, and then with some effort forced Kish away. He wobbled with his glass in one hand, and unable to steady himself, he slipped off the sofa, his head colliding with the edge of the mahogany coffee table.

Kish lay on his back, wine-soaked and motionless.

'Oh my goodness, no!' Vilora cried, and leaped up. She sped from the lounge, her sandals making a loud slapping sound with every step across the hall's Victorian tiles and into the kitchen. There she grabbed a roll of kitchen towels, a hand towel, and rushed back.

'Are you okay?' she asked, kneeling down beside Kish.

'Crickey. What happened?' Kish groaned back, and scooped himself off the floor and flopped onto the sofa.

Satisfied Kish had not sustained injuries, Vilora began dabbing the drenched, stained carpet, working fast, not looking up. She eventually left the room with a handful of wine-soaked tissues, then made her way upstairs. Seconds later Kish heard a bedroom door quietly clicked shut. *What the hell had just happened? Perhaps she didn't want a kiss after all?* Everything seemed confused. *No doubt things'll be clearer in the morning.* Seconds later Kish was in a deep sleep, his lips still red with Vilora's bright lipstick.

Kish did not notice the figure stood silently in the doorway, lingering for one more moment then turning her back on her son, and weeping all the way to bed.

In Putney Ferret, Elise put down her mint tea, and looked at the smudged image from the twenty-week scan. Geoff hovered over her, eyes wide. 'And a whole twenty centimetres in length,' she said. Elise had chosen this moment to tell Geoff about the recorded meeting Kish had left on her phone several weeks ago. 'Whether he deserves it or not, Kish is in trouble at work and I don't know what to do.'

THIRTY-FOUR

Kish awoke at 6:20am on the lounge sofa, and instantly groaned. Once the events of last night became clearer, he decided to leave for Putney Ferret well before his mum or Vilora emerged. In his opinion, the brief note he slipped under Vilora's door would adequately explain his regretful actions last night. Writing it was a risk; she might show someone. In the kitchen, he quickly re-read his note to his mother. It mentioned some issue at work that needed his urgent attention, and how he didn't want to wake her up unnecessarily. He propped it beside a vase of flowers that provided a pleasant centrepiece to the ancient breakfast table, and knowing he needn't rush, gave the kitchen one last look around. He knew he might not see it for a while. It was not long before he was drawn to the photo on the windowsill, the one of him as a very small boy. He picked up the frame and stared at this image of him smiling, taken . . . maybe twenty-five years ago? It was around then that his dad had begun to call him Kish. 'Kish' was how as a small boy he'd mispronounced his own name. Next to it was that damned photo of his mother, stood alongside Fadim and Vilora. But the pine frame had been replaced with the silver frame Vilora had presented her a few weeks back. No indication of when the photo was taken. Intrigued, he unclipped the back of the frame. Perhaps his mum had written something on the back of the photo. As he removed the photo mount card, a smaller photo dropped to the floor. He picked it up and read the scratchy handwriting.

St James' Park, London, November 1981. Please remember our special time together. Then as in now, I love you. Fadim Dimas. (December 2002).

Kish turned it over, revealing small colour photograph of a young, happy-looking couple sat on the grass under a tree, their arms around each other, heads touching. It was his mother and a young man. Kish's heart began pounding and his ears thumped at the words. *St James' Park . . . a photo . . . taken in St James Park in 1981?* Then he remembered. Of course, the perplexing note from Fadim that was in that brown envelope in his mothers folder marked '2002'. The envelope, it was marked 'FD—EU Kosovo'. FD must have stood for Fadim Dinas. Kish stared at the photo then the works on the back. 1981 . . . the date, the maths . . . *But Mum was already with Dad around then?*

'Chris?' It was his mother's voice.

Kish hastily returned the photos into the frame.

'Chris? There you are.'

Kish span around to see his mother stood on the kitchen door threshold. She saw him holding the silver photo frame; his eyes looked like they were burning. It was a look she'd seen many times before. The little boy who couldn't work out why something wasn't as he thought it should be.

'After last night I thought you might be gone already,' she said ambiguously, momentarily leaving Kish unsure if it was he or her who should feel more upset.

Kish decided to cut with the pleasantries. 'I left you a note, trouble at work. Time to go I'm afraid, Mum.'

'You sure that's the only reason?'

Kish looked down. 'Well that and I don't think you want me around.'

'Really?' Diana was not one for over-reacting these days, though she felt torn by a mother's intuition to both love and discipline an errant child.

For Kish this was it. Time to get this off his chest. *Say it and be out the door in minutes.* He drew his breath. 'Face it, you don't want me here, so why keep up the façade.'

'I'd be very upset if you meant that,' said Diana.

'Of course I mean it. And it only took a few weeks, but I can see it so clearly now. You want me out of the picture. You've got someone else who calls you Mum, and you love that. What, she adopted or something?'

'You mean Vilora? I'm unsure what right you have to even discuss her. Fact remains she asked if she could call me Mum, and I was honoured.'

'But she's not your daughter.'

'You don't need to be related to love like a mother to a daughter.' Diana remained standing.

'Okay, so if she is so damn important how come you never told me much about her?'

Diana paused before responding. 'Perhaps the real question you should ask is to yourself. Why you chose not to take an interest and find out.'

'Well I . . . Jesus, it's like I've just entered into a relationship that I never knew existed, then find out my mother has taken in a complete stranger from some poxy country in southern Europe, who I'm suddenly expected to embrace as an adopted sister? Is that it?'

'You should calm down a little. In fact—'

Kish wasn't listening. 'And another thing, where are the letters I wrote?'

'Letters you wrote?' Diana said incredulously. 'Exactly what letters Chris? What letters or emails have you ever sent me?

Kish scrambled. 'I can't exactly remember too much correspondence from you either. Postcards usually, and the odd Easter card. Whereas, judging by the volume of stuff from Balkan-kid, you must have sent her a similar boatload.'

'Chris, that's unfair. Of course I want to be in regular communication with my only child. I've made many an effort over the years. I'm the one who initiates a phone call with you, rarely is it I get a call out of the blue, unless of course it refers to something you need. And you rarely acknowledged any such postcard or letters at Easter. I got the message you'd rather not be bothered by your interfering old mum. Even now, when I send you a lengthy email, all too often I get nothing more than a quick response that appears to have been run off between meetings, and without much thought. An email back that's more than being told your fine and work's okay and Elise is fine and the house is messy. Or even a phone call to say hello for just a minute or two. But you don't. You never did, so I've just grown to accept it. It hurts me to write and know from the moment I begin, it won't lead to much in return.' Diana paused, maintaining an unfaltering stare into Kish's eyes. 'Sooner or later you will have to realise that maintaining a relationship takes dialogue and communication, of any sort. Do you even keep my cards I've sent to you?'

Kish sniffed. Highly unlikely, and even if he did keep anything, they were probably scattered around the house back in Ferret, dispersed across communal drawers shared with receipts, spare keys, old batteries, and other detritus belonging to God knows who. But most likely, scooped up and binned along with old bills and window cleaner flyers. 'You know what your problem is?' he fired back tersely.

'No but I imagine it's better for both of us if you told me,' Diana replied calmly.

'You just can't get emotionally close with your own. You only get close to strangers and their problems and get your kicks from feeling wanted by newly formed acquaintances. Of course Vilora's going to need you more than me for Christsake. I'm living in Britain, self-sufficient and well off. What's she got before you came along? Nothing, so you become steadfast for her, she feels totally smitten by your love and ends up limpet-like on you. Within a few short years gives you the title of mummy. And you, you're not close to anyone else, so you feel fulfilled at long last.'

'What are you saying?' There was pain in Diana's voice for the first time.

'I'm saying, you thrive on the attention of strangers in need. Being loved. In fact I'd go further. Vilora gives you some meaning.'

Diana recoiled. 'And you think that meaning has come at the expense of something? Or perhaps it's filled a void? I have always loved you unconditionally, but I have gradually had to accept you don't need me. It hurts so much, of course it does, especially now, but I accept it.'

'Don't need you?' Kish stood up and faced his mother. 'Did you ever ask if I needed you? Oh, and then you have some cancer scare just to get me here and bloody rub my nose in the fact you need someone else more than me.'

'Chris, don't say that,' she pleaded. 'I called you and Vilora because I wanted to spend time with you both before its too late. Of course I needed your support. But I wouldn't dare demand it.'

'Save the emotion. Rather late for that.'

'Do you know what you are saying?' Diana wanted to reach out, but stopped. 'I'm still your mother. And what I face is something you can't possibly imagine.'

Kish curled his lip and barged past his mother. 'All I see is you putting a bloody stranger before your own son. Feeling guilty now?'

'Guilty? Why on earth do you say that?'

'She's the living memory of her father. Yeh, I know now how you loved him.' Kish tossed Fadim's note onto the breakfast table. 'More than you loved dad? But I'm guessing now that Dad was second best from the outset. No surprise neither you nor he in all likelihood invested in it, so it cracked and ended. I guess that makes me cracked, soiled goods too. Not all clean and virtuous like lovely young Vilora, because she is part of someone who you loved. I'm not.' Kish barged past his mother and into the hallway.

'Chris, please,' quivered Diana as she followed him down the hallway towards the front door. 'You need to realise something.' His image blurred as her eyes filled. She still had so much to tell him.

Vilora stood halfway up the stairs, wearing a pair of green pyjama-bottoms and a blue t-shirt. As he rushed along below her, she said, 'Kish, why are you so selfish and pathetic?' then tossed his crumpled note at him. 'And who is the real Kish anyway? I am person who thinks you was so nice, in stories from your mother to me. I felt I might have friend in you, brother maybe even. I keep thinking you were in my mind as a kind and warm man. But you are not. Your mother may die and I know what it is like to have a parent dying. But you just think about you.'

Kish spun around and bore his face directly into Vilora's. Like last night but this time without a smile. He saw the fear in her eyes, she saw the utter hatred in his. Kish collected his holdall and without looking back he sneered, 'Button it. Nice trade, Mum,' then grabbed the door.

'She kept everything you ever wrote to her!' Vilora shouted. 'Since you were a baby. She tell me!'

Kish slammed the door. No going back on this one. Not ever. Closure on an already decaying relationship.

Ten minutes later, a few miles up the A46, he indicated left and broke hard, coming to a complete stop in the hard shoulder. Kish stepped out from his car and began gasping. *Mum may die.* It hung there in the cold morning air. Vilora knew the true extent of his mother's illness, because she was the only one who his mother had probably confided in. As cars dashed past on the busy road, only now did he realise why Vilora was over. His mother might not last much longer. He stared westward again, then got back in his car.

Two hours later Kish entered his house on Ferret Rise, and immediately headed to his bedroom. He could simply phone his mother and apologise, tell her he loved her and that he was just a selfish little boy who put his own small concerns before anything or anyone else. He could confess he was close to losing his job. He could tell her why. He could explain that Elise was pregnant. *Elise.* He'd left her reeling, alone, and he had no idea what she was thinking. What his mother must be thinking of him. What anyone was thinking of him. An email from Rachael Frears' PA popped up on his mobile. He was required in the office on Tuesday morning, 9:00am. *Get sentenced.*

Kish turned his mobile phone off and slid under his duvet.

Three miles away in Wandsworth, Geoff put down his tea. 'I've got to get back, Elise.' He saw her smiling, and paused before adding, 'But I really think you should tell Kish.'

'Like I said, I will think about it.'

Geoff kissed her and wandered down past the Alma Tavern toward Wandsworth Town train station. Elise poured herself another cup of mint tea and began to well up. This emotional mix-up with Geoff made things far less black and white. Somehow she wasn't the only victim now, no matter how she justified herself. Kish was still a bastard, but she was not going to leave the bastard hanging, even if he did deserve all he got. Elise logged onto her laptop and replayed the 'wav' file she'd downloaded from her voicemail weeks ago. She'd need to contact the right person in Mironic—sending it to Kish would have been easier but she couldn't communicate directly with him just yet—she was unsure how she'd react with him. Elise trawled through the biographies of key people featured on Mironic's main website. All bigwigs in the US. She needed to get to the local office. She navigated her way to the Mironic UK site and began the same trawl as before. The name of someone heading up their Legal or HR organisations. Nothing came back. *Another approach was needed.* Elise logged onto Linkedin.com and in the site search bar typed 'Director of Human Resources Mironic', and for good measure added 'UK', then clicked 'search'. At the top of the list of names returned was someone called Rachael Frears. She was ranked as a '2nd' connection meaning one other person knew both of them. Chris Reece. It also meant that Elise could invite her directly to connect. Elise paused then wrote:

Important information concerning your investigation of Chris Reece:

Dear Ms Frears,

Sincere apologies for the unconventional introduction. I hope I have the right person. I understand Chris Reece is on leave pending investigation for misconduct. I know this only because I am his girlfriend, and I have in my possession a recording of what appears to be a conversation between Chris Reece and another employee at Mironic, who I think is Mike Gribbin. I urge you to call me as soon as you get this so I can send it to you or the relevant person at Mironic. I have no interest in pursuing this issue further or publicly other than making you personally aware.

Best regards, Elise Hall.

Elise signed off with her mobile phone number and logged off. Like every other day for the past seven weeks, she felt nauseous and needed to lie down.

THIRTY-FIVE

The next morning, Monday, Kish flicked on the TV in his bedroom. Jeremy Kyle was performing his usual interrogation-cum-DNA test on his latest guests, a young looking couple. According to the screen subtitles, the young man *"denies he's the father of his girlfriend's child, and doesn't care even if he is"*. Kish studied the man. Twenty at a push, unkempt hair and clothes, feral looking with translucent teeth and a pasty complexion, and now busy denying any responsibility in front of a gobsmacked, baying audience. Jeremy Kyle asserted he had no self-respect, zero respect for others, and little hope or care for the future. A self-harming, self-defeated man, barely out of his teens. As Jeremy Kyle prepared to read out the results of the DNA test, Kish looked at the girlfriend. She didn't look much healthier than her boyfriend, except for one thing. Her eyes. The eyes were alive and determined. Tired looking and a little bewildered, she hadn't been broken, gone under. She apologised to the presenter for being there at all, said she felt shameful, and told her boyfriend she just wanted what was right for her, their baby. Two people thrown into parenthood, and how differently they'd approached it. Kish leant back. The pathetic young man on TV hadn't had his education, his money or any of the other advantages he'd been afforded. With that he fell asleep again.

Kish woke at 12:00pm and turned his mobile back on. Nothing from Elise. A missed call from his mother though. 'More insults no doubt,' he mumbled, and didn't bother listening to her voicemail. His phone rang a moment later, it was Natalie Watson and before he could think, he'd already answered.

'What the hell do you want?'

'Please don't put the phone down on me. I am in so much trouble and I don't know what to do.'

'Heart bleeds for you,' said Kish, now regretting taking the call.

'I'm entirely to blame for all this hell you're going through . . . Gribbin promised me your job, if I played along and did exactly what he wanted. I found out you are due back in tomorrow to face the music. I had to get hold of you first, and tell you.'

'Tell me what?'

'Tell you that I agreed to say things to support his case against you to edge you out. He reckons he's got enough now to do it.' Natalie spent the next ten minutes telling Kish about Gribbin's plan, about how he'd coerced her into helping removing Kish. About her getting too close to Gribbin, crossing the line. 'I am so very sorry, I didn't know what to do.'

Somehow Kish remained calm. 'Well I do. Are you in the office still?'

'No, I'm up in London. Just met with the Communities and Local Government bods up near Victoria.'

'Good. Meet you in one hour. The entrance to the Grosvenor Hotel on the Victoria Station concourse. We can talk over a coffee there.'

An hour and ten minutes later Kish and Natalie were tucked inside the Grosvenor Hotel bar, huddled over two cappuccinos. Kish said, 'so this is what I'm proposing.'

Kish and Natalie parted company forty minutes later. Considering his current relationships with various females, for Kish, meeting Natalie was a fillip. Tomorrow was going to be a good day and she was his ticket out of Mironic.

As Kish made his way to platform sixteen, Kish's phone buzzed. It was his mother again, and he ignored it.

Natalie was walking in the opposite direction when she switched her phone back on. A bevy of texts instantly appeared, all of them from Gribbin.

1:27pm Urgent you ring me asap!

1:30pm Tried u again. Why you not answering? Your diary says you are free

1:40pm Left office. HR suspects. Need to speak. Ring please. Not good.

Natalie called Gribbin, and he instantly picked up. 'Jesus Christ! Finally! Do you think I have all day to piss about!' he hissed. 'Did you speak to him?'

'Calm down Mike. I did one better. We met up and based on what I told him, Chris is out. I suggest that when you meet with HR, tell them exactly what we agreed. I'll stick up for you, honey, I promise.'

Gribbin exhaled slowly, then ended the call with a hasty goodbye.

Kish was stood at Clapham Junction Station waiting for the Putney train when Gribbin's name flashed up on his mobile's screen. It was the call he was waiting for. 'Hello Mike.'

'Chris, I trust you've seen the HR mail?' he asked coarsely.

'Yes, of course.'

'Good. Tomorrow morning, nine o'clock. Rachael Frears' office. I imagine it should only take thirty minutes. And don't be late.' Gribbin hung up abruptly.

Looking forward to it, thought Kish as he boarded the train home.

THIRTY-SIX

Shortly before 9:00am the following morning, Kish peered into Rachael's office through the glass frontage. The seating plan was the same as the previous, memorable occasion several weeks ago: Rachael sat behind her desk, and beside it, another chair, presumably awaiting Gribbin's bony arse, and a lonely-looking third chair Kish guessed was for him. Rachael was on the telephone, and Kish knew not to enter until explicitly directed to.

'Well this is a pretty thing isn't it?' Gribbin snarled behind him.

Kish turned round calmly. Gribbin's damp eyebrows suggested he must have just freshened up in the nearby bathroom. Nervous then. 'Not sure I'd call it pretty Mike. Besides, I can't see how your word can weigh more than mine, particularly as half of it is complete fantasy.'

Gribbin double-checked Rachael's door was closed, then motioned Kish to step a few feet away. 'You really think this is about the truth? Oh, you amateur. Her complaint merely served a purpose. Allowed me to imply a few things about you, spin just a little. And guess what, Natalie has ended up telling me all sorts of things about you.'

'Meaning?'

Gribbin hesitated. Say too much, Kish could formulate a defence. Then again, Kish needed softening up before seeing Rachael, and thus capitulate quicker and more dramatically. Who knows what he might reveal if he suddenly felt truly cornered. 'Lets just say you've compromised your integrity as a manager by consorting with a female report, tut-tut, and worse, deliberately holding her, i.e. Natalie, back. Rachael is very keen on conserving a woman's professional integrity in this organisation. And here's the sweet irony, Reece. Natalie told me everything over a pleasant weekend away.' Kish said nothing. Gribbin's whole rationale for getting rid of him began to make sense. He'd gone visceral. 'The trouble with

286

you Reece is you got in the way. You chancing on me and Natalie in the stairwell that time, I don't like the thought of you peeking into my personal life, and I don't want you around professionally. I need conformists. People I know will do what I want, and who I can subdue or trust to behave. With you I don't get either. I just don't think it's in my best interests you stay around.'

Kish stared back, recounting his own unfortunate timing in the stairwell those few weeks ago, something Natalie hadn't told him about last night. 'So it was Natalie and you up there?'

Gribbin paused, then snorted with laughter. 'Hilarious! There was me assuming you knew it was us, when you didn't? Well now you know for sure.'

'So who is my replacement then Mike? Let me guess. Natalie?'

'You catch on fast,' Gribbin wheezed softly, 'but with the re-org I've been influencing, the wonderful thing is she won't be reporting to me.'

'Just how you wanted it. After all there's no rule about having a relationship with a colleague who doesn't report to you.'

'Quite. In fact,' Gribbin pointed towards Rachael through her glass-fronted office, 'I wouldn't be surprised if it's her on the phone with Rachael right now.'

Gribbin's insipid smile left Kish cold. The terrible truth now dawned on him. Natalie had used last night's meeting not to help him, but to help Gribbin. Before Kish could remonstrate any further, Rachael swung her office door open.

'Good morning Gentleman.' Her voice was firm. 'Please come in.' Gribbin smiled smugly, and the back of Kish's knees began to sweat.

'After you Chris,' Gribbin said. He'd make certain that this time round, Kish couldn't make a break.

Rachael wasted no time outlining the facts to Chris. 'This meeting follows a previous meeting in late March when I informed you of a serious allegation made against you by a colleague, Natalie Watson.' Rachael took off her half-rims and looked plainly at Kish. 'Chris, following discussions this morning, I need to inform you that Natalie has revised her story. This forms the basis of a new, but equally serious charge of misconduct.'

'I'm afraid I don't know what you are talking about,' started Kish.

Gribbin jumped in. 'Of course you'd say that. Well what you think doesn't really matter.'

'Mike, if I may remind you of the correct procedure.' Rachael paused then said to Chris, 'Mike has instituted formal proceedings about you regarding your relationship with Natalie Watson. Mike, feel free to explain.'

Kish's phone buzzed. Another missed call from his mother. And a text, which he deleted without reading.

'Certainly Rachael,' said Gribbin, visibly pleased. 'Natalie Watson has confirmed that Chris' highly public fraternising in the Chiswick bar in March was one of several instances where Chris made suggestive and inappropriate comments to her. Mironic forbids any such misconduct. The offence is all the more appalling when undertaken between managers and their reports. Furthermore, it is my assertion that Chris Reece deliberately held her back from promotion when his sexual advances were not welcomed.'

Rachael turned to Kish. 'Chris, do you wish to confirm or deny your behaviour with Natalie?'

The back of Kish's knees felt damp and itchy as he responded slowly. 'I firmly deny ever having had a relationship with Natalie or talking with her in any compromising manner. For full disclosure, Natalie and I may have had a very brief kiss over a year ago. It was while celebrating a great quarter, it was convivial, not what you might call sensual, but yes, we both felt a little stupid the following Monday morning in the office nonetheless. Other than that, I've been polite, smiled and confided with her on a couple of things but that's as close as it gets. I've certainly not fraternised.'

Gribbin rocked back. 'So it's your word against hers. That's rich, because I have evidence from Natalie that-'

Rachael's stare over her half-rims cut him short, before Rachael said, 'Chris, at anytime have you tried to hold Natalie back, or compromise her professionally in any way from moving up.' Rachael flicked through what looked like annual assessment printouts. She'd spot inconsistencies, any indicators he was marking her performance incorrectly, from a mile off.

'Never,' Kish replied flatly. 'Natalie is a top performer, and the performance ratings I've given her clearly reflect her attainment and skillset. She is young, ambitious and capable. The concerns I raised with Mike shortly before I was put on leave was that she'd only got eighteen months' sales experience, no management experience, and I truly believed then, as I do now, that she needs a further year or so before she is ready to step up into leading a team of salespeople. At no time would I deliberately hold her back though.'

Rachael made some notes and read from her screen. 'Following a call with Natalie Watson late last night, I have asked her to kindly join us.' Rachael motioned to Natalie, who had been stood outside, to come in. Gribbin smiled. Kish tried in vain to catch her eye as she sat down. Rachael continued, 'Natalie, I know from our conversation on the phone last night has been a most sickening and disturbing situation for you. It is your turn to give your side of the story. Please, take your time.'

Kish looked down at his feet and prepared for the worst. Gribbin rocked back and looked hatefully at Kish.

THIRTY-SEVEN

Natalie cleared her throat. 'A few months ago at a bar in Chiswick, Chris Reece took me to one side and told me that I was to be careful not to attract the wrong attention from certain male managers in Mironic.'

'Define "wrong attention",' said Rachael.

'He was clear. He told me I was young, physically attractive and that in certain work situations, I might expect the odd flirt.'

'You see now, Rachael?' Gribbin blurted. 'He was clearly trying to fraternise with her, discussing her physical appearance in a very inappropriate manner. He's unbelievable.'

Natalie continued. 'And when we spoke again last night, he asked me flat out if I was having an affair with Mike.'

'How dare he make such preposterous allegations!' Gribbin's face creased. 'It's clearly stated in our ABC policy that such behaviour won't be tolerated.

'And Natalie, how do you wish to respond?'

Natalie paused. She glanced at Gribbin, then to Kish. *This is it,* thought Kish who was still staring at the floor. Gribbin smiled.

'Mike Gribbin and I have indeed been have been in a relationship. It more or less started when he took over as the Head of Government Sales. At the beginning he said he'd mentor me, get me promoted faster. He started telling me how I could head up security sales, and that he just needed to work on a few things first. Initially it was quiet chats after work, up the pub, and Chris' name came up a lot. Mike would talk about him negatively, asking my opinion. Then, just after Chris got put on leave, my relationship with Mike got physical. Very casual and discreet. A few nights away here and there. I was flattered by the attention, quite honestly.'

'Can you tell me how your initial complaint about Chris arose?' asked Rachael.

'It was at that bar in Chiswick. At the time Mike and I were increasingly spending time together outside work. It was later on, and Chris joined me at the bar, thanked me for my efforts, and again told me to watch out for unnecessary attention. But Mike, well he'd been watching on, and I guess he didn't like seeing Chris holding me, hugging me almost. It was a compliment he was giving me, a professional one too, and when Chris left the bar, he-, Mike that is, got angry with me. Told me I had hurt my own reputation by overtly fraternising with my manager in front of Mironic customers. He said a few customers had remarked on it to him. I told him I was very sorry for any harm caused, and how might I fix the issue. Mike said he'd consider stepping in and support me, should any complaints arise that is, provided I made a formal complaint about Chris, basically stating he'd overstepped the mark in the bar, behaved inappropriately to a female colleague. Panicking, I agreed. But I honestly didn't get offended by anything Chris did. He wasn't being lewd. A bit friendly but that's it. Not a problem for me.'

'I see. So why did you decide to speak up?' asked Rachael.

'From the moment Chris went on leave, I felt terrible about it. But I couldn't say much to him or anyone else, just in case I got implicated. I was in a relationship with his boss. But it got to the point, a week ago, when I realised that everything that Mike was accusing Chris of, he was himself guilty of. So when I learned from Mike that Chris was going to get his marching orders at this meeting today, I decided to act. Yesterday I called Chris to tell him everything. And I called you too.'

'And Natalie, for the record, you have never had an extra-curricular relationship with Chris Reece,' asked Rachael.

'No. Like Chris said, we briefly kissed at a quarter-close celebration a year or so ago, if that counts. The gossipers had a field day, blew it up more than it was.'

'I tend to hear most of the gossip myself', said Rachael, nodding. Then she turned to Gribbin. 'Anything you'd like to add, Mike?'

Gribbin was pale and shaking. After ten seconds waiting for a response, Rachael said, 'Well perhaps I can for you. I spoke with Natalie late last night on her concerns and also received a recording of a meeting you had with Chris shortly after we last convened in my office several weeks ago.'

'I'm sorry?' asked Gribbin, weakly.

Rachael pressed play.

At first Kish couldn't place it. Then it became clearer. It was him and Gribbin. *In that room, straight after he'd fled Rachael's office. The earpiece.*

When it finished, Rachael said, 'I must say it does shed light on your management practices, Mike. As well as your interesting opinions of this company's HR team.'

'Rachael, I assure you this is all a colossal misunderstanding,' said Gribbin.

'Mike, I spoke with Ruud prior to this morning's meeting regarding the situation. We also spoke regarding certain personal expenses claimed on trips away with Natalie. You have broken our strict code of conduct on at least two counts. I am therefore authorised to inform you that you are hereby dismissed from the company. You will be supervised by one of the security staff as you gather your personal effects. Goodbye.'

Kish looked at his watch. At least Gribbin was right about one thing. The meeting indeed lasted thirty minutes.

At 9:54am, a security guard was seen escorting Gribbin through a busy atrium full of whispering employees and bemused customers, past reception and outside the main entrance. Kish decided to retire to his favourite toilet cubicle for a couple of hours. No laptop and no mobile phone. No one to bug him. He sat alone with his thoughts. Elise had saved him, and he knew just how much he'd royally screwed up.

Earlier that same Tuesday morning, at Gladstone Villa Diana was sat on the window sofa in her dressing gown, watching her neighbour's cat take its post-breakfast stroll. She hadn't slept much since her son had left on Sunday morning, and had got through far too many painkillers for her liking these past forty-eight hours. In vain, she'd tried to call Chris yesterday evening, but it was no use.

Vilora drew a chair alongside, and handed Diana a cup of camomile tea. 'Why did you never tell him about me coming here to go to university, to stay for a while?' Vilora had asked. She hadn't wanted to burden Diana, but it seemed right to ask the question.

'Oh my darling,' started Diana, sympathetically. 'When you've known someone all his life, you just know when discretion is called for, and when it is not. Of course I wanted to tell him, but I'd fear he'd go off in such a rage he might crash his car or something. I can't lose him.'

Vilora smiled back, and took Diana's cold white hands, thinking of the wonderful things Diana had mentioned about her son in her letters, cards and emails. A love for a son that came alive only in words and letters. It saddened Diana. If he had read them, or simply trusted her in the first place, maybe he'd be sat there too. She'd tried to call him, give him the opportunity to vent, and also let her speak and explain. Maybe he'd listen to her voice message she'd left this morning, perhaps not. Diana felt more aches, and took yet another painkiller. She now realised she had peddled false witness all this time. Those letters to Vilora had created and sustained a false picture of him, one that had kept her loving him. With little direct dialogue between them, she'd coveted that image of him in the photo frame by the kettle—a young boy smiling in the garden wearing a cowboy hat, and assembled words and emotions around him. A boy who once loved his mother, yet who now rarely bothered calling her at all. For the past decade, it was the letters and emails written between her and a young girl living at the other end of Europe that spoke of her love for him.

Diana sighed deeply and blew her nose. 'My son really doesn't need me.' She was determined not to cry as she turned to Vilora and said, 'And I don't know if you need me, but if you do, I am here. Please tell me you do.'

Vilora held her hand. 'From before I knew it, I always need you.'

Diana squeezed her hand back, and took a sip of tea. As she breathed into the cup, hot moist air blew back across her cheeks, and tingled her chapped lips. Diana thought back to that sunny late August day in 2002 when she first met Vilora. A happy little girl, all smiles and a runny nose, who ran up to her and simply hugged her. It was the day after she'd run into Vilora's father Fadim in that hotel in Pristina. That absurd text message from her idiot husband, precipitating the end of a twenty-year marriage, but which made way for a new world of love for her in Kosovo. Then in 2007, when Fadim died suddenly from a huge heart attack, Diana had stepped in to help Vilora, and more formally so in 2009. Two further years of wading through administration and seeing all the papers were in order for Vilora's eventual move to England, under her guardianship. And with it time for Diana to think about Vilora's father, a man she'd never got over since university.

'Goodness,' Diana exclaimed, her mind now back in her lounge. 'Drifted off there.'

'Are you okay?' asked Vilora.

'I'm fine, it's nothing,' Diana replied. *Why didn't Chris once mention Elise during his stay? And if asked about her, then why were his replies so curt? Why did he behave so stupidly with Vilora? The sight of him on the sofa on his last night, so pathetic.* Diana's thoughts collided with one another, sending them off in new, more fearful directions, rather than connecting and giving her reasons to forgive. *Enough.* There and then she made up her mind. So determined was she now, she'd not felt numbness setting in along her arms and legs.

Vilora could live here permanently.

Vilora should and would share the estate equally with her son. The practical reasoning sat well with her. Clearly, Chris was solvent, whereas Vilora needed financial security when Diana was gone. But she had another reason. Something she now realised she should have told her son years ago. And Vilora too. Something she'd fretted over for nearly thirty years.

'Vilora my dear.'

'Yes?'

Diana felt odd as she stood up. 'Both Chris and you needed to hear something . . . tired all of a sud-'

Diana lost consciousness and collapsed onto the lounge foor.

'Oh my God!' shrieked Vilora. She frantically confirmed Diana's pulse, gently tapping her cheek. No response, Vilora's instinct was to contact Kish on his mobile phone. She tried three times in quick succession, with no luck. She rushed to the kitchen and got a glass of water. As she returned, Diana was reviving but mumbled something about a doctor. How could Vilora get to a doctor, call an ambulance? Desperation took hold as she'd rushed to the neighbours on both sides and hammered on the front door. No one was in. It was a weekday—they'd be at work. She looked at her watch and decided to do what she knew best, take things into her own hands. With huge effort, she dragged a semi-conscious

Diana towards her car and lay her out along the back seat. Despite her best efforts, Vilora couldn't quite secure a seat belt around her, and then jumped in the driver seat and turned on the engine.

'Mum, where do I go now?' asked Vilora frantically.

'Go right . . . bottom of the hill,' mumbled Diana from behind her. 'Keep . . . keep going . . . See signs for-'

'Signs for what? Please tell me?' Vilora tried to remain calm as she jerked madly into second gear, trying to remember all that Diana had taught her over the past few weeks.

'Hospital . . . signs, follow them . . .' Diana said weakly, before fainting.

Vilora began a frantic drive.

THIRTY-EIGHT

Kish returned to his desk and turned his iPhone on. He'd had three missed calls from Vilora apparently, and a text from Geoff. He ignored Vilora's voicemails and went instead to Geoff's message, which simply read:

All ok? ;-) ;-)

Kish was halfway through some irreverent response when Ruud Wankhuizen motioned to join him in his office. 'We need to speak, my friend,' started Ruud, closing his office door behind him. 'I know you are barely out of that last meeting with Rachael, but I do want you to know I will support your decision to stay. Run all government sales for me. I see no reason why this shouldn't happen immediately. Senior Director level, naturally. I also understand you came up with a great idea for improving how we collaborate more effectively internally? We'd be very interested in having you lead a cross-company initiative to improve our workplace processes and culture. Introduce new governance, ways of working, execution models. I'd assign you a team. Great profile and above all secures you on the executive manager bench. And me as your manager and top sponsor for at least the next fiscal.'

Kish sat back. Ruud's offer basically amounted to hush money. Not because of Gribbin's extra-marital indiscretions. No, this was about that little phone recording. If employees ever got wind of it, Ruud's own credibility would be undermined. He being the one who promoted Gribbin up through the ranks. If it found its way onto the internet, the press would have a field day.

'Well Chris, what do you think?' Ruud asked.

Kish considered that down payment on a place in St Leonard's Avenue. In the past week alone, three very nice flats had come on the market on this one road. With this offer from Ruud, he could be in one by Christmas, near enough a year earlier than planned.

Kish considered himself three years from now, still working for Mironic. Certainly some accomplishments under his belt by then, plus he'd probably have been be promoted again, have larger team maybe. Definitely more Mironic stock. Perhaps he'd receive some credit for certain changes in working practices that had resulted from his recommendations, in some way positively impacted the company's culture. But no matter how capable he was, or how great his ideas were, he knew his impact would be limited by the very culture he was trying to change. The reason was simple: Mironic was becoming staid. An increasingly un-innovative CEO and COO, sat there barking increasingly stale, US centric orders across their Silicon Valley offices and down to emasculated local leadership around the planet, while they and their circle quietly vested millions of shares. No matter how widely used its software was, Mironic's work culture was silently shaping its external brand, and it was starting to stall. On the face of it, Kish's ideas to improve Mironic's workplace culture were simple. No more email, no more physical office environment unless you had to be working physically in a team session. Replace it all with more dynamic, socially interactive communication like you have at home with your friends through Facebook and such. A few more dynamic CIOs had started to think about a 'zero email' workplace. Some insisted on sections of their workforce staying at home for a few days a week. Heresy to the upper echelons of Mironic, brought up on a factory mindset—having people physically present to produce goods, and deliberating through over-populated meetings and endless exchanges of overwritten monologue.

No, the wholesale cultural change of a business never worked unless it came from the top. The same people far more powerful than him, who would resist anything that threatened their own dull conventions.

'Ruud,' Kish started, 'I need to focus on the most important things in my life. Being a Director in Mironic isn't one of them.'

Ruud raised his eyebrows and tapped his fingers on the table. Two line managers leaving his business in quick succession presented a large problem for him and keeping Chris on, even for the next six-to-twelve months, had been his plan to best contain this sensitive issue. Then again, as Ruud knew all too well, Chris might very well continue to exploit the situation to his own advantage if he was still here, which might only compound problems for Ruud at a later date. It seemed the best idea was to let him go now. Giving Chris what he wanted now in return for a watertight non-disclosure agreement avoided any further mud-raking, this at a point when the UK subsidiary was suffering from its lowest morale in six years.

Ruud cleared his throat. 'In view of your decision, which I totally support, I am sure we can arrange something amenable.'

'Good,' replied Kish. 'And if you let me leave today on agreeable terms, I'll keep more than quiet.'

As soon as Kish left his office, Ruud called Rachael to relay the discussion and move to closure. At 12:55pm, Rachael Frears called Kish to her office.

'In view of your treatment, Mironic can offer you a lump sum of eighteen months pay tax free, in addition to all end of year bonuses already entitled to you, and will bring forward the vesting date for your Mironic stock allocation currently scheduled to vest next June. You will also receive full references, and may leave immediately with no penalty.'

'Okay. And in return?'

'The offer is conditional on you signing a non-disclosure agreement prohibiting you from discussing the circumstances of your departure, and Mike's.'

One hour later, Kish signed the non-disclosure, and set his 'Out of Office' to state he no longer worked at Mironic, and instructions on who to contact going forward. Shortly after came the announcement mail from Ruud. Entitled "Chris Reece leaving Mironic", Ruud led with the ambiguous sentence that Chris was keen to pursue personal interests outside the company; Ruud thanked Kish for eight years of sterling effort in sales and marketing and for being an exemplary employee.

Within minutes of the email hitting corporate inboxes, Kish received several texts, tweets, and messages on Facebook from twenty or so colleagues—colleagues he'd been on stag weekends with, seen get married, one or two he'd once dated, written plans with, coordinated customer activity with, drunk lattes with, shared a concern over a beer with. Others simply wanted gossip. Kish then began to type out two emails from his private Gmail account. The first was to his team who he genuinely wished well. He knew each of their email aliases off by heart—no problem there. The second one was to Natalie. He felt he owed Natalie something more; his note would cut through all the crap and warn her of the perils of working in a sanitised, introspective bubble. He warned her about taking herself too seriously, not allowing self-worth to grow unchecked, but also to remember who she was when all those about her had forgotten who they were. And lastly that no one is indispensible. Lastly, Kish knew that any email received by an Mironic employee was a record—another reason it remained high-level, professional and compliant with the non-disclosure agreement.

At 4:40pm Kish had finished boxing up any personal paper files worth keeping and dumped the rest—papers, old magazines, campaign articles and training CDs, into a variety of recycle bins. It had taken him thirty minutes to wrap up nearly eight years of activity. Bag packed, Kish made the final rounds with his still shocked team, and promised them all a goodbye drink in a fortnight. Next he went round to see Ruud. He wasn't in his office, but Anne his PA was sat at a desk located opposite.

'I'm off, Anne. I'd like to say goodbye to Ruud but he doesn't seem to be around.'

'No worries—I'll pass it on when I see him. Well best of luck with the next adventure. Out of all this madness,' she said, smiling.

'Thanks Anne, you too.' In that smile he remembered how processed one's life really was in this place, and why some people chose to be there. He smiled back.

Next, Kish made his way to the Security Office on the ground floor—taking the back route meant he avoided the busy corridors. This was not a day for handshakes, backslaps and brave faces, but a day to just quietly slip away. Security thanked him for his ID badge. 'We've got everything else from when you left . . . last time,' said one of the assistant guards. It was the security guard called Andy who led him to the exit. 'Good luck mate, take care.' The handshake had no pretense and Andy's eyes confirmed it. Kish pushed his way through the revolving glass entrance, stepped into the early evening air, and turned his iPhone back on.

Natalie was stood outside waiting for him. 'Well this is all a bit of a turn up, eh?' she said.

Kish nodded then said, 'Now you be good, yeh?' He kissed her cheek, and walked off.

Natalie saw Kish disappear among the herd of polished cars. She'd got two scalps in one day.

Twenty metres away, Kish also smiled. He had his little pot of gold. A place in St Leonard's avenue was now within reach. He'd just joined the M4 Eastbound when his car's comms system alerted him to an incoming telephone call from Geoff.

'Good day at work?' asked Geoff instantly.

'Oh the usual . . . got called in by HR to get fired, got exonerated, got boss fired instead, resigned all the same with some benefits attached.' Kish paused. 'Basically Elise saved my bacon.'

'Really?' Despite you being the biggest shit in the world to her, which you are, she still couldn't see you fry.'

'You knew the circumstances about me and her falling out then?'

'Enough to know what a complete twat you've been. Stop pricking about Reece. You've hurt her more than you could dream possible. That girl needs you.'

Twenty minutes later, a mile or so before the Slough turn-off, Kish activated his mother's number. Feeling good about his professional circumstances meant he could feel more buoyed about his private life. He could stomach speaking to her again, humble himself. Instead, Diana's answer phone kicked in. 'Hi Mum it's me, look I am really, really sorry I rushed off, but everything's good now with me. Everything. How are you? Anyhow I'll pop back down if I may. I think I left things a little up in the air. Mum, I know I should have said this before but I am truly, truly sorry.' For an instant Kish contemplated driving down to Bath there and then. It was just gone 5:30pm, and if the traffic proved favourable he'd be there by 7:30pm at the latest. A massive apology from him, a genuine one, then a warm cup of tea for her, and a long, long, long, chat right up until bedtime. Hell, he could even apologise to Vilora. Feeling conciliatory, Kish dialled into his voicemail. The first was from Vilora:

'*Kish it is Vilora. Get here quick. Mum is in Hospital. I am here too but okay. Please come!*'

'Oh Christ,' Kish said loudly. He activated the next voice message.

'*Kish please it's Vilora. Mum she is in intensive care and very ill. I drove her there. Please call me or hospital.*

Kish dodged several vehicles as he swerved across two lanes and made the Slough turn-off. As he circled back onto the westbound carriageway of the M4, he frantically called Elise's mobile. He got her voicemail. 'Elise, no time to explain. Mum is in intensive care in Bath. Bath Royal Edward Hospital. I'm on my way to her now. Please call me! I know you helped me at work. Please call.' Then he called the Bath Royal Edward Hospital. What he heard was not good.

Two hours later Kish tore into the Accident and Emergency Reception.

THIRTY-NINE

The A&E Receptionist calmly instructed Kish to wait nearby, and within a few minutes one of the Intensive Care Unit team arrived. 'Mr. Reece,' said the Sister, 'earlier today, your mother was involved in a serious collision with a lorry. She'd collapsed earlier at her home and was being driven here when the accident occurred. She received serious head and neck injuries as well as internal damage on her left side to her lower organs. She underwent emergency surgery and is now out of theatre, but remains in intensive care, in a coma.'

Kish stopped dead. 'What the hell happened?'

The Sister said, 'We are still getting the full picture, but from what the driver has said, the left hand side of the car took the impact apparently.'

'Can I see her?'

'Of course.'

The backs of Kish's knees were sweating as he walked into the Intensive Care Unit. It was busy, with medical staff issuing and executing vital instructions between rooms. For Kish it neither smelled nice nor optimistic. It smelt mortal.

The Sister directed him to a room toward the end of a corridor, then paused to say, 'Mr Reece before you see your mother, I have to tell you that she is in a very critical condition due to the extent of the injuries sustained, and we are doing all we can, but you must prepare you for the worst.' She put her hand on his forearm, and guided him slowly towards the chair at his mother's side. Kish stared at his mother as she lay motionless on her back, hair crumpled beneath a heavily bandaged head and face, metal structure around it. A tube was placed into her nose and a machine checking vital signs bleeped away.

From behind him came a quiet voice. 'Oh thank God you are here.' It was Vilora, eyes red raw. She sobbed as she limped towards him, then hugged him. Kish leant and took hold of his mother's hand. He couldn't remember the last time he did. Vilora knelt beside him and gently clasped Diana's other hand. Eventually she said, 'I am so sorry Kish. I was driving. She was ill and big truck came out from nowhere and just hit into us. And then I cannot remember anything. She was lying down in back seat, and had no seatbelt . . .'

Kish rested his head on the bed beside his mother hip, and after a while began to mutter, 'I will make it better, I promise. And Mum-, Mum, you're going to be a grandmother. You see, Elise and me, we're having a baby.'

Kish felt Diana squeeze his hand just a little. 'I know dear,' he heard her whisper, 'And I know you'll make a wonderful father. I love you Chris. Always remember that.'

'I love you too, Mum. I love you too. I am so sorry.' Kish felt his hand being gently squeezed once more. 'You know I've got to go to sleep now, don't you.'

'Yes.'

'Night night, dear.'

'Night night, Mum.' He took her mother's hand and kissed it, tears running past his mouth and down between her knuckles, then fell asleep beside his unconscious mother. A few minutes later, Vilora watched her slip away. Once again she'd witnessed firsthand the death of someone she cherished.

The Sister gently nudged Kish awake. He was told his mother had passed away peacefully as he'd slept with his arm gently curled round hers. At midnight, Kish left the hospital alone and returned to his mother's home, emotionless. Vilora, on the consultant's insistence, stayed overnight at the hospital for observation.

Kish was up early the next morning, and left a message on Elise's mobile telling her the sad news. He didn't deserve any sympathy and he was glad she hadn't picked up. He then called his father for the first time since Christmas, then spent twenty minutes breaking the news to his uncle James, Diana's brother, who was left making urgent flight arrangements from New Zealand to the UK. At Eleven-ish, he returned to the hospital to pick up Vilora. She had just finished an initial interview with the police, who seem satisfied with her account of the crash; two independent witnesses had come forward with details that appeared to corroborate her story. The lorry driver was being detained.

'Mum said goodbye to me,' Kish said to Vilora later that afternoon. They were back at Diana's home, sat quietly in the lounge. 'And I said goodbye to her.'

Vilora smiled. Even though she knew Diana had been in a coma, unresponsive and motionless, perhaps she too needed to believe what Kish believed. Regardless, she'd never correct him. Who was she to question what's communicated between mother and son in a dying moment.

'I'm just popping upstairs to sort through a few things, Vilora,' said Kish, smiling. 'Then I'll put the kettle on and make us some coffee.' He clapped his hands and made his way upstairs. There, he locked himself in the bathroom and sat up against the bath, closed his eyes and imagined his mother lying motionless in the mortuary cubbyhole. The immensity of sudden and permanent separation became real to him, and he cried for the first time in years. It would be easy to remain there much longer, locked away in a warm, familiar bathroom. But something bigger in him eventually made him get to his feet, wipe his face and go downstairs. *Vilora needed comforting too.*

Returning to the lounge, Kish immediately put his arm around her, on that same sofa he'd attempted to force a kiss from her just a few days before. He knew that, and so did she.

After a long silence Vilora eventually said, 'you know why I came over to England now. I came over because, like you, that is what you do when someone you love is ill, however far away they are.' Yesterday she'd seen another person she loved slip away before her eyes, through a violent injury and premature death. 'I want you to know how much I loved her,' she said, 'and what she did for me. But you must never think she didn't love you. In all my letters and emails from her, she always mentioned what you mean to her, how close she hoped we would all be one day, and always said you will one day say you love her once more, ever hoping. I think I will never forgive myself.'

Kish turned to Vilora. 'I am now so grateful that she knew you. You did everything you possibly could. Don't ever feel guilty about Mum. I am the one who must feel guilty forever, not you. Not now. Not ever.'

ONE MONTH LATER

FORTY

At 5:20am, Humphrey exited No. 47, Ferret Rise as prim as a clipped privet hedge. He glanced up toward an opaque sky. It had rained overnight and the air carried a musky tar-like smell from moisture evaporating off fast-drying tarmac. While Geoff continued the hunt for his house keys, which he eventually found in a pile of discarded underwear, Humphrey was in the purple delivery van double-checking his gear, including tonight's impressive party attire, and just ensuring the contents of the wine boxes matched the brand embossed on them. To his relief they did.

Compared to recent van journeys, today's one to Southampton, proved pleasingly quieter and more straightforward, as was the ferry across the Solent to East Cowes on the Isle of Wight, and a short drive to their Bed & Breakfast. Humphrey spent most of the trip contemplating a variety of matters. Contemplating the fact that today was the first time he felt more in charge of his circumstances, perhaps for the first time ever. And circumspect that today was also his thirtieth birthday—time to plan afresh rather than spend it bemoaning the close of the last 'mercurial' decade. It felt good to be thirty.

'Actually quite looking forward to tonight's party. You?' he asked Geoff as they parked up near the B&B.

'Of course. Plus I was thinking. When we get home we can celebrate a little more. Dinner party next week perhaps?'

'Perhaps. Only this time none of your silly cross-the-table sniper skills on show.' Humphrey smiled and thought back to birthday celebrations laid on for him a year ago. If his memory served, also the last time he had any amorous contact with a girl . . .

~

Humphrey's birthday celebrations at No. 47 were in full swing. The star of the ensemble was Elise's moist lamb stuffed with pistachio, whole garlic and rosemary, closely followed by Geoff's contribution: a selection of cold cuts, relishes and cheeses, courtesy of Fromage de Ferret, a small delicatessen that would not look out of place in a quaint village in Limousin. Geoff kicked off a debate on whether, fluid mililitre to fluid mililitre, expensive wine, and just for examples sake, a Montrachet he'd acquired, was a more effective giver of gout than a less expensive version of say, port. He did not care for the right or wrong answer, nor whether it was a viable question to begin with. The point of it was to divert Humphrey's attention, and while he postulated before assembled guests, Geoff quietly took a palm-sized lump of stuffing from his own plate and began moulding it into three small balls, each roughly the size of a marble. Checking no one was looking his way, he quietly took three party poppers off the table, and out of view carefully removed their cardboard bottoms and streamer filling, and pressed one of the balls into the small cavity, then replaced the cardboard disc to secure them. When Kish and Humphrey concluded their views on gout, Geoff tapped his glass.

'Before I toast the birthday boy, can I ask Humphrey to tell us what he really thinks of his birthday present.' Humphrey and the table turned to the mantelpiece. Sat proudly at the centre, just two or three feet from where Kish sat, was Humphrey's gift, a clock that had been presented at the beginning of the meal by his housemates. Made entirely from Styrofoam, and the size of a dinner plate, the clock face was in fact the exposed face of a friendly, purple hippopotamus, with the clock's hands mounted on a pin in the middle of the hippo's nose. The hippo's body and ears moved left and right with each tick. 'Let's just say it's the thought that counts.'

'Who on earth makes a clock from styrofoam?' asked Kish, as Geoff lined up his sights and aimed the business end of a party popper, heavily charged and crammed with stodgy Montrachet-dyed stuffing.

With eight glasses of Montrachet in him, Humphrey was at best non-plussed. 'Chap?' he enquired finally. 'Are you trying to shoot my hippo with a party popper? I mean, you might want something a little more powerful than a bunch of ruddy streamers. Hippos have thick hides. Even styrofoam ones.'

Sniper-like, Geoff leant across the table holding the three poppers in his right hand, their cords in his left and took aim, training his left eye along the short barrel. Kish sensibly ducked right, and barely four short feet from his quarry, Geoff pulled the short cords. *The poppers went of simultaneously, propelling their musket balls of stuffing with surprising velocity toward the happy hippo's pink snout. On impact, the hippo exploded, sending styrofoam body parts in various directions. Humphrey looked down at his fudge cake to see a hippo's left ear resting on it. He then looked back at the mantelpiece. Where his hippo clock had stood happily ticking away just seconds before, beige splats now marked the eggshell paint wall, plus an (indeterminable) remnant of the hippo's once pendulous torso.*

Geoff raised his glass. 'A ferray happy birthday Humph. More Montrachet, anyone?'

'Well tonight shall be different, because I feel different,' said Humphrey as they grabbed their room keys from the B&B reception. 'Given the surroundings, I shall of course be in my chosen maritime attire. Reading off HQ's email he'd printed out, he added 'I mean with such a broad definition like 'maritime attire', the options extended to us by Debrays are simply endless.' Humphrey was determined that this time he'd look the part. Others would be left standing.

Geoff read a message on his phone. 'Kish'll be sailing on some boat most of the day,' he relayed to Humphrey.

'What's this about him blagging a spot on a boat for the day?'

'Some bigwig he knows in the IT trade. He hopes to join us on Titus at eight.'

'And his special lady joining us too?'

'Oh she'll be there for sure.'

Once registered, Humphrey finished unpacking and read the instructions from HQ again. The Debrays wine reception was from 2:00pm to 6:00pm, held aboard the splendid sixty-foot yacht the Titus Vente moored in the main Cowes marina, before being prepared for tonight's end of season VIP party, which kicked off at 8:00pm. Geoff and Humphrey would work the reception and were guests at the evening party, thanks to Kish's continued access to corporate hospitality. 'Okay Geoff. We need to have all the wines unpacked by eleven, and that gives us just forty minutes.'

Across the water at Port Solent, Kish smiled as he held a very attractive young lady's hand. Not long now before they'd join their hosts aboard Calleva, a magnificent forty-eight foot Bowman yacht. The wind was already picking up—there'd be little need for its Perkins 4-236 engine. Today he was a guest of Comitsu, who like any ambitious IT Services company keen for an angle on their competitors, were using his well-timed departure from Mironic to coax him into a plum job running a sizeable chunk of their government business across Europe and the Middle East. Kish had already had time to consider the attractive offer on the table. Sixty percent increase on his old salary at Mironic, plus crucially, an uncapped bonus. The sort of cash that Mironic never gave him until faced with him leaving.

How he and Geoff ever got out of the whole wine-swapping, van-crashing, food poison debacle was beyond Humphrey. Karen Williams had been surprisingly quiet these past few weeks as there was no proof the inventory was awry. The van theft had seen to that. As Geoff said in a statement to the company's Managing Director, *'the unfortunate circumstances with the stolen van and significant loss of expensive wines could have been avoided if my immediate management had heeded my detailed, recorded concerns regarding the store's poor security.'* In other words Karen's persecuting hands were tied.

Today, on their fourth and final gig with Debrays, Geoff and Humphrey, once admonished and now pardoned employees of Bacchus Braves, acted to perfection that afternoon. The selected guests, by invitation only, sauntered amongst themselves on board the Titus Vente, plied with well fashioned tasting notes from Humphrey, and the charming compliments from Geoff. Champagne flowed. Just once or twice Humphrey caught himself double-checking the label of the bottle he was pouring, as Toby Sarber-Collins watched on. He wished he knew what really happened at Glyndebourne. If he ever discovered that that trumped-up Massey fellow had fiddled him, he'd break the little sod's . . .

'What did became of Roger Ashton?' Humphrey asked Geoff during a quiet moment.

'Simply disappeared,' said Geoff, ensuring he was within earshot of Sarber-Collins. 'And who were we to tell he was an imposter?' Geoff smiled wryly.

'That's very true.'

Bang on 6:00pm, Geoff slapped his hands. 'Right, we're done. Debrays can clear up the empties. Time to get ready for the evening event. Got your stuff here?'

'I have it back at the B&B,' Humphrey replied.

Geoff resisted smirking as best he could. On one hand he surely owed it to Humph to explain tonight was not in fact a fancy dress party, after everything that had happened these past few months. Humphrey hardly needed yet another prank played on him. Then again . . . Geoff's impish side won over. 'I have my stuff with me. I'll shower in the marina. I hope you don't still outshine me though.' Goading was good.

'I think you might just pip me,' Humphrey replied modestly, unsure what he was competing with, but determined nonetheless not to be upstaged by his housemate.

An hour later, dressed and ready, Humphrey stared into a mirror on the B&B bedroom wall. 'Ding dong, you're not wrong,' he announced proudly to his beaming reflection.

Aboard the Calleva, Kish had spent much of his afternoon in pleasant conversation with his host and fellow guests. Yet he found his mind still strayed elsewhere when given half the chance. Like every day this past month, Kish's mother remained uppermost in his mind, along with the other two women in his life, one of them with him today.

'Chris, got to say, I love a man who knows his own heart,' said Simon Wildman, who'd captained the boat today but who also happened to be Comitsu's Senior Vice President of Global Sales. Kish had known Wildman over many seasons of selling, and knew whatever he'd ever agreed with him usually proved mutually beneficial.

Kish squeezed his companion's hand. Elise smiled back. She was nervous still, having spent weeks convincing herself he was capable of the truth and not chancing at every opportunity. Throughout he seemed, well more honest. Eye contact for starters. She was very happy to smile back today.

'Wind's picking up Mr. Reece,' bellowed Wildman, 'Now let's get that spinnaker out and grab some wind!'

Kish scooted over to unfold the spinnaker, leaving Elise stood at the helm with Wildman's wife, Hazel, while Wildman worked on steadying the boom.

Approaching 6:00pm Calleva put into Cowes Yacht Haven. Kish and his companion bid farewell to Wildman, Hazel and their other guests, then disembarked. At the Yacht Haven's marina changing rooms, Kish shaved slowly and precisely, then scrubbed himself clean of the fine briny crust that had accumulated on his face today. The shower was hot, just as he liked it. On went the black, loose-fitting linen trousers, the leather sandals, and a cream linen shirt. Fancying his attire needed something to top it off, Kish popped off to the Cowes Crew Shop, and selected a cap. 'Crew', he chuckled. *Crew of what?* Perhaps that was the point. Kish paid for the cap, put it on and strode back to the busy marina. Having collected his companion from outside the female changing rooms, they weaved towards the moorings. He soon spotted the Titus Vente, a beautiful wooden boat with deep blue stern, with yellow flag and bunting.

'You first,' Kish said offering Elise the gangplank. Geoff, stood in a white deck top, cap, and impossibly white deck trousers, was there to greet them.

'What-ho,' said Geoff, shaking Kish's hand, and then wrapping his free arm around Elise's waist. 'Sorry, not sure I should manhandle you. I mean, in your state.'

'Don't be silly, it's a lovely hug,' replied Elise.

Geoff looked at Kish and then to Elise. He raised his can of diet Coke. Kish kept his gentle gaze fixed on Geoff, and squeezed Elise's hand. As he did, Elise felt another kick inside her. She clenched Kish's warm hand and said nothing. He'd been dry for a month. She'd attended Diana's funeral with him, and they'd started talking again. First, about the baby. Then about them.

Humphrey's evening stroll from the B&B to Cowes Yacht Haven was marked by a few odd stares and several wolf whistles from some local youths gathered around at various points along the high street. He didn't care though. Outside he might look like a pretentious twat heralding a bygone era, but inside he was Everyman. He received another blast of wolf-whistles as he passed the chip shop, including one from the shop owner, outside on a fag break, to whom Humphrey doffed his hat. He felt comfortable to make a detour into one of the local pubs, where he sat and polished off two pints, determined to just relax.

Onboard the Titus Vente, Elise's senses were enlivened by the variety of music coming from various boats. A few boats away, various deck shoes were tapping to upbeat jazz tunes, whereas on the pontoon behind her, they seemed more partial to salsa and mamba. Then there was the marina marquee, a good hundred metres off and cornering the market in cheesy hits. Melodies merging and drifting in chorus out into the winking Solent.

It was another hour before a loud, familiar voice boomed from the floating walkway. 'Permission to board!' bellowed Humphrey. He then tooted his whistle—a long low note, then a screamingly high one, and then a low longer one. The several people stood on deck immediate formed an opinion. Only those who knew him simply chuckled. Even the various sound systems seemed to have turned their volume down, as if caught up in the moment.

Given his choice of dress, there was little doubt that tonight Humphrey would cut a dash in any port. That is if tonight was any night between the years 1795 and 1820. This evening, Humphrey was a very authentic-looking Rear Admiral in His Majesty's Navy from around the time of the Napoleonic Wars. Humphrey straightened his waistcoat, and placed his whistle back in his breast pocket. Finally, he checked that his bicorne hat was unlikely to fall off anytime soon, then proceeded up the gangplank, as a gentle breeze fluttered the tail of his long seaman's overcoat. Half way up, he removed his hat and tucked it deliberately under his left arm. He caught Geoff's eye, who promptly winced.

'Avast!' Humphrey called out. 'Splice my giblets and brace my main.' Humphrey felt he was on fire, liberated. Wearing such attire from Britain's finest naval period seemed to work wonders for his self-esteem.

Toby Sarber-Collins piped up first. 'Who the bloody hell invited Horatio Hornblower?' He laughing at his own joke. 'You. Yes you. The one who should have been hanged from the yardarm for screwing us over at Glyndebourne.'

Humphrey squinted a smile at the brightly back-dropped silhouettes, the low sun directly behind them, and looked Geoff up and down. 'And where's your fancy boat dress? You look more like a tubbier version of George Michael in some Wham video.'

'Quite,' Geoff replied. 'And no socks, obviously. Got to show off my yachtie ankles.'

'And Kish,' added Humphrey, 'your cap looks like you put it in the wash with a red sock. It's gone pink.'

'Bought it like that. Genuine maritime attire, apparently,' Kish replied.

Sarber-Collins was less controlled. 'Not sure how you misread the term 'maritime attire', Horace.' Good God, everyone else knew the form.' Sarber-Collins paused and necked his mojito before picking up another. 'Geoff, you must feel a bit of prick again, hanging around with this tiresome trier.'

'What do you mean, bit of a prick, *again?*'

Sarber-Collins smiled. 'Well what with your sidekick's total arse-up with the van at the Boat Race, not to mention the peculiar wines sold at Glyndebourne, *allegedly*, you must wonder if he'll ever get a break. Perhaps situations get the better of him. I've seen it in certain men before. No composure. No elan. Not one of us.'

Geoff interjected. 'Toby, I can accept Glyndebourne was not one hundred percent satisfactory, but the replacement wines were my decision, and not Humphrey's.' Geoff did not take his eyes of Toby.

Sarber-Collins sipped on his mojito and considered his response, his eager supporters sensing a challenge afoot. It took a similarly observant American to intervene and calm things. 'Quite, now let's toast your birthday, Admiral!' said Elise. 'In fact Geoff's got a card from us all. Hope you find it funny.' Geoff prized his stare away and handed Humphrey a mud-brown envelope.

'Awful colour,' muttered Sarber-Collins, still keen to get a rise. 'A sort of turd brown, isn't it.'

'I should have told you Humph,' said Geoff, ignoring Sarber-Collins. 'About the evening attire. Sorry.'

'Compared to everything else you've ever inflicted on me, my friend, it hardly matters,' said Humphrey.

Geoff watched on as Humphrey opened the envelope then smiled at the amusing prose on the front of the card. Humphrey then re-read the familiar prose on the front. *Odd.* They were his words, sat in speech bubbles coming from a roughly sketched lavatory. Humphrey looked up at Elise. *The idea of her rifling through his bedroom and creating something so personal had a certain appeal, but it was odd all the same.* Humphrey then opened the card up and read on. *Yep, my poem.* 'Which of you got this done so nicely? It looks so professional. Nice artwork too.'

Elise frowned, then said, 'Actually, I bought it yesterday from the card shop near your place. I picked it because I liked it.'

Humphrey flipped the car over and read the back. It read *"Suzies Toozies, published by Haggard Ltd. Number 2, in a series of 7"*. Humphrey felt a sudden panic and disbelief. He was holding a professionally-made card bought in his local card shop, and most concerning of all, the words and design had been copyrighted. His words. He dipped his head, and immediately Elise grabbed his hand.

'What's wrong, Hun? We haven't offended you have we?'

'I can't work it out. You see, I—I wrote this poem.'

His shaking caught the eye of a bemused Sarber-Collins, who grabbed the card. 'Semi-funny I suppose,' he concluded. 'Not my taste personally, I mean, finding humour in a woman taking a dump. Hardly high-brow is it now. Drawing is a bit rudimentary, too.'

Geoff looked at Humphrey's red temple, which had a sinuous vein running all the way down it. 'Humph, I've seen them too in a shop, a whole line of them,' he said, barely keeping straight-faced. Looked like they were selling nicely.'

'A whole line?' Humphrey kept his eyes glued to the card. 'This is crazy. These poems, they were in a folder in my bedroom, and—' Humphrey's heart pounded harder.

The humiliation-by-porn soundtrack, the electrocution, not to mention countless pranks before. Since then, the submerged van, being fired for deception and fraud, the food poisoning, the stolen van. And today, turning up at a remarkably un-fancy dress event as some old-fashioned Admiral, then receiving a birthday card containing a poem passed off as Geoff's. All inflicted upon Humphrey, and all involving Geoff.

Very slowly, Humphrey turned to face his housemate. Geoff's smirk confirmed his worst betrayal yet. Humphrey lowered his head then slowly shook it. His jaw trembled uncontrollably, his mouth dry as he began to draw air noisily through his nostrils.

By the time anyone could react, Humphrey had made his way onto the gangplank, which flexed as he galloped down.

'Humphrey, wait! I can explain!' Geoff pleaded, levity in his voice still. Humphrey accelerated off the gangplank and suddenly lost his footing, sending his left ankle crumpling beneath him. Instinctively Humphrey threw his left hand out to take the impact. He hit the ground and felt one of his fingers bend back and crack in an instant. Humphrey screwed his face up with the sudden, excruciating pain, then without turning round, picked himself up and limped away along the pontoon, his left hand braced under his right arm.

Elise fixed her stare menacingly at Geoff. 'What the hell have you done to him?! I thought you were better than that.' Geoff was no longer smirking.

Like Humphrey, Elise had also trusted him these past few months. She'd needed him and got close as a result. But Geoff was still the same selfish, thoughtless shit after all.

Suddenly Elise felt guilty too.

FORTY-ONE

The pain shooting up from Humphrey's left ankle was unbearable, and after a hundred and fifty metres, he pulled up in a dark corner at the far side of the marina. He sat against the wall, hidden from view. Humphrey clawed up his trouser leg with his right hand, and in the darkness gently touched the podgy outline of a hugely swollen ankle. On the rare occasion of making a major public exit, he'd tripped and tumbled down some blasted walkway. Tonight's episode was the final straw. Kish, Geoff and Elise—they were all in it together against him.

After everything that has happened. Getting Geoff out of trouble, tolerating his constant stupidity. What a backstabbing, thieving bastard, who right now is probably howling behind my back. Well, I just hope the sad, sordid life you lead finally catches up with you and really makes you weep. Damn shame I didn't just plant my fist squarely on that superior smirk of yours when I had the chance. Kish, you sanctimonious, self-centred money-grabbing prick. That's all you are. Elise, you . . . sad, sorry victim. And as for Putney-sodding-Ferret . . .

Humphrey's instinct for peace, to simply roll with it, let things lie, had finally failed him. *This time I won't let myself forget or forgive.*

Several minutes passed before Humphrey realised his legs were shaking violently. They'd not shaken like this for years. The last occasion . . .

The last occasion . . .

Humphrey was stood in a large marquee. There was laughter, and he was holding a violin, and wearing a bow tie. His parents were there, and family. Some friends. But this was not a memory of him performing as a small child. The memory was of an older him. A summer party. Warm with a slight breeze, bit like tonight. His twenty-first birthday . . .

On that night, nine years ago, Humphrey had a sense of who he was—or who he might be, thrust upon him. Instant provenance-in-a-box, courtesy of his father. Humphrey began recalling a particular conversation he'd had that night with his Grandfather. It concerned that that stupid, wretched, pathetic little ring he'd just received. Humphrey staggered upright, and rested his weight on his un-injured leg. Carefully he hobbled a few steps out from the dark recess and into the field of light cast from a gantry opposite. He stared down at his golden signet ring, tightly wedged around his puffed-up little finger. A badly-scuffed family crest glinted back. *What on earth had he inferred by wearing it all these years? What did it prove? What had it given him, other than a false sense of self-importance and petard?* He had once felt proud and resolved whenever he looked at it. Now it had made him feel false and flimsy. His thoughts returned to his Grandfather once more. Now there was man who knew who he was. No way was Humphrey leaving Cowes Yacht Haven with that worthless piece of flotsam on his finger.

A boistrous hen party clearly up for a very big night, rounded the corner. As they did one of them noted a curious shadow cast up the marina's back wall twenty metres away. 'Look, an enormously huge cock!' a young woman blurted, catching the group's collective attention. She traced its outline with her index finger. The penis-shaped silhouette suddenly wobbled, as Humphrey took his weight off his throbbing ankle, and they all burst out in laughter. 'Look, the cock's a wobbler!' The group sourced the shadow back to Humphrey, who turned to face the wall and realised what they were laughing at. Somehow, his fancy dress had created the prefect silhouette of a four-foot wide vas deferens, sat bulbous atop a fifteen-foot long, by approximately three-foot wide, shaft. Humphrey gently tilted his bicorne-topped head left and right, and the bell-end shadow obliged by performing a comical sailor's jig.

For Humphrey, what happened next was all a little confusing to say the least. Initially he was expertly rugby-tackled by one of them. 'You dirty bloody perve,' she joked, who for the next thirty seconds, proceeded to treat him like an insolent mustang being broken in at its first rodeo, bouncing herself on his rump, pounding his groin into hard, unforgiving tarmac beneath. Occupying a disbelieving dream-state, Humphrey sensed it was most probably best he go along with it. 'Ride a cock horse to Banbury Cross!' she shrieked, yanking the back of Humphrey's shirt collar like some sort of makeshift rein, before manoeuvering off him, and slapping his flaccid rump farewell. From the corner of his eye, Humphrey spied the group sway off in the direction of the evening's live entertainment, and left alone once more, he groaned quietly. Along with a likely cracked ankle and a ballooned finger joint—also probably cracked, he possessed a screaming groin too. Humphrey slowly stood up. *Time to get the hell out of here.*

The ring. He never wanted to see the bloody thing again. Calmly, Humphrey moistened his finger with spit, breathed in, and began pulling it. The pain was beyond anything he'd felt before. He tried again. *More pain, no movement.* Humphrey paused, then bit down on his finger just behind where the ring sat, and began wrenching his finger from his mouth. As he applied more force, the ring gathered up skin around the raised, swollen joint. Finally his finger joint capitulated and his finger zipped out from his mouth, leaving his ring clanking around his back teeth. After a minute doubled-up in pain, he slowly straightened himself, and stretched his left hand out in the flat yellow light. His broken finger kinked leftward at the joint, and revealed a thin, clammy band of light skin which once lay beneath the ring. He clutched the ring in his right hand, and waited to feel something. An emotion. Nothing nostalgic came, no memories worth remembering. Something else though. *Liberty.* Humphrey began to hop towards the Marina exit, and passing by a drain he tossed his ring unceremoniously over his shoulder. Behind him came a satisfactory 'clang' as it hit the drain's wrought iron grill. *Bullseye.*

Forty metres from the marina exit, Humphrey's slim cloaked silhouette caught the attention of a couple of doormen stood stiff at the Cowes Marina's east exit, counting down the final minutes of tonight's security job, and the warm promise of a locals-only lock-in at the pub round the corner. Humphrey squinted towards them. Seeing them in their black overcoats reminded him of his own comedy uniform, only his involved polished brass buttons, long tail and braided epaulettes. One of the doormen gestured to the other, clearly bemused by this figure limping toward them. Their gaze remained fixed and confident, as did his. As he passed, he looked straight at them, nodded politely, and moved purposefully through the arch, and into Cowes High Street. In the streetlight's pale yellow luminescence, Humphrey looked at his Breitling watch. Only forty-odd payments to go and the glass was smashed, the hands standing still at 9:46pm. The moment he'd tripped off the Titus Vente.

Humphrey wound slowly through Cowes and reached the B&B about twenty minutes later. He hunted through his trousers. *Bollocks. No key.* He cursed the earlier gangplank moment as he wrapped himself in his cloak, then sat down on the top step leading to the B&B's front door. Despite the pain, he felt buoyed as he gently touched the band of white skin where his ring once sat. Nine years since that quite ridiculous ceremony on his birthday that marked the moment his parents set their expectations of him. Suddenly that same strip of skin seemed, well almost iconic.

Alone and calm, Humphrey rested his head on the front door, and began to study the events that led to his departure from the Titus Vente. Controlled, enabled, he did the right thing by walking away in pain. But the loss of Geoff's friendship stung more than any of his other injuries.

In a matter of minutes Humphrey nodded off, sweat cooling his brow.

Below deck on the *Titus Vente*, upbeat conversations continued on house prices and loopholes to avoid paying too much income tax; anything that could be used to compare ones own fortunes with those of others. Above deck, at the bow, it had taken Geoff nearly an hour to explain himself to Kish and Elise. Sarber-Collins looked on, bemused.

'You didn't make any cash yourself from his idea?' asked Elise.

'No,' shouted Geoff. 'Not at all. Look. See the back of the card? They are his original poems. I didn't steal them, I helped him, by getting him a deal. I've even got a few of the designs with me. If he hadn't gone and crashed off the boat, I was going to show them to him.' Geoff paused. 'After a bit.'

'After you'd seen him wound up you mean,' Elise snapped.

'I didn't expect him to run off like that. No chance to explain.'

Elise slammed her drink down angrily. 'Can you imagine how he feels? Do you ever imagine how he feels each time you ridicule him? It's not just tonight. Tonight's simply the icing on the cake. And somehow you get a kick from it, is that it? Helps you get through the day, taking your mind off all your own issues, tackle where you've gone wrong yourself? No, far easier to pick at Humphrey.'

Geoff finished his drink, and eyed a bottle of chilled beer wedged in an ice bucket. He motioned to grab it, but Elise stopped him. 'Not the answer. Not now.' Geoff dipped his head and his eyes began welling up.

'Oh do come on,' said Sarber-Collins. 'All this soppiness over nothing. Your winestore lacky comes aboard fresh from the chorus line of some Rogers and Hammerstein musical, then simply wimps off.' Sarber-Collins took another swig of whisky. 'Best let him go, he doesn't fit in here. Clearly one of life's losers.'

What happened next surprised even Geoff. The red mist had not come down for years. Last time, it was because he'd got caught having his end away with a teammate's girlfriend. He grabbed Sarber-Collins by his Debrays rugby shirt collars, allowing Geoff to spin his entire body around like a plumb weight on a string, grinding the reinforced cotton hem of Sarber-Collins' collars unforgivingly into his sunburned neck. Geoff then brought a knee up sharply under Sarber-Collins' jaw. Geoff's knee glanced just a little—that patella now needed surgery for sure, and Sarber-Collins fell limp, dropping his mojito. Geoff slowly lowered his now stunned victim to the deck.

'My fuggin tung! I bit frew my tung!' Sarber-Collins groaned.

Geoff calmly leant down into his ear. 'Once upon a time, someone called me one of life's losers and it took years to get over it. Mind your tongue next time my friend, and don't tell me what 'sort' I settle for. Okay?' Geoff grabbed a bottle of Sol beer from an ice bucket and broke it open for Sarber-Collins. 'Here, this'll wash down the pain.' Geoff stood up, and turned to a silenced Kish and Elise. 'I will explain everything to Humphrey. Perhaps I should find him before he does something stupid.' Geoff then launched himself off the boat onto the marina pontoon and made for the marina. As Sarber-Collins sputtered something crude at

Geoff, Kish told some concerned onlookers that it was a personal tiff between two old muckers—Mr. Sarber-Collins started on his old friend Geoff without any provocation, and Geoff acted in self-defence. Elise nodded.

Jogging now, Geoff thought harder than he could remember. *Humphrey the Pretentious Snob. Humphrey the Disagreeing Housemate. Humphrey the Insecure. Humphrey the Thoughtful. Humphrey the ex-Friend. Need a slash. Running . . . not helping. Dark corner, go there . . . I can think now more clearly. Smile as three girls walk past. Hear some tinny calypso music coming out of the large marina tent—its sides lit up by synchronised disco lights. Gives way to the opening violin riff to 'Come on Eileen', then delayed cheers. The B&B keys are still jammed in my pocket, that's good to know. I fix my eyes on the marina exit. Get closer. Acutely un-maritime-looking bouncers looking back at me. I make out their earpieces, the sheen on their black nylon jackets and their gelled-hair cuts. Their dark eyes, half flitting, half dosing, but always menacing. Cowes attitude. Two locals, tired of us tossers taking over their town every year, but bringing in some seasonal employment for those who stay here. Reliance on us lot. They must hate it. What's glinting there? Looks like a coin . . .*

Geoff picked up the signet ring, and immediately recognised the crest.

Geoff ran the kilometre or so from the Marina to the B&B. As he approached, he noticed a dark object crouched on the B&B's steps, and failing to spot a kerb, tripped and ploughed headfirst into a dustbin, sending both him and it flying. The clatter woke half the street. 'Thank Christ, your alive!' shouted Geoff languishing at Humphrey's feet, clearly ignorant of the several curtains twitching about him.

'Piss off,' mumbled Humphrey from under his cloak.

'Okay. Why do you say that?' replied Geoff pensively.

'Funny isn't it. Just when I've actually created something I could be proud of, something that could have some value, it turns out you've stolen it. You are a thief. A rogue. You think of no-one but yourself.' Geoff usually cut people short. His pride would not get the better of him this time, and he remained silent. Humphrey continued, 'you do absolutely nothing yourself, you simply exploit anything and anyone around you. That's why you can afford to live so idly. The shop, and the thievery, even stooping to steal from your own friends. Yeh, you might be off the hook with Bacchus but not with me.'

'I'm truly sorry,' began Geoff earnestly. 'I owe you so much.' Geoff then extracted something from his pocket. Humphrey remained cocooned. 'For God's sake Humphrey, can you please remove that idiotic overcoat, so we can talk face-to-face.' Humphrey deliberated for a few moments before pulling the cloak off over his head. 'Bit crumpled now I'm afraid,' Geoff said, as he thrust a crumpled card into Humphrey's hand.

Humphrey studied the front. 'Are you taking the piss?'

'Just read what I wrote inside,' said Geoff. Humphrey sniffed as he opened it.

'Dear Humpy,

By my calculation this card just earned you 12p in royalties—you're on your way pal. Thank you for everything. Best, Geoff'

'So?'

'Read the back.'

Humphrey reluctantly flipped it over. *Suzie's Toozies. Number 2 in a series of 7, by FerayNotFerret.*

'But how?' asked Humphrey.

'Look, sheer boredom got the better of me a couple of months ago, so I went wandering in your room. I may have needed a clean pair of socks or something. Anyhow I found a notepad with your absurd toilet poems inside, and well, I pitched them to a greetings card company. Not sure what I was thinking at the time, but I added some drawings and, well, basically they decided to take them on, print them into proper cards.' Geoff paused for breath, then said. 'I guess I genuinely couldn't find anything fancy to improve my own life, but that doesn't exactly stop me helping you find something in yours. Now, we might need to unpick the legalities as technically I said I was acting on your behalf, but provided you're okay me being the artist still, as my naive style of drawing is apparently perfect for this genre, I am sure we'll pull this off.'

'Meaning?'

'Let's not bother with the details. Safe to say I have this for you.' Geoff handed him an envelope, as crumpled as the card was.

'All yours Humph. All yours.' Humphrey looked inside and pulled out a receipt and a cheque paper-clipped together. 'Couldn't get a cheque directly payable you, so had them paid into the business account, hence the receipt. But the cheque is from me to you.'

'It's three grand.'

Geoff smiled. 'Happy birthday. And bloody well run the race you were designed to.'

'On three grand?'

Geoff resumed a familiar brusqueness. 'Can't you see? It's what it represents. You've been fiddling around trying to carve a career out of wine displays and checkout tills, because the alternative just looked too hard. I see the alternative career in you every day, and the cheque proves what you do have is unique and worth something.'

'Like some Colour Sergeant, first he breaks me then he rebuilds me,' Humphrey sighed.

'Hadn't thought of it like that. In any case, was thinking about some alternative themes on the way over to Cowes actually. A dialogue between two latte glugging Ferret Yummies? I mean, if you can't sum up coffee shop pretentions then who can, Mr. FerayNotFerret?' Humphrey looked up at Geoff. 'Your Twitter name,' said Geoff. 'I twigged, and as your nemesis, CompleteChief, I enjoyed every single moment of our online jousting. Your tweets have most of the neighbourhood following them.'

'I like that. I'm still not one hundred percent comfortable with the cards idea. I mean selling low-brow poems?'

'You wrote the low-brow poems. Besides, I'll make it work for you, if you'll let me.' Geoff noticed Humphrey's grazed hand and warped finger. 'What happened?'

'Did it as I fell off the boat. It's a bit painful, yes.'

'Humphrey, your ring. I-'

'Oh, that little impediment. I threw it away.'

Geoff checked himself, and like Humphrey sat quietly with his thoughts.

Back at the boat, Elise finished what she had to say to Kish. 'Well?'

Kish nodded and squeezed her hand. Elise smiled nervously, and Kish kissed her more tenderly than he'd ever kissed her before. As tender as Geoff's, only this one meant everything to her.

August 3rd, 2002

Hampshire, England

Humphrey was making his way to the dance floor when his Grandfather Ernest called him over. The old man stood up from his chair and gripped Humphrey's arms. 'I'm very proud of you, old chap.'

'I'm so glad you are here,' Humphrey replied, slightly taken aback by the affection shown by this reserved old man. 'Not up for a dance then?'

'I leave that to those with younger legs. I'll just puff away here.' Ernest took drew on his pipe. 'Humphrey, when the disco's died down and people have gone home, use the moment to ask yourself something.' Humphrey gave a cautious smile. Ask yourself, even for a moment, who you are going to be.'

Humphrey frowned, then smiled. 'Who? Don't you mean what?'

Ernest paused. Perhaps not the most ideal time for a serious word. 'Sooner, rather than later, work out who you want Humphrey Massey to be. Don't wait for it, let it hang in the air and one day find you. And when you do know, do everything, and I mean everything you can to be that person. And lastly, don't expect it to be easy.' Ernest pointed at the ring. 'And be careful with that thing. Might make you forget it's your own legacy that counts,' he said sternly.

'Oh I don't know about that. I feel quite motivated when I'm reminded of my Massey heritage. Your roots after all. Look, it's even got our family motto beneath the family crest. You never wore one?'

'I've never had one to wear. Your dad's idea.'

Humphrey might have continued the heart-to-heart but Neil Diamond's Sweet Caroline began belting out. Humphrey hugged his grandfather then joined a gaggle of university friends prancing in a wide circle on the small dance floor. Humphrey felt buoyed by his Grandfather's eternal care for him, despite his occasional mistimed reverence. Tiredness probably. Tonight Humphrey felt he'd arrived.

He'd got provenance. And that meant something. Especially in front of his university friends.

The evening ended soon enough and guests slid off to their beds. Sat alone in the corner of the marquee, Ernest Massey re-lit his pipe. At eighty he was the only one of six siblings alive. He served his country in the Second World War and survived, unlike his two eldest brothers—one dying during the Dunkirk retreat, the other in occupied Belgium a year before. Heart disease or cancer had seen the others off. Still, seeing the young folk dancing merrily in such pleasant surroundings made him feel it was all worth it. How different to his own upbringing. He left school at fourteen to join his father at the local tanners, before his father convinced a family friend to take young Ernest on, working six days a week and selling fabric at Durham, Hartlepool and Middlesborough markets. The business grew steadily, and after the war, now in his mid-twenties, the newly married Ernest went to work for a company supplying tough fabric for industrial clothing across the North East. At thirty-one and now a father of two, Ernest was managing the company's new man-made fibre business, having moved the family down the road to Middlesborough. In 1963, aged 41, Ernest was made Chief Executive and his son Paul got into the local grammar school. It was Ernest's shrewd business mind that brokered the company's acquisition by Imperial Manufactures, at the time Britain's second largest industrial chemicals and materials company. In 1982, Ernest sold his shares and retired with his wife Abigail to the pretty market town of Yarm. He earned a prominent role on Middlesborough's Chamber of Commerce, successfully championing foreign investment into the North-East region and becoming a major benefactor of Teesside Polytechnic, as it was then known. In 1988, Ernest, already a Member of the Order of the British Empire was promoted to Officer of the Order of the British Empire for Services to the UK Manufacturing Industry. In 1997, he was given the Keys to the City of Durham, his birthplace. His lasting regret was that his beloved Abigail had not lived to see him on that memorable day. Ernest's thoughts then turned to his parents. His poor mother had died during his birth, something his father never quite forgave him for. He was never quite good enough for Dad.

Ernest wondered where on earth he'd been when this so-called family 'tradition' of signet ring-wearing had begun. Not on his say-so, that was for sure. Then he recalled something he'd heard countless times through the years. That you don't know how good a parent you've been until you see how your grandchildren have turned out. Perhaps it was his fault, he lamented. After all, he'd given his son Paul and his brother things he'd never dreamed possible when he grew up: a good education, a chance to go to university, a large garden to play in, foreign holidays. A little 'touched' is how he'd have privately described his son Paul these days—someone who, somewhere along the line, had forgotten his humble roots. He hoped to God that this grandson of his would not turn out the same. Ernest drew on his favourite pipe and sighed.

Pattaya, Thailand

Kish and the Dutch girl casually weaved through a small lane that led them to the beach road, passing by neat piles of garbage—beer cans and street food containers mainly—before they felt their sandals sink into the soft sand. After a short walk they came to a boat that was wedged upright by wooden props, close to a low stand of salt-tolerant trees.

'Let's tuck ourselves behind there,' said Kish.

For the next twenty minutes or so they got as much as they could possibly get from each other. She was on top, scratched him passionately and he gritted his teeth, both frantically smudging kisses until their lips were stinging. When they were done, their minds drifted off briefly with the shallow tide's slow ebb and flow, and brought-to by a warm, gentle breeze. They sat up and shared the Dutch girl's last cigarette. As she half-heartedly tried to locate her underwear, Kish asked just enough pleasant questions for her to think he cared. He kissed her one last time as she began to doze. Looking at his watch, and then convincing himself she'd be fine being left there asleep behind the old boat, he made his way off the beach, and toward the main drag, working on his patois with this Elise chick. He hoped she'd picked up on his wink, and would still be up, waiting for him. Pull this double off, he thought, and he'd win the bet with Stan, the barman at the Yabba-Dabba-Doo! bar. His chances were high. He'd played the 'dumb Brit' card with the rich American girl for two weeks now. She seemed only too happy to supplement his lifestyle, feed him, keep him in beers, all—it seemed—in return for making her laugh out loud.

As Kish approached the entrance to Elise's small, tidy apartment, he stuffed the Dutch girl's panties into his jeans back pocket. In an hour he was sure he'd have an additional pair, and with them, proof to win the bet with Stan.

A week's free Singha beer.

East Midlands, England

Geoff walked the long corridor, rehearsing the lines he'd say to his awaiting father. It didn't help and just before the exit, he darted into the gents. At the sinks, he rummaged through his bag and grabbed a pewter hip flask. He looked at himself in the wall mirror and considered the three charges that had resulted in tonight's dismissal. The first came in late April: he was caught drinking alcohol at half-time and narrowly missing being fired there and then. He spent the whole of May on the bench; the official word was a bad case of flu, everyone in the club's inner circle knew the truth. The second came in late June: missing one-too-many off-season training sessions because of hangovers and late night partying. The third, the most serious, resulted in him spending the night in a police cell on a charge of physical assault following a widely witnessed affray at a Nottingham nightclub. It was over a teammate's girlfriend, in itself bad enough, but irreparable given it was the very night before the B's pre-season game against Wasps, and the teammate in question was now unable to play through injuries sustained by Geoff's left hook.

Geoff unscrewed the hip flask, cocked his neck back and let neat whisky tumble down his throat. He barely flinched when he realised he'd emptied it. Instantly stiffened, he made for the exit toward the double door exit and the yellow neon lit car park outside. Beside the glass door exit stood a tall, burly man, the one he'd had the fracas with in the street just a week ago.

'One of life's losers,' muttered the ex-team mate as he passed, his nose still bandaged. Geoff stopped briefly, then seeing his father stood outside beside the Land Rover, walked straight out of the door.

His father saw his face and instantly knew the outcome of the meeting. It broke his heart to think his beautiful son, barely knee high when he first picked up a rugby ball, could self-destruct so easily. He reached out and took Geoff's holdall. Not for the first time he smelt alcohol on his son's breath and his eyes red with pain.

'Come on, Son. Things to sort out.'

Pristina, Kosovo

Diana and the man she now recognised as her one-time love, Fadim Dinas talked on in the quiet hotel bar beneath grand, marbled walls and intricate ceiling architrave. She thought back to two decades ago. She, the bookish graduate at London University. He, the promising post-grad engineer who'd just enrolled there, one of only a few ethnic Albanians to be sponsored through Belgrade University to study overseas that year. All part of President Tito's ambitious plans for a Yugoslavian tourist industry that would indeed become a reality in the early 'eighties, concentrated in pockets along the Adriatic coast and not much elsewhere. She remembered how Fadim left London and her back to his home city of Pristina, to his parents and a new role in the city's engineering department. And back to a girl that he should marry the following spring. Diana remembered how upset she'd felt, but not surprised. They'd always known that theirs was an untenable relationship, she from a Catholic family already engaged to another, and he a Muslim. Theirs was a secret love where she'd have done anything for him. And he for her.

Fadim was now working with the EU's EAR effort. He'd noticed Diana one morning in the Pristina HQ, conducted discrete enquiries to confirm it was her, then procrastinated for weeks for the right opportunity to approach her. When he discovered that tonight was her last night in Pristina for several months, he let his heart lead him to her hotel lobby.

'Diana, you are ever more beautiful than I remember. And before you is a man suddenly alive for the first time in years. These past few years have had their toll . . .' he paused then smiled. 'What keeps me going is my child, Vilora.' Fadim spoke warmly of his cherished daughter, a bright and bubbly ten-year-old. The youngest of five. He then told Diana what happened when their home took a direct hit. 'It was the Serb and Yugoslav forces that did it. All my three sons, and one daughter died, along with my old mother, and a cousin. Only my wife survived along with little Vilora, she was around seven at the time, and me. Then we were harassed out of Pristina by Serb-backed paramilitaries, like so many other Albanian Kosovans.'

'That is truly terrible. Where did you go?'

'It was May 1999. We made for the Albanian border. But on the way, NATO mistook our refugee convoy for a Yugoslav military convoy, and bombed us with their warplanes. Very sadly, my wife was among the many dead, God keep her safe.'

Diana gasped, groping for words. 'Fadim, I am very familiar with that awful incident. I am so very sorry.' She held his arm.

'Yes, NATO admitted its terrible mistake a few days later, but it did not bring my wife back. After her burial, I swore I would not let any harm come to little Vilora. Whatever it took.' Fadim paused. 'But enough now of me, what of you? The years have only made you more beautiful.'

'I have been lucky,' she said. She saw Fadim was looking at her left hand, her wedding ring.

'I left London shortly after you did. When you left, I was still seeing Tim, you remember Tim Reece? He was a research graduate in your electrical engineering department.'

'Of course I remember Tim,' Fadim replied gently. He felt her guilt too.

'You see, I—,' Diana paused to choose her words carefully. 'I got pregnant more or less around the time you left. For that reason, Tim and I married pretty quickly as you can imagine, in fact while I was still at London. Not exactly the done thing having a bump while waddling up the aisle, and all that. I had a son called Chris, all grown up now. Without hesitation Diana produced a photo of her son when he was a little boy, wearing a big cowboy hat and grinning from ear to ear. 'He's in Thailand at the moment, he's been backpacking round Southeast Asia with a wonderful-sounding eco-tour group. Comes home in a week or two, but he told me in his last postcard he was in the forests for the next few weeks so pretty much incommunicado. Diana leant in. 'Plus he's not one for writing or emailing generally.'

'Wonderful to hear how our children become adults. Do you have any other children?'

'No, just the one. After Chris, turned out I couldn't have anymore.' Diana put the photo back in her purse. 'We moved out of London and *settled down in South West England. Tim went into the Ministry of Defence and I began lecturing . . .'*

Tonight's encounter with Fadim was the first activity in months, other than her work, that had made Diana forget about being a lonely mother and wife. It was well past 8:30pm when she looked at her watch. 'Goodness! Where has all the time gone? I must pack.'

Fadim signalled the waiter for the bill. 'I am honoured to have shared this evening with you, Diana. Although in my heart, it is a great pity you are leaving, just as we talk for the first time in years. If you stayed tomorrow, I would have you meet my little daughter, Vilora.'

Diana found herself wanting to take Fadim's hand. 'I would have loved to, Fadim. Perhaps when I return in the spring of next year. I need to get back home for a husband who still can't cook for himself.' Diana's mobile phone lit up with a text message. 'Speak of the devil. It's Tim, texting me. Do excuse me.'

It was the first communication from her husband for days, despite several from her messages telling him she'd be home tomorrow evening. At first Diana thought the text was a bit of an odd joke—humour never being one of Tim's stronger points. Then she read it once more.

Deanne, coming over in ten. Looking forward to kissing you all over. Wife's not back until tomorrow, so expect some fun! Timmy x o x o x o x.

The smile dropped. For some time now, Diana had suspected her husband was up to something behind her back. He was increasingly going on about feeling 'unfulfilled and misunderstood', working late, and wearing jeans again for the first time in years. And now the idiot had inadvertently just sent her a text, clearly meant for someone a vowel off her own name, and who called him 'Timmy'. Probably someone both younger and easier to impress than a boring old wife who'd never even looked at another man in twenty years.

Diana calmly sent a text back:

Darling "Timmy", I think you meant your last text for someone else? D.

She hit 'send' then switched her phone off.

'Fadim, you know, I would love to meet your grandaughter tomorrow. I am sure Tim will cope. Looks like he's got a lot on his plate right now. I shall make the necessary arrangements to stay another few days.'

Her husband could damn well hang now. She'd not take him back. And as for Chris, he was away still, saving the planet in Thailand.

Fadim smiled graciously. 'We would be honoured to have you as our houseguest. Our apartment, it is small but clean and most importantly, much safer now.' He placed his hand on Diana's shoulder. 'And best of all you can meet my little Vilora.'

Diana smiled. She and Fadim would always have an unspoken understanding. After so many years though, it made no sense letting her doubts concerning her son resurface.

FORTY-TWO

It was Monday morning, a little over a week since Cowes. Humphrey spied his bedside alarm clock. *7:01am*. Early start today. He felt the bare finger where his ring once sat, and smiled. No doubt the bloody thing was still lodged in sludge at the bottom of a greasy drain, somewhere back in that damn marina. He glanced across his bedroom, now laid bare—just a lamp, a chest of drawers and the bed he currently lay in. Most of his possessions were already moved out. No. 47 Ferret Rise, his home for the last three years, would be someone else's rented space within the next few days, someone else's launch pad into Putney Ferret and its foibles.

Showered and packed, Humphrey bashed out a few tweets while waiting for Geoff, then checked his follower count. His months of prattling had now earned him 18,729 followers, half of them in the past four weeks. Someone had called it a "tipping point". He chuckled over a few recent ditties on signet ring observations and the merits of putting one's Tesco shopping into a boutique-branded bag. He grabbed the doorknob, and lingered a moment to look around the clean, stark room. It looked strangely vulnerable, stripped of the framed photos and occasionals which, paired with the polished wood floor positively shrieked *urbane sophisticate* to the very rare few who'd seen it over the past two or so years. He placed the holdall strap over his shoulder, and with the help of a single crutch, hobbled downstairs where Geoff was waiting with one large holdall—his parents had paid a visit yesterday, and cleared most of his stuff and transported it up the M1.

House checked, utilities alerted, windows secured. Geoff dragged Humphrey's holdall outside. He hesitated at the front door then patted the portico a final farewell. 'Time for that coffee. Kish and Elise are already there.' He grabbed both holdalls, groaning with clothes and anything not stored and followed a slow, hobbling Humphrey into the gentle hum of London's morning traffic.

Much had happened in the short week since Cowes. Bacchus Braves Winestores Ltd had finally succumbed to the stuttering economy; Toby Sarber-Collins was on a sabbatical in Portugal, rediscovering his port-producing roots, and resting his jaw.

Inside the Latte Pharté café, Lucia the waitress served two more hot mugs of coffee. Geoff watched Kish gently pat Elise's large tummy. He still wasn't entirely convinced that Kish deserved her. Her humility, her patience, her kind heart. But Kish had shown he was determined to change and Geoff simply had to hope Kish meant it for good.

Coffees drained, they paid up, and hugged one another in succession.

'Thank you,' Elise whispered into Geoff's ear. She stood back and looked at him for a moment.

'Take care boys,' said Kish and taking Elise's hand left the café for his car. Not the expensive Mercedes anymore, but something a little smaller and anonymous. Kish helped Elise into the car, pleasantly surprised he was showing the concern he knew he should always have given. It was too late to make amends with mother, but not too late to learn from it. Kish got in and adjusted his belt. He had promised Elise that once they'd moved in, together they'd sort out the nursery first. At the same time a tear trickled down Elise's cheek. Her mind went back to the sticky night in Thailand nearly ten years ago when she met Kish, and laughed at his failed, drunken attempt to seduce her. She'd invested too much time in this to see it fail just because of a man's immaturity. It seemed her investment might still prove to be a wise one.

Kish's first priority was towards Elise and their unborn baby. Vilora's immigration visa and the final paperwork to secure her university place were his next. Vilora, a young lady who a few months ago he'd never met nor spoken to, yet who was so close to the woman he'd so neglected. He turned to Elise. 'You know, perpetual devotion to what a man calls his business is only to be sustained by perpetual neglect of other things. Some insightful guy called Brasher said that.' The quote on Diana's fridge hadn't been placed there to passively attack her son's attitude to life. It was her quiet admission of her own past, a conclusion no doubt arrived at while fiddling with pea sticks in the garden for hours on end, and a painful reminder every time she'd read it. Kish knew that now.

Kish gently moved off the curb and headed down Ferret Rise. In two hours they would be at his old family home in Bath, where Vilora would be waiting for them, and if the good weather held out, they could all wander along his mother's clematis collection and gaze at the frieze of late-summer colours. Among the varieties now grew the clematis with dazzlingly bright sunburst-yellow flowers. It had a name now: simply "Mother Diana".

The former staff of the Putney Ferret branch of Bacchus Braves Winestores made surprisingly short work of the stroll down Putney Rise to Putney Train Station, despite Geoff being lumbered with two large and cumbersome holdalls, and Humphrey hobbling alongside. 'No taxi chap. No need.' At platform one, they stood amongst the morning's commuters, awaiting their collective ride to work.

'Why do we remain in our comfort zone?' Geoff asked.

'Dunno. Perhaps it's something to do with being in denial.' Humphrey replied wryly, and then turned to his old housemate. 'Besides, anyone who insults, belittles or scuppers people to the extent you did must yourself have an itch to scratch.'

Geoff laughed. 'Which reminds me . . .' he retrieved something from his pocket, and handed it to Humphrey.

'My ring! But I chucked that away in Cowes. How did you find it?'

'It was winking at me when I came after you after you fell off the boat in your Nelson suit. So I picked it up.' Humphrey grimaced at the ring. Broken finger joint or not, he would never be putting that ring back on.

Geoff stared across the platform. 'Funny, these past nine or ten years, I've thought I'll never amount to anything, so hardly a surprise it's actually turned out that way. Turns out my only true pursuit was pursuing the act of doing bugger all. Like you say, denial.'

Humphrey nodded. 'For us both perhaps was also a fear of failure. I've been too scared to do something I might actually enjoy, and cock it up. I've lived passively, in limbo, accepting myself as being pretty blah-blah. Average-man. Always the observer never the player. Boozing doesn't exactly help, takes the edge away.'

Geoff looked down and said, 'The demon drink has done more than take the edge off me. Dumbed me down. And I've long known I can't be sort-of-sober. My family knows, have done for years. It hurts me because it hurts them. Going back up there to the farm now makes sense because they will make me face up to a few things.'

'It's a true gift is your family.' Humphrey looked down at his ring. 'They are empty without true bonds aren't they? As if some piece of gold jewellery defines what it means to be part of one.'

A train approached, and Humphrey put the ring in his pocket. An assembly of office workers jostled on the platform, one or two feral-like, many others simply looking like they'd be better off laid out on their sofas right now, victims of a super-Sunday, stress, or plain lack of sleep. Geoff and Humphrey glanced knowingly at each other and calmly hopped aboard, their uncommuter-friendly bags causing minor irritation amongst those crammed beside them. As the train set off, Humphrey gazed across the collage of anonymous expressions spread throughout the crowded carriage. Professionals in the main, educated folk who as Theroux once remarked, simply live in quiet desperation. Quiet, save the occasional voice breaking the silence with unabashed, self-aggrandising chatter into his phone. Like a cold wind blown into an empty vessel, howling loudly.

'Okay pal, this is where I bugger off,' said Humphrey as the train drew up at Wandsworth. They shook hands, nothing valedictory. 'Call you soon. By the way, in a spare moment, google Putney Ferret. He stepped off and onto the platform.

'Doors closing!' yelled the Guard. He blew a shrill whistle that sliced through a trainload of private thoughts. On board, Geoff thumbed 'Putney Ferret' into the search bar on his mobile's screen. Two clicks later he was reading a description on some fancy website. He closed his eyes and smiled. He'd be back home in Leicestershire by early afternoon. They'd have to see how it went, but he was looking forward to it. Farming was in the blood, after all.

Humphrey checked his text messages again. A 9:00am meeting with Des Orr of Haggard Cards, then over to join the rest of his belongings at his new rented flat over in Sheen. When he had a moment, he'd post the ring back to his parents, with a polite explanation. He remembered his late Grandfather, Ernest, who'd once told him it took more than a piece of metal to define you.

Humphrey Chris Massey placed his holdall over his shoulder and headed for the exit.

He now understood what that old man meant.

The train guard blew his whistle and another train dragged itself off towards Waterloo. On that whistle, there were those who instinctively checked their watches and huffed quietly at the delay. There were those who'd made a last minute dash, beating the whistle by seconds and were left confident that the day would continue to go their way. There were those who were roused from a daydream, miles away, returning to a perennial ennui. Alongside them sat those who plotted their tactics, deciding who they'd screw over and who they'd suck up to this week; there were those who sat in solitude, unflinching, mellowing towards uncertain retirement; there were the commuter couples, unsure how to communicate affection to one another on a crowded train. Lastly, there sat the kids in their neat school uniforms or scruffy college mufti, busy tweeting and texting hormone-jumpy wit to one another, their happiness sustained by iPhones, twitter, and the prospect of Kinect and football practice later, all paid for by their parent's labour, credit cards and re-mortgages. And yet blissfully unaware they'd already set a course to join all the others.

Some might speculate anyone trying to escape the fray is naïve—foolhardy to question where their finite lives are heading. But you'd do well ignoring such Ferret talk.

An introduction to Putney Ferret, continued

The word "Ferret" has increasingly been used on Twitter to denote a young aspiring individual of approximately 25-35 years old, associated in particular with South West London, who still enjoys a parent-subsidised lifestyle, and is typically noted for self-aggrandising his or her social standing. The definition is widely attributed to the now infamous yet still anonymous Tweeter, "FerayNotFerret", a self-confessed reformed Ferret, who enjoys a considerable public following, bemoaning local ferret-isms through short, rhyming couplets.